The single poker light hanging above the table cast dancing shadows across each wall of the smoke saturated room. The tell tale glow of joints being drawn every few seconds signaled the location of each occupant.

The man with the ponytail hesitated for a moment until the glowing joint at the center of the table turned. Then he whispered something and the pitted face man replied, "Dead? I thought they were locked up somewhere. How could they be dead?"

"I don't know, Jefe. I talked to our source at the cops. He said they were at the county morgue. I went down to get our gang mark, you know, the gold ring in their ear, but the rings were gone. Their bodies were all twisted and mangled like pretzels. Maybe you should let this one go."

Without a word, the gang leader grabbed the man's long ponytail and jerked his head down till it crashed onto the table. Then he yanked on the gold ring in the man's ear until it ripped through the ear lobe.

"No one disses me, understand, no one. You see this," he pointed to his broken tooth, "He did it, and he's going to suffer."

Pit-face looked at the other three men at the table, and waited for a response, but none was offered.

The man with the ponytail picked himself up and used his hands to stop the bleeding from his nose and torn ear. He stepped back and tried a second time. "We raped and killed his wife. Isn't that enough?"

"When his nuts hang from this lamp, then that'll be enough." Pit face and the three others at the table laughed.

A dog outside the abandoned building howled. After a moment, it stopped, and after several seconds, the dog started barking again. Pit-face squawked to the man at his left, "Juan, if you don't shut up that damn dog, I'll shoot you first, and then him."

As if on cue, the dog went silent. The gang leader looked at the other members seated at the table, and then changed his mind. "Juan, go see why that mutt stopped barking."

After several minutes of waiting for Juan's return, something scratched at the door. "I swear I'm going to slit that dog's throat."

Pit-face directed one of the guards. "I've had it with that dog. Take him out behind the dumpsters and beat him to death."

The guard opened the door, but nothing was there. He glanced toward the pit-faced man for guidance. "Go find him, now."

Pit-face looked back at the two men at the table. "I told Juan to keep that hound out of my face. Now I'll going to turn him into maggot food."

The men at the table continued their card game. After several minutes, there was a muffled noise outside the window, as if someone tried to yell, but there was no air in his throat to make the sound. The dim room instantly darkened, like a sponge had consumed every ray of light. Only the red ash from the joints being smoked by the four men who remained lickered as their breath became erratic.

In the void, the distinctive snarl of pit face demanded, "Must be a hit by the Diablo Soldado gang. Give me the shotgun!"

Before anyone could respond, the sound of a door swinging open could be heard.

Pit-face felt something edge by his left leg. "Tomas, is that you?"

From the far corner of the room, the remaining guard reached for a black metal bat, but it was gone. The heavy breathing was interrupted by a loud thump, as if a pumpkin had been cracked open. The room stilled. Then a muffed sound struggled in the dark, someone gargling in their own blood. Again silence.

An agonizing scream reverberated around the walls, accompanied by several shots, and then a thump on the floor.

More shots rang out. The crash of boxes, barrels, and furniture could be heard as something angry moved through the void. A low guttural growl, like a predator preparing to pounce on its victim, greeted the sole survivor.

A single plea into the darkness could be heard, as the prey stumbled and searched for the exit, desperately trying to flee. "El Dios me ahorra."

Another torso collapsed onto the floor, followed by repeated raps of someone kicking their feet against the floor, struggling to escape. Lungs gasped for air. A final kick of the door signaled the end.

Something was dragged back into the room. The door closed, and the room filled with silence.

Champagne Books Presents

Tainted Hero

By

Michael Davis

Tainted Hero

This is a work of fiction. The characters, incidents and dialogues in this book are of the author's imagination and are not to be construed as real. Any resemblance to actual events or persons, living or dead, is completely coincidental.

No part of this book may be reproduced or transmitted in any form or by any means, electronic or mechanical, including photocopying, recording, or by any information storage and retrieval system, without permission in writing from the publisher.

Champagne Books
www.champagnebooks.com
Copyright © 2007 by Michael W. Davis
ISBN 978-1-897445-39-6
December 2007
Cover Art © Trisha FitzGerald
Produced in Canada

Champagne Books
19-3 Avenue SE
High River, AB T1V 1G3
Canada

Dedication

Thanks to my Sons, Sean and Craig, for their editorial contributions and valuable insights.

Tainted Hero

One

BOOM!

The explosion ripped the three-man team off the ground and tossed them into the air. Eric slammed face first in the sand. He pushed up on his knees, pressed the detached flap of flesh back down on his forehead, wiped the blood from his eye, and fought the pain hammering inside his skull. He turned toward his friend, but Mac was gone, only a hole remained where he had been seconds before. Eric saw Duke lying in the sand...

The sound of the vehicle pulling into the driveway brought him out of the dream and back to the kitchen in his small house. Eric stood up from the table, walked over to the window above the sink, and stared at the two figures in the black car. The glow from the streetlight was insufficient to see their faces, but he knew, there in the passenger seat, it was her. The head of the passenger disappeared below the edge of the car window. When the head of the driver leaned back, Eric gripped the sides of his coffee mug. He watched for a moment to confirm his suspicions, and then he closed his eyes and lowered his head. He fought the impulse to end it all, to rush outside and set things straight.

Perhaps she's right. Maybe if I had been here, things would have turned out different.

He took a deep breath, started to glance out the window one last time, but instead returned to his seat at the table, and waited.

Eric tapped his knuckles on the table as he sat alone in the dark. His eyes bored into the kitchen door until he heard the key turn in the lock. He listened to the door close and the light footsteps echo through the small two-story house, and advanced on his position. When the entry to the kitchen opened, the woman flipped the light switch and was startled.

"Damn, you scared the hell out of me. I didn't know you were home from your trip. Where's your car?"

"In the garage."

"Why are you sitting in the dark?"

Eric surveyed his wife's attire: the three-inch heels, the opal earrings he gave her on their first anniversary, and the strapless black dress. The same outfit she used to wear when they went out; the one that made him proud she was his and no one else's.

"It's a bit late to be coming in, isn't it? Where have you been?"

Karen paused for moment, tossed her keys on the counter, and responded without looking at her husband. "I was out with friends."

"Do I know these friends?"

"No."

"It's really getting old, to come home to an empty house every night, and find out you're with your…friends."

"Then stop traveling everywhere for that damn job. Besides, why the hell should you care what I do when you're gone? I'm aware you're not alone on those trips. I know you take one of your sluts with you, like that red headed major."

Eric stood up. He scanned the hard expression on his wife's beautiful face, the glistening black hair he longed to stroke. He glanced at the tight lips that once smiled whenever he was near, the soft lips he needed to touch, to taste. "No matter how many times you accuse me of infidelity, it doesn't make it true. I swear I have not been with any other women during our entire marriage. Can you say the same for yourself?"

With an expression barren of emotion, Karen ignored the comment and turned toward the doorway to leave, but not without making one final cutting remark. "I don't believe you. You haven't been with me for a long time, so you must be screwing someone else. As always, this conversation has given me a headache. Don't wake me when you come to bed, or when you go jogging in the morning."

He remained alone in the kitchen with only the light beneath the doorsill stretching across the floor. While he stared past the door into the next room, he whispered after the only woman in his life, "Where did it go, Karen? You loved me once. Is it so easy to forget what we used to have, together? I still remember. I've tried hard not to let it go, but it becomes more difficult each day."

~ * ~

Eric listened to the clock on his nightstand, and resisted the need for sleep. He knew it waited in the shadows of his nightmare. After two hours, he lost the battle. While he slept, the vision that hounded his dreams for so long returned: the fawn grazed toward the edge of the woodland, unaware of what lurked just inside the trees. In an instant, the beast lunged onto his prey. While it consumed her innocence, Eric was helpless. Chained to an oak tree, he was forced to observe while the demon mocked him. He could only watch from the hill as he lost her forever to that ruthless bastard. He ripped at the chains as they cut deep into his skin. He struggled against the bonds until the shackles that had imprisoned him all these years were covered with his blood. He ignored the gnawing pain, pushed against the tree with his feet, until the steel tore deep into his flesh and exposed the bone, but the chains remained, stopped him from saving her. Eric looked away and closed his eyes, but the tears continued to pour down his cheeks. The beast grunted with pleasure as it wrested the life from her small slender body. Eric screamed in agony, but no one was there on the lonely hill to listen. While he watched her die alone, he wept.

Eric sat up in bed. The nightmare left him soaked in sweat. He gazed at his wife lying next to him, and started to reach for her. He needed to feel her soft skin, touch the taut ridge of spine that flowed down her back. He yearned to be absolved of his guilt, or to achieve some semblance of comfort, but he pulled back, afraid of being rejected, again.

He felt alone, as always, all alone. He got up, walked into the spare bedroom, and curled up on the bed, lying motionless and staring out the window at the stars in the night sky, until the tremors from the nightmare disappeared. After thirty minutes he fell asleep again, by himself, in the dark room.

~ * ~

The rhythmic pattern of his stride along the asphalt offered some relief from the stress of a fractured marriage. As Eric approached his house, he remembered when they were first together and his wife greeted him at the door. Without a word, she surrounded him with her body, and consumed him completely, right on the Persian rug.

Now there was no passion, no tenderness. Only silent nights together in distant parts of that lonely house, except when she wanted verbal retribution. He had apologized a hundred times for being overseas on assignment the night she lost the child, but the very act of contrition made it worse. He wanted it back, to recapture what they once shared. He had to try, until it was finally over. He had to try.

After his shower, he ambled into the kitchen and greeted his wife in an appeasing voice. "Good morning. I hope you feel better this morning."

Karen continued to sip her brew without lifting her head.

He tried again. "I see you're already dressed. That outfit looks good on you."

Still no response. "Is there any coffee left?"

She pointed to the pot behind her and continued to read her magazine.

Eric poured the remains of the liquid into his cup. "What do you say we spend the entire day together? We could go down to the square before our appointment with the counselor and do some window-shopping. Then, maybe we could take a stroll on the boardwalk. In the evening, we could have dinner at that new seafood place on the pier called the Bullfish. Doesn't that sound like fun?"

She stood up from the table and combed her fingers through her long black hair. "I can't. I have plans to shop with some of my friends. I'll see you at the marriage counselor's office at one o'clock."

Without glancing at him, Karen walked out of the kitchen and departed the house.

Eric stood by the window and watched her get into her car. With a somber expression he murmured, "Goodbye, Karen."

Two

Eric sat on the bench in front of the counselor's office. As he shifted the position of his legs for the tenth time, he clenched his fist and looked at his watch. *She does this every damn time I try to soothe her feathers. It's her way of reigning lord and master over me. I don't think she really cares anymore whether we mend things.*

He scanned the square for any sign of his wife. He noticed a couple across the street as they pointed at infant apparel in the display window. The young man tenderly placed his arm around his wife while she rested both hands on her bulging tummy. Ten yards to their left, an overweight mother scolded her son for playing in the street. Further left, an elderly couple ambled down the sidewalk arm-in-arm, disappearing together around the corner of the two-story red brick pharmacy.

He caught the sound of a girl's laughter. He turned toward a small pond thirty yards to his left in the community park. The young female smiled flirtatiously at her partner. He watched the two teenagers touch indirectly, and verbalize suggestive affections. Eric saw the young man's lips move as he pretended to whisper something in the girl's ear to steal a whiff of her enticing scent. The girl played her part in the ritual; she giggled seductively, flipped her long blonde hair and softly patted the young man's chest.

Eric envied the couple's playful banter as they enjoyed the natural splendor of initial romance. He remembered that wonderful period in relationships when everything was simple and innocent. The motivation of intimacy was clear and understood, not complicated by insecurity and scars that evolved from years of argument and confrontation.

When he leaned back into the bench, there came a faint smell of the ocean mixed with steamed seafood being prepared a few hundred yards east on the boardwalk. He fixated on the yellow leaves rustling in the breeze from dwarf maples bedded within wooded frames around the edge of the sidewalks. The tension in his neck eased. Somehow the sight of others gaining pleasure from their lives made him relax. He took a deep breath, uncrossed his arms, and raked his hand through his coal-black hair.

Eric noted the familiar pattern of high heels scuffing the sidewalk, behind and to his left. He turned to catch Karen's austere visage as she shuffled toward her husband. He attempted a smile, but the greeting was returned by a frown.

"I'm here. Let's do it," she said.

The momentary smile disappeared and Eric shot back, "What do you mean, let's do it? This was your idea. You were the one who demanded we come to these damn sessions, not me. You insisted we use your old college sweetheart, just to dig into me a little deeper. All we do is spend the hour exploring how screwed up I am and how I ruined your life."

What I fool I was to think this would bring you back to me. That you actually wanted us to be the way we were before we lost the baby.

When Eric stood to follow his wife into the office, she smirked. "It sure helps me. I feel refreshed after every visit."

Before the couple could proceed with their routine argument, tires squealed across the street. A man with a mustache in a blue vintage Pontiac with a white convertible top and mag wheels pulled out a .357 revolver and pumped multiple shots into a red Firebird parked next to the curb. In an instant, the street that had been busy with activity became deserted. Like critters scurrying into their burrows when the predator steps into the field, everyone disappeared. Even Karen rushed into the counselor's office and peered cautiously around the doorsill.

A small girl with blonde pigtails walked out of the treat shop next to the counselor's office while her mother paid the bill for a scoop of rocky road ice cream. The six year old was intent on licking the streams of chocolate dripping across her hand and down onto her white pleated dress when the loud gunshots first frightened her. She grabbed the first thing in sight, Eric's leg. As he scanned the empty square, two tiny hands clenched his right leg as events rapidly unfolded across the street.

The man with the mustache got out of his car, removed a briefcase from the victim's vehicle and inspected its contents. Once the shooter had finished the examination of his bounty, he tossed the black leather case into his car and turned directly toward Eric. While the shooter strutted across the street, Eric reached down and positioned the girl behind him. The man with the mustache advanced to within four feet of Eric, and with a sneering grin on his pitted face. "You want a piece of this, asshole..."

Before he could fully raise his weapon, Eric pushed the girl backward, grabbed the assailant's arm, and sent him arching through the air. The shooter landed directly on his face two yards from Eric's feet. A knee pushed deep into his back forcing his mouth firmly against the concrete. Eric heard the man on the ground verbalize various threats toward him and his family. With each attempt, Eric pressed the pitted face harder into the concrete until he could hear the sound of teeth scraping against the coarse surface.

"Yeah, I'll take a piece of that, pus face," Eric informed the shooter, then reached down and inserted his right hand under the thick silver chain from which dangled a religious medallion of the Virgin Mary. "You keep mouthing off, and I'll keep twisting. Let's see who gives up first."

Eric twisted the chain tighter and tighter around the man's neck until the shooter silenced. He fought the urge to twist further while his hands trembled as he struggled against his instincts. He wanted desperately to sweep this trash from the street forever, but not here, not now. He reached down and removed the gold ring from the man's ear and placed it in his pants pocket.

The whine of a police siren approached from the direction of the boardwalk. The vehicle jerked to a halt next to the two men on the ground. The small girl returned to Eric's side while the mother remained frozen at the window in the treat shop. Two officers jumped out of the car and drew their weapons.

"I don't think you'll need them," Eric said. "He's decided to cooperate."

The senior officer removed his sunglasses and looked down at the man lying motionless on the ground. He lifted his eyes toward Eric and smiled. "I think you're right." After holstering his weapon, he turned to his rookie partner. "Go talk to the people coming out of the stores. See if we can get any witnesses before they run off. I'll handle things here."

When Eric stood up, the young girl re-established her grip on his leg. The mother rushed out of the treat shop, removed her daughter from Eric's side, and hurried down the street without a word of gratitude. He surmised that she was too focused on fleeing the scene to acknowledge the man that had just saved her daughter's life.

Eric helped the officer drag the shooter into the police vehicle where he was handcuffed to the steel cage in the back seat. The senior officer closed the door, turned back to Eric, and pulled his casebook out of his pocket. "I'm Officer Simms. Could I have your name sir?"

"Eric Emerson."

At that instant, Karen came out of the counselor's office, moved next to her husband and demanded, "Come on. We're late for our appointment."

"I can't leave until I've told the officer what I saw."

She frowned and whispered into his left ear, "I don't want you to get involved in this. It will just lead to trouble."

"I can't ignore what happened. This scum tried to kill me, and that little girl, for no reason. Someone has to stand up against these assholes. Just cancel the appointment for today. We'll do it next Saturday."

Karen crossed her arms and opened her mouth to voice her objection, but nothing came out. She bit down on her lip then looked hard into her husband's blue eyes. "I guess you can get home on your own." She turned and walked away without a parting word.

Officer Simms placed the pen back in his shirt pocket. "Looks like you're in hot water."

"I'm starting to get used to it. Go ahead and ask your questions."

After ten minutes the officer completed his interview, folded up his casebook, and placed it back in his pocket. "You'll need to come down to the station and make a formal statement. If it goes to trial, it'll be twelve to eighteen months but in the meantime, the prosecutor will probably ask you to be a witness at a hearing so a judge can evaluate the evidence. You could be our only witness by the time we get to trial. People have a tendency to fade away as the court date gets closer. With a record like this guy's got, most people get scared off."

The rookie approached from behind. "Officer Simms, no one seems to be sure of what they saw. Not one person felt they could identify the man who did the shooting. What should we do next?"

The stout senior officer replied, "Looks like Gonzales is coming to. He's screaming and kicking the doors. You need to go read him his rights, and make sure he understands them."

Eric listened as the rookie officer arrived at the front door to the police vehicle and Officer Simms warned, "Be careful he doesn't bite. You'd hate to have to go through the required series of rabies shots. It's very painful."

The rookie, bamboozled by his partner, replied, "Yes Sir. I'll be careful." The junior officer opened the front door of the patrol car and carefully eased into the passenger seat. Officer Simms turned toward Eric and grinned.

"Rookies can be a lot of fun."

"Do you think the guy will get out on bail?"

"I doubt it, with his record. We do appreciate your cooperation. Hopefully, with your testimony, he'll be locked up forever this time."

The two men shook hands. Eric pulled out his cell phone, dialed the number of his friend, Samantha Cassidy, and waited for her to answer while he watched the police vehicle depart. "Hi Sam, it's your bud, Eric. I'm stranded again. Do you think you can pick me up at the corner of Clemson Street and Oceanside Avenue, just off the beach? I'm stuck here without a car."

"What happened this time; did your car break down or something?"

"No. I'll tell you all about it when you get here."

"Alright, it will take me twenty minutes, but I'll be right there."

"I appreciate it. I'll see you shortly."

Three

Samantha glanced at Eric, then back at the road. "Boy that's some story. You had one heck of an afternoon didn't you?"

"Yes."

"I know you're schooled in the art of self-defense, but weren't you scared, just a little bit?"

"No. I was pissed. When the asshole pulled his gun, I was close enough to penetrate those hollow, empty eyes. There was no soul, no heart. Just hate, for everyone. He was pure evil. I don't understand how someone could be that empty of any compassion for others. It was like looking into the pit of hell."

"But why did he come at you, did you say something to piss him off?"

"Hell no. There was no reason. Even with the small child clinging to my side, we were nothing to him. He was willing to kill us both for no purpose other than the fact that we were standing there. It infuriates me that such trash is allowed to manipulate our inept legal system and roam free."

Sam glanced at the stain on Eric's leg and jested with her friend. "Did you get excited and drop your ice cream? Looks like chocolate."

"That little girl had very sticky hands."

"You're just Mr. Hero today, aren't you? What a man."

"Hey carrot-top, why don't you just kiss my butt."

"I appreciate the offer, but I wouldn't want to get you in more trouble with your wife."

Eric looked at the woman beside him. Even through the

foundation of makeup, he saw a smattering of light freckles. Eric had always thought of Sam as a beautiful, feminine woman. The dimple on her right cheek and the eternal curl that twirled just above her right eye projected the image of a young adolescent. Even after thirty-six years, she still portrayed the look of youth. The tight skin, small nose, green eyes, and puffed lips had always affected him. But even with her shapely figure, he never crossed the line. It wouldn't be right. Besides, it might hurt their friendship. They'd been close friends since they were classmates ten years ago. Eric would do nothing to risk that relationship. He wondered how things might have been different, had he met Sam first, but he would play the cards he had been dealt, until things were all burned out.

Sam interrupted the silence. "How are things on the home front, any progress?"

"I'm afraid not. Just seems to keep going downhill."

"Hasn't the marriage counselor helped at all?"

"No. Karen spends the entire time listing off what a bastard I am, and then the counselor asks me what I'm going to do to straighten my butt out."

"It can't be that bad. Aren't you exaggerating just a bit?"

"Sam, I'm not kidding you. It's exactly like I said."

"What are you going to do? Do you think there's any hope of reconciliation after all this time?"

"I don't know. Since she lost the baby, it just keeps getting worse. I think the fact that it damaged her inside so that she can never have children anymore is at the core of everything. It's like she blames me for the miscarriage, and it's gnawing at her gut." Eric turned his head to the right and watched the houses rush by. It was a minute before he spoke again. "It wasn't always this way. You remember when we were classmates at Monterey? You saw how good we were together. She was in heaven out there: all the shops in Carmel, the restaurants on Cannery Row, the scenic drives along Seventeen Mile Drive. She was into everything, especially me. We were very happy. She made me happy."

"I remember how close the two of you were, always touching each other. You always seemed so happy back then."

"We were, both of us. Even when I would deploy on deep SpecOps missions, and I couldn't contact her for months, she wrote me every day. The guys in base camp were always jealous at the boxes of letters waiting for me. When I got back home, we were wrapped around each other for weeks, until we were exhausted."

Eric turned toward Sam. "Now it's all changed, and I miss it. She doesn't look at me anymore with tenderness or passion like when we were first married. All I see now is anger and contempt each time she turns my way. I've tried to hold on. She's just all eaten up inside. No matter what I try to do, nothing works."

He paused a moment. "Hell, now she's started accusing me of screwing around on her. Sam, I've never been unfaithful in my entire marriage. She's even portrayed you as one of my many whores. Those are her words, not mine. That's what she calls any woman I work with. We both know that's bull. I don't see any resolution of this rift between us. I keep hanging on, but I don't think she even cares any more. It's like she sticks around just to punish me for something she's concocted in her mind."

Eric shook his head. "I shouldn't dump all this on you. It's not your problem. It's wrong to share these feelings about my wife with someone else. I'm sorry."

"It's alright. Really, you need to talk with someone who cares about you. If there's anything I can do, just ask. I wish there was some way I could help. Please, if you ever need to talk to a friend, just call."

Sam hesitated and he could tell there was something she wanted to say. For just a second, she parted her lips, like the words were right there on the surface, fighting to get out. Then her month closed and she bit down on her lower lip. After a few seconds, she turned and offered, "If you still want to have children, you can always adopt."

"I've always loved kids, but I would never bring a child into a relationship so torn with distrust. I do want kids someday soon, but I don't know if it will ever happen." As they approached his house, Eric requested, "Drop me at the corner?"

"I'm not afraid to take you up to the driveway. I can take care of myself."

"It's easier for me this way. Just let me off here."

Sam complied. As Eric got out of the car, he paused, "Thanks for coming to my rescue again."

"No problem. You know I owe you for a lot of things. Anytime you need me, I'm here. Even when I move to my next assignment, just pick up the phone. I mean anytime."

"I wish things were different for you. I hate seeing such a good person suffer."

Eric waved while she drove off. He stood gazing down the street at his house, and sighed. He didn't know how much longer he could put up with this. A person can only tolerate such behavior for so long. He'd have to bring things to a close soon. *I'll give it two months. If nothing changes, I'll have to give up and finish things.* Eric walked the last hundred yards to his house and another night of squabbling.

~ * ~

Sam bent down to kiss her son on the lips. Ronnie pointed to his cheek. "No Mom, not there. Do it here. Remember yesterday was my birthday. Nine is too old for that, now."

Sam expressed a solemn smile. "You're not too old to kiss your mom, are you? You're the only man I have in my life."

The young boy hesitated, and then when he scanned his mother's face, said, "No Mom, I didn't mean it that way. I still love you two tanks and two towers. Just kiss me on the cheek from now on, okay?"

It's all happening too fast Ronnie. I'm not ready yet. She obediently kissed her son on the cheek. While Sam pulled up his covers, she capitulated, "Alright, I can live with that, if I must. Sweet dreams, handsome. I love you, Ronnie."

"Me too, Mom."

Sam planned to read for half an hour, but after ten minutes her head nodded. When she heard the book hit the floor, she switched off the light, and turned her head toward the window. The full moon beamed its mellow light down on her peaceful slumber.

Then it came back. From the deepest part of her memory, it returned to haunt her dreams, and inflict the pain. Sam pushed back, as hard as she could. "Stop. Please don't do that. Help me. Someone please get him off of me." Sam continued to fight, but it was no use, he was too big. Tears trailed down her face when she realized there was nothing she could do.

Something touched Sam on the shoulder and brought her out

of the horrible nightmare. She looked over and saw Ronnie patting her arm. "Mom, are you all right? You were screaming in your sleep again."

"Yes sweetheart, I'm alright. It was just a real bad dream."

"Do you want to talk about it? It always makes me feel better when I tell you my dreams."

"Thanks, but I'm okay, really I am."

"What if I sleep with you tonight? It won't come back if I'm there to protect you."

Sam smiled at the small boy with his hands on his hips. "Works for me, Son." As he crawled in next to his mother, Sam pulled him in snugly.

"That's a little tight Mom, but if you need it, I can handle that."

Sam kissed her son on the cheek. "Have to enjoy this while I can. Someday you won't want to be cuddled by your mother."

"I'll always love you, Mom, and I'll always be there to watch out for you. Now go to sleep. You have to work tomorrow and I've got school."

Sam tugged gently on her son's ear. "Good night, my little soldier."

"Good night."

Sam wiped the tears from her cheek and eased into a comfortable sleep.

Four

    The senator peered over the top of his specks at Mr. Harris and Ms. Dickerson seated across and to the right of his desk. Then he focused again on the document they had delivered for his review.
    While he read the report, the young woman stared out the window at the small pond where the mallard gracefully led a newly born set of ducklings. The senator watched her legs flitter up and down nervously as she stared at the small stream feeding into the pond. He noted the similarity between the girl and his youngest daughter; the same full face, pale skin tone, chocolate eyes, and thin lips.
    "Ms. Dickerson, do you have a problem?"
    "No sir, there's no problem here."
    The senator watched as the young woman scanned the rustic surroundings of the large log house; the twenty-foot ceilings with exposed wood beams, and the cedar-stained tongue and groove natural wood planks. He caught the motion of the young woman when she turned toward the massive stone fireplace that consumed half the wall.
    "The chimney and mantle come from right here on my farm. Those are water-worn granite stones from the river running through my lower eighty acres."
    "I've never seen anything like it, and the copper inlays over the mantel are exquisite. Is that image engraved in the top picture the view from your window?"
    "Yes. My daughter is an artist. She did that inlay for my

birthday several years ago." He returned to the report, but remained aware of the discomfort the young woman continued to endure.

After a few minutes, he could no longer bear her obvious predicament. "Young lady, I recognize when a woman is in distress. It's okay, there's no need for you to suffer. Go into the hallway and turn left, it's the third door down on the right."

Both men smiled while she scurried out of the room and pressed her hands securely to her sides.

"She reminds me of my Emma, when she was that age," the senator noted. Then he removed his glasses and tossed them gently onto his desk pad. He pulled the document to within six inches of his eyes and returned to studying the details printed on each page. Every few sheets, the senator shook his head slowly as he interpreted the significance of the results. After he finished the last page, he placed the document down in the center of his desk and turned his attention outside to the large collie that strained at its chain to devour the ducks swimming in the pond.

Without turning his head, he pronounced, "What I have feared for so long is finally here, but much sooner then anyone expected."

"I'm sorry Senator, but we can't discuss the specifics of the report in this unsecured environment. Maybe you should request a mobile secure enclosure for discussing classified material."

"I probably won't be here long enough to justify expending the taxpayer's money for a mobile SCIF. We can just discuss in general what all this means to us as a nation."

As the young woman reentered the room and returned to her chair, the senator's attention returned to the report lying on his desk. "Mr. Harris, tell the director I appreciate what your team has done for us. The question still remains, what are we going to do about it?"

"I'm not sure, Senator, but something has to be done before it's too late."

"I agree, however, the solution will be very complicated technically, politically and socially. There are global ramifications to this, and the way we approach the problem could explode in our faces."

The room silenced as each person searched for something profound to say or share, but nothing was there. The senator stood up, rubbed his left leg, and walked over to peer out the wall of glass that formed the entire south side of his house. "I want to thank both of you for driving down here all the way from Langley to see me."

"It was a pleasant trip, Senator," Mr. Harris said. "I love your farm. It's very peaceful and serene. The mountains seem to reach up and envelope you from all sides."

The senator turned toward the scenic view just outside his window. "I searched for years to find this place. We're nuzzled at the far northern edge of the Shenandoah mountain range. To the right you can see the eastern ridge of Brown Mountain, and off in the distance to the left you can see the tip of Massanutten Mountain. The South Fork of the Shenandoah River forms the lower boundary to my sanctuary."

The young woman interjected, "I bet it's really beautiful out here in the winter."

"When the snow blankets this side of the mountains, the view is simply breathtaking. I can sit here for hours and watch nature slowly paint a white canvas along the ridgelines of the surrounding mountains. The pines along the ridge form fingers that stretch down from the sky. I can't get enough of it. No matter how long I stare out this window, it always consumes me. Regardless of how much pressure and tension they send my way, this view grounds me to what really matters in the grand scheme."

The two guests stood beside the elderly gentleman while he surveyed the twenty-acre pasture positioned at the back of his horse stable and training corral. All three watched the seventy-foot ponderosa pines at the far end of the field waltz back and forth to the rhythm of the wind.

The young woman pointed at the edge of the clearing. "There are three deer coming out of the woods."

"I plant Ladino clover in that field to feed the wildlife. This time of year the does have just dropped their fawns. That one has a set of twins. You can still see the white specks on their coats. I'm also frequently visited by wild turkey, black bear, and occasionally I'll see a bobcat. This place has brought me much peace and happiness over the past twenty years. It saddens me that I don't have much longer to enjoy this gift from our Maker."

The senator paused for a moment, and then limped back

toward his desk to pick up the report. "Have these results been validated? Are you sure they're correct?"

"I wish the report would have turned out differently, but we ran the projections several times. There's no mistake. It will happen, and soon."

The senator shook the hands of the man and woman from Langley. "Tell the Director I am in his debt, and I will stop by when I get back to D.C. next week. Also, I request that these results be tightly held to a small group of people. I'm sure they will eventually be leaked to the press, but I would like some time before the report becomes the Sunday morning media frenzy."

Harris walked over to the desk and placed the report in the courier pouch. Then he locked and secured the contents for the trip back to Washington and placed the key in his pocket. "No problem, Senator. The Robertson Report has already been designated Top Secret."

As the elderly gentleman escorted the two guests to the door, he called into the hallway. "Davis, I need you. Come on in here."

The senator walked over to his rocking chair and sat down. While he watched the two visitors from Langley depart along his long driveway, he rubbed his left leg vigorously. "Damn these old bones are really starting to ache any time I move around much. I guess I'll have to go back to the doctor and have them checked out."

At that moment, a young man in his late twenties knocked on the door and entered the room. "Yes, sir. You wanted to see me?"

"Brian, pull up a chair and watch the evening activities with me as we figure out what our next move should be."

"How did the report turn out, Senator? Was it anything like we discussed?"

"It's worse than expected. I thought we would have more time, but it will be upon us sooner than anyone has imagined. I hope I have enough time left here on Mother Earth to get them to do something before it's too late. Now that we have data that proves I'm not just some silly old crackpot, I want to establish a study to help evaluate potential solutions to our dilemma. We need to determine our best strategy for dealing with this situation before it gets here. If we act immediately, we may still have time to delay the catastrophe until a more prolonged solution can be derived. At least, that's my hope."

"Should we have Langley do this one too?"

Robertson canvassed the energetic young man, his curly brown hair, and muscular frame. He had selected Brian as his aide, but not just because the young man was determined and full of drive. He saw his own image from so long ago; a fresh face wanting to change the world, make a difference, unwilling to realize how naive it was to actually believe he could set everything right.

"No," he replied. "It was all right for them to do the research to verify my hypothesis, but I don't trust those guys to come up with any realistic alternative courses of action. They have a tendency to leak things to the media for their own political purposes. A lot of them want to kick out the incumbent president. We need someone like him in charge with enough guts to make the hardest decision in the history of this nation. I just don't trust them to keep their collective mouths shut, not even for the good of the country."

The young man looked over at the senator. "What if they leak the results of this study?"

"Hell, I'm counting on it. It just might light a short-term fire under my colleague's butts long enough to foster support to get this other study up and running. I'm not worried about this report getting out. It just talks about what's coming. The public will forget about it in a few weeks. They always do. But what we plan to do, that's something else. Some of the strategies we have to consider are likely to be drastic and terminal to everyone involved in the decision process. I don't mean just from a political angle. I believe that many of the actions we need to evaluate will stretch the bounds of our legal authority."

"Then what about the military? They're experienced at conducting this type of study."

"I agree, and generally they're not politically driven. Let's contact the Army to lead the effort. They're familiar with most of the data sources and models needed to conduct this study. They can bring in the other services and think tank groups where they see fit. Let's have them develop optional strategies for dealing with this horrible situation, and I want this study to be compartmented as a Special Access Program. Keep the SAP clearance to no more than two-dozen people. The organizations on the periphery can provide supporting data and analysis without knowing its specific purpose. It's imperative that we keep the study SAP if there's to be any hope of success. Make sure I emphasize that point during our initial preamble meeting."

"What should we call the analysis, the Robertson Study?"

"No, I want no credit for what we have to do. Besides, Langley has already dubbed this one as the Robertson report. It would get confusing as hell. You studied ancient history didn't you? What name do you think would be appropriate?"

The young man thought for a few seconds. "How does the Osiris Study sound?"

"I'm familiar with that Egyptian myth about life and death. I think it fits well. Osiris it is. Now we have to decide who we want to lead the effort."

"What about Colonel Perry Clark? He just got transferred to the Pentagon. He was schooled at Monterey as a green suit modeler, and his father continues to push for the colonel's first star. You could use it as a carrot stick."

"Damn, Brian. I like the way you think. You've been around me too long. I can use it as political leverage on Senator Clark the next time I need help. Maybe he will stop taking shots at me on the Sunday morning circuit, and I would love to see his son get his just dessert. I never liked that guy. He's crooked as a country road."

Davis beamed at the accolades from his mentor. "Senator, I think the colonel is overseeing the Viper missile system Operational Evaluation at White Sands next month and won't be available for three weeks. Do you want me to call him and set up a meeting before he gets wrapped up in the tests? We could set the preamble meeting for next week."

"I forgot all about the Viper OPEVAL. The results of those tests are really important, and I'm aware that Senator Clark has been trying to get those jobs for his constituents. What do you want to bet that Clark had a hand in getting his son to oversee those Viper tests?"

The senator scratched his gray sideburns for a moment. "Get General Williams on the line for me. I want him to send an independent observer to the Viper tests. We'll have the general forward a copy of the report to us without any filtering through the chain of command. Williams is a good man, he will comply with the request when he understands my reasons. Also, set up a meeting with the two lead members from both sides of the Armed Services Committee. I'll have to get their support to establish the Osiris Study. Have Colonel Clark and his daddy come as observers. That should be enough bait to hook them good."

"Yes sir. Is there anything else I can do for you?"

"On the way back to your office, ask Rose to bring me a big glass of her wonderful tea. I'm really thirsty for some reason. By the way, if you want to invite your fiancée down to ride the horses and spend the weekend with us that would be fine. That girl has a beautiful set of legs, kind of reminds me of Rose when we were young. They were something to see. I'll even give you Saturday off so you can spend some romantic time at the pavilion down by the river, but your tail is mine again Sunday morning.

We've got tons to do and there's not much time. Now get me that tea, get on the phone, and call that girl before she decides to get someone else for the weekend. I'm just going to sit here for a few minutes and wait for my animal friends to come out and visit me."

"Thank you, Senator. Julie will appreciate coming here again. She is starting to rag me about all the hours I spend away from her. I'll be right back with that tea."

"Thank you, Senator. Julie will appreciate coming here again. She is starting to rag me about all the hours I spend away from her. I'll be right back with that tea."

The young man hurried out of the room and left the seventy-four year old senator to enjoy the scenic view unfolding as the evening sun began its descent behind the distant mountain ridge.

Five

The colonel leaned forward in the chair. He twirled his hat as he waited impatiently in the senator's reception area.

When the phone on the secretary's desk rang, the woman seated at the computer screen picked up the receiver. "Yes Sir, I'll send him in."

The secretary tilted her head down, and looked over her glasses at the man with the thin mustache and raven eyes. Although it was difficult to relate to the colonel, his dry personality, the cold stares, she still felt sympathy for his isolated life, and the harsh nature of the relationship with his father, the senator. The way the senator screamed at his son and treated him like a dog made her skin crawl. Her heart sank to hear anyone treat their own blood in such a cruel manner. She cleared her throat and informed Colonel Perry, "Your father will see you now."

The colonel took a deep breath, walked in and saw Carlson, with his crew cut hair and square face, positioned in his typical catbird position three feet to the right of Senator Clark's desk.

Without a greeting, Senator Clark began drilling his son Perry. "How many times do I have to tell you to stop screwing around with subordinates? I'm working my tail off to get your star and you can't keep your whacker corralled in your shorts. This is the last time I'm going to warn you, I swear. I can cover up a lot of your foul-ups, but this is different. You're going to blow all my work to get you into politics. Coercing any junior officer to grease your johnson is a court martial offense. It will end your military career and any hope of a seat in Congress. If you can't get a regular woman to hump, Carlson has a list of very discreet whores you can hound."

Perry glanced at the person he called father. He surveyed the fat man's oily scalp, his protruding double chin, and yellow faded teeth that projected spittle with every tenth word. He redirected his eyes out the window, listened to the senator's harsh voice hammering at his offspring, issuing a relentless stream of verbal assaults toward his son. Periodically, Perry glanced toward Carlson to see him shake his head and grin at each bullet the senator fired at his son.

"I'm not going to talk to you about this again. Is that clear? Next time, you're on your own. If this shit gets into the press, it will cost me a ton of votes. I can't let you screw up my career too. Understand?"

The old man looked at his son with the same piercing stare he always used.

The colonel glared hard into his father's eyes. He wanted to say what he really felt. It was bubbling in his throat, trying to get out. All these years he had been forced down a path he despised. The military, the politics, the lies, everything he had surrendered to, it twisted and pulled at his insides. He wanted desperately to throw it back in his father's face. He never gave a shit about any of this, but he was never asked. No one really cared what he wanted. He opened and closed his lips twice to let it out, but nothing came up.

Impatiently, the older man demanded, "I asked you a question. Did you understand what I just said? A simple yes or no will suffice."

Perry looked down at the left leg of the desk and nodded.

"Fine. Now I want to discuss something else. My contacts over at Langley inform me that Robertson plans to commission an important study, and I want to be part of this one. I need to keep tabs on that old fart."

The phone on the senator's desk rang, "Yes, Mrs. Johnson, what is it?"

"There's a call from a Mr. Brian Davis. He's an aide for Senator Robertson."

"What the hell does he want? If Robertson needs to talk, tell him to call me personally."

"The young man says it's about you and the colonel

attending a meeting on a new study Senator Robertson has organized, but I'll give him your message."

"No wait, I'll take this one. What did you say his name was?"

"Brian Davis, Senator."

Clark sat straight up in his chair, cleared his throat, and pushed the blinking light on his phone. "Hello Brian, how can I help you this morning? Yes, I heard something about that study. When is it? Yes, I can be there. Really, my son too? Tell Senator Robertson that we would be happy to attend his meeting. Yes, I understand, flies on the wall for this one. No problem. Tell the senator I appreciate the invitation. No, you don't need to call him. I'll inform my son. That's fine, we'll see you then."

Clark leaned back in his chair and grinned while he informed Carlson of the news. "Well I'll be damned. Ask and you shall receive. I must be living right. Robertson wants me on the oversight committee for the new study."

Finally the senator turned toward his son. "Guess who Robertson recommended to be the task leader for this effort? You."

The empty expression on Perry's face transformed to one of apprehension.

"Don't look so scared, damn it. This is exactly want we need. This could push you right over the top. These opportunities don't come around often. We need to keep close tabs on what's going on in the background. They plan to have the Headquarters for the Department of the Army run this one out of the Pentagon for some reason."

The senator turned to the man seated next to him. "Carlson, I'm going to get you a temporary position over there at Army Headquarters. Help Perry any way you can, and make sure he doesn't mess this one up."

The senator turned back to his son. "One more thing before you go. This Viper Operational Evaluation is very important to both of us. It has to go off without a hitch. We need that contract and those jobs back home if I'm going to have any chance in the next election. I've talked to the company and assured them that you will help to make this happen, no matter what it takes. I had to call in a lot of favors so you could lead this one. Do this right, Perry. Don't screw up this time, you got it?"

The colonel nodded, turned and exited his father's office.

After he'd closed the door, Clark looked at Carlson. "I want you to watch my son on this new study. Your position will be in the computer security group for the Army Headquarters. You need to get a list of the people that will be working on his team. Keep an eagle eye on everything that goes on. Report anything suspicious back to me. Understand?"

With a grin, Carlson replied, "Yes, I understand completely."

"There's one more thing. I set it up so that you would be my personal observer for the Viper test. You'll need to leave today to get there for the opening meeting in the morning. I made him schedule the firing two days ahead of when everyone else gets there. That way we can blame the assistant for sending out the wrong schedule. It would be too costly for them to run the live shots again. Call me immediately after the tests are done and let me know how it goes. Hopefully, the company has worked out the bugs this time. Now get going."

While Carlson walked out the door, Clark called to his secretary. "Mary, get General Hamilton on the phone. He's the oversight authority for the Viper OPEVAL. If he's not in his office, he's probably on his way to White Sands. Buzz me when you get him."

The thin haired man looked out the large window. He'd make sure Hamilton funnels all results through his office. The right tone could mean everything.

Six

As Eric sat on the worn brown-leather couch in the waiting area, he studied the abundance of memorabilia scattered around the room. Each piece represented a fragment of a long career dedicated to the service of his country and his men. There were emblems from each tour and assignment Major General Williams had served across his twenty-eight year career. Eric stood and walked the perimeter of the small entry space to the general's office. Just below a plaque of his tour in Korea was a bookcase with an assortment of cups. Eric surveyed the two-dozen coffee mugs for each program the general supported; Apache, ATACMS, JSTARS, and numerous other weapon systems that had been fielded over the years.

"Damn, he still has it." Eric picked up one specific cup and ran his fingers over the embossed symbol of a Doberman chewing on the body of a large dead snake.

The receptionist seated off to the right of the entry turned his way. "I'm sorry, what did you say, Mr. Emerson?"

"This one, he still has it after all these years. I gave him this SpecOps cup just before he left the theater. We made him an honorary member of the Snake Eaters after he flew in under fire and recovered my team and I, or what was left of it. During the extraction, he took shrapnel in his butt and a large chunk of the fuselage in his right knee. He was one hell of a pilot. That's why he limps, and he never lets me forget it either."

The receptionist pushed her pearl-rimmed glasses higher on her nose and inclined her head. "I wondered why he limped. I figured it was from a football injury or something. That intel on the steel in his derriere is priceless. He's got a birthday coming up. Now I know what picture to put on his cake."

Eric grinned. "Guess I better keep my mouth shut. Don't tell him I spilled his secret. I don't need something else for him to razz me about."

The phone interrupted the conversation before the receptionist could respond. "Yes sir, Mr. Emerson is here. I'll send him in." She hung up the receiver and motioned Eric toward the door. "He's all yours."

When Eric entered the office, he was greeted by a second array of mementos that the general had carried with him across the years. Eric glanced at the large man while he talked on the phone and waited for the general to finish his call. He walked over to the corner curio cabinet to admire the variety of iconic models of different weapon systems. The detail in the models was extensive. The small version of the 7.62 Vulcan gun had bullets passing through the ammo chute. The nine inch long AH-1J Cobra helicopter had a loaded pod of 2.75 inch Zuni rockets. Even the AHIP version of the OV-58 chopper had a functioning main and tail rotor. The collection was truly impressive.

"Yes, Mr. Davis. You can tell him we will be happy to participate. No, it's not a problem. Yes I understand. Goodbye."

The general stood up, walked around his desk to Eric, rubbing his knee along the way. "Hey you old Snake Eater. Man, this knee still hurts me. Do you sleep well at night knowing you cost me my wings?"

"I sleep like a baby. General, you play that guilt trip on me each time I see you. It just isn't going to work. I didn't tell you to fly your MH 60 right over that ZSU-23 unit. After your Blackhawk got shot up, we were lucky to get back at all. It must have been that damn fine co-pilot of yours."

The general smiled. "You say that every time too. Good to see you again, Eric. Sorry I don't get down to visit you guys as much as I used to. This damn Future Combat Program consumes every minute I've got. We've put a lot of our eggs in this FCP basket. We've got to make it work or we'll be in trouble ten years downstream."

Eric pointed to the furnishings in the office. "You've moved some fancy furniture in here since the last time I came to see you, General. This didn't come out of any GSA catalog. The curio and coffee table look like antiques."

"They are. I love the simplistic rugged look. I bought them for my wife at an estate auction when I was on tour in Germany. It's out of the English Arts & Crafts style over a hundred years ago. When my wife passed away in January, I brought them in here with me. They were two of her favorite pieces of furniture. Now that she's gone, I spend most of my time here at the office, and I like to have them around on those long nights. They'll go with me on my next assignment. That's why I wanted to see you, Eric. They've called me up to work at the Pentagon. I'm going to be the central focal point at headquarters for the airborne component of FCP."

"It sounds like they're prepping you for that third star. Congratulations."

"That's what I figured too. That's why I wanted to see you. I would really like to have you on my staff at the Pentagon. We'd make a hell of a team again. You could do some really good things up there. It would likely be a promotion to a Fourteen for you. What do you say?"

"General, I can't think of anything I'd like better than to continue working under your command, and I recognize it's one hell of an opportunity for me. Unfortunately, I've got some major difficulties at home right now. Relocating would make everything worse. I still want to try and work things out."

"Tell you what. I'll leave the invitation open for three or four months. If things straighten out at home, give me a call. I have two positions on my staff for Operations Analysts. Do you know anyone else that's the cream of the cream?"

"Yes I do, General. Major Samantha Cassidy. She is top notch analytically, and a real team player. She's a single mom with a nine-year-old son, so she would only be able to work a ten-hour day, but she'll give you 120%. She would be my choice."

"The major worked with me on the Orion effort several years ago. She did a damn fine job. Not bad on the eyes either. It's a good suggestion. I'll call her in and talk to her myself. One more thing, guess who's taking a trip to the White Sands Missile Range?"

Eric offered an assessment that he knew to be wrong.

"You're going out to WMSR to help them on the Viper Operational Evaluation. That's mighty good of you sir. I'm sure you'll do a fine job out there."

"Think again, hotshot. Pack your bags and clear your schedule. The tests are planned for next week. You're to act as an independent observer for me. Your report is to come straight back to this office. I'll distribute copies of the report from here before I leave."

"Sir, you're aware that I'll tell it exactly like it is. I'm not going to pull any punches. It's likely to draw a lot of heat. I think they've pushed that system toward deployment too damn fast. I won't shy away from reporting anything I see."

"I'm sending you because of your reputation, not in spite of it. Call it like you see it."

"General, they're obviously grooming you for your next star. Are you sure you want to be associated with this firecracker?"

"You let me worry about that. I'm not going to pass a live one on to someone else. It's on my command so I'll deal with it. You just write up what you see."

"I'd prefer not to wait till next week. I've worked with this team before and...I think I should be there tomorrow, just in case they are so good they do the test early."

"You're referring to Colonel Perry Clark. I've seen you two have words before."

"Yes sir. He forgets I'm not a green-suiter anymore, and I love to remind him."

"Remember, he is a colonel and you should respect the uniform, if not the man."

"I do, General. Every time I look at the bird on his shoulder it gnaws at me how the hell they let one slip through."

"Fortunately, all those years in a chopper have affected my hearing. Are you going to need any support?"

"Yes sir. A second pair of eyes will help short circuit any claims of personal bias. Have the second person prepare their report separately and forward it directly to you."

"That's a good idea. Anyone in mind?"

"Major Cassidy."

"I'm starting to see a pattern here. All right, if you trust her that much, so do I. You tell her to drop what she's working on and prepare for a fun trip, but I'll talk to her myself about the Pentagon assignment."

"You won't be disappointed, General."

"Hopefully, things will work out at home and I'll see you up there. Get that Viper report to me by the day you return so I can handle it on my shift. See you, Eric."

"Will do, and good luck at the Pentagon. Don't let them swallow you whole." Eric departed from General Williams' office and headed down the hall to see his friend Sam.

Seven

Eric walked into the office, nodded at Tanya seated in the counter, and then quietly eased in behind Sam to watch as she studied the analytical model running on her computer console, typing feverishly with those slender delicate fingers. Even at this distance, he caught the faint smell of her natural feminine scent blended with the mild fragrance of some type of cologne. He picked up a few rubber bands from the dark gray metal desk to his left, and dropped them onto her head.

Sam removed the earphones from her MP3 player and turned around. "Just like a little boy, always playing games."

Eric pulled up a chair and sat down. "Hey, guess where you're headed tomorrow?"

"Rome, London, Paris, somewhere glamorous like that, right?"

"Not exactly. You've been directed to participate as an independent observer for the Viper Operational Evaluation. That's, of course, assuming that you're interested in the assignment."

"Are you kidding me? I'd love to get away from here, especially on something that important. Is anyone else going with me, or is this a solo flight?"

"You're looking at him."

Sam smiled. "I smell a rascal at work. You set this up, didn't you? Just so you'd have a woman to take notes for you."

"When have I ever treated you like that? You're to make your own separate report directly to General Williams, and I had nothing to do with this. I know what a pain in the butt you can be on

TDY trips, always late, and always telling me what to do."

"I was joking with you. You've never treated me with anything but respect."

Sam looked over at her office roommate, then back into Eric's dark blue eyes. She leaned over and whispered, "Thanks, I do appreciate it."

"If you like, I'll make the arrangements. We can fly out together, that way you won't talk some poor stranger's ear off, but we have to leave tonight. I don't trust Clark."

"Colonel Clark will be there?"

"Yes, he's leading the tests. Is that okay, or do you want me to get someone else to attend the test in your place?"

Sam hesitated. She looked down at the floor for a moment, and then back up at her friend. "Will you be there the whole time?"

"I'll be standing right beside you."

"Then I'm your man, so to speak. Should I pick you up at your house?"

"It would be great if you could drive us to the airport. My second car is still stranded and I can't leave my wife without a vehicle for two weeks. It would probably be better if I meet you somewhere else. There's no sense in upsetting Karen. I'll take a taxi to the library and you can pick me up there. I'll call you later when I schedule our flight. Remember, you have to be there two hours early. Don't make me miss the flight like last time."

"A girl is entitled to one mistake. You wouldn't have appreciated rushing through security with me after Ronnie threw up all over everything. I felt terrible the whole trip leaving him that way with Mom and Dad."

"Hell, they loved it. Everyone looks forward to getting up all night with a sick kid. I've got to get back to my office and read up on the Viper system and the test plan. I suggest you clear your slate for the rest of the day and do the same. I'll send you the material as soon as I'm done with it. I assume that you'll take Ronnie over to your parents this afternoon so I'll try to send the stuff to you in an hour."

Eric stood to leave. "Remember to wear your Flak jacket and watch your words when we get there. This one could become a political nightmare."

"I can take care of myself. You don't have to worry about

me."

"Maybe, but I think you can still turn that gold leaf to silver. If there's heat to bear, let me take the brunt of it."

Sam cocked her head slightly and motioned Eric away with her right hand. "Always the hero, now get out of here."

As Eric walked out the door, Sam's sole roommate pushed her chair across the small room next to where Sam was seated. "Girl, don't go chasing a white knight away from your doorstep. The man has always treated you like a princess, and that's a rare thing these days. Such a handsome fellow is prime for the pickin'."

"Tanya, Eric and I are just good friends. We've known each other since we were classmates at the Postgraduate School in Monterey ten years ago."

"I've seen his wife. At the office party last Christmas, she treated him like a dog. Girlfriend, there is a window open in that marriage if you just climb on in."

"There may be problems at home, but the man respects his vows, and I respect him for that. I don't plan to interfere or cause any additional turmoil in his life. You are right, though. He does see me differently than the others around here. He has always treated me with respect, someone that can contribute to the mission. Most of the others see me as a competitor, or someone who has been given a free ride because of my gender. I studied and trained just as hard as they did to serve my country, but they don't look at it that way. Then there are the few obnoxious ones that see me, not as a colleague, but as an object to ogle. Not Eric. He sees me as a person with a brain."

"Girlfriend, where in the world have you been? That boy is looking at more than your brain."

Sam grinned. "I'm not blind. I'm aware there's an attraction, but it's different, it's like it's supposed to be between a man and woman. You know what I mean, admiration from a distance."

"Are you saying that when you look at his handsome rugged face, your blood don't churn?"

Sam continued working silently at her computer.

"You're going to sit there and tell me you haven't noticed that rock-hard body and tight butt? Have you checked your pulse lately?"

Sam still did not respond.

"I know what the problem is; it's that dark side that all SpecOps guys have. They're asked to do some really harsh things on those deep attack missions. That's what it is. He scares the hell out of you."

"Think again. He only did what he had to in order to survive and complete his mission. It just adds to his mystery and charm."

"That's what I thought. He does get to you. You just don't want to admit it."

"Like I said, he's married. If he wasn't, maybe, but he is."

"He is one fine looking man, even with that scar. Was he in an accident or something?"

"No, it happened in combat. He actually got a Silver Star for the mission. I'm not privy to the specifics because it was a classified covert operation, but I've heard he saved the life of his surviving team member after he himself was badly wounded."

"Damn. I wish he had it for me like he does for you. I'd do something about it. I'd get a lock on him and never let go, but I'm sure you wouldn't understand what I mean by that would you, Miss Innocent?"

Sam felt herself blush. She turned back to the screen. "Okay, I've heard enough. Go back over there and get to work. I have to finish this if I'm going TDY tonight."

Tanya pushed her chair back over to her desk. "Got you thinking and the juices flowing didn't it? You may fool him, but Tanya sees all and knows all."

Sam put her MP3 earphones back on her head. "I'm not listening to any more of your gossip…Girlfriend."

Eight

Eric sat on the bench at the foot of the library entryway. Despite a stiff wind, his eyes remained fixed on the path leading from behind the brick building. He detected the distinctive sound of small wheels speeding along asphalt. The noise became progressively louder until four boys on blades launched from the parking lot onto the walkway. He followed the kids snaking around the occupants of the sideway. The convoy of rollerblades barreled toward the road, then darted back and forth between the vehicles paused at the stoplight. He noticed the sign, 'No bikes or rollerblades', and smiled.

A horn beeped twice and Sam drove up in her silver tone Elantra. When he circled around to the back of her car, she got out grinning cheek to cheek. "Aren't you proud of me? I'm fifteen minutes early. I thought I would beat you here."

"Shocked is more like it."

After Eric put his single bag in the trunk, they both got back into the vehicle for the twenty-minute ride to the airport. Throughout the short trip, he listened as she chatted about the things she had to do to get ready for the trip.

At the ramp to the airport parking lot, Eric inquired, "Why the big grin? Is there something you want to share with your bud?"

"I'm just happy to be taking this trip."

"What's so good about waiting two hours in a line to be crammed into a butt-crushing seat for three and a half hours? Then we have to spend ten days at White Sands to monitor the tests on an air defense system being rushed into production. I'm only doing this because General Williams made it a direct order."

"It's all about perspective. I love to travel, and I don't get to do it all the time like you. I plan to enjoy every minute. You'd have a different slant if you were a single parent stuck in a small apartment with a nine-year-old boy full of energy. When I get home at night, Ronnie is ready for some time with his mother. I love my son but he's like a rubber ball bouncing around the apartment."

"It doesn't take long to get burned out of living from a suitcase every other week, and it can levy a heavy toll on relationships."

Sam pulled into the satellite parking lot and searched for an empty space. "Maybe, but for me, these trips are a mini vacation. I'm out of my green suit and actually get to look like a woman for a while. Plus I love trying out new restaurants. I never get out much with all the hours we work. You probably wouldn't understand this, but when you're an officer in the military; you don't get to work an eight hour day like you civilians."

Eric replied, "Woman, you're so full of it. You always leave the office before me." They walked to the rear of the vehicle and when Sam bent inside the trunk to remove her suitcase, he noted, "I will admit, you do look nice in blue jeans."

With her face still directed inside the trunk of the car, Sam smiled, but when she turned toward Eric, she replaced the smile with a frown. "No wonder you stay in trouble with your wife."

"I said I was faithful, I didn't say I was dead. There's the shuttle bus. Hurry up or we'll miss it."

Eric grabbed both their bags and hobbled toward the bus. In slow motion Sam closed the trunk, brushed back her hair, and spun her keys around her finger before tucking them leisurely into the pocket of her skintight jeans.

Eric looked back and yelled, "I'm always waiting on a woman. Come on, or I'll tell them to leave your tail behind."

Sam took her time. She knew he would never leave her stranded anywhere, and she loved to make him wait. She meandered slowing behind her friend, admired his buttocks as he tossed their bags into the bus, and whispered to herself, "Not bad, not bad at all."

~ * ~

When Sam returned from the restroom just outside the boarding area, she caught a slight grin as Eric gazed at the two girls seated two rows to his right. "A bit young for you aren't they, guy? Been a long time, has it?"

"Always with the smart ass comments, aren't you? I just got tickled at the conversation they're having."

Sam looked back at the teenagers. "I wasn't aware you understood sign language. What are they saying?"

"They've been comparing notes on their dates last Saturday. Those are two energetic and inventive young ladies."

Sam leaned over and whispered, "Come on, share the gossip. What are they saying?"

"Ouch, that's a bit spicy. Girls are a lot more adventurous today than when I prowled the streets. Oh, this is just getting too kinky. It's been a long time since I even considered that stuff. Better tune out before they get me all spun up and I have a heart attack."

With a tone of frustration Sam demanded, "Darn it, are you going to clue me in or not!"

"Not. You'd have me up on harassment charges if I told you what they said. I can't afford the lawsuit."

"Eric Emerson, if you don't tell me, I'll never speak to you again, and I mean it."

He leaned over and motioned her closer. As she did so, he became momentarily distracted by the smell of her strawberry scented body lotion.

"Yes, go ahead. Tell me."

Eric whispered a portion of the conversation. She smiled. "Boy that is spicy, isn't it?"

"That's only the mild stuff. I'll save the rest for another time when conditions are just right."

Sam slapped Eric lightly on the leg, and as he opened his journal on discrete event simulations she asked, "Where did you learn to sign? Can you read lips, too?"

As they boarded the airplane, Eric replied, "Yes I can. I lost a portion of my hearing in combat when I was in the service and a mortar round landed next to me. I taught myself to lip read to help compensate. It comes in real handy sometimes, so you better not talk about me while I'm in the room."

"What about the signing? You always avoid my questions, don't you?"

"You shouldn't be so damn nosy all the time."

"I'm going to keep asking until you tell me, so you might as well fess up and save yourself the aggravation."

"My sister was a deaf mute. Everyone in my family learned to sign."

"Now I understand why that young girl Judi, up in the Office of the Under Secretary of the Army, lights up every time we visit the Pentagon. I just thought she had a crush on that handsome sad-sack face of yours. I guess she likes crusty old men that speak her language. You do realize that she's got it bad for you."

"Cut it out. Judi is a sweetheart, and she has a really nice boyfriend. It's amazing what she's accomplished with the challenges she's had to overcome. The girl never asks for a free ride or special treatment. I do care for her, but as a mentor and nothing else. I help her professionally whenever I can. She's going to be a great operations analyst one day. She reminds me a lot of my sister. Same size, hair color, even her gestures mimic my sister."

Once positioned in their assigned seats, Sam continued her stream of questions. "I've never heard you mention your sister before. Do you get to see her very much?"

Eric paused, and then looked out the small window of the plane across the aisle. "No."

"Does she live far away?"

"She's not here anymore."

What do you mean--she doesn't live locally?"

"No, Robin died a long time ago."

"I'm sorry. What happened?"

He fought the visions. He bit his lip to shield the old wound, but he found it difficult to deny Sam anything she wanted. "Robin was killed. She was murdered by someone that should never have been allowed to walk among normal people."

"I didn't mean to make you revisit sad memories. I'll just keep my big mouth shut for the rest of the trip."

He looked into Sam's sparkling green eyes. "That's an impossible feat. I'll bet you twenty bucks you can't last the trip without another word."

"You're on, Mister."

Within twelve minutes, she forgot about their bet and restarted the stream of dialogue. "Look at all the lights out there. It's really pretty to fly across the country at night and watch people scurry around in the cities."

Eric glanced at his watch. "You did real well. Twelve minutes without stopping me from reading this article."

Sam smirked. "So I guess you expect to be paid, do you?"

"I'll just put it on your bill."

He looked out the window and gazed at the dotted lights creating a web-like pattern in the early twilight. "I think there's a lot more today compared to when I started traveling for the Army. Back then, you could go eight to ten minutes before viewing one of those clusters of city life, now they're back to back, every two minutes."

Eric noted the growing blanket of urban sprawl. "When I was a young boy, I built model airplanes on the kitchen table as I listened to the radio, I remember one night hearing the news that the census had just tabulated 175 million people in America. There are three hundred million in the country today. Do you realize that's roughly a seventy percent increase during my short life? It amazes me this country is able to flourish with that many mouths to feed, homes to heat, and cars to drive. I wonder how far we can go before we hit a wall."

"Man, you don't get to pick the topics anymore. You're just Mr. Negative aren't you? Sit back, read your article, and listen to my story about Ronnie. Can you believe that he already has a little special friend in his life? I thought boys were only interested in snails and snakes and dirt at this age. I think…"

Eric grinned as Sam dominated the conversation. He actually enjoyed hearing her felicitous banter. The only other feminine dialogue he experienced of late was the constant barrage of accusations and stones tossed his way whenever he and Karen were together. He had planned to take a nap, but this one-way discussion was actually refreshing. Being caged with a nine year old night after night obviously demanded a little adult conversation. He put his magazine away, and listened as Sam shifted the discussion to the opportunity General Williams had offered her at the Pentagon.

Nine

Eric was seated in the lobby of the motel when Sam came up and tugged on his ear. He glanced down at his watch, then back up at the smile on her face. "Twenty minutes. I've been sitting here in this damn lobby for twenty minutes."

"I'll make it up to you. Let's stop at the donut store across the street and I'll treat for breakfast."

"From now on, I'm going plan on being late every time you and I go anywhere together. Maybe I'll just lie and tell you we have to meet thirty minutes sooner, that way you'll be on time."

"It would only work for a while. Besides, I always like to see your attractive face waiting for me, kind of makes me feel like I actually control something."

Eric stood up and mumbled something as he walked toward the exit.

"I heard that Mr. Emerson. That's not very nice to say to a lady."

"Come on, I need a cup of coffee. I can see this is going to be a long trip."

As Eric munched his second cruller, she looked out the window at the pecan orchards spattered across the landscape intermixed with patches of barren desert. "It's really beautiful out here, in a desolate sort of way."

"I thought you had been to White Sands before?"

"I have, but we flew in by helicopter from El Paso. I was too scared watching General Williams try to remember how to pilot a helicopter again. I had my eyes closed the entire flight. Besides, it doesn't look the same from the air rushing by at 150 miles per hour. I thought we were supposed to stay at the Bachelor Officer Quarters out here. Weren't there any rooms available?"

"There probably were, but have you ever stayed at the BOQ?"

"Yes, I have."

"Did you like it?"

"No, I did not."

Eric continued driving up the mountain road toward the base. He forced a serious expression onto his face and turned to his riding partner. "You aren't happy we're staying in town? Would you prefer to eat in the cafeteria at the base? I thought you liked to sample restaurants in new areas. Isn't that what you told me? Maybe you don't like this pleasant morning drive, is that what you're saying, because if you're not happy, I'm not happy. We can turn around, go back, and check out of the motel."

"I should never have let you get prune juice for breakfast. It's made you too cantankerous this morning, Mr. Smarty. I was just wondering how you arranged for us to stay thirty miles away in Las Cruces instead of at the BOQ, that's all."

"You're not cleared for that kind of information."

"Let me reach into my briefcase and take out a ruler, then I'll whack you were it really hurts."

Eric grinned but kept his eyes fixed on the road. "I had our itinerary set up to visit the University of New Mexico in town. I figured that if we have time, we might visit their interactive simulation lab. It's supposed to be quite impressive. They can run 3D force or force scenarios. I figured you might enjoy it, but again, it you'd rather not see where our profession is moving technically, then just let me know, because my aim in life is to make sure you're happy, Miss Cassidy."

"Aw, shut up and watch the road."

Eric parked the rental car at the visitor center outside the gate of the White Sands Missile Range. He held the door open for Sam, and then they both walked up to the guard at the desk.

"Good morning. I'm Eric Emerson and this is Major Cassidy

from the TRADOC Analysis Command Headquarters at Fort Monroe. We're here for the Viper Missile operational evaluation. Our clearances were passed to your security yesterday."

The guard turned toward the computer screen. "Hold on a minute."

After checking his monitor, the guard turned toward Eric and Sam. "I'm sorry sir, but according to my system, your tour on base is not scheduled till next week."

Eric pointed to the line on the screen entitled, *Clearance effective date*. "You can see our clearances are effective today."

"I can see that, but your visit is not authorized till next week."

Eric reached across the counter and picked up the small note pad next to the guard. He jotted a number on the first sheet of paper under the title *Major General Williams*. "Call this number. It's his direct phone. When the general answers, inform him his representatives were blocked from attending the pre-firing brief today. You should also contact Senator Clark and tell him his favorite contract will be postponed. All because the general's representatives were refused entry to the test *Mr. Griffith*. That is your name, right? I suggest you have a good explanation, seeing our clearances have been approved."

The guard glanced down at the pad of paper. Then he looked at the screen, and back at the two visitors. Finally, he scratched his head. "Can I see some identification please, a driver's license will do." After both visitors provided identification, the guard instructed, "Please sign here."

"What was that all about?" Sam inquired as they drove toward the test facility.

"Whenever I've worked with Colonel Clark before, he had a tendency to play games with the schedule. He'll give you the wrong time for a meeting because he doesn't want you there, then he blames it on his secretary. You should be prepared for a scuffle when we arrive. I'll bet you dinner tonight that they don't expect us to be here yet, and that they're not going to be happy when we stroll through the door. If you take anything from this trip, never let political games or incompetence deter you from getting the job done. Understand?"

Sam smiled and chopped out a mock salute. "Yes sir."

~ * ~

Sam stopped just past the doorframe of the briefing room and pulled on Eric's shirt.

He raised his eyebrows. "What?"

"You didn't tell me all this brass would be here," she whispered. Even in the dim light, she saw half a dozen General Level Officers, and two prominent Congressmen.

"What are you saying, you want to go sit in the car or something?"

"Don't start that crap again. I'm serious."

The man at the podium pointed a laser pin at the slide on the overhead projector. He glanced up in irritation at the voices at the back of the room. "Excuse me, you're interrupting a closed briefing."

Eric stared at the thin man at the podium. Clark had always reminded him of one of the villainous figures on the Saturday cartoon shows. The same slicked down black hair parked in the middle with a French style cut, the small pencil sized mustache, and the extended Adam's apple that protruded from a scrawny neck like a studding turkey gobbler. "Sorry Colonel Clark, but someone gave us the wrong time. It must have been a clerical error."

The man at the front of the room began to twirl the laser pointer in his hand. "I'm sorry but participation in this Viper OPEVAL was by invitation."

As if choreographed, the heads of the visitors in the room bounced like a ping-pong match as they watched the contest of wills.

Eric volleyed, "I understand. We have been directed by General Williams to observe the test. I'm sure you know the general sits on the Army Headquarters Acquisition Review Board." He reached for the phone next to the door. "But if you prefer Colonel, I'll call the general and suggest he convene a special meeting of the Board, to understand why his representatives were denied participation in the Viper OPEVAL."

Eric started to dial. The colonel glanced over at one of the men seated in the front row. When Carlson nodded, Clark turned back toward Eric and relented. "That won't be necessary, Mr. Emerson. We would be glad to get your inputs on what we're doing here."

Clark continued to turn the laser pointer, as a shade of red spread across his face. He turned back to the audience and suggested, "It's time for a ten minute break. There's coffee and donuts in the back so everyone help themselves. We'll assemble at nine twenty, then we'll head over to control center Baker to commence phase one of the tests."

When Sam and Eric moved over to the refreshment table, a hand came down on his head and mussed his hair. "How the hell are you doing, Hammer?"

Eric turned around and came face to face with a large-framed man roughly two inches taller. "Duke, you son of a bitch, you're still alive."

The two friends shook hands vigorously, and then Eric reached down and knocked on the man's thigh. "How's the leg, Pinocchio?"

"Aches all the time, but I'd rather be the bionic man than dead."

When Sam cleared her throat, the large man looked in her direction. He surveyed up and down her frame, like a fox eying a hen.

"Who is your gorgeous escort? Has she got a friend?"

"Cut it out, or I'll kick your one-legged ass out the window. This is Major Cassidy. She and I work for General Williams at TRADOC. We're here to observe the Viper tests. Sam, this is Harry Myers, but everyone calls him Duke. He and I served together in the 75th Ranger Regiment."

"Eric, what do you say we have dinner tonight to bull over old times? We could meet up at Pete's Pig House; say at 1800. How's that sound?"

"Man that would be great. I haven't been out there in years."

The major requested, "Can a woman participate or is this just a guy thing?"

"This place is a bit rustic. I'm not sure you can handle it."

"I'm a country girl. If they have great food, I'm up for it."

"Major," Duke encouraged Sam, "you would bring color and class to the whole meal, but you need to toss the green suit. They don't take kindly to people wearing a suit and tie, and if you're there, I promise to be a gentleman."

Eric turned to his old friend. "Why are you here?"

"I work for the company that's building the Viper missile system. Can you believe it? I'm a highly paid contractor now. How come you haven't come over to the money side yet? With your experience and reputation, you could draw a hefty paycheck."

"I keep telling myself I can still make a difference from the inside, but I do consider it from time to time."

Eric turned his head back toward Colonel Clark as he reentered the room and started to talk to Carlson. "Maybe one day I'll get fed up with guys like that and say the hell with it."

Harry grinned. "That was like old times watching you snip his balls. Oh, I'm sorry, Major. Sometimes I forget my manners."

"Being in the military with all the grunting testosterone, it's not like I haven't hear it before. Where do you know Colonel Clark from?"

"Old Knuckles failed out of the Rangers. Couldn't even make the first cut."

"Why do you call him Old Knuckles?"

"Watch him when he gets nervous or starts putting up a humma humma. He'll twirl whatever's in his hands around his knuckles."

When Sam saw Eric was about to explain the jargon, she put her hand in front of his lips. "Give me a break. I know that humma humma means a smoke screen. I've been in the Army long enough to understand what a smoke generator sounds like, thank you. Now if you two civilians don't mind, I'll go sit over there while you boys rag on the colonel. I'm not permitted to belittle a senior officer."

As she walked away, Sam offered a final word. "That's not to say it wasn't fun to listen to you two guys do it."

After Sam moved out of range, Duke suggested, "Man she's a wild filly. She reminds me of my ex-wife. She was a red headed fireball too. Have you tapped that sweet thing yet?"

"Stop it right there. I'm serious, Harry. The major is a good friend of mine, nothing more. I respect her, and she's an outstanding officer, so cut that shit out. Got it?"

"Sorry Hammer, I didn't understand. You mean you never even entertained the thought?"

"I didn't say that, but I would never verbalize it in the foul crude way you did."

"I got you, no more gutter talk. I promise. By the way, it was great to watch you and Clark jockey back and forth."

"It was no big deal. The colonel never could learn you don't screw with a snake eater. Once you've bitten the head off a snake, cutting into a Colonel's ass pales in comparison." He nodded in the direction of a small group of men. "It looks like they've started to head over to the range house."

Eric walked over to Sam. "Come on, I don't want to miss a minute of this test."

Ten

While Clark waited for everyone to file into the room, he looked out over the visitors in the range house and tried not to focus on the one person he admired, envied, and despised all at the same time. Since their first encounter at Fort Benning, before Perry was dropped from the Ranger group, the two men had been enemies. It wasn't what he wanted, but Perry had never found relating to other men easy. With Eric, it was something else, the distrust he saw in Eric's eyes, heard in his voice, it always made Perry feel uncomfortable, like someone was watching him, waiting for another mistake.

Clark took a deep breath. "There will be three segments to this phase of the test. First, we'll perform a one on one live fire, and then two on two. Finally, we'll witness a launch against a drone configured with a coded Identification Friend or Foe transponder to mimic a friendly aircraft with a functioning IFF device. Gentleman, remember the Viper missile system has independent target recognition, and it integrates both Radio Frequency and Infrared data from the target. This unique capability affords a kill probability of ninety percent or greater in an active and passive countermeasure environment. Alright Mr. Ames, you may begin the test."

For the next two hours, the group watched through the explosive-proof glass as each missile fired from a tripod positioned seventy yards in front of the range house. As the white exhaust trail of the olive green missile disappeared into the distance, the visitors would shift their attention to the large screen at the left of the room.

Roughly twenty seconds after each launch, a small puff of white smoke appeared in the center of the large screen at the middle of the room. The instant after the explosion, the technicians at the consoles let out a cheer, and the colonel confirmed with relief, "That's a kill."

Finally, when the Drone configured with the IFF device came onto the range, the missile, as intended, did not fire at the friendly target. Clark provided an interpretation of the results. "If the missile had been launched from a concealed position behind terrain, then it would self-destruct when it cleared the mountain and acquired the IFF signal from the friendly aircraft."

"Has that been done yet?" Eric asked.

The colonel quirked an eyebrow. "Has what been done?"

"Is this an Operational Evaluation or a developmental test?"

"It's an OPEVAL of course. What's your point?" Clark answered.

"There's several." Eric pointed at a technician in a white lab coat performing adjustments on the missile loaded into the launch rail bolted to the yellow tripod. "I see a company technician tinkering with the missiles before each launch, your firing from a tripod and not a HUMVEE configured with a launch container, and you have no real soldiers in the loop as would occur during real combat operations. So I ask again, have you ever fired a missile from behind terrain and seen it self-destruct, successfully? Also, when will we see a live fire in both a jammed electronic and infrared counter measures environment?"

The group absorbed every word, then turned back to the colonel as he twirled his pen.

"Those are very good questions, Mr. Emerson. Let me talk to you offline so we don't get behind schedule. If everyone will follow me to the test lab, we'll conduct the self diagnostic test to evaluate the ability of the Viper system to expedite the corrective and preventive maintenance cycles."

As the group walked out of the range house, General Hamilton intercepted Eric and Sam, with Colonel Perry following in close pursuit. "I want a word with you two."

After the group departed the room, the general made his position clear. "Your attendance at these test is at my discretion, and no one else. Anything you document or say outside of this facility will be approved first by the colonel or me. Do I make myself clear?"

Eric smiled. "Sure General, no problem."

"Major, do you understand this is a direct order?"

Sam looked up at General Hamilton. "Yes sir."

Then both Hamilton and Perry walked out of the door without another word.

Eric looked at Sam and murmured, "Just like I thought. The whole damn test is a sham. This is not an Operational Evaluation, and this system is not ready to go into production. They want to control everything that goes out on these tests. I expected this from Clark, but I don't understand General Hamilton pushing this line of bullshit. Someone up the line must really be anxious about these tests and what they will reveal."

"What are you going to do?" Sam asked.

"I intend to do exactly what I was sent here to do. I will watch the entire test, document my observations, and forward them to General Williams. I wouldn't waste time asking any more questions. The answers they give, if any, will be bullshit."

Sam hesitated a moment. "Are you going to filter your report through the colonel?"

"You're pulling my leg, right? I don't work for either one of those guys. I told General Williams not to send me here if he didn't want the truth. I'll tell it like it is, but neither of those two will get a copy from me. They'll hear what General Williams wants to share with them."

Eric saw his partner's face tighten with apprehension. "Sam, I understand it's different for you because you're wearing that uniform, but I told you this was going to be a very political assignment. You have to live with your own choices, just as I do. I'll still be your buddy either way you go. If you're uncertain, ask General Williams when we get back, but if you do, you're going to lose some credibility in his eyes."

Sam took a deep breath and with determination affirmed, "No Eric, you're right. You gave me a heads up on this, and I'm here for the soldiers, not for the colonel by any means. My report goes to General Williams, period."

"Damn, I've created a red haired beast. Take pity on me,

Major."

    Sam slapped Eric gently on the arm.

    They started out the door. "Let's go with the group before they lock the door on us. This is kind of fun isn't it?"

    "I think you're really enjoying this way too much. There is a dark side to that handsome face of yours, but you're still my bud."

Eleven

As they headed deeper into the desert, Sam looked across at Eric. "Tell me about this restaurant. Is it fancy?"

"Remember, I warned you that this place is a bit rustic. I would never have suggested you wear jeans if it were fancy."

"I know why you wanted me to wear jeans Mr. Emerson, you don't fool me. Now tell me about the place."

"It's a very unusual establishment. I promise, you've never had dinner in this kind of surroundings anywhere else."

"What does that mean, and why did they put it all the way out in the desert? There's nothing else around here."

"The ambiance of Pete's Place requires the type of environment offered by the open range."

"I have no idea what you just said, you're speaking gibberish."

"You'll understand shortly, there it is."

Sam scanned beyond the six-foot fences, 360 degrees in all directions to the dark building. There were no windows, no paint, just gray sun-bleached lapboard covered by a rusted tin roof. "That place? It's a barn. Is that where they park the cars?"

"No, that's the restaurant."

"No way. You're playing with me again, aren't you? Where's the restaurant?"

Eric pulled onto a compacted dirt driveway, leading into a gravel lot, and parked the white Camry rental car. He opened the passenger door and instructed, "Come on, wait till you see the inside of the place, it's a hoot."

Sam walked along the gravel trail bordered by five to eight inch stones, with an occasional marker light. When she came to the entrance of Pete's Pig Barn, she stopped abruptly. She panned to the right, and then to the left. She turned around and projected a confused expression at the man who'd brought her to this place out in the middle of nowhere.

Eric pressed gently on her shoulders to encourage her to advance along the passageway toward the structure that appeared more like a livestock building then an eating-place. Sam resisted. She was reluctant to walk down the dirt path between the two corrals of longhorn steers positioned on each side of the entrance.

Sam shook her head. "Is this a joke or something? Looks like a slaughter house, not a restaurant."

"I told you it's a bit rustic, but their food is unbelievable."

While they moved along the fenced corridor, Sam pinched her nose to block out the smell of sweat-drenched hides and cow pies. "I'm supposed to enjoy a meal when I'm surrounded by the fragrances of a barnyard? This reminds me of when Dad made me clean out the horse stable because I let my grades slip."

"The smell disappears inside, at least most of it."

"I'm a sporting woman, I really am. I will go along with most anything, but I think you've crossed the line this time."

"You wanted to come. At least give it a chance. I'm sure you'll change your mind once you get inside."

Sam eyed the parking lot, as if she was formulating an escape plan. Finally she looked back at her friend and sighed. "I guess I did invite myself, but next time I get to choose where we eat, and it's going to have pink tablecloths, two-foot tall menus, and eight pairs of silverware on each side of the plate."

"I can't wait; now come on before Duke eats everything."

Sam looked at the two-dozen steers meandering around the corral, each averaging roughly half a ton of beef on the hoof. "I don't think any man can eat that much. Guess I can have a salad."

"Read it and weep, woman." Eric pointed to the sign above the door of the restaurant; *Within these walls we serve red beef. Not pork, not seafood, not little green things, but BEEF.*

"No pork? I thought that's why they called it the pig barn.

What gives?"

Without expression, he responded, "It's just a name. Come on, I'm starving, move it along or I'll leave you out here with the coyotes."

Sam scanned the desert, tried to peer behind the dunes, around the prickly pear cactus, and searched for any signs of wild critters. Eric grinned when a small pig like javelina scurried from behind a mount and Sam flinched. She turned back and offered a warning. "Sometimes, you go too far, Mister."

Sam ascended the warped and noisy steps leading into the Pig Barn. When she walked through the doorway, she examined the décor distributed randomly around the room. There was a rusted double "T" branding iron, several pairs of spurs and bridles, a series of chafe guards and in the corner, a campfire with a real Dutch oven surrounded by cowboy figurines. Sam paused and examined the boards that lined the inside of the dining area. She noticed what appeared to be tuffs of fiber lodged in the lower portion of each wallboard.

"Why did they put those tufts of fiber in the walls?"

Eric positioned himself between Sam and the exit to block her escape route. Then he admitted, "That's pig hair. These are the original boards from a pig barn, hence the name. Swine used to wipe their backsides on these boards to scratch their hides. Don't worry; I'm sure they've been disinfected. At least I would think so."

Sam stepped back, lowered her voice two octaves, and insisted, "No, no way. You would never bring me to a place where they stored swine. I mean an actual pig barn."

Eric replied with a smile and one word, "Yep."

"You really understand how to impress a woman don't you? Now I know why this place is out in the desert. It couldn't pass the health codes in town. I can't believe I considered wearing a dress with nylons. Thank God I wore jeans. We'll sit in the center of the room."

Sam's eyes had not yet adapted to the dim yellow hue cast by the oil lanterns on each table, so she held onto Eric's shirttail until her eyes could adjust to the light.

"What in the world is all over this floor? It feels like I'm stepping on crushed glass."

"Those are pistachio shells. The owner provides a bottomless bucket on each table."

Sam's eyes began to adjust and she noticed that the establishment was actually crowded with men, except for one large woman—who appeared to have arrived on the back of a chopper—attired in black leather. Sam watched as the hungry female tossed a rib bone on the large mountain next to her plate, licked her fingers, ripped off another chunk, and started gnawing again.

When they approached the center of the main section, Sam heard a familiar voice, "Hey guys, I'm over here."

Duke grinned as Sam moved cautiously toward their table. "I'd tell you how gorgeous you look Major, but I promised Hammer I'd watch my manners."

Just as Eric pulled out Sam's chair, his cell phone rang. "Hello. All right, hold on a minute."

"I have to take this outside guys," Eric informed his friends. He looked at Duke. "Remember what I said, you're on your best behavior, and I mean it."

While Duke initiated small talk, Sam listened politely, but every few minutes, she was reminded of her surroundings by the bellows of live cattle around the outer perimeter of the establishment. She was puzzled why any restaurant would operate in the center of a herd of cattle. The reason became clear when she read the bold red sign with the white border over the cast iron stove: *Please forgive the smell, but our steaks are fresh because we keep them so close.* She pulled out a tissue from her purse and wiped down all her silverware. Then she started on the thick blue-rimmed plate and the water glass formed from an old mason jar.

Once she had removed all the bacteria from her eating utensils, she looked across the table at Duke's lime green and yellow Hawaiian shirt and khaki shorts. "Why do you call Eric 'The Hammer'?"

"I always have, since our earlier days with the 3rd Battalion, 75th Ranger Regiment at Fort Benning. That's what everyone called him back then, or at least all those that served with Hammer in the force."

"But why?"

"You've been friends with Hammer for a long time, right?

Have you ever seen him when he gets under pressure?"

"You mean like giving a briefing to the brass, sure I have. I haven't noticed anything that would warrant the name Hammer, in fact, I think he enjoys it."

"No, I mean gut ripping tension. Like when you deploy on a hot mission in a real hostile zone and you know you're out there on your own. There are a few moments in the drop vehicle where the team turns inward. Everyone goes silent. I guess some pray they'll come back alive from the mission, others think about their wife and kids, whatever it is, we would all go through it. Hell, Old Mac, our Comms and language specialist, he wouldn't leave the vehicle till he had recited the SpecOps prayer out loud, you know 'God grant us wisdom from Thy mind, courage from Thine heart, and protection by Thine hand' and so on."

Sam focused on every word. "I understand. My dad was in SpecOps. He used to talk to me about what it was like when he was deployed on deep operations, isolated behind lines, with no one to help you, except your fellow members of the team."

Harry grinned. "Even for macho guys like me, it can be a soul searching experience. Eric was different. I think he liked it. No, I think he thrived on it, except just before we were dropped in the zone. He would sit there quietly with his eyes focused on the wall of the vehicle, like he was trying to penetrate the side of the fuselage and peer into God knows where. Then you would hear a grinding sound. When you looked over, his fists would be knotted like a hammer, and pressed hard into his thighs. I'm surprised he has any teeth left to eat with as hard as he would grind them."

"Within a few seconds, he would look up with total peace in his eyes, like he had just been awakened from a three day sleep. He would say, 'Let's do it' and we all knew he was ready. It got where no one wanted to step out of the door until they heard the Hammer grind his teeth."

Sam wanted more. For years, she had thirsted to understand what made Eric the person he was, and now she had a source capable and willing to provide a rare glimpse into the hidden psyche of her quiet friend.

"Are you familiar with why he was awarded the Silver Star?"

"You bet I am. Hell, I was part of the team that he led on that mission. I'm the one whose life he saved. He couldn't do anything about this leg I lost, but if it were not for Hammer, I wouldn't be here today."

The waiter sidled to the table. "You guys figure out what you want yet?"

"No, we're still waiting on a friend. Come back in ten minutes."

Duke turned back toward Sam. "Go ahead, Harry. Please continue."

When Duke looked into those sparkling green eyes, he knew. Like a sponge absorbing each word, she was hooked. Not for mere curiosity, but from something deeper. He recognized that look on Sam's face. This relationship was more than either Eric or Sam admitted. He now understood why Eric had reacted so strongly when he came on to Sam. They both were trying to hide it, not just from others, but also from themselves. Harry owed so much to his friend. He would allow them to maintain the facade that they were just friends. They could continue their joint admiration from a distance without anyone violating their secret.

"All right Red, I'll tell you the story, but if Eric ever finds out, I'm dead meat, do you understand?"

Sam closed her two fingers and ran them across her mouth. "I swear, zipped forever."

"Eric led a three-man team for a direct action, deep interdiction mission. When I say deep, I mean our team was only a few hundred yards outside the town with enemy patrols scurrying all around us. We were responsible to take out various adversary high payoff assets from the Joint Integrated Priority Target List prior to the main ground assault phase of the campaign. Things like command centers, communication assets, mobile air defense units, whatever popped up from their Intel sources, the Joint Intel Center directed us to help take it out. We had just target-designated a communication node for a MK 83 Laser Guided Bomb when we got a new assignment from the JIC. A High Value Target of opportunity was uncovered in our area. A tip-off from HUMINT sources placed the officer in charge of the royal guard for the local district within two miles of our location. We were told to beat feet to the general's position, and prepare him for extraction. Once we arrived at his strong hold, Hammer told us to provide perimeter guard."

Harry picked up his glass of water, and downed a few sips, slowly, for affect.

"Go ahead, then what?"

"I've seen a lot of guys that were good at clandestine missions. I mean men that could crawl like a cat into an enemy position. But Hammer, he was…I guess you'd say he was like a shadow. Something you knew was there but still couldn't pick it out. When Eric and I were in sniper training together at Fort Benning, he received the best scores they ever awarded for concealment and closing on the enemy. Some of his classmates at sniper school actually dubbed him 'the shadow'. I never liked that name. It was too corny, but the image of a fading silhouette edging slowly across the dunes and merging with the mud huts is what it was like. It was really spooky to watch. You knew he was there, but you couldn't see him, and with the toys they gave us; I was always glad to be on his team, rather than his target."

"What kind of toys?" Sam inquired, "You mean night vision and that kind of stuff?"

"I'm referring to devices much more sophisticated than standard night vision equipment. Over the years, Special Operations Command has contracted with various research centers and universities to create tools and devices that gave us an advantage over the bad guy for deep penetration missions. For example, we used Night Sight Enhancement goggles. They look something like what swimmers use, only the lenses were twice as big, yet they weigh roughly the same, just a few ounces. Nighttime was the enemy of our adversary, but it was our friend. It made them blind, yet we could see and hear almost everything. The NSE goggles provide roughly two thirds the resolution of night vision sets for inanimate objects, like buildings, but they had infrared capability so that you could see and distinguish humans. They also had embedded acoustic receivers that amplify low volume sounds ten fold, while muffling loud noises to protect your ears from explosions and small arms fire. Plus, they diffused light so that it would not reflect off the lens, or your eyes. We also had adaptable camouflage to adjust to various degrees of illumination, from total darkness, to a moon lit night.

With this stuff, you were virtually invisible at night. This equipment is really sensitive. The rest is compartmented. You had to be a Snake Eater to talk about it."

Sam glanced at the entryway to the restaurant where she could still see Eric leaning against the outside doorframe. "I don't mean to be rude, but you need to get back to the mission, before Eric returns."

He smiled. "The third member of the team and I provided cover while Eric went in. Like a morning mist sliding silently across the terrain, he penetrated their defenses without tipping off any of the lookouts. There was no sign, no sound, just this dark silhouette that seeped into the torture chamber. Within fifteen minutes, Hammer returned with a naked and battered young girl barely alive. She was severely beaten, at the edge of death. The four interrogators and the general had raped her repeatedly. They made her watch while they went at her mother before they killed her. I never told anyone else, but I think Eric lost it."

"What do you mean he lost it?"

"Are you aware of how Eric's little sister died?"

"I know she was murdered."

"This mission took place eight months after he lost his sister back in the states. When he saw what they were doing to that poor young girl, it was to close to what his sister had suffered. He forgot the rules of engagement, just totally ignored the real reason we were there, to extract the general. Somehow those fiends in that room became the demon that haunted his dreams since he lost his sister. Right there, in an instant, he judged their fate, and he took them out, every last one of them, by himself. Our assignment was to capture the general and to remain detached from the indigenous personnel, but Hammer only returned with the girl. He violated the mission order. He never said it, but I'm sure that's what he did. He didn't care. He just made the verdict on the spot to do what was right. He terminated all the scum and I agreed with his decision. We've never discussed it to this day. I'm still convinced he made the right choice, even though it cost me my leg, and Mac his life."

"How did that incident make you lose your leg?"

"We took the girl to a doctor that we thought to be friendly. It was against the rules, but it was necessary if she was going to survive. After we dropped her off, we were moving back into position to continue designating targets, but because we diverted from our original escape route, the enemy made us. They started to direct mortar fire at the team. The first two rounds hit forty yards to the left, but as we moved behind a dune, their spotter picked us up. The next round took out most of our equipment, and Mac. One minute I'm yelling at him, and the next minute he's gone. Only his arm was left sticking up out of the sand."

"The forth round took my leg and laid Hammer's head open from his hairline down to his ear. Hammer tossed me on his back while blood poured down his face and hauled me along the dune line out of sight from the spotter. Then he took his rifle and silencer, and disappeared. After ten minutes, the mortar fire stopped, and he returned with what was left of our supplies.

We called in to tell them our unit was down and we needed immediate medical extraction, but the main assault had started. We had to wait almost an hour for recovery. Hammer stopped my bleeding. Then, that magnificent bastard, with his head caked in blood; he went back and continued to designate targets for the next fifty minutes, till he passed out from loss of blood. I watched the whole thing. There isn't anything he could ask of me that I wouldn't do for him. That kind of courage and strength doesn't come along very often. I know that incident with the girl and all, took a toll on his psyche, but there isn't anyone that I want beside me as a friend more than him."

"I feel the same way, but what kind of toll did it take on Eric, you mean his emotions?"

"This is not stuff guys generally talk about, but when we were in the hospital together, he had some bad dreams, I mean some real hummers. Somehow, the guilt of losing his sister, and seeing that young girl her age brutalized and raped that way, I think it was really hard for him to get over."

Sam saw Eric returning to the table. "You just gave me insights into a special man that I would never get from anyone else. I really appreciate it." They stopped talking and waited for Eric to weave his way back through Pete's Pig Barn to their location.

Twelve

Eric looked at his two best friends. "I apologize guys, but that was the boss checking up on me."

"Is everything all right?" Sam asked.

Eric hesitated. He glanced at Duke, then at Sam. "Yeah. She's going away with a friend again. Said not to try and contact her, she wouldn't be taking her phone."

After several moments of silences between the three friends, Eric asked, "What were you two talking about?"

"Just what good taste you have in restaurants," Sam interjected. "That's all. Now let's order something. I think even I'm in the mood now for a piece of juicy red beef."

As Sam scanned the menu, both Eric and Harry looked at each other and raised their eyebrows. Harry smiled at Eric. "We'll make a man out of Red yet. A little raw beef, and we'll put some hair on that gorgeous…"

Duke looked at Eric. "Sorry, almost forgot myself."

Sam pulled the menu in front of her face, and grinned. "That ain't ever going to happen. Now stop jawing and order, I'm getting hungry. If you're going to take me to a pig barn, then at least feed a girl."

Eric motioned the waiter over to take their order.

~ * ~

"I hate to say it guys," Sam admitted, "but that was one heck of a steak, if you like meat with blood oozing onto the plate. I wouldn't want to make a habit of it, but for this one time, it was mighty good."

Eric raised his cup to his face, sniffed the aroma of hand-ground fresh coffee, and took a sip. "Harry, you did several assignments with the guys from Langley, didn't you?"

"Yes I did. We were teamed with several men out of their Operations Directorate to coordinate attacks with the Northern Alliance when we were sent into Afghanistan to eliminate the Taliban. Most of them were really good guys. Not like their management that sat on their butts back at headquarters. Those guys were assholes. They would sample the political currents to determine what they would and would not do. But the field units, they were no bullshit guys. I had no problem serving with them. I thought you served with a couple Langley Ops guys yourself?"

"I did. We were sent in as a sniper group after the Cole incident. We were told our mission was to take out Bin Laden before he did something worse. We had him in our sights. I mean literally in our sights. When we called back for the go ahead, the National Command Authority could not get the release from the Executive branch to execute the bastard. After we risked out lives, the man in charge had a change of heart. I was called back for a different assignment.

Two weeks later they sent them back in again, but this time the Langley guys were killed, both of them. Their family, their kids, no one ever knew what they tried to do to protect this country. All because someone didn't have the guts to do what was right. Our leadership back home took the easy solution and just ignored the problem."

Duke frowned at his friend. "Always mister negativity. That's why you're such a loner. It's like you keep this damn dark cloud floating over your head all the time. You scare the hell out of guys that try to be buds with you. I'm going to buy a black hat for you with the name *Darth* stitched in it."

"See Eric," Sam chimed in, "it's not just me. We're going to have to get Obi Wan to banish your dark side."

Eric ignored his two best friends and repeated, "As I was saying, do you have any viable contacts at Langley that you haven't pissed off yet with your babble?"

"Yes I do. Why do you ask?"

Eric first looked at Duke, and then directly at Sam.
"Remember Judi who works for the Under Secretary of the Army out of the Pentagon? I was looking at an email on my blackberry while Karen was reading me the riot act. Judi's been asked if she would like to work on a new study they're gearing up for at Army Headquarters. She said it relates to an effort called the Robertson report conducted out of Langley. I suggested that it sounds like a good opportunity for her. She'll actually be the sole analytical modeler. How can she give that up? Harry, would you check your contacts to see if they know anything about it? If you get any Intel, send it to me through the secure SIPERNET network, here's my account."

"All right, I can do that for you, but it will take me a few weeks. Till then, will you try and smile a little bit. You won't freak out so many people."

Harry pulled out his wallet. "It's been great seeing you again Hammer, and meeting you too Red, but I have to go. My new honey is flying in tonight to stay with me during the Viper missile OPEVAL. She's a carrot top too, and what a firecracker. Don't want to miss one second of personal time, if you get my drift."

Duke placed a hundred dollar bill on the table. "This one is my treat, guys."

Eric insisted, "Is it your treat or are you billing the company?"

"I said my treat, you need to chill out and go have some fun. I'm off to the airport, and a whole lot of loving. I'll probably be in late tomorrow for Phase two. I'm not on call until Phase four of the test, so I might as well enjoy life while I can. Think about that, bud."

He waved as he departed. Eric turned and apologized, "I'm sorry about Duke. He can be a little coarse sometimes, but he's a great guy, and a true friend."

"You don't need to apologize to me, I actually like the guy. He's charming, in a strange way. I can't quite figure it out but he reminds me of someone. The way he walks, kind of saunters back and forth, and the way he moves those big shoulders. I just can't place it, but it seems familiar."

"Imagine a big strutting dude out of the old west."

Sam pondered for a moment. "John Wayne. You call him

Duke because he resembles John Wayne."

"Exactly."

"Duke was right, though."

"Right about what?"

"You do need to blow away that dark cloud you hang up there above your head."

"I'll work on it."

"One more thing: try to smile more. You're too handsome to tout a frown all the time."

"Yes ma'am. Now let's head back. I'm tired from all this excitement and worn out from all this advice."

Eric walked around to pull out Sam's chair. "What did you think about this place? It's really got a unique atmosphere. Worth the hour drive out here, wasn't it?"

"It was definitely like no place I've ever been before. I think my mother was right. A man's instincts revolve around two things, his stomach and his little friend. Cater to those elements and you have his heart forever."

Eric smiled. "I can live with that."

Thirteen

Eric reached the south wall of the building next to the general's position. He removed his M4A1 rifle with the QD suppression unit from his back, switched the sight on IR mode, and positioned the barrel across the brick wall. He waited for the distinctive signature of a human thermal image. After a few minutes, two targets appeared on the roof eighty yards from his location. In four seconds, there were two low tone puff sounds, and the two lookouts disappeared from view.

He silently worked his way up the abandoned street. He heard Farsi conversation in the alleyway thirty yards to his left. He tucked down behind the carcass of a burned out pickup truck. Two men strolled out of the alley, one with a shouldered RPG unit, and the other with an AK47 clutched in his right hand.

He waited until both men crossed the street, walked up a stairway to a second floor and disappeared through a doorway. Then he stood up, edged out from behind the pickup, and crept toward his destination. When he reached the wooden door, he placed the optical fiber under the sill and confirmed the general's location. He counted the occupants in the room, noted the layout, and then removed the viewing device. He took several deep breaths, knocked on the door, and pulled back several feet into the shadows. When the soldier opened the door and saw no one, he closed it behind him and stepped out on to the street. Before he reached the stone wall, Eric covered the soldier's mouth and snapped his neck. Then he placed his rifle around his back, removed his MK23 pistol with suppressor *and LAM unit from its holster, and his Yarborough knife from its sleeve. He stepped in front of the door and gently tapped on the soft wood with his boot.*

This time, when the door opened, Eric shot the first soldier in the forehead and noted the red mist as it sprayed out the back of the man's skull. Then he kicked the soldier backward into the doorway, and burst into the room. Before the two soldiers standing guard near the door could fire their rifles, Eric shot the man on the right and knifed the second guard in the throat. The remaining soldier positioned in front of a young girl tried to grab his gun, but he was shot twice before he could stand up.

The general could not disengage from sodomizing the teenage prisoner quickly enough before Eric ripped him from her back and slammed the man hard against the dirt floor. Once he placed his knee in the chest of the naked man and his hand on the general's mouth, the enemy offered no resistance. Eric looked up at the small girl tied down to the table. He gazed at the bleeding stripes along her small frame, the two chucks of flesh ripped from her shoulder and exposed by the buckle of a belt. He saw her fear, the pain in her young eyes, and the tears streaming down onto the filthy wooden table.

Eric turned back and looked deep into the dark eyes of the man responsible for the girl's torment. He searched for some explanation, but there was nothing but hate and iniquity. His vision blurred. The fiend deserved no convention of fair treatment. If returned for interrogation, this animal would be released after the conflict, and not be held accountable for his cruelty. Eric knew this would be the fate of the man that had brutalized the innocence of this girl and that course was unacceptable. The demon had to be expunged now, here before his victim. Eric discharged a low guttural growl, and issued a final verdict, "Enjoy hell, you evil bastard." He raised his dagger and thrust it deep into the throat of his adversary. He watched as the life oozed out of the creature he had dispatched. Then he walked over to the tormented girl and...

"Mister Emerson, are you alright?" The buxom blonde squeezed Eric's leg to get his attention.

Eric sat up in his window seat and scanned the inside of the airplane. "Yes, I'm fine. I'm sorry, but I must have been dreaming."

The young girl in the seat next to him smiled. "It must have been a wild one. You were cussing some guy out and sending him straight to hell."

Eric looked down at his leg and noticed that the attractive young lady continued softly rubbing down the inside of his right leg. She gently pulled her French nails towards his groin and he felt a surge run through his abdomen. "Sorry Heather, but I have to go to the rest room. I need to get by you."

"That's okay, I'll still be waiting here for you when you get back."

On the way to the lavatory, Eric passed Sam in her seat at the rear of the plane. When she did not return his smile, he noted her attention focused toward the front of the plane. He turned back and saw the attractive young lady positioned next to his seat following his rear as he walked toward the restroom.

Two hours later, Eric departed the plane and moved up the ramp into the airport. When he entered the lounge area, he saw Sam waving her hand. While they both walked toward the baggage claim area, he asked, "Are you glad you went on this assignment?"

"I'm always glad to spend time with my bud, but I didn't like that return trip at all."

"It was very crowded. I don't think there was an empty seat on the plane. I tried to convince the passenger next to you to switch seats but he wouldn't budge. I think he had a thing for you."

"Uh, you think. The guy was all over me the whole darn flight, all four hundred pounds of him. He overflowed onto half of my seat. That was bad enough but the air conditioning didn't work in my section and he perspired all over me. Look at this. My pants are wet."

Eric recognized that she was void of her typical upbeat attitude. "A bit testy aren't we? Where's that positive outlook you're always telling me about, Miss dark cloud?"

"Don't go there, Mr. Emerson. I didn't see you offer to swap seats with me so you could get Mr. Sweaty and I could sit next to that Twinkie who had her hands on you the whole flight."

Eric caught an expression, a look in her eye, like something had slipped. She glanced down at the floor, then back at Eric and explained, "Sorry, it was just a bad flight, but next time we travel together, I'll make the arrangements."

He saw the opportunity for one more jab. "You're forgiven. But you were right about that young girl. She was a very touchy person, and very friendly too. She invited me over to see her CD collection. Look at this; she made me take her phone number."

As he held out a piece of paper, Sam grabbed it. She ripped up the paper declaring, "Just what you need; more woman trouble. Men just don't know how to keep their butts out of hot water."

Then Eric cracked his typical stoic expression and cut loose with an uncharacteristic deep-throated laugh. When she realized she had been played, Sam returned the smile. "You turkey."

While they tossed their luggage into the trunk of Sam's car, Eric attempted to call his wife again.

"No luck with Karen?" Sam asked.

"I guess she's still with her friend. I tried to call her several times today and there was no answer."

"What do you say you and I share a banana split? I would never indulge in one by myself, but a split really sounds good right now. What do you say? It will even be my treat. No sense returning to that lonely house if Karen's not there."

"I've never had a woman treat me to an ice cream before. You've got a deal. Let's try that new parlor by the park."

Eric carried their luggage off the shuttle bus to the silver Elantra and placed it in the trunk. As they headed down the exit ramp of the airport, he glanced over to Sam and smiled. It had been a long time since he had felt so comfortable, at ease, with a...friend. The opportunity to extend their time together just a little longer offered a pleasant excursion from his solitary existence with Karen.

Fourteen

Eric stopped after his third bite and focused on the woman across the table as she made a ritual out of the simple task of eating ice cream. "Well what do you think, is it good?"

With a full mouth, Sam returned, "Uuuuuh."

Eric watched as she enjoyed every morsel of the double-sized split. He was immersed in the sensual image of her purring, as her tiny slender tongue slowly consumed the marshmallow, pineapple and chocolate oozing down the side of the center mound of strawberry ice cream. The appealing vision came to an abrupt halt when she bit a large chunk out of the banana.

Sam devoured two thirds of the split. The scent of rich cream blended with vanilla extract, and the signs of tasty colorful treats scattered around the parlor reminded him of the Cream Palace in Monterey. Eric and Karen had only been married a year. Once a month they stopped by the Palace for dessert after dinner at the Fish Factory on Cannery Row. He enjoyed watching Karen revel in her hot fudge sundae with the same enthusiasm as the woman seated across from him now, chocolate smeared on her nose. In the first few years of their marriage, each time he was near Karen, he felt warm inside. The smell of her mild fragrance of Boucheron perfume, the touch of her cool skin, and her soothing feminine voice, all the pleasures in life seemed better when he was near Karen. He missed those sensations, the private moments with a woman that he cared for deeply.

Eric had just returned from his daydream when he heard

Sam ask, "What--have I got some on me?"

"Yes you do," he said, then dipped a napkin in his water glass and gently wiped the spot off of her nose.

"How do you feel about the trip?"

"A little more contentious and political than I thought, but I learned a lot."

"Remember, we have to turn in our report day after tomorrow."

"I've already done mine Mr. Bossy, and you?"

"Of course, Major. Seeing we both have completed our reports, and would never go back and change anything, I'll show you mine if you show me yours."

"It seems I've heard that on the playground before."

"Just summarize what you saw the last two weeks, and I'll do the same."

"First, this was not an OPEVAL by any stretch. An operational evaluation is intended to test how the system will perform in an environment that emulates true combat conditions. In this case, there were no soldiers operating the system, only contractors messing with it the whole time. Second, in a real combat situation, you would assume the worst scenario of autonomous battery control, which means that the fire team would not know the direction, azimuth or elevation of the incoming target. Yet, the contractors fed the known coordinates into the missile system prior to each launch. Third, they did not test the weapon system in any extreme conditions. No sandstorm, no rain, and no cold weather. Everything was in a totally controlled environment."

"That's pretty good, Sam."

"What about you?"

"You mean in addition to what you just said?"

"Of course, I would never expect to catch something Mr. Smarty pants didn't see."

Eric smiled. "Let me add a fourth issue to your list. All test shots were in a countermeasure free environment. No electronic or infrared countermeasures were used at all."

"So what's your bottom line?"

"They're trying to push production without support of a true Operational Evaluation. Frankly, I would have expected more out of

General Hamilton. I didn't see any of the normal engineers that White Sands typically uses for these tests. It was all contractors that operated and directed everything. It smells rotten, the whole damn thing. When our report goes in, it's probably going to raise a fire storm, and halt the production decision until they do a true OPEVAL."

"That's what I figured too. Fortunately, I've decided to jump ship after I drop my bomb and accept the job on General Williams' staff at the Pentagon. You're going to be left on your own to deal with the aftershock. Isn't that nice of me?"

Eric grinned. "Just like a woman. Kick up all this dirt and leave me to clean up the mess."

"I've got a little intel that's really going to make your day. Are you ready?"

"Go ahead."

"I talked to one of my girlfriends and she gave me some real juicy gossip. Guess who's going to replace General Williams as the Commanding Officer of TRAC Headquarters in Fort Monroe?"

"Who?"

"Think of your worst nightmare right now."

"No way. Providence could not be that cruel to me."

With a grin, she confirmed, "You got it, General Hamilton is your new boss. The same man you and I are about to send through the roof."

"I'll be damned." Eric noticed Sam's expression. "Wipe that grin off your face, you nasty female. You look like you're taking pleasure in my agony."

"I am."

"Samantha Cassidy, I thought we were friends."

"You lied to me. And you never want to fib to a woman. That's bad juju."

"What are you talking about? I've never lied to you."

"You just did it again, shame on you. I have a friend who works on General William's staff. She told me the general offered the same position to you before he asked me. That's why he called you up there in the first place, isn't it? I got the position after you talked to him. You said you had nothing to do with it, and that was a fib. Just admit it and clear your conscience."

Eric shook his head and confessed. "You got me. You women and your damn intel sources, a man can't get away with anything, but that should make you happy. Why do you want to see me suffer, just because I fibbed about helping you? Man, that's mean."

"I am happy, and you know I really appreciate what you did."

"Then why the hell the apathy over my plight?"

"I figure that if General Hamilton makes your life miserable enough, you'll get fed up and take the second operations analyst position at the Pentagon. General Williams gave me a direct order to try any way I could to coerce you into joining the team up there. I'm just obeying orders from a superior officer, that's all."

"Everyone plots against me around here."

"What do you say, are you going to take the job or not?"

"I have to keep my options open, Sam."

"Why not just take it. It's one heck of an opportunity for you, and I could keep mentoring you like I've done for the last two years at TRAC."

"I can't do that right now. Not with what's happening at home. Maybe later if it straightens out, but I just can't do it the way things are."

"I understand. I do, but I'm going to call and bug you every week. I need Mr. Dark Cloud up there to keep me straight."

"What are you going to do with Ronnie?"

"Mom and Dad will keep him here for six weeks so he can finish out the school year, then he'll come up to live with me. I should have things all fixed up by that time."

"No, I'm referring to your work hours. At your current job, you can put in a regular nine hours five days a week, and it's no problem. At the Pentagon, it will be eleven hour days, and many times on the weekends too."

"I hadn't considered that. Darn, why did I miss that? I thought I had everything all planned out."

"I may have a solution for you. Have you picked out a place to live yet?"

"No, not yet, why?"

"I have a cousin who lives in La Plata, Maryland. With the

traffic, it's an hour drive to the Pentagon. Amy has two great kids of her own. She would be glad to help. You could drop Ronnie off before you head to work and he could get the school bus with her kids. In the evening, he could stay there till you picked him up. I'm sure she would do it for free, but you could pay her a stipend of ten or fifteen bucks a day just to clear your conscience."

"Please don't take this wrong, but I have to ask. Does she have a good family environment there, I mean with the other kids and her husband?"

"Let me tell you a little story about the women in my family. I was born and raised in the hills of North Carolina. I still have a 278-acre farm passed down from my grandfather to my dad and then to me six years ago when he died. Have you ever heard of SWOTS?"

"No."

"It stands for Strong Women Of The South. For some reason, the women in my family possess a character that provides strength during adversity. They are true SWOTS women. They take no bullshit from anyone. Don't get me wrong, they're sweethearts to be around unless you try to do them wrong. Consider my aunt Molly. She's been central to my life since I was six. What I know about surviving in the woods, fishing, and hunting, I learned from that wonderful lady. Her husband, Henry, was a boozehound and womanizer. He had a thriving profitable business until he blew it on liquor and hard women. My dad used to track him down on paydays at the bars to try and get money for the employees in the company. My aunt finally got fed up with Uncle Henry running around on her all the time, and she issued an ultimatum: the next time she heard a rumor regarding another woman, she would shoot off his willy. Two weeks later, there was a picture in the local paper of Aunt Molly in her apron with my three cousins huddled around her legs. The caption read *Woman attempts to castrate her husband*. Seems when she caught him this time, she took his .38 pistol and tried to shoot off his privates, but she missed and hit him in the leg."

"I bet he didn't do that again."

"Maybe, or at least he became more careful. The point is that my cousin Amy is Aunt Molly's daughter. Like all SWOTS, she is an angel until you try to screw with her. And I think that's the way it should be."

"Are you saying her husband is like your uncle?"

"Not anymore."

"My God, did she kill him?"

"No, but it was close. Ten years ago, Amy was pregnant with their first kid. She got a call from a neighbor who said she'd seen Amy's husband's car at a local strip joint. Being a pregnant woman with her hormones raging, the prospect of her husband out on the town, lusting after some nude woman, while she was bulging from his seed, did not sit well with Amy, not well at all.

As the story goes, a police officer saw a pregnant woman with a hammer and ice pick taking out all four tires on Billy's car. When he confronted her about the crime, she informed him that it wasn't a crime if it was her car. Then he inquired why she was disabling her own car. Without stopping she informed the officer that her husband was in the bar ogling other females and she wanted the bastard to walk home. The policeman made a quick assessment of the situation and informed Amy to just be careful so she did not hurt herself. Then he got back in his vehicle and left her alone to complete her revenge."

"What happened when Billy got home?"

"Unfortunately, some of the men on that side of the family are deprived of a portion of their gray matter. Amy felt a bit guilty, so when Billy got home, she offered him the opportunity to redeem himself. When she ask if he had learned his lesson to stay away from those places, the fool responded that he just planned to hide his car better next time. It was probably the booze talking because I can't fathom anyone being that damn stupid, especially to turn around on a SWOTS that was pregnant and cooking bacon in an iron skillet."

"She didn't! You're playing with me aren't you?"

Eric reached into his pocket and pulled out his wallet. "Here is a picture of Amy and Billy three weeks after the incident. See the stitches in his temple? You'll also notice how his right eye is off center and cocked upward. The doctors said it's a permanent result of the whack on the head. I carry the picture so I can remind his two boys what happens when you screw around with women in the south. One more thing Sam, you can't get upset when Ronnie starts saying things you don't understand."

"Like what?"

"Like 'butter my butt and call me a biscuit' or 'jumpy as spit on the griddle'. Remember, Amy's from the south. Are you still interested?"

"Are you kidding me? That woman's my idol. I think it would be great. Give me her phone number."

Eric jotted down his cousin's number. "If you're finished with your ninety percent of that split, I better get home."

While Sam paid the bill, she admitted, "I did kind of make a pig of myself, but I don't get those treats very often. Besides, you didn't eat your share, and I didn't want it to go to waste."

"I never got a chance. You were on that split like a piranha before I could get my fourth spoonful."

"Guess next time you share food with me, you'd better eat."

Eric grinned. "I don't mind. I like seeing a woman enjoy herself. It's something I don't get to see much anymore."

He opened the door as they departed from the ice cream parlor and watched Sam saunter toward her car in those darn snug jeans.

Fifteen

Sam turned the car down Eric's street and pointed at the red lights swirling in front of a white Colonial with black shutters. "Isn't that your house?"

Before she could come to a complete stop, he had vanished, headed down his sidewalk. An officer with a familiar face, and the sight of a gurney being lifted down his front steps, blocked his advance. Sam had just reached his side when the motion of the gurney caught the blanket placed on top of the body. The cover slowly peeled back and exposed the battered and bloody torso of a woman.

Sam gasped and covered her mouth. "Oh my God."

Eric's stomach knotted. The voices around him faded to a low rumble. All of his senses focused on the limp figure covered in blood, the face beaten beyond recognition. He gazed at the opal pierced earrings he gave Karen for their anniversary, at the missing tip of the little finger she lost in an accident. His temples throbbed, his ears began to buzz, and he knew without a doubt, it was her; the woman he once shared his soul, his essence, and his dreams.

Then he saw it, the telltale signature of her murderer: the gold earring worn by the Guerreros Demonio Gang. It had been forced through the center of her nose as a warning. An intentional signature left behind so he would understand; Gonzales had carried out his threat of revenge.

As Eric closed his eyes, the images he had fought for so long rushed back, the nightmares of his sister's murder, and the young

Iraqi girl penetrated by so many demons. His mind flooded with emotions; anger, hate, and guilt. He looked into the sky and opened his month to scream, but no sound issued, just the voices around him whispering through the red haze in his mind.

He became aware of a soft hand stroking his arm. "Eric, are you all right?"

He regained his control, pushed out the red cloud. "I'm okay."

Eric turned to the familiar face of Officer Simms, the same man he had met during his encounter with Gonzales two weeks ago. "Go ahead, explain to me how this could happen." He had already surmised the truth, but he wanted to hear it out loud, in front of everyone as the EMT replaced the blanket over her tortured body.

The officer hesitated. He glanced at Karen's body being lifted into the back of the ambulance.

"I asked you what happened. You let him out, didn't you? Your useless bullshit system let him out. Tell me. I want to hear you say it."

The officer looked down at the ground. "I'm sorry, Mr. Emerson."

"What's the excuse this time?"

"Gonzales was released because he wasn't read his rights according to the law."

"What the hell are you talking about? I heard your partner give him his rights in the backseat. What did he claim, that he was asleep?"

"No."

"Well what then?"

The officer started to speak, but stopped.

"What, say it damn it! What?"

"He claimed he doesn't speak English. The rookie did not follow procedure. He was supposed to read him his rights in both languages."

"You and I both know that's a lie. He threatened me in English. But that doesn't matter, does it? Because he's a thug and our system is so screwed up, they protected this asshole, and at what cost? Tell me! What good are you and your damn fouled up worthless system? Tell me!"

Again, the officer looked at the ground, paused for several seconds, and finally answered, "I'm really sorry, Mr. Emerson. I am. I have a wife, too. I can see her body lying there and..."

"Stop it. I don't want to hear any more of your bullshit. I give up on you and your useless laws."

"Mr. Emerson, you need to understand that you're at risk. There's no way we can link this murder to Gonzales. Most likely, one or more members of his gang were responsible for your wife's death. I doubt he would come this close to your house with us watching him."

"If you were watching the son of a bitch," Eric barked, "how the hell did he kill my wife?"

Simms hesitated before responding, "We weren't watching your house; we were monitoring his movements. We had no idea this would happen. It had to be someone from his gang. You should let us provide surveillance so we can protect you. Mr. Emerson, let us help..."

"The same way you helped my wife? Or all of the other innocent women across this country rotting in their graves because the legal system is useless? No, I don't need you. I won't be here."

"Excuse me, what do mean?"

"You don't think I trust you guys to protect me? I would rather have a goat stand guard at my door. I'll stay with a friend."

"Officer," Sam interjected. "He can stay at my apartment with my son and me. I'm moving out in two weeks. He can use the extra room till we leave. When we're gone, he can live at our place until he gets things settled, all right Eric?"

"Okay."

"That's fine, but I wouldn't tell anyone where you're staying. And you still need to be careful."

"How long do you suggest I hide like a scared rabbit and put my life on hold? And what good will it do anyway? You'll just lock him up again for a week, and then let him out."

"As I said Mr. Emerson, I'm truly sorry for what happened here." The officer shook his head, turned and walked away.

Eric reached for Sam's hand. "Let's go. I want to get out of here, please."

After driving in silence, Sam offered, "I think it's a good

thing that you'll be staying with us. You shouldn't be alone in that lonely house, especially right now."

Sam waited, but there was no response.

"Eric, did you hear what I said?" she asked softly.

"I'll stay with you tonight, until they clear out, but I'm going back tomorrow."

"You can't go back there now. You heard what the officer said. It's not safe for you to be there."

"I'll be fine."

"Please Eric," Sam pleaded. "You're not invulnerable. I don't want you to get hurt. Don't do this, please."

He turned toward the driver's seat and touched Sam's shoulder. "I care for you too. I've always considered you one on my best friends, but I have to do this my way. And you have to trust me. I will be all right. No harm will come to me."

"Don't do anything that would put you at risk, not now. You still have a life and people that care about…I care about you. Please be careful."

After a few moments Sam continued. "I'm aware that this may be the last thing you want to think about tonight, but in a few days you should consider that now might be the right time to change your life. There's nothing to hold you here any longer. You can come up to the Pentagon with a clear conscience."

"Right now, I have to focus on something else. Maybe in a month I'll consider it, but at this moment, there are things I must take care of here."

They drove in silence for several minutes. Then she reached over and gently grasped his hand.

Eric continued to stare at the road with a vacant expression. "Sam."

"Yes."

"Thanks for being here, and for being my friend."

She released an almost imperceptible sigh.

Sixteen

Eric responded to the knock at his front door. "Hello Reverend Harper. How can I help you?"

"Good evening Eric. Since you wouldn't return my calls, I decided to come to discuss the arrangements for your wife's funeral."

"Whatever you feel is appropriate. I trust your judgment, Reverend."

"We need to talk. You have to be involved in this, for your future peace of mind. Son, its part of the bereavement process. May I come in?"

Eric paused, and then he stood back from the door. "All right, come on in."

The two men entered the dining room and sat at opposing ends of the small table.

"I know that you are not an active member of our church, but Karen was well known to our congregation. She often came to me for consultation and support. She also confided to me that the two of you were having some difficulties in your marriage. It's important at these times that we deal directly with the loss of a loved one, and the passing into the next realm. I understand that it's hard to make sense of these tragedies, but there is a purpose in all God lays out before us."

Eric gazed at the man across the table and surveyed his gaunt appearance, the thick horned glasses, and the flap of hair combed across his scalp. *Karen, did you have to share our problems with everyone? Why is he telling me all this? He lives in a sheltered world. He has no idea how they walk among us.*

"Reverend, I know you've studied the Holy Scripture and were trained to preach the word of God. I respect that. I'm just not sure we share a common interpretation of God's plan."

"What do you mean? You don't believe in the Lord and all he's done here on earth?"

"I do believe in God. I just believe he operates differently, that's all."

"In what way?"

"Do you think we are each children of God, and that he cares for us equally?"

"Well of course, he loves us all."

"Then if we accept God, and we are each his children, he would not help one of us at the expense of another, right?"

"I'm not sure I understand exactly what you're suggesting."

"I remember somewhere in the bible that Jesus prayed to God to protect and deliver us from the demons that walk among us."

"Yes, it's in the Book of Paul."

"Then you do believe evil walks with us everyday, that there are those who service the will of the evil one?"

The Reverend was speechless. He looked confused.

Eric summarized his view. "So God loves us each the same. He sees the evil that threatens all of us, and he would not ignore any of his children at the expense of another one. Would you agree?"

"I'm not sure. I guess that would be correct."

"Then, there can only be one explanation why some are shielded from the demons and others are not."

"What do you mean?"

"He's so busy that some slip through his shield. Sometimes God actually needs help to shelter the lambs from the wolves. His flock is so large; he expects some of us to protect others that are incapable of defending themselves. Then again, there are times when we cannot be a shield; instead, we must be the sword."

Eric watched the reverend fidget in his chair, as if he was uncomfortable with something. Then he realized it was his argument; the man of cloth was alarmed by the supposition Eric had put forth.

"If you're saying God wants us to help our fellow man, I agree. If somehow you have interpreted that God's intent for us is to take things into our own hands, I think you are very confused."

Eric remained silent.

"Son, evil is the whore and temptress of the devil. Even the most righteous man can be lured into her bed. It is God's burden to deal with the evil ones among us, not ours. In the eyes of God, to try and do his work against the demons will turn us into the very wickedness that you wish to overcome."

Eric looked directly into the eyes of the man seated in the opposing chair. "Reverend have you ever consoled someone, or taken a confession, only to discover that their intent was to do harm to others?"

The Reverend glanced down at his hands. He hesitated for a moment, and then replied, "Yes I have."

"And what did you do with that knowledge?"

"By the doctrine of the church, I am required to maintain their confidence."

"Then you allowed harm to come to the innocent you are obliged to protect."

"What are you saying, by observing the rules I have been told to obey, I have sinned? Is that what you're inferring?"

"No, I'm not suggesting you sinned, Reverend, but as moral men, each of us is honor bound to defend the helpless. Like many others who are given the chance to do the right thing, you have failed your personal struggle with the moral paradox. As a result, you are responsible for the pain and suffering others were required to endure because of your decision. You were caught between two opposing forces.

Do what is just and right, and you will guard the lives of others. Do what is socially acceptable in order to adhere to principles and rules you were taught throughout your life, and you will bring harm to those you are obligated to protect. This conflict between what is right and what is socially compliant is a test most people fail. They cannot break the chains that bind them to rules they've been taught keep us civilized, regardless of the price the innocent must pay."

The Reverend was visually startled by Eric's statement. "Son, you cannot prevent evil by doing evil."

Eric spoke without emotion. "I am confident that when we come face to face with the suffering of those we love, the only way to resolve the moral paradox is to listen to the voice within each of us. In so doing, we ensure that others do not experience such pain."

The Reverend stared directly at Eric for several seconds. "Deus absconditus."

Confused, Eric inquired, "What does that mean?"

"Hidden is the mind of God. As mortal men, we can never totally understand or interpret the intent and methods of the Lord. I'm afraid you have confused God's will. The loss of your wife has twisted your perception of right and wrong. You are on a dangerous personal journey if you believe his intent is for each of us to fall prey to our own emotions. The path you just presented will contort your soul and haunt your existence on earth. I encourage you not to take any action based on what you're feeling during this time of sorrow."

Eric looked past the Reverend, through the front door, and paused for a moment. "I understand, and I appreciate your advice."

Eric felt the Reverend examining his purposely-blank expression. "Are there any memories or experiences you would like me to discuss during the services for your wife?"

"I will always think of her as she was during the early years of our marriage when she saw the world as a happy place, and enjoyed everyday for the wonder it brought to both of us."

"I can include that for you. Now I must go, and remember what I said. Only the Lord determines what is just, not man."

"I enjoyed our talk, Reverend Harper. It helped provide insights to me on certain issues I've been struggling with. I will see you at the service."

Harper paused for a moment on the front steps. He started to leave then turned back. "Remember, I'm always available if you need to talk, about anything."

"I appreciate the offer, but I think I've got things figured out now, thanks, and good bye."

Eric closed the door and walked back to the kitchen.

Seventeen

Like the night before, Eric unlocked the back door to his house and slid two tacks between the doorframe and the top of the outside kitchen door. Then he did the same at the front door, and switched off all the lights in the place, except for a small florescent unit over the sink. Eric walked back into the hallway around the corner from the kitchen, and sat quietly in a chair that he had placed at the very back of the dark corridor at the entrance to his home. The faint light from the kitchen washed the path toward the front of the house, but left him in complete darkness. He adjusted the goggles over his ears, and waited, alone, to ponder the past. *Why did you give me this skill and take me away, when I needed to be there, to protect them? If you refuse to watch over them, why stop me? Why?*

As he sat alone, in the dark, Eric considered that perhaps Karen had been right all along. His continual desire to do what was right in his job, and morally correct in his life had taken its toll on those close to him. His sister's death may have been prevented if he had not been overseas serving his country. If he had not ignored orders and had forgotten about the life of the young Iraqi girl, and the removal of her torturer, Harry would not have lost his leg, or Mac his life. If he had been there with his wife, instead of TDY on assignment, he may not have lost his unborn child, or his marriage. And if he had ignored what he witnessed in the square the day he took down Gonzales, then Karen would not have lost her life. All these attempts to take the right path and hold on to his moral principles had levied a tremendous cost, but what was the alternative, to ignore the evil that surrounds us, like so many others do?

The choices, decisions, and repercussions were unclear and confusing. The chains of morality that bind us to right and wrong, and to a faulty legal system, prevent us from defending those close to us. The things he should have done, how they would have altered the outcomes in his life. Everything swirled in his head—and then he heard the slight echo of metal bouncing on the kitchen floor. In the shadowy void, the sound of teeth scraping together stopped, while two figures approached the front of the corridor.

BAM...BAM

There were two shots. Someone screamed and then another voice shrieked several times, like the life was being twisted from their body. Then, the house was silent again. Only the sound of heavy breathing filled the darkness.

~ * ~

The officer knocked hard on the front door, then he moved to the side and shouted, "This is the police, open the door!"

Officer Simms pounded the panel again. "This is your last warning. Open the door or we'll knock it down!"

Eric twisted the knob and pulled the door open. At first glance, he saw no one, then realized that, not knowing the situation inside the home, the officer had moved to the left—out of sight, and range. He had his gun raised, ready. "Come on out, and keep your hands above your head," he said to Eric.

Eric slowly inched the door the rest of the way open and poked just his head out. The officer's alert face relaxed. He lowered the gun, and smiled.

"Evening, Officer Simms," Eric said, dryly.

"Mr. Emerson, a Mrs. Grossman, your neighbor, called to say she heard gunshots. She said she also heard someone screaming. Are you alright?"

Eric pointed behind him. "I'm fine, but these guys are having a real bad night. I don't think things turned out the way they planned."

Officer Simms stepped through the door and looked at the two men sprawled in the corridor, both twisted into contorted positions.

"Tell me something, Simms. Why do you guys always get

here after an incident has occurred, why not before? Have you ever pondered that question?"

The officer opened his mouth and then closed it. "Mr. Emerson, what are you doing here? You told me you were going to stay with friends."

"I had to get some things for my wife's funeral. You remember her, don't you? She was slaughtered by these demons just two days ago."

Simms looked down at the broken torsos. "You want to tell me what happened here?"

"I was upstairs in our bedroom getting an outfit to bury my wife in, and I heard a noise down on the first floor. I eased toward the stairway and saw these two coming up the steps. I waited till they got to the top, and then kicked the lead guy in the nuts. He fell back onto the second man, and as they tumbled down the stairs, the guy with the gun shot his partner, I assume accidentally."

Simms examined the two bullet holes in the closest corpse. "He shot his partner accidentally, twice?"

"Yep, you can see it was a long trip back down those steps."

The officer scanned the bodies. "This guy's arm is broken backwards around his neck. And him—I can't even imagine how his leg got twisted under his belly like that. Are you telling me a fall down the stairs did this?"

Eric's face was hollow, all emotions stripped bare. "Of course. How else could they get that way?"

"There will have to be an investigation."

"An investigation of what, the fact that I had to defend myself against two armed assailants because your messed up legal system is incapable of protecting us? The media would have a field day with that one, don't you think? The only prints on that gun and knife are theirs, not mine. You and your useless organization lost this one. Go screw with someone else."

Simms face flushed. "I'm not your enemy, Mr. Emerson. It wasn't my fault you lost your wife."

His face twisted with absolute contempt. "It's your face standing here tonight, isn't it? If you work for the system, you are the system. Unless you've got any more stupid questions, get this trash out of my house. I've got a funeral to prepare for, and I'm done with you guys."

Eric closed the door as the last corpse was removed. Then he dropped into the nearest chair. He should be fatigued, drained of every ounce of strength, but mysteriously he felt refreshed. He breathed a deep sigh and felt oddly at peace as he looked at the ceiling. *I'm sorry Karen. I should have been there when you needed me. This was for you. It's the best I can do, for now.*

~ * ~

Simms watched his co-workers as the two bodies were thrown into the vehicle. The man's stance belied his frustration. "Damn it. He's right, we're useless lately."

"What are you talking about?" the second officer asked. "We couldn't stop this. It's not our fault. We can't be everywhere at the same time. We don't have the resources, and the politicians don't give us the laws that we need to protect the citizens. They can't lay all that on our shoulders."

"That's bullshit and you know it. We are responsible. We enforce their corrupted laws. We arrest them, and treat them with kid gloves so the judges and lawyers can put them right back on the street to reap havoc on the public. It wasn't always that way. When I was young, I had a positive effect on the community. People looked at me with respect, and we were able to keep the scum off the streets; but today, our legal system has become so liberalized, we're helpless to stop this insanity. I hate this job. I've got my years in, to hell with it all."

He removed the badge from his shirt, tossed it into the back seat, and ended his shift, for the last time.

Eighteen

Sam walked into the grand room of her small apartment and saw her son glued to the TV. "Good morning, Ronnie."

"Morning, Mom. I fixed your breakfast, it's on the table."

Sam glanced at the bowl of soggy flakes covered in warm milk and smiled. "Thank you." She placed the two bowls in the sink full of dishes. Then she poured coffee into a large navy blue mug with a gold Patriot missile engraved on the side and sat down at her dining room table. She removed two yellow Splenda packets from the small white porcelain bowl, emptied the contents through the steaming mist, and steered the black liquid in a slow lazy circle.

Sam pulled out the chair beside her and patted the seat. "Come in here and sit with me while I drink my coffee."

"I'll be right there. This show will be over in just a minute."

Sam smiled as she thought about how such a small boy could provide so much joy in her life, and help to fill much of the loneliness that visited her. She watched as her son sat locked on the screen with his head tilted to the left. Sometimes she forgot how Ronnie had to compensate for his inability to coordinate both eyes and look up at objects above him by cocking his head to one side. She remembered the birth trauma and damage to his facial nerves, the hours she patched each eye to maintain his vision, and how she wept each time she had to shock his tiny face to prevent loss of muscle control. All the pain, the tears, even the guilt she often felt that somehow her son was being punished for her mistakes; it was worth all the suffering, because she had Ronnie. And except for a loss of his upper visual field, he had retained sight in both eyes.

The boy turned off the TV, walked over to the table and sat down next to his mother.

Sam looked up from her paper. "What were you watching in there?"

"It was neat, Mom. They were fishing for these monster catfish in South Carolina at a place called Santee Cooper Lake."

Sam grinned when he moved his arms apart as far as he could to indicate the enormous size of the fish. "When can we go fishing?"

"I don't know. I'm sorry but I don't really understand how to catch fish. It's not something my dad taught me when I was growing up."

"Do you know any guys who might want to take us fishing?"

Sam hesitated for several moments. It had to be difficult for a young boy with a single mother, moving around every few years to a new assignment, making new friends, ones that would not be cruel about his wandering eye. Sam stroked her son's cheek. "I'm sorry sweetheart, but I'm afraid I don't have anyone to ask."

"What about Mr. Emerson, I bet he knows how to fish?"

"He might."

"When he comes to pick us up today, can I ask him if he will take us? Mom, please?"

"Maybe soon, but not right now. Mr. Emerson is going through some rough times since his wife passed away. We have to allow him some time to mourn his loss."

"I understand, but once he's over his mournful period, can we ask him then?"

"I think so."

The young boy looked down and paused for a moment. Then he tilted his head and looked up at Sam. "Mom."

"Yes."

"I like Mr. Emerson. He's really nice. Do you like him?"

"Yes I do."

"Like Mrs. Emerson did before she passed away?"

"Ronnie, it's time we get ready for the funeral. Are you sure you want to go? There will be a lot of sad people there."

"Mr. Emerson doesn't have anyone else anymore. We're his

friends. We have to go."

Sam leaned across the table and kissed her son on the forehead. "Go put your nice pants on and that clip-on tie. Forget about your little sport coat. You've outgrown it anyway. Hurry up because we don't want to be late. Eric will be by to pick us up in forty minutes."

"You too Mom, you know how you always make me wait."

Sam shook her head as the young boy prepared to attend his first funeral.

~ * ~

"Let us say a final prayer for Karen and those who loved this dear woman so deeply. Lord, please open your arms and heal the hearts of all those suffering today at the loss of Karen. Please take her to your breast and let her look down and continue to share her love. And please help Eric in his pain and struggle to understand your way. Amen."

Eric walked over and placed their wedding picture on the casket. "Karen, I'm sorry our life together did not turn out the way we planned. I have purged the pain from my heart and will keep your memory the way we were when you loved me. Good bye, my wife."

As they got into the car, Sam turned to Eric. "I hope you didn't mind that Ronnie came to the funeral. He wanted to be here for you, and I wanted him to understand your loss."

"It was fine." Eric looked into the mirror and saw Ronnie gazing back. "What did you think about all that, Sport?"

"It was sad. I'm sorry Mr. Emerson that you lost your wife."

Eric turned toward Sam. "That's one perceptive young man. Would you two like to go with me to a get-together at Karen's sister's house? There will probably be refreshments."

"We would be happy to go with you, wouldn't we, Ronnie?"

"Sure, do you think they'll have any ice cream?"

Eric glanced at Sam. "I wonder where he gets his sweet tooth from."

When the door to the large house opened, the woman offered a dry greeting, "Hello Eric, and Eric's friend, and her little one. We're happy all of you could come."

"Charlie, this is Sam. Karen and I have been friends with

Sam for ten years. This is her son, Ronnie. Guys, this is Karen's sister Charlie."

When Charlie reached down to shake Ronnie's hand, the young boy remarked, "Wow, you're as pretty as Mrs. Emerson."

Eric whispered to Sam. "That is one smart boy. He's already got the touch."

A smile spread across Charlie's face. "I bet you like ice cream. We have three flavors in the kitchen."

"Oh boy, you don't have to tell me twice."

As Ronnie ran toward the kitchen, he stopped half way. "Sorry ma'am. Thank you." Then he continued toward his destination.

Sam scanned the lush surroundings while she strolled with Eric around the large estate. The numerous antiques, the hand woven Persian rugs, the Swarovski crystal, the marble floors; the entire dwelling conveyed a statement of wealth and luxury.

"Your sister-in-law has done well for herself, hasn't she? I doubt that six months of my salary could purchase a single item in this house. Does she own a bank or something?"

"You're close. Her husband is a defense lawyer for some of the worst elements in our society. Charlie figures that her role in life is to find new ways to spend his dirty money."

"I guess the two of you are real good buds, huh?" Sam jested.

"Guess again."

Ronnie came back from the kitchen with a double scoop of dark chocolate.

"Let me fix that before you drip it all over everything," Sam said, reaching toward him.

"All right, but only one lick this time. Don't eat it all."

Eric watched Sam remove a tissue from her pocket, dab it on the tip of her slender tongue, and wipe the chocolate smear on Ronnie's cheek. There was something in the way she gently wiped his face, tugged at his little red tie, and pressed his shirttail beneath his belt. It was more than the maternal reflection of a loving mother. There was feminine grace in her motion, her gesture, her flow. The image conveyed a confusing mix of warmth and passion in Eric, even in these surroundings.

While Sam attended to her son, Eric smiled. "He's obviously had to share with you before." Then he looked down at the boy. "I know how you feel. I've been there myself. She ate all of my ice cream last time I tried to share with her."

Sam shook her head. "You two guys should be more gracious."

She wrapped a napkin around the cone, and when she attempted to lick the streams tracing down the side, two drops leaped onto her blouse. "Doggone it. Ronnie, stand over here on the marble floor so you don't get any on their rug. I can't afford that cleaning bill. Stay there until you're finished."

While they meandered across the various cliques of conversation and opinions being aired in the living room, Eric overheard a middle aged female with a large mole on her nose. The woman was positioned on the settee in the center of the room. He stopped and digested the supposition that the husky woman offered to the group that surrounded her.

"I'm convinced that if our military officers were better educated, they would be less interested in involving this country in constant conflicts across the globe. It's obvious to any intelligent person that wars are fought so that the military can play with their toys."

Eric moved so he stood in front of the woman. He waited till she glanced up and looked directly at his face. "Madam, have you ever been associated with anyone in the military?" Eric's tone caused everyone within the vicinity of his voice to stop and turn in his direction.

She looked at those around her, and then back up at Eric. "Excuse me?"

"Based on your comment, you obviously have experience on the topic you were discussing, so I'm curious. Have you ever worked with any officers in our military forces?"

"No I haven't. How is that relevant to this conversation?"

"Have you ever entered into a verbal exchange or discussion with one of our officers?"

Again, the woman responded. "No, I have not."

"Maybe you were educated at the Institute of Military History. Is that where you gained your extensive insights?"

This time the woman did not respond. One of the guests rushed into the kitchen to inform the host of the activities unfolding in the living room, but Eric continued offering his assessment of the situation.

"You have never interacted with the military, nor studied the history of how the men and women in our armed forces have dedicated their lives to protect you, yet you feel qualified to slur their capability and motivations."

Charlie stormed into the living room and planted her hands on her hips. "Eric, stop this. She's my guest."

"We're just exchanging ideas, right? Free country and all. Lady, let me introduce you to a concept you've probably never experienced before in your circle of friends, it's called reality. The officers you so malign do not make the decision to go into conflict. They are given orders by the executive branch. They don't ask if the military wants the mission, they tell them specifically when to go and were. Then, with their very lives on the line, they do their best to protect their fellow soldiers and the welfare of this country.

In terms of their education, except for the warrant officers, all of our military leaders have been schooled at the best institutions in this country. They spend a major portion of their career advancing their knowledge of politics, history, foreign cultures, and a dozen other topics to help them figure out ways to circumvent conflict. Compared to other nations, we have the best-educated military in the world, and that's by design, not by accident. Before you cast aspersions on the very people that protect your world so you can enjoy the freedom and luxury you have grown accustomed to, pull your head out of the sand, and get your facts straight."

"You should leave," Charlie said.

Eric scanned those in the room who had observed the discussion. It was clear that his point had generally fallen into a vacuum. He turned to the woman with the mole and offered one final witticism, "My friends and I will be glad to leave, but ponder the first words of a well known passage written by Theodore Roosevelt. 'It is not the critic who counts, not the one who points out how the strong man stumbled or how the doer of deeds might have done them better. The credit belongs to the man who is actually in the arena, whose face is marred with sweat and dust and blood'."

Eric gathered up Sam and Ronnie and walked them toward the door. As they departed, Charlie exposed her true emotions. "I don't know why you came. My sister was killed because you were off running around with one of your sluts. Karen told me about all your women."

Eric stopped and turned to face his sister-in-law. He returned her hostility, not with anger, but with resolve. "Regardless of what Karen told you, I was never unfaithful to your sister, not during our entire marriage. Not even when I found her in the arms of another man. I still remained loyal and tried to work things out. I came here out of respect for Karen, and what we used to have. Even you can't take that away from me."

While Eric and Sam moved to the door, Ronnie turned and walked back toward Charlie. "I'm grateful for the ice cream ma'am, but it doesn't taste good anymore." He placed the cone on the antique table, walked toward his mother, grasped her hand, and left.

Nineteen

As they drove away from Charlie's house, Eric turned to Sam. "I'm sorry you two had to witness that."

"You never have to apologize to me for who you are. Don't take what your sister-in-law said to heart. She's just suffering from her loss right now."

"She was right about one thing. If I had been here for Karen, instead of traveling for my job, she would still be alive today."

"You can't control everything. You're not God. You're a man, a very good man. I never knew you were aware of Karen's indiscretions. I'd seen her around town with other men, but I was reluctant to mention anything, for fear it would cause you more pain."

"I've known for a long time. I probably should have left her, but I kept hoping she'd come to her senses. I guess that makes me out to be a wuss, doesn't it?"

"Not in my eyes. You're just a very forgiving person. I do have one suggestion, though." Sam grinned. "Next time, when you share your views with someone, like that woman with the mole on the tip of her nose, don't hold back so much. Tell them how you really feel."

Eric looked in the mirror at the small boy in the back seat, engrossed in everything being said by the adults. "Sorry about all that, Sport."

"It was not your fault Mr. Emerson, but what did that woman mean when she called my mom a slut?"

Sam looked at her son. "Ronnie, she was just trying to hurt Mr. Emerson and me. She misinterpreted our friendship."

"That's what I thought. That lady was pretty, but she wasn't very nice. Let's not go back there again."

"You got it, Sport." Eric turned to Sam and whispered, "Damn, he's a smart kid."

"Sometimes he's too smart. I can't keep up with him."

"What do you say that I make it up to you guys? How does a pizza with the works sound?"

From the back seat, a young voice responded, "I can live with that, how about you Mom?"

"Alright, but drop me by the apartment first so I can run in and change this blouse. I can't go out to a restaurant with chocolate smeared everywhere."

As the two males waited for Sam to return from the apartment, Ronnie inquired, "Why was that lady so nasty to you and my mom?"

Eric turned around in his seat so that he could look into Ronnie's eyes. "That's a good question. There are some people who think outwardly. They are aware of how others feel, and try to make them feel better. Then there are those who only look inward. They focus on themselves; they don't care how they affect others."

"I don't understand, Mr. Emerson."

"Call me Eric, Ronnie, or you'll wear yourself out."

"Okay Eric, I still don't understand what you mean."

"Let me put it another way for you, but this has to be man to man, you can't tell your mom. Can you do that?"

"Yes."

"All right here goes. Some women are like your mom. They always think about everyone else; they're called angels. Some women are like my sister-in-law; they never think about anyone else. They would be called a...well certainly not an angel. Something much lower on the totem pole. Understand?"

Ronnie hesitated for a moment, and then looked up with a grin. "I got you."

"Eric."

"Yes, Sport?"

"Do you like my mom?"

"Why do you ask?"
"Are we talking man to man?"
"You bet."
"I think she likes you a lot."
"Really, what makes you think so?"
"She talks about you all the time. She says she is going to miss you a lot when we move up to DC. Mom says you might move up there, too."
"I just might do that."
"That's good. I like you, too."
"I'm glad. I think you're a pretty neat guy myself. Tell me something; does your mom have any other guy friends? I mean, does she ever go out on dates with other men?"
"No. There's just Grandpa and me. And you, too."
"That's good."
"Eric?"
"Yes?"
"You didn't answer my question. Do you like my mom?"
"Yes."
"How much do you like her?"
"More than you can imagine."
"That's good. You should tell her. I think it would make her real happy."
"I will, I promise."
"When? When will you tell her?"
"With a woman, you have to pick the right time to share feelings. The moment has to be just right. Girls are special like that."
"I understand."
"One more thing."
"Yes Eric?"
"Keep that between us."
"I understand, man to man."
"Right, man to man."

Sam opened the door and tossed a shirt in the back seat for her son. "Put this on, no sense going out in a soiled shirt. What were you two guys talking about?"

"How one woman could keep two men waiting so long. Isn't that right, Sport?"

"That's right, Eric."

Sam looked back at her son, "Eric?"

"He said to call him Eric. I'm just being polite."

"He did, did he?"

"Yes I did, now let's go get that pizza with the works, I'm hungry."

"Me too," Ronnie replied.

Eric looked in the mirror, and winked.

The young boy tried to return the wink, but he couldn't quite get just one eye to blink, so he took his finger and pulled down his right eyelid.

"What was that?" Sam asked her son.

"It was just a guy thing, Mom. You know—man to man."

Sam looked over at Eric, but he maintained his focus on the road as they headed for a large pizza with everything on it.

After consuming the large pizza, the threesome returned to Sam's small apartment. Eric parked the car at the curb and walked around to open the door for his passengers. As the three friends advanced along the walkway to Sam's apartment, Eric offered a parting thought, "Guys, I hope you enjoyed our time together today, at least most of it. I sure did."

"Anytime you need someone to help eat a pizza, we're you're team. Isn't that right, Ronnie?"

"You bet."

"If you need help packing for the move, or anything else, just call Sam, for anything."

When they arrived at the entry to the apartment, Sam started to lean over toward Eric, and then she stopped and looked at Ronnie. As she gently touched his arm, Sam offered, "Thanks Eric, for everything. Please think about taking the job in DC."

Ronnie reached out his hand to offer a parting handshake. "It would be real nice to have you around, now that we're good friends."

"You too, Sport. Goodbye."

~ * ~

Sam hung her coat on the brass rack next to the door, and then gazed at the far wall, as she stood motionless next to her son.

The young boy looked at the wall, and then at his mother as she stared at some unseen object in the distance.

"Mom...Hey Mom?"

"Yes. What is it?"

"Do you like Eric?"

"Well of course."

"I mean the way a woman likes a man."

Sam glanced down at her son. Then she sat on the edge of the chair. "Where is that clever little mind of yours going with this?"

"He seems like a real nice guy."

"He is."

"Sometimes, don't you miss having a guy like Eric around?"

"You mean like a dad?"

"Yes."

"Sometimes I do."

"Do you think of Eric that way?"

"It's been a long day. You need to get ready for bed."

"Mom?"

"Yes, what is it?"

"Do you think we'll ever have someone like Eric with us, all the time?"

"I don't know. I hope so."

"But you do like him, right?"

"Yes Ronnie, I said I like him."

"Have you ever told him?"

"Told him what?"

"Have you ever told Eric that you like him, the way a woman likes a man?"

"No, I have not."

"Why?"

"It's complicated. For adults, things are more complicated. Why are you asking me all these questions?"

"I think he like's you a bunch."

"Really, what makes you say that? Did he say something to you?"

"It's the way he looks at you, like he wants to be with you, all the time. You should invite him over sometime. I can go stay with Grandpa and Grandma, if that would help."

"Maybe we will have him over sometime, but together. Now go to bed."

"Okay, but think about it, he's a really nice guy."

Sam watched her son disappear into his room. *I want it too Son, as much as you do, but I can't force things to happen. I'm sorry things came out the way they did. I always dreamed of a child conceived from passion and love. It just didn't happen that way. But I'm not sorry for having you. Everything, the nightmares, the loneliness, you make it all bearable, my little soldier. Maybe someday, we will both have what we want, so much, together.*

Twenty

When the doorbell rang, Ronnie ran to greet his grandparents. "They're here Mom. They're here!"

The elderly woman walked in and hugged her grandson. "Hello Ronnie, are you ready to move?"

"If I have to, Grandma. Where are Tucker and Jimmy? I don't see them with you. Are they in the car?"

"Sorry, but we decided that they would just get in the way while we packed everything up for your move. You're going to be with them for four wonderful weeks while you stay with us before you go up to DC with your mom."

Ronnie's grandfather gently pushed his wife inside the door. "Come on old woman, you're blocking the door."

As the woman eased into the apartment, Ronnie's grandfather reached down, picked up his grandson. "How much do you love me, Spud?"

"Always two tanks and two towers, Grandpa."

Sam's mother greeted her daughter with a hug. "Hello Samantha." She glanced back at her husband and small grandson as they talked in the doorway. "It's amazing, but after all these years, Ronnie still remembers that expression. He was just four when he asked your dad how much he loved him, and your father pointed to the radio tower and water tank outside your window, and said, 'I love you two of those and two of those'."

"I'm relieved that he still says it," Sam confessed. "The other day he asked me not to kiss him on the lips anymore. I didn't think that would happen so soon."

"I know what you mean, sweetheart. I remember when you said the same thing to your dad and me."

Her father wove his way through the half-filled boxes to the open arms of his daughter. "Princess, is that French vanilla blend I smell brewing? And cinnamon rolls? I smell fresh cinnamon rolls."

"Yes Dad. I made them both just for you."

Sam and her family sat at the kitchen table, enjoying the light breakfast before they began the chore of packing for the move.

"How's retirement, Dad? Have you adjusted to civilian life yet?"

"I'm getting there. It is different, not having the stars on my shoulder any more, and not worrying about the lives of the young men and women under my command. I miss it a little, but I'm sure I'll get used to it soon."

"Who are you kidding?" Sam's mother added. "Max? It's driving me crazy having the old goat around the house all day long. He needs to get some hobbies and some more golfing buddies before I kick his wrinkly old butt out of the house permanently."

Sam's father changed the direction of the conversation. "Princess, when are you going to get a good man in your life?"

"Not this again. Please tell him not to start up with this again."

The retired General ignored his daughter and began the inquisition. "I want you to have someone who will give you the love you deserve. You don't seem to be out there searching for him. Any targets on the horizon, or do you plan to fly solo the rest of your life?"

"There's no one on the radar screen, but I promise, the minute a bogey appears I'll pass it up the chain of command."

The young boy seated at the table offered his insight, "What about Eric, Mom? You said you liked him a lot, remember?"

"Ronnie!"

"What? Didn't you say that to me the other day?"

Sam's mother grinned. "Who is this Eric? Anyone we know?"

"He's just a friend. We've known each other since we were at the Post Graduate School in Monterey ten years ago."

"Is he military?" Sam's father inquired.

"He was an Officer in the Army, and now he works as a civilian for TRADOC. When he was in the military, he was part of a SpecOps unit until he was seriously injured during deep operations."

"This wouldn't be Eric Emerson by any chance, would it?"

"Yes, do you know him?"

"I know *of* him. He was a damn fine soldier, and a good man. Have you told him yet how you feel about him?"

Ronnie joined in the inquest. "That's exactly what I told her, Grandpa. See Mom, I know what I'm talking about; you just don't listen to me."

"Hey guys, stop ganging up on me will you? Mom, make them stop, please."

"Maybe I should call this Eric and see what his intentions are."

"Dad, I'm serious, stop it. Mom's right, you need more hobbies. You have too much time on your hands. If Eric and I advance this relationship, it will be on our terms."

"Don't wait too long, I'm getting up there in years and I want a granddaughter."

"I agree with Grandpa, Mom. You need to move faster."

"Alright, that's enough. Let's get back to packing up these boxes, and Mom, you need to tell Dad to give me some space."

"Sorry sweetheart, but I agree with your father on this subject. You need to move things along a bit. If you care about this young man, you should show it, and soon."

Sam walked over to the counter, picked up a roll of masking tape, and started to secure one of the boxes she filled earlier. "That's it. Just go ahead and talk amongst yourselves, because I'm not listening anymore. I'm working over here, and I thought you came to help, not to hound me the entire visit."

Sam's parents smiled at each other before her mother suggested, "Alright Ronnie, let's give your mother some peace for now and go help her pack."

Ronnie whispered to his grandparents, "Don't worry, I'll help Mom with Eric. I know she likes him a lot. She's just shy."

Sam's father chuckled. "You do that Spud, and if you need help, just let us know. Now let's go help your mom before she really gets mad at us."

~ * ~

Eric walked out of General Hamilton's office. That was fun. Only took two weeks for the report to bring the wrath of hell down on his head. He hadn't been yelled at like that since boot camp. He guessed it's time to call in his chits. There was nothing left for him around here anyway.

Eric started to head back to his office but then changed his mind. There were too many phone calls from Washington about the Viper decision. He walked down to the library, sat in the first empty cubicle at the back of the room, and dialed General Williams' new office in the Pentagon.

"General Williams' office, this is Major Cassidy. Can I help you?"

"Hey Major, are you causing a ton of trouble up there yet?"

"Eric. Is that you?"

"Now that you're in Starsville, you've already forgot your old friends."

"There are definitely a ton of General level officers up here. It's a bit scary with all this brass walking the halls. How's your new boss? Are you two getting along yet?"

"What do you think? Did you see the paper yesterday? The production decision on the Viper missile program has been postponed. I wonder why."

"I know. Our report caused a real uproar. We felt the quakes all the way up here."

"I've been tongue lashed before, but General Hamilton left welts on my hide. He essentially handed me my walking papers and suggested that I look elsewhere. I've got calls from both Senator Clark and Senator Robertson's office. I guess they want to see me for a little more target practice."

"What did they say?"

"Nothing yet, I've been hiding since the production halt was announced. That's why I called. Do you think there's still a job up there for an old Snake Eater?"

"You're kidding me! Do you really mean it? The general will be ecstatic. He keeps telling me to bug you into submission."

"How does Major Cassidy feel about it?"

The phone was quiet for several seconds. Then Sam whispered, "I miss you."

"I miss you too. I've been thinking a lot in terms of you and me, and Ronnie."

"What do you think we should do about it?" Sam inquired.

"Nothing over the phone, but do you think we would cause people to cross their eyes if we actually went out on a date?"

"Who cares? When can you get up here?"

"There's one more thing I have to take care of here, and then I should have everything wrapped up. I'll turn the house over to an agent. I plan to sell all the furniture. Too many memories for me. I'd like to start fresh.

I can report on board in two weeks. I'll transition my projects over to someone else by this Friday. Think I'll take leave until I start the new job. I'll drive up this Saturday and probably get there between six and six thirty."

"Outstanding. Why don't you come directly to my apartment? I'll have some dinner ready, and you can stay in our spare bedroom. Ronnie's been asking when he was going to see you again."

"Tell him I miss him, too."

"Would you like me to find you a place, maybe near us? That way we could carpool together. You know, save gas and money that way."

"That works for me. I'll stay in touch; maybe call each day to make sure things are working out."

"It sounds great handsome. Hey, is it alright if I tell the general I convinced you to come?"

"A little brown nosing never hurts, does it?"

"Do you mind?"

"Of course not, you'll really be telling the truth, anyway."

Sam understood the meaning of the words, but she wanted to hear it from him. "What do you mean?"

"You are the biggest part of why I'm coming up there. You understand that, don't you?"

Sam paused before replying. "I can't wait to see you."

"Me too, Sam. You need to email me directions to your apartment. I'll see you soon. Goodbye."

"Goodbye."

The secretary that had been standing at the door placed her lunch on the desk. "Thanks Major for watching the phones. I'll take over. Where did that big grin come from? It wasn't there when I left."

"It's just such a beautiful day outside. Don't you think so?"

"Sure, that must be it. Couldn't be that phone call I overheard, could it?"

"No, it's just a great day, that's all. I've got to go in and see the general. I'm about to make him a happy man."

Sam bounced into General Williams' office. The general looked up from a newspaper article when she knocked on the doorframe. "Man, we started a real firefight didn't we? I knew once the media got hold of the story, the fur would pop off the hide. We had to tell it like it is no matter who got upset. Better to pay the piper before the system hits the field.

You and Eric did a real good job on this one; no matter how many flaming calls I get from Washington. What's that big smile for, Major? Did you win the lottery or something?"

"Something better, Sir. Guess who finally decided to join our team?"

"Outstanding, I knew you could talk him into it. I've got a dozen problems for the two of you to solve. I want things set up so you can hit the deck running when he gets here. Top of the list is to work with White Sands and reschedule the Viper Operational Evaluation. I want all test plans previewed through our office. Let's make sure they do it right this time.

Senator Clark insisted his son stay involved, and I went along with the request, provided we approve all actions relative to the test and the fielding of the system. I don't understand exactly what's going on there, but we'll make sure they do it right this time. Did you staff out the new combat vehicle Cost and Operational Effectiveness Analysis?"

"Yes Sir. Everyone except the Deputy Chief of Staff for Operations has their comments on the COEA plan back to us. Their staff officer said he would have them up here by 1300 today. I'll run down there and pick them up for you."

"Thanks Major, and good job on getting Eric up here."

As Sam walked back into the reception area, the secretary pulled a tissue out of a box. "Come here, Major."

Sam walked over and bent down. "What, did I smooch something?"

"No, I just want to wipe that smile off your face so that we can get some work done around here."

"Not today Mary, not today."

Twenty One

A heavyset man with a ponytail walked past the two-armed men that guarded the entry into the secluded room. He navigated around the broken furniture, the mildew stained barrels, and piles of bundled cardboard scattered around the dim room, until he reached the man with the mustache and pitted face seated at a table with chipped red paint.

The single poker light hanging above the table cast dancing shadows across each wall of the smoke saturated room. The telltale glow of joints being drawn every few seconds signaled the location of each occupant.

The man with the ponytail hesitated for a moment until the glowing joint at the center of the table turned. Then he whispered something and the pitted face man replied, "Dead? I thought they were locked up somewhere. How could they be dead?"

"I don't know, Jefe. I talked to our source at the cops. He said they were at the county morgue. I went down to get our gang mark, you know, the gold ring in their ear, but the rings were gone. Their bodies were all twisted and mangled like pretzels. Maybe you should let this one go."

Without a word, the gang leader grabbed the man's long ponytail and jerked his head down till it crashed onto the table. Then he yanked on the gold ring in the man's ear until it ripped through the ear lobe.

"No one disses me, understand, no one. You see this," he pointed to his broken tooth, "He did it, and he's going to suffer."

Pit-face looked at the other three men at the table, and waited for a response, but none was offered.

The man with the ponytail picked himself up and used his hands to stop the bleeding from his nose and torn ear. He stepped back and tried a second time. "We raped and killed his wife. Isn't that enough?"

"When his nuts hang from this lamp, then that'll be enough." Pit face and the three others at the table laughed.

A dog outside the abandoned building howled. After a moment, it stopped, and after several seconds, the dog started barking again. Pit-face squawked to the man at his left, "Juan, if you don't shut up that damn dog, I'll shoot you first, and then him."

As if on cue, the dog went silent. The gang leader looked at the other members seated at the table, and then changed his mind. "Juan, go see why that mutt stopped barking."

After several minutes of waiting for Juan's return, something scratched at the door. "I swear I'm going to slit that dog's throat."

Pit-face directed one of the guards. "I've had it with that dog. Take him out behind the dumpsters and beat him to death with the bat in the corner."

The guard opened the door, but nothing was there. He glanced toward the pit-faced man for guidance. "Go find him, now."

Pit-face looked back at the two men at the table. "I told Juan to keep that hound out of my face. Now I'll going to turn him into maggot food."

The men at the table continued their card game. After several minutes, there was a muffled noise outside the window, as if someone tried to yell, but there was no air in his throat to make the sound. The dim room instantly darkened, like a sponge had consumed every ray of light. Only the red ash from the joints being smoked by the four men who remained lickered as their breath became erratic.

In the void, the distinctive snarl of pit face demanded, "Must be a hit by the Diablo Soldado gang. Give me the shotgun!"

Before anyone could respond, the sound of a door swinging open could be heard.

Pit-face felt something edge by his left leg. "Tomas, is that you?"

From the far corner of the room, the remaining guard

reached for a black metal bat, but it was gone. The heavy breathing was interrupted by a loud thump, as if a pumpkin had been cracked open. The room stilled. Then a muffed sound struggled in the dark, someone gargling in their own blood. Again silence.

An agonizing scream reverberated around the walls, accompanied by several shots, and then a thump on the floor.

More shots rang out. The crash of boxes, barrels, and furniture could be heard as something angry moved through the void. A low guttural growl, like a predator preparing to pounce on its victim, greeted the sole survivor.

A single plea into the darkness could be heard, as the prey stumbled and searched for the exit, desperately trying to flee. "El Dios me ahorra."

Another torso collapsed onto the floor, followed by repeated raps of someone kicking their feet against the floor, struggling to escape. Lungs gasped for air. A final kick of the door signaled the end.

Something was dragged back into the room. The door closed, and the room filled with silence.

~ * ~

Eric pulled onto I-64 and started the two and a half hour trip to La Plata, Maryland. He was determined not to look back, only forward. The only things he retained from his past were his clothes, and the contents of the green shoebox placed next to him in the passenger seat.

He felt at ease and more relaxed then he could remember for a long time. It was like a hand had reached down and released his spirit from the cage where it had been imprisoned for so long. The horrible dreams, the guilt, the specters that gnawed at his soul were finally gone.

He had battled with his internal turmoil and survived. The conflict was no longer ambiguous. Everything was clear. It was not within his purview to always protect the flock. He could not be everywhere, shield everyone important in his life. He knew that now. If the eternal shepherd would not protect all the lambs from the wolf, neither could he. But he could be the hunter that destroys each demon when it reveals itself, and prevent the beast from devouring another. This was his charge, the reason he was here. The nightmares haunting his soul were gone, and he was at peace with what lay behind.

Eric was actually enjoying the drive as each mile moved him closer toward his destination, and the person he wanted to be with. After listening to the local all-talk news station for twenty minutes, he decided to tune in some music.

As he reached down to change the station, the announcer stated, "The streets may be a little safer tonight. The Guerreros Demonio gang just lost their kingpin and a half of their thugs. Rodriquez Gonzales was found dead yesterday, along with numerous members of his gang. It appears he was killed in a ritualized act of retribution from a rival gang. Officials would not release all the details, but a correspondent from our sister station was there as the bodies were removed. Police at the scene shared that Gonzales had been strangled and his neck broken, before he was castrated. We can all sleep a little better, at least for a while.

Our listeners may recall that Gonzales had been charged on numerous counts of murder over the last six years, but the courts were incapable, or unwilling, to stop this fiend. It appears judgment was finally served tonight, if not by the law, then by the hand of his own kind."

Eric rolled down his window, took a long breath, and sighed. He tuned the radio to some light jazz, and continued his journey to a new life.

Twenty Two

Eric crossed the Harry Nice Potomac River Bridge twenty miles south of the small town of La Plata. It had been several years since he visited his family off Carmel Road close to the college. As he drove up Route 301, he noticed the quiet town had changed some, but still maintained its charm as a friendly community, a rebel to the urban explosion eight miles north in the sprawling city of Waldorf.

Sam had rented an apartment in a new complex just behind the town library. The brick architecture used on the majority of structures in the town provided a common sense of unity and pride in one's neighborhood. Eric rang the bell and Sam's beaming face greeted him, followed by a prolonged, but warranted hug, and a soft kiss on the cheek.

"Boy, am I glad to see you. I bet you're hungry."

He inhaled deeply. "Smells good: spaghetti and garlic bread, my favorite."

"I know, I made it just for you."

As Eric walked into the freshly painted living room, Ronnie extended his hand upward to greet his large friend.

"Good evening. We sure are happy to see you again."

Eric smiled. "Handshake? I was looking for a kiss, or are you too big for that now?"

"Yes sir." The young man paused and then offered, "Will a hug do?"

"I can live with that, Sport."

When Eric picked Ronnie up, the young boy remarked,

"What happened to your neck? It looks swollen."

Sam glanced where Ronnie was touching. "My Lord Eric, what did you do?"

"It's no big deal, guys. I just cut myself shaving, that's all."

"With what, a dagger? It looks infected."

"It's fine. I put some peroxide on it this morning. It will be gone in a few days. We men heal fast, right Ronnie?"

"Right, Eric."

"Remember Sport, pain is just weakness leaving the body."

Sam held her finger up to Eric's lips. "Oh no you don't. I've heard Dad use that expression before from when he was a SpecOps instructor. You guys need to let my little boy figure out what he wants to be on his own, no indoctrination of my nine year old, understand?"

"Yes ma'am," Eric replied, but when Sam looked down at her son, Eric winked at him.

Sam stared at Eric's wound again, and then at Ronnie. "Guess we'll have to get him an electric shaver for his birthday. I don't think I trust him with a razor. Ronnie, show Eric where he can put his things for tonight." Sam turned back to Eric. "Ronnie is going to sleep on the couch tonight so you can have the bed."

"No. I appreciate it, but I'll sleep here. The sofa looks comfortable."

"Are you sure you don't mine the couch?"

"I've slept outside in sandstorms, with rain pouring down…and buried in a field of thorns. I think this will be great. Besides, you can't kick a man out of his bed, right Sport?"

"Right."

"Okay then, the couch it is. I got you a furnished apartment three bays over. You can see it through the window. I thought we could go shopping tomorrow to get you the little necessities, like curtains, soap dishes, toothbrush holders, spices, and kitchen candles. All those things you guys would never worry over, but make a place look and feel like a home. I'll even help decorate the new apartment, but only if you want me too."

"I'll take any help I can get."

Eric looked down at Ronnie and winked. "You're probably right about us guys. We men have no idea about all that frilly stuff.

As primitives, we would just lay the toothbrush right on the counter. A few germs strengthen a man's constitution, right Sport?"

"Right. Hey Mom, why are you fixing up a place for Eric?"

"He's our friend. It's nice to help your friends."

"No, I mean why does he have to live in a different place? Why can't he just stay with us? He can share my room, or maybe yours."

"Ronnie! I'm sorry Eric, but there appears to be a few areas that I have been delinquent in explaining to my son."

"No problem." Eric bent down and whispered, "Let this one go. I'll explain why later."

"Okay. Hey Mom, when are we going to eat? I'm really starving."

"Me too. When are we going to eat, Mom?"

"It's ready. Guys and their stomachs, that's your primal motivation in life, isn't it?"

"Food is important, but we do think about other things on occasion, don't we?"

"Yes we do, like baseball, cars and stuff."

"That's exactly what I was thinking."

"Right," Sam replied, "cars and stuff. Now let's get in there and eat before the food gets cold."

"It does smell good. Hope she's got enough for two hungry men."

Ronnie grinned. "Me too, I'm so hungry I could eat a mule's butt."

Eric looked over at Sam as she offered an explanation. "Ronnie's grandfather says that all the time. I just let it go."

The three friends sat at the small table in the tiny dining area and enjoyed a good meal with good conversation. Eric discussed how things turned to crap once she left. Sam explained how much work was stacked up at his new office, and Ronnie inserted a word or two on his favorite new topic, fishing.

~ * ~

Eric pushed back from the table, and patted his stomach. "Great meal, Sam. I don't think I could eat too many like that or I'd need a new wardrobe."

"Me too, Mom."

"A meal like that deserves a good cigar. I use to smoke one every night, but I gave them up several years ago. I do miss them after a great meal like this."

Ronnie added, "A good cigar would be nice right now."

Sam uttered three words, "No stinky cigars."

"What about ice cream?" Eric suggested. "Can we get some ice cream?"

"Hey Mom, what about some ice cream?"

"I'm sorry guys, but I don't keep it around here because I have such a weakness for it."

"Would it be all right if Ronnie and I ran down to April's Treat Shop and got us some ice cream? It's right off Main Street and they provide an outlet for those with a sweet tooth. They make their ice cream and many of their candies right on site."

"Yeah Mom, I could use some ice cream."

"I thought you said you were full."

"There's always room for ice cream, right Eric?"

"I think if I unbutton one belt loop, I could fit at least a scoop in there, but it's up to your mom."

Sam looked at the two males seated across the table waiting for her consent. "It's Saturday, and kind of a special night. All right, we'll bend the rules a bit. You guys go ahead; I'll stay here and clean up the kitchen."

"Is there any particular flavor you would like?"

"Surprise me."

"Okay, we'll be back in thirty minutes."

As the guys got into the car, Eric instructed the young boy, "Put your seat belt on."

"I always do."

After a few minutes, the young passenger turned to his friend. "Why can't you just stay with us?"

"Men and women require a period of courtship before they get that close together in their relationship, understand?"

"No."

"Your mom and I are from the old school. Today, many people just hook up without getting to really know each other. When things don't work out just right, they split up and go their separate way. To make sure a man and woman are compatible to live together forever, a period of courtship is traditional."

"Oh. What does courtship mean?"

"A woman needs to feel that a man will always be good to her, love her and her alone. Courtship is where a man does things to make the woman understand that he really cares."

"Like what?"

"Like taking her out to places she likes to go, bringing her presents like candy, flowers and stuff, things like that."

"I see. So are you and Mom going through courtship?"

"You sure ask a lot of questions."

"Well are you?"

"I think so."

"Good."

Eric glanced over at Ronnie sitting in the passenger seat with his arms crossed, and wondered if he would ever be given the chance to have a kid as great as the one Sam had raised, all on her own.

Twenty Three

Ronnie paused in the doorway of April's Treat Shop. First he panned left, then right. To a nine year old, the store offered a cornucopia of delights in every conceivable variety. Chocolate coated everything, chewy nuggets of every kind, rainbow drops of any color, anything a child's fantasy could imagine, the establishment could satisfy.

He folded his hands across the top of his head and declared, "Wow, this place is great!"

Eric moved Ronnie gently into the store. "That's just what my little cousins said the first time I brought them here."

Overwhelmed by all the choices, Ronnie staggered through the rows of sugar treats, like a drunk high on his addiction. Then he stopped abruptly. He rubbed his eyes to confirm his vision. A glass counter that spanned twenty-five feet left and right in front of the young boy contained every imaginable flavor of ice cream known to man.

Eric watched as he read each flavor, and then started over again. "Hard to choose just one isn't it? See anything you like?"

"Everything, I like everything."

"Let's try to keep it down to just four flavors. We'll get a pint of each. Pick out two for you and two for your mom."

Ronnie supervised as the lady packed every ounce of delicious sweet flavor into the four containers. When she was done, the boy walked over to the candy counter. He gazed up at his large friend. "Eric, these would make good courtship presents."

Everyone behind the counter stopped serving customers and

focused on the young matchmaker's plans.

"They would. Are you sure she likes these things?"

"Pretty sure, I know she loves the chocolate-coated cashews, and she's crazy about the cream filled chocolate covered cherries. Those are really her favorites of all time."

Eric handed the boxes to the cashier. "We'll take these too. Now we need to get home before this stuff melts."

While they drove the two miles back to the apartment, Eric asked, "Does your mom like to do anything specific?"

"Like what?"

"What kind of things does she like to do in her free time?"

"You mean courtship things?"

"Yes."

"You mean like baseball and race cars."

"Sort of, but more tuned to what a woman would like to do."

The young boy thought hard. "I know she loves to fish, and she's always wanted to go crabbing."

"Really?"

"Yeah, she talks about it all the time, the way she would like to fish and crab if she only had the chance."

As they pulled into the parking lot, Eric grinned down at his young adviser. "I'll keep that in mind."

"Mom, we're back! Wait till you see what we got. You've got to see that place. It was... fantastic."

Sam had been bent over, placing pots in her bottom cabinet. She stood up and turned around. "My goodness. Looks like someone went a little overboard. Go wash your hands before you chow down again."

Eric reached toward Sam with two boxes of candy. "These are for you. Ronnie said they were your favorite of all time."

Sam examined the contents of the bag, and then looked back at Eric with a smile. "Looks like you've been conned by a nine-year-old, on the ice cream flavors too."

Eric grinned. "I sensed that after he picked out huckleberry bluebird swirl for you. I know for a fact you love straight dark chocolate, so I made him pick that one, too."

"I'm glad someone watched out for me. I'm sorry. He doesn't get to do this often. I guess he just went crazy."

"That's what little boys do. They remind us of how wonderful life can be if we just enjoy the simple pleasures. I guess fishing and crabbing are not things you've been dying to try either?"

"Hardly, he really homed in on your weak spot, didn't he?"

"Not really. I wouldn't mind teaching him how to fish and crab. Every boy has to be snipped by at least one crab claw. It's the rite of passage to manhood. Think you could come along and pretend to have fun. There's no sense letting him know we're onto his game."

"I'd like that. I'll even hold a rod, as long as you bait it and take off anything that bites."

"I think I can handle that, but I've got a better idea. If you'll wear a nice swimsuit, I'll fish for both of us. How's that sound?"

"I'll have to think about that request, Mr. Emerson."

"Don't give me that look. Ronnie has his dreams, and I have mine. Tell him we'll plan a fishing trip right after I get situated at work."

"He'll drive you nuts until then talking about it."

"That's the way it's supposed to be. What are kids for if they can't bug us every now and then? Let's eat this ice cream. I'm not used to all this food and excitement. I'm worn out."

"You don't think with all these sweets he'll be getting to bed any time soon, do you?"

"That's your problem."

"That's not very nice. What kind of friend are you?"

"The same kind of friend that sets a fire under General Hamilton and leaves me to take the heat."

Sam eyed the grin on Eric's face. "You turkey, you planned all this."

"Revenge is sweet when served cold."

Sam smiled. "Touché, guess I deserved that."

"I could stay up with you until he goes to bed. I enjoy hearing you fill the air with all your ideas and stuff."

"Think I'll take you up on that. Let's get started consuming these sweets so we can watch him bounce off the walls."

Ronnie came back into the room. "Hey Mom, how do you like the courtship presents Eric got you?"

Sam stared at her son. "The what?"

Eric eased over to the young boy and whispered,

"Remember the words man to man, Sport."
"Oh, never mind, Mom."

As Sam listened to Eric and Ronnie discuss how to catch slimy fish and prickly crustaceans, she watched the two males bond, and it felt good, like it was supposed to be. It was something that Sam knew her son needed, and wanted. Then she pondered her needs. Someone near that cared about her, made her feel warm inside, like a woman, not a mom. Someone that wanted her, and her alone, that she could share the days with, and the nights. Sam felt different. For some reason, tonight, she didn't feel alone, and it felt right. For all of them, it felt like it was meant to be.

Twenty Four

Sam pointed to the small desk positioned to the rear of the nine-foot square room, "Here's your space behind mine. If you need any supplies, see Mary in the general's office."

The room was small with a thick coat of cream-colored paint. There were no decorations, pictures, or adornments of any kind. Except around Sam's desk where several colorful posters of far off cities had been taped to the bland walls. Not to mention the dozen or so snapshots of Ronnie. "It's a bit small. I could fit two of these rooms in my office back at Fort Monroe."

Sam smiled. "I prefer to think of it as cozy. Space is a real commodity at Headquarters for the Department of the Army here in the Pentagon. The HQDA gets the leftovers when it comes to office space. You should see the offices for the blue suitor's. Those guys really live in luxury."

"I think you planned it this way, so you could keep an eye on me."

"You always see right through me don't you?"

A man with a flat top haircut was just finishing some work behind Eric's computer. The stocky man offered no greeting, no expression of any sort. He picked up his case and walked out of the room without any conversation.

"Who was that guy messing with my console? Is he part of the general's staff?"

"You mean the man with that big gaudy ring?"

"That was a star sapphire stone. He wasn't very friendly was he?"

"No. I asked Mary at the front desk about him. She said he's with the computer security group in the basement. I've tried to start up a conversation but he just grunts. I think his name is Carlson."

"What was he doing to my console?"

"It's part of their computer security procedures here at the Pentagon. They have anti-tamper indicators they check randomly to make sure no one penetrates our security measures."

Ericnodded to indicate he understood and then asked, "Has the general decided which tasks he wants us to tackle first?"

Sam pulled a sheet of paper out of her notebook. "General Williams is touring the major Commands to get their inputs on the Future Combat Program specs. He won't be back at Army Headquarters for two weeks, so he gave me his list of priority actions that he wants us to focus on while he's gone."

Eric scanned the paper. "God save us, the general put a woman in charge for two weeks. We're in real trouble."

Sam lowered her head and cocked her right eyebrow. "Don't forget it either, Mister. It's probably the only time in our lives I'll get to tell you what to do, and I'm going to enjoy every minute of it."

Eric grinned. "I think I'll be taking orders from you for a long time, if Ronnie has his way."

Sam blushed and then looked down at the page. "You'll notice he put the Viper OPEVAL, as well as some study their running out of the Pentagon called Osiris, at the top of his list. General Williams wants us to see if we can get some Intel on this Osiris effort. He needs to know if this particular study deals with force structure or JROC needs associated with the Future Combat Program. Oh, and you'll love this: Colonel Clark works out of the office for the Under Secretary of the Army now. He's the team leader for the study."

"Crap."

"Your words, not mine." Then she conveyed a more serious expression, "Just a suggestion, it's different up here. A lot of stars cross each other with their own agendas. It's hard for us at the staff officer level to see all the warning lines. Seems there are a lot of turf battles around here every day. It's kind of like stepping your way through a minefield at each meeting. It's impossible to keep up with the pet projects of each General Officer. A person can say something apparently innocent and BANG, they hit a mine."

Eric watched as Sam pushed the curl of auburn hair off her forehead for the fourth time. "You know I thrive on confrontation, even with a General Officer. Besides, you don't have to worry. You're just too damn cute. They would never take you down."

"Maybe, but I just got you here. I don't want one of the big guys to send you off to some distant assignment."

"Just for you, I'll pull back on my caveman ways, but just a little. A man's got to follow his own tune, or he's no good to anyone."

"I knew it was a waste of breath, but I figured I'd try."

"Don't worry, I've got a lot of experience wading through minefields. At the first sign, I'll make sure you're out of range from any collateral damage. Have you talked to Judi about the Osiris study? I think she's assigned to the project."

"I tried, but she's zip-lipped about the whole project. Just says it's a compartmented program. Of course, she's got a thing for your granite face, she always has. Maybe you should try and see if you can get anything around the edges."

"I keep telling you, she's like my sister, nothing more, so chill. I'm just into green eyed redheads, you know that."

"So you keep telling me."

"What room is she in? I'll stop by on my way to personnel. There's a foul-up on my transfer papers. Where's her office?"

"Room 2D928."

"While I'm down there, think you could check with security and get a list of who's cleared for the Osiris Study?"

"They're not going to share those details with me on a compartmented program."

"Sure they will. That particular information is only classified at the Secret level. If it's a guy, charm him. If it's a woman, use the sisterhood thing."

"I thought I was in charge for the next two weeks."

"You are, I'm just offering a strong suggestion."

"Alright, but first tell me why."

"If we can figure out who's been assigned to work this effort, and what organization they work for, it can provide some insight regarding the type of data and skill sets they need. If it's a Special Access Program, we'll never find out anything from the inside, but we can use some peripheral information to speculate on what they're up to."

"That sounds reasonable, anything else, Mr. Bossy?"

"The Viper contractor has a satellite office over in Crystal City. Could you set up a meeting to discuss their plans for the follow up tests? Also, ask if they can give us a list of who worked on the first OPEVAL you and I attended, and what each of them was responsible for during the test."

Sam turned around with a parting assessment. "I don't know what made me think I was ever in charge here."

He smiled. "I kind of wondered about that myself."

~ * ~

Eric turned the corner of corridor nine and started down D ring when a young girl loaded with files, a purse, and a coffee cup clashed arms first into his chest. He looked into the young girl's face. Then he pulled gently on her ponytail and smiled. "Hell of a way to greet me on my first day. I was just coming down to see you, Judi."

In a muted tone deeper then would be expected of a petite young girl, she apologized. "I'm sorry. I was so looking forward to seeing you again, and working with you, now I destroyed your shirt. I'm so sorry."

With an uncharacteristic tenderness for a professional setting, Eric gently pinched the chin of the attractive girl. "Don't sweat it, the coffee will come out. I see you still have the cup I gave you."

Judi looked at the mug with the Doberman chewing on a snake and grinned. "It's my favorite. I never let it out of my sight, not for a minute. Too many people admire it all the time. I hide it each night in my drawer so no sticky hands can get it."

"Looks like you're running off to somewhere."

"I'm headed to the SCIF. We're briefing the preliminary results of that study I emailed you about. We meet with a bunch of stars and congressmen once a month. I'm a bit nervous, to tell you the truth."

"You'd better go ahead then. I don't want you to walk in late with all that brass. I'll stop back by later when I get settled in, and good luck on your briefing." Eric tapped the young girl on the shoulder and walked toward personnel.

Twenty Five

Judi inserted her badge into the Special Compartmented Intelligence Facility PIN reader. Then she entered her personal security code and opened the outer door. She signed in at the security guard and waited for him to activate the release to the SCIF inner electromagnetic shielded enclosure.

She sat her mug and purse alongside the computer console positioned at the back of the chamber. She pushed the large circular glasses back onto the bridge of her nose and played with her long ponytail as she scanned the stars, ribbons and suits positioned around the mahogany table in the center of the windowless room. Then Judi looked to the front of the room where Colonel Clark waited impatiently on the podium, twirling his laser pin knuckle to knuckle. She wished they'd moved her closer because the lights were too low and she couldn't see his lips. If she missed one of his darn signals, he'd yell at her again, right in front of everyone.

Judi edged toward the screen hanging down behind the podium. In a muted tone she said, "Colonel, I'm sorry but I can't see you very well with the lights so low. I'm afraid I'll miss your cue."

The colonel reached over to the dimmer switch, turned it up slightly, and then with an irritated voice responded, "Can you see me now? I'd rap on the podium, but that wouldn't help would it?"

She blushed. "Colonel, I'm deaf, not stupid." As she started to walk back to the console she added, "Nor am I a dog either."

I don't care who he is. He has no cause to be so rude to me all the time. If I wasn't learning so much, and getting to work with

Paul, I'd ask to be transferred to a different project. They never tell us what this is all for anyway. I've worked hard to make him look good and all he does is snarl at me. I bet he doesn't introduce us to the group again this time.

As the last member of the Executive Oversight Board arrived, the colonel began his presentation. "It looks like we can get started. Based on the guidance provided by the Board at our last meeting, we altered the assumptions that were used for the model runs. We also added two additional scenarios, per your direction."

The colonel pointed to the red light positioned above the screen with the word SAP highlighted. "Just a reminder, the briefing and all its contents are classified as a Special Access Program. None of the results can be discussed outside the group of twenty-four people cleared for the Osiris Study. After we present the preliminary runs of the PRES model, the remainder of the team will leave so we can continue the executive session. Now we can begin."

The elderly gray haired gentleman in the wheel chair requested, "Excuse me, Colonel."

"Yes, Senator Robertson?"

"I understand your team has worked long hours to support this effort. I didn't get their names at the last meeting. Think you could introduce them to us, please?"

Reluctantly, the colonel replied, "Okay, in the very back we have Paul Levin, our programmer and data collector. At the console is Judi Cohen. She's our analytical modeler. We also have a dozen people feeding data into the study from CAA, CDC, and several Federally Funded Research and Development Centers. They are all SAP cleared into the project, but only the six members of the oversight board and myself see the actual model runs, and discuss their interpretation. Everyone else who's cleared for the program just provides generic data without an explanation of how it's used in the final analysis."

"I am grateful Colonel for what your team has done," the gray haired man replied. "Please be sure to tell the rest of the team that we appreciate their contribution."

"All right, if we can get back to today's briefing, on the screen you'll notice a matrix that depicts the Measures Of Effectiveness for each scenario we ran. We used two central MOEs to represent the effectiveness of each solution strategy, namely: how long before we achieve 60% realignment, and second, how many years does the correction remain effective before we reach catastrophic limits again? The columns indicate what method of realignment we might employ, while the rows define four levels at which we can choose to apply those methods of realignment. The matrix on the screen uses generic categories, like minimum and maximum level, or method A and method D. When we transition to the executive portion of this meeting, the team members will leave and I'll fill in the actual data from the model runs.

"To get a sense for how the model works, we will run one sample scenario. For this illustration, we've picked four levels of severity, ranging from minimum to extreme, for using method B to achieve the realignment."

The colonel waved his hand sideways at the young woman seated at the computer console. Judi typed in a few numbers, and then the model generated a series of four lines of different colors that traced left to right on the overhead screen. The graph displayed the 'percent of realignment achieved' plotted against a timeframe extending from 'today to eighty years into the future'.

"The model uses a technique referred to as system dynamics to correlate all the variables that drive how the global system will respond, then it predicts what we can expect to see each year if we take the prescribed course of action. Now, if the team in the back of the room will leave, we'll discuss the actual runs and their implications."

~ * ~

After Judi and Paul exited the SCIF, the colonel placed a new slide on the projector, "Gentleman, on this exhibit you can see the actual result of our model runs across the various scenarios. We've made hundreds of runs, and these results are consistent across the board."

Senator Robertson raised his hand. "Colonel, I have two questions. First, does your team have any idea of the intent of this analysis? By that I mean, just exactly what we are attempting to achieve?"

"No sir. As I said before, they have only been given the raw data to input into the model, but with dummy headers. They know we are using global population data, but they have not been told the specific means we are considering for realignment. You'll also note that I did not provide you any copies of these results. This is the only version, and it remains in the double combo safe here in the SCIF with 24/7 controlled access."

"That's fine," Senator Robertson added. "My second question deals with the source of your input data. The board requested that you validate your methods data from two independent sources. Has that been done?"

The colonel began to twirl his light pin across his fingers, "Yes sir. It's all been validated from independent sources."

"Go ahead then and explain to us what these results mean."

The colonel stopped rotating his laser pointer and turned toward the screen. "Per your request, we deleted the more immediate and destructive methods of achieving the desired goal. From your guidance at the last meeting, we examined only the biological agent. We evaluated four modes or degrees of application severity, ranging from a DO NOTHING option, to the extreme case of executing an ACTIVE AGENT."

"You can see on the screen that with the DO NOTHING option, our dilemma remains dominant and breakdown occurs in twelve to twenty years, with a probability of 90%. If we elect to use the passive agent and the PRECLUDE RECOVERY option, we can halt the dilemma in six to nine years, and the problem remains dormant for sixty years with a probability of 70%. The course of action I recommend is Option 4, specifically, to execute an ACTIVE AGENT. Such a solution will have almost an immediate affect. In roughly three years we will achieve our 60% realignment goal, and it will prevent the dilemma from reappearing for ninety years, with a probability of 95%. That's our best option gentleman."

The four-star General from the Joint Chiefs of Staff demanded, "Colonel, are you actually suggesting that we employ an active agent?"

"Sir, I don't like the implications either, but situations like this can require extreme measures. Otherwise, it is very unlikely that we will be able to resolve this catastrophe before it's too late."

The senator in the wheelchair cleared his throat, and then slapped his pencil hard on the table three times to refocus everyone's attention.

"Gentleman, I'm the individual responsible for this study. I commissioned it because I wanted reasonable solutions to save our civilization from total chaos. I must tell you, Colonel, with no disrespect intended, I believe your Extreme Option is not a solution. It's a callous and deliberate action that could be characterized as mass murder."

Senator Clark insisted, "Senator Robertson, you asked my son to deliver viable solutions. Don't cast aspersions when you can't stomach the results."

"Clark, do you think any of us in this room would survive the repercussions if we recommended, let alone executed, such a course of action? When what we did got out, and it would get out, other countries would declare war, and carry out God knows what kind of retaliation against our nation.

Hell, our own people would revolt and throw all our old bones to the wolves. It doesn't matter that our intent was to do the right thing and save the world. Nobody would care. The only realistic and plausible choice is Option 2. When the agents occur through the normal dynamics and interaction of a global population, we offer no recovery provisions; we just let nature take its course. That's our only viable solution. How many here agree with my assessment?"

All but two of the individuals in the room agreed.

"Other than the colonel and his father, how many on this Board agree that we should commit suicide and select the active agent option as the solution we recommend to the president?"

No one in the room signified their concurrence with the colonel.

"Good, we have a decision. Colonel, I appreciate your candor. I want you and your team to repeat your analysis. Please double check all your data, and validate your prediction algorithms. I prefer that you employ a different analytical construct to verify your results. If they remain valid, I want you to work out a preliminary operational concept to implement the PRECLUDE RECOVERY Option. We'll reassemble again in a month. This meeting is adjourned, gentleman."

Twenty Six

Eric walked into room 9A238. "Excuse me. Where does Judi Cohen sit?"

The Army officer pointed at the hallway to the left. As Eric worked his way through the cubicles, he saw Carlson come out of Judi's cubicle.

Eric looked over the top of the partition and saw Judi working feverishly at her terminal. She studied the screen and periodically pushed her large circular glasses up the bridge of her nose. The sequence of, type, poke the glasses, and type was interrupted every few minutes when she picked up her favorite mug.

Eric smiled when the girl embraced the porcelain with both hands as if it were her best friend, absorbing the warmth of the hot tea into her tiny fingers. Then she inhaled the aromatic stream rising from the cup, and slowly sipped the mixture of gourmet tea. The ritual was repeated again and again; altered occasionally when Judi removed a wooden pencil wedged into her blonde ponytail, scribbled a note on the pad beside the screen, and repeated the cycle through the same set of steps.

Eric noticed the three-inch square reflector Judi kept fixed to the top of her screen. The small detachable mirror provided an early warning system signaling the approach of someone from behind. The similarity between the petite woman at the screen, and Eric's deceased sister established a unique bond with the attractive young girl. From behind, it was as if he were watching his sister Robin pull the pencil from the ponytail in her blonde hair, write some juicy event in her daily diary, and then read the day's events back to herself.

Eric reached around the side of the cubicle and gently tugged on Judi's ponytail. When she looked into her mirror and saw her good friend, she quickly stood up, turned and hugged him.

"That's a better greeting then this morning. How have you been? Has that boyfriend of yours realized what a jewel he has and proposed yet?"

Judi placed her finger in front of her lips to indicate they could be heard across the cubicles. She signed, *"Not so loud. Paul sits three spaces over. I keep waiting for him, but there's no ring yet."*

It had been a while since Eric had signed, so he slowly formed his response. *"Maybe I should talk to that young man before some good looking dude swoops down and steals you right from under his nose."*

Judi blushed before grinning. *"No, if he's going to do it, let it be on his own."*

"Don't wait too long Judi. Life has a way of rushing by. You'll turn around one day and be searching for those kids you keep talking about, but there'll be none there."

"I know. My sister bugs me constantly over the same thing."

"Has Paul learned to sign yet?"

"No, he tries but he gets his letters mixed. At first I thought he was being nasty, but eventually I realized he couldn't keep the letters straight. I've wonder if that might be part of the problem."

"What do you mean?"

"There are so many pretty girls out there that are whole, not damaged like me. Maybe that's why he won't commit."

"Don't start that self-pity crap. It's not your style. I've seen the way he looks at you. He adores everything about you, and why not? You're cute as a button. Besides, I've seen that spark in his eyes. You could look like a warthog and he would still be hooked on what he sees inside. What we all see in you."

"Then why won't he ask me?"

"He's shy. You girls scare the hell out of us men. You grab our hearts, but you never send clear signals. Everything is ambiguous. We need it spelled out in big letters, TAKE ME I'M YOURS. He's probably afraid he'll be rejected. You need a Cupid to

break down the communication barrier. I know the perfect matchmaker. You should get Sam to loan you her son next time you go on a date. He really tells it like it is, in the courtship department."

"I might just do that Eric. He is a sweet little boy, and just as cute as can be. Sam is really lucky. Any man would be fortunate to become part of that family."

"Not you too. Don't worry; Ronnie is exercising his prerogatives in that area. He doesn't need any help."

With the personal discussion completed, Eric verbalized his question. "Sam said you wanted to discuss an analytical problem you had on the new project you're working on."

"I know you're familiar with system dynamics theory. We are using a model based on that technique for this project. The problem is that the sponsors of the study want us to construct a Rough Order of Magnitude secondary model that we can use to validate the runs from the primary system dynamics based model. Do you have any ideas on quantitative methods we might use that are good enough to generate ROM estimates?"

"Possibly, but you have to give me a better feel for the phenomenon you're trying to model."

"I can't tell you any specifics because the project is compartmented."

"If you want me to help, you need to either give me an analogous situation, or generalize the problem."

Judi paused for a moment before grabbing a piece of paper and drawing a two-inch circle. "Imagine this circle represents some system with objects flowing in and out." She traced several arrows leaving, and several entering the circle.

"There is also internal flow between sub-elements of the system."

"I understand. It's the classic system dynamics paradigm. You establish differential equations to represent the flow rates in, out, and within the system, then step your model across time increments with differences equations to emulate how the system will behave."

"Exactly. My question is: are there any other analytical techniques that could approximate dynamic performance of such a nature?"

"Yes there are, but I need more specifics. Is the system you refer to a mechanical or an electronic entity, like a weapon system?"

"No."

"Is it a social, political, or economic system?"

"Not exactly."

"Is it any derivative of a demographics model?"

"What do you mean?"

"Think of a system inhabited by objects that consume resources, like the population of a country. Things flow into and out of the country based on the needs and habits of the population. People have to eat, farms produce food, trucks deliver products, pollutants are generated, fuel is consumed, people are born and die, and everything interacts with and is dependent upon the habits and numbers of consumers. Would the system you are modeling be analogous to that situation?"

Judi opened her month, and then stopped. "Something like that."

Eric wrote three lines on the sheet of paper in her notebook. "There are three other analytical methods that can be used to approximate the behavior of your system. Time stepped input/output analysis comes from the discipline of econometrics, and it's probably your best bet. They use it during mobilization planning to gear up entire economies to dramatic changes in the system, like war or a catastrophe. Markovian chains are also possible, but you would have to make the transition probabilities time dependent.

The third approach, nonlinear dynamics is possible but it's based on solving complex sets of tensors and non-linear equations. It can be difficult to apply to large problems like yours. I would try the econometric based method first and see how well it compares to your current model. There are numerous books down in the library that demonstrate how to use these methods. Give it a shot. If you have any more questions, just call me and I'll give you a hand."

"Thank. I knew you could help. Sorry I have to be so vague."

"No problem. If you're done with me, General Williams has a few hot potatoes he wants Sam and I to work on. Maybe the three of us can have lunch soon. Better yet, what do you say we do a picnic and you invite Paul? Ronnie can help bring the guy to his senses."

"Now who's being the matchmaker?"

"I'm just trying to help a young girl out, that's all." Eric stood up, put his chair back in place and waved as he exited Judi's cubicle.

~ * ~

Judi removed four texts from the library shelves, and carried them to a desk behind the math oriented topics. The desks were isolated from the main tables, but once she placed her mirror on the top of the single wooden shelf built onto the back of the desk, she was still able to view anyone that might approach from behind.

After studying for a while, Judi detected movement behind her, in the far corner of the library. When she looked up, she saw Colonel Clark remove the *Military Times* newspaper from the second shelf and sit at the only desk in that counter. She continued to read the book on econometric methods. After a few minutes, she noticed the man who'd inspected her computer earlier in the day sit down directly across from the colonel. Judi periodically glanced into the mirror, and casually followed the side of the conversation she could see.

Several minutes into their discussion, her interest shifted from random curiosity, to apprehension. She continued to pry into the private dialogue, until the heavy set man got up and walked away.

As the colonel returned the newspaper to the rack, Judi quickly removed the mirror, and scrunched her shoulders down into the seat. The second man left and Judi remained locked in her seat, afraid to move. After a few minutes, she slowly raised her mirror and looked at the room behind her. When she was sure that they were gone, she considered what she had just witnessed, and what she should do. If she disregarded what she saw, her life would continue unaffected, but how could she just ignore it? She had no idea which path to take. She needed guidance from someone she could trust, someone she respected. Judi picked up her belongings and hurried out the library door, leaving behind the four textbooks that were the very reason she had ventured to the Pentagon library.

Twenty Seven

When Sam heard Eric enter their office space, she raised her head from the report she was reading. "Hey handsome. Did Judi give you a big hug when you saw her?"

"Yes she did, Miss Nosy. Did you get a chance to stop by security?"

Sam pulled out a sheet of paper from her notebook. "You were right, it was only classified *Secret*. A little girlfriend talk with Jenny in security and she printed me a copy."

"Did she ask why you wanted it?"

"Yes. I just told her we were looking for presenters at the next meeting of the Military Operation Research Society."

"That was very smart Major, brains and beauty." Eric thought for a moment. "Sam, I know you squirrel things away. Roughly six months ago, I seem to remember an article in the PHALANX magazine about some professor who was going to present at the upcoming MORS conference. I think he had created a system dynamics model that could be used to predict trends on a global scale. Do you still save those newsletters?"

Sam moved over to her file cabinet. "Why should I want to help anyone that referred to me as a squirrel?"

"I said you were a beautiful squirrel, didn't I?"

As she searched through her files, Eric scanned the list of individuals cleared to work on the Osiris study.

Sam handed Eric her copy of PLANLAX. "Here it is. You were close. A professor at Virginia Tech announced he would present the results of his research to predict the impact of catastrophic events in terms of their global implications and the way civilizations function. I actually went to that symposium and I don't remember seeing his presentation on the schedule."

"Can you contact the professor and see if we can talk to him regarding his project? It might give us some insights on the Osiris Study. Judi would not provide any specifics, but I did learn that their analytical construct uses system dynamics methods. I got the sense they're modeling some type of global demographics system. There's a chance these two things are related. Can you check it out for us?"

"Sure. Did you get any insights from the list of people cleared to work on the Osiris Study?"

"I'm familiar with most of these guys, not the suits or brass, but those at the worker level."

Sam examined the list. "That's strange."

"What?"

"Look at where these guys work. If they were modeling a combat system, you would expect for the functional area schools to be involved. If it were artillery or deep attack, Fort Sill should be there. If they were evaluating air defense, Fort Bliss would be involved. If it were an intel system, Fort Huachuca would be on the list. None of the functional area schools are involved in the study."

"You're right, but look who is there. All centers that perform macro level or cross service analysis. For example, look at this guy. He graduated with us from Monterey. I know he works over at the Concept Analysis Agency in Bethesda. Or what about this lady here, I worked with her on the chemical cloud penetration test of the Bradley seal modification. She works up at Fort Derricks in Fredrick. They specialize in chemical and biologic agents. Here's Al Jones. He's out at the Atmospheric Analysis Lab. You also have several people from the private think tank groups that specialize in environmental and resource trends."

"Why would the Under Secretary of the Army be leading a study that has nothing to do with combat systems? Why would the Army be involved in global trend analysis? It doesn't make sense."

"I don't know. Can you tell me why two Congressmen would be on the oversight committee for a military study? I understand why they review the results of our studies once they're completed, but why would they be directly involved in issuing executive guidance? I don't understand it. And look at the names. Robertson's staff tried to tongue-lash the hell out of me after we sent in the Viper report. So did Clark. I knew they were going to chew me out, so I just ignored their phone calls."

Eric paused. "I just figured out why the Under Secretary's office was assigned to work this one. Senator Clark is Perry's old man. He's still trying to get the colonel his first star. That's why Perry is the lead on this effort. What a bunch of crap."

"But why the military?" Sam asked again. "Why not select one of the intelligence agencies or a Federally Funded Research and Development Center?"

"That's a good question. I've seen studies dealing with global trends conducted by the CIA before. Wait a minute. Duke was supposed to contact his sources at Langley for me. I forgot about that. I'll call him and see if he found out anything. I also want to ask if he can get a list of those from his company that participated in the Viper operational evaluation."

"I thought you asked me to set up a meeting with the guys at Crystal City, and that was one of the questions we were going to ask them?"

"It is."

"I don't get it. Why would you ask your friend for the same list of people?"

"I know Duke. No matter what they paid him, he's a soldier and an officer first. I trust his list."

"Then why ask the guys at Crystal City?"

"Anyone who appears on the list Duke comes up with, and is not on the list the Crystal City guys give us, is a gray ghost. Someone they don't want us to associate with the study, for whatever reason."

"That's very clever. What other magic tricks can you show me?"

"Someday I intend to show you a lot of tricks."

Sam grinned. "I look forward to that…I think."

"Would you mind contacting that professor at Virginia Tech and see what information you can get out of him? I'll call Duke on the secure STU phone. We can get together at the lunch counter in an hour. Does that sound okay to you?"

"Only if you plan to treat me to lunch. After that squirrel comment, you owe me."

"I think I can scrounge up a bag of nuts somewhere."

"I'll settle for a salad."

"You got it, Sam. See you in an hour."

~ * ~

Sam scanned the small lunchroom and saw Eric sitting in the corner reading a book. As she approached the table, she saw a plate of salad positioned across from Eric's seat. Alongside the plate was a paper bag.

"What's this?" she asked.

Eric pointed to the bag. "It's for you."

Sam opened the bag, and then snapped it closed. "You turkey, you really understand how to please a girl."

Eric turned the bag upside down and a handful of peanuts wrapped in cellophane fell out. "You started it."

"So I did. You win. I give up. Did you find out anything from Duke?"

"His contact at Langley said Senator Robertson commissioned the CIA to analyze trends in population growth across the world and the impact it would have over the next several decades."

"What kind of impact?"

"The results of the analysis were *Top Secret* and available only on a need to know basis. I would presume that for some reason, Robertson is interested in understanding how populations interact on a global scale with their surroundings. I guess things like how we're screwing up the environment and stuff. Duke's buddy said that after Robertson saw the results, he asked the military to conduct the Osiris Study."

"What for? I mean, how is it connected to the analysis that was done by Langley?"

"Woman, you just think I can figure out everything, don't you?"

"Yes. What else are you good for if you can't answer my questions?"

"What about you, did you talk to the guy at Virginia Tech?"

"Yes. He said that after he wrote the announcement in PLANLAX about his global trends model, he got a call from his sponsors. They instructed him not to brief his model at the MORS conference. Since they controlled his funds, he withdrew his presentation from the conference."

"Did he say who his sponsor was?"

"Indeed he did. It was the Under Secretary's office here in the Pentagon."

"I'll be damned. We've come full circle."

"Why would they stop him? You can brief classified models at MORS. What's the big deal?"

"I don't know, Sam. Did he discuss the model itself, in terms of what it does?"

"He was a bit hesitant to say anything. He did let slip that this model was based on some work he had done for the Remsen Center of Advanced Studies in Washington four years ago. That's why the Under Secretary's office contacted him in the first place. They read an article he published in one of the Operations Research journals."

"Maybe I'll head down to the library and see if they still have that back issue. Did he say which issue it was?"

"I'm two steps ahead of you, Mr. Emerson. I went down and made a copy for us."

"What a partner. Did you read it yet?"

"Yes. Here's the copy. Would you like me to summarize it for you?"

"Only if it's free."

"No, it will cost you a real meal. You're choice of the place and time. Have we got a deal?"

"I think I can handle that. Chinese, your place, tonight."

"Works for me."

"What about my summary?"

"The professor developed a dynamic model called PRES, which stands for Population Realignment Evaluation Simulator. It predicts the interaction between global population densities and various drivers that impact the expansion and contraction of those densities. It was created to help analyze how governments could respond to various types of mega disasters, like super tidal waves, coastal flooding from global warming patterns, major meteor impacts, pandemics, things like that."

Eric paused for several seconds, and then interjected, "Great, tells us what it is but not why they're using it for the Osiris Study. At least we can tell General Williams it has nothing to do with force structure or combat system requirements. Guess we can scratch the Osiris task off his list."

Sam raised her voice, "Wait a minute. Aren't you still curious what they're using the model for on the Osiris Study?"

"No."

"Not even a little?"

"No."

"Why not?"

"Because I'm not a Miss Nosy like you are."

With a smile Sam jested, "Listen buster, them are fighting words."

"I guess if we don't find out what they're doing with the model, you won't be able to sleep, and you'll make life miserable for me."

"You've got that right."

"All right, for your peace of mind, we'll keep at it a little while longer. I know several of those guys on the SAP list pretty well. I'll call them and see if I can squeak anything loose from around the edges. Will that make you happy?"

"Yes. Oh, and guess who I saw in the library when I looked up this article. One of your most favorite people here at the Pentagon."

"Knuckles? What the hell was he doing in the library? I thought he already knew everything there was to know in the world."

"Remember that guy we were discussing this morning, the one with the ugly gold ring?"

"You mean Carlson?"

"That's right. They were seated in the back jawing about something."

"What in the world do those two guys have in common?"

"I can't figure that out either, but they were seated off by themselves, acting kind of spooky."

"That's very interesting. I don't know what to do with that

factoid, but it does make you ponder why those two apparently disparate individuals would be chatting with each other."

Eric paused. "I'm sure you have sources scattered everywhere in this building by now. See if you can find out more on this guy, like where he came from."

"Now who's being Mr. Curious?"

"It must have rubbed off from you. I've got to go see Judi. Let me know what you find out when we carpool home tonight."

"Twice in one day. Are you trying to make me jealous?"

"I got this really weird email from her. She said she needed to talk to me regarding something urgent, but not in her office."

Eric saw Sam's lips begin to form the words, so he placed his hand on her mouth. "Don't say it...I don't understand what it's about, but I'll give you a full report after I talk to her."

"See that you do."

As Eric stood up to leave for his meeting with Judi, he informed his ride home, "I'll meet you outside the PT exit at 1700. Later, Trouble."

Twenty Eight

Eric saw Judi outside the main entrance, seated on a stone bench in the garden area. He approached from the left and observed her frown as she gnawed nervously on the side of her pencil.

He tapped the young woman on the shoulder to gain her attention. "Hello Judi. What's got you so excited? Did Paul finally propose?"

"I need your advice on a legal matter."

"A legal matter. Did Clark make a smart-ass comment about your physical difficulty? Did he come on to you?"

"No, it's nothing like that. Have you ever seen something at work that you knew was wrong, and you felt it was your duty to report it to someone in the legal chain?"

"Sure, there have been many times throughout my career where I witnessed things that were wrong, and difficult to ignore."

"What happened, did you report them? Did it affect you professionally?"

"Why do you think I'm still A GS 14? People with half my experience and credentials have been promoted above me."

"Then why did you do it?"

"At some point in your life, you will come to a crossroad. If you go to the left, you make the choice to ignore everything around you; incompetence, corruption, or people content to do nothing on the job but watch the clock spin. You can lead a peaceful life, without any concern over how you contributed, and how you're being there had a positive impact. The problem is that you become a slug, leaving nothing but a slime trail wherever you've been. You can never look back and say with pride, *I made a difference in the world.* All you did was deposit slime everywhere you touched, but it is the easy way, and many people choose that course."

Eric paused to allow her to consider his advice. Then he added, "Take the right path, and you can contribute to your full potential. You never have to apologize to yourself for what you ignored. When you reach the end of the journey, you can look back with pride, not from others, but from yourself.

There is a price. Those on the left trail will do everything they can to take you down. They will direct aspersions at your character, and call you a liar. I decided to take the right path when I was roughly where you are in your career. Only you can make the choice, but once you start down the trail, it's hard to turn back. If you turn left, you become comfortable with letting things slip, this time, then the next, until nothing has meaning anymore."

Judi stared down at the concrete between her small feet. After several seconds, she turned back to Eric. "If I did decide to do the right thing, what would happen?"

"It depends how serious the infraction is. If it's minor, like someone stealing a pencil, or sleeping on the job, or falsifying their timecard, tell your boss with an email, and let them work it out, but lock a copy of your email away someway. If it's broader than that, something that affects the Army, or involves a senior officer, you have to go to the Inspector General's Office. They will require you to complete a statement of what you witnessed before they'll conduct an investigation. If your suspicions are confirmed, you may be required to give testimony, especially if there is only circumstantial evidence."

Eric looked at the troubled expression on his young friend's face. "Do you want to tell me what it is you witnessed?"

"Not yet. I have to decide what I'm going to do first."

"At my age, it's no big deal. I've moved up the food chain as far as I can go in my job. You've just started your career, and you need to think hard before you take that leap. Remember though, if you do nothing, that decision will sit on your shoulders and stare back each time you look into a mirror. I know from experience that with issues that involve morality, they usually float back into your psyche and haunt the view you have of yourself for a long time. Whichever path you choose on this issue, I'll still be your bud."

"I appreciate your thoughts on this, and your honesty."

"That's what we old farts are good for. Remember Judi, you're young, and your life is good. As long as you have your health, everything else pales in comparison. Keep that in mind as you grapple with this decision. Make your choice, and then move on, that's how you have to deal with this stuff. Okay?"

"Okay."

"I've got to run and meet Sam for the ride home. If you need me, just call my cell phone."

"Thanks, I'll see you later."

Eric watched as Judi walked back into the building, with the world on her shoulders. He wanted to do more, but he knew this had to be her decision. He had been there before, struggled with the difficult choices, and he knew he was stronger from the experience.

~ * ~

As they crossed the Wilson Bridge headed for home, Sam asked, "So what did Judi want?"

"The poor girl has a real whale of a decision on her hands. I think she saw something that upset her principles, and she's having trouble deciding how to handle it."

"Like what, you mean something illegal?"

"It could be; she wasn't ready to discuss it with me yet. She just wanted to understand what her options were."

"What did you tell her to do? She's a young girl with her whole life ahead of her. She's not a macho tough guy like you."

"She has to make the choice herself. Either path she takes, she will live with it the rest of her life. When a person is placed in the wrong spot at the wrong time, no one else can tell them the right thing to do. They have to struggle with their own moral dilemma and decide what's right for them. I can't do that for her. I'll be there to help her, but she sleeps with her decisions. She can't pass them off to anyone."

"I just hate to see someone so young lament over such a difficult issue, that's all."

"I know Sam, I do too, but what choice do I have? If I could transfer the burden to my shoulders, I would without hesitation, but I can't do that to her. If I shield her from the realities of our world, how can she grow and be expected to deal with life on her own?"

Sam thought for a moment, and she knew he was right. As much as she wished otherwise, Judi would have to determine what course to take on her own.

"You're right, I'm sorry. How bad is it?"

"I really don't know yet. I figure once she makes her choice, she will share it with me. If it's as serious as she thinks, I'll support her either way. If she goes to the Inspector General's office, I'll go with her. I'll stand beside her the whole time. I promise you, I won't let her go through it alone, like I've had to, but she has to take the first step."

As they approached Sam's apartment, she requested, "Let's talk about something fun. What's for dinner?"

"How does Ronnie like Chinese?"

"It's midway down his priority list, but it's one of my favorites."

"Chinese it is then. I'll stop by the Red Dragon and get a bunch of stuff from the menu. I'll be back in thirty or forty minutes."

"First, there's something I've wanted to do all day, but the office wasn't quite the right place."

"Like what? Hit me upside the head."

"Hardly." Sam reached over, placed her hands on Eric's cheek, turned his head toward her, and kissed him right on the lips.

"That was nice. Not right for the office, but still nice."

"I thought so too. I just wanted to send you off with a smile. I'll go pick up Ronnie at your cousin's house. Hurry back with the food, handsome."

As Eric drove away, Sam noticed that a smile had indeed replaced the typical stoic expression on his face.

Twenty Nine

Ronnie answered the knock at the door.

"Hey Sport. Hope you like Chinese. I got a little of everything."

"Hey Mom, Eric's got food! Let's eat."

Sam had set the table, and placed two candles on the breakfast bar. She dimmed the lights and opened a small bottle of wine.

"Hey, what happened to the lights? I can't see the food, and why the candles, and why the wine?"

"It's called atmosphere, Sport. It makes the food taste better."

After several bites, the young boy looked over at Eric. "It tastes the same to me. I don't get it. What's the big deal?"

Eric leaned over and whispered, "It's a courtship thing, go with the flow."

"Oh, I see. Candles are kind of nice, Mom. Sort of like a spooky campfire. Where's my glass for the wine?"

Eric held his fist up to his mouth, but the chuckle escaped.

Sam smiled and poured a half an inch in her son's tiny glass. "Okay, but just a little."

The boy tasted the white wine. "Yuck, that's terrible."

"You have to develop a taste for wine over time. It's what adults do."

"Why?"

"Because it demonstrates that you have class and culture."

Ronnie took a second taste. "I see. It does grow on you. Good wine, Mom."

After dinner, Eric noticed Ronnie had become very quiet. When he looked down, he saw the young boy struggle valiantly to stay awake, but a few nods of the head signaled he had lost the battle.

"Ronnie, it's past your bedtime."

"No, I'm all right, I was just thinking, that's all."

"No Son, you're about to fall in your plate. Eric, let me get him in bed, and I'll be back."

"I'll clean up the table; good night, Ronnie."

"Good night Eric. It's Friday, why don't you just sleep over tonight? Then we can do something in the morning."

"Go on in and put your pajamas on, I'll be right there." When Ronnie exited the room, she added, "I'm sorry, but my son does have a mind of his own."

"You don't need to apologize for him. He's a terrific kid. He sees what's really there, and we've been fighting for so long. What he wants, the two of us together, it's not wrong is it?"

Sam knew the answer, but she wanted to hear it out loud, from him. "What do you mean?"

"This thing between us that we keep skirting around. Everyone else can see it, they all sense how we feel, even the boy. You have to be aware that I've always been crazy over you. If I had met you before Karen, I would have trailed you like a bloodhound. Then that wonderful kid in there could have been yours and mine. I'm not missing something, am I? You do feel the same way, don't you? I mean, you have to, you and Ronnie are all I want, all I've ever wanted."

"Go ahead. I'm listening."

"Go ahead and what? I thought I just said it."

"For being so darn smart, you're a little dense Mr. Macho." Sam reached over, wrapped her arms around his shoulders, and planted a juicy smooch right on his smacker. "How's that for an answer?" But before Eric could recover, a young voice called, "Mom, hurry up, I'm tired."

Sam kissed Eric again. "Hold that thought." Then she hurried off to ensure that her son was secured for the night.

Sam lit the last of the six candles flanking the mirror on her dresser in the bedroom. She walked back into the kitchen where Eric had finished washing the last dish. Sam softy called out, "Have you got a minute?"

When he turned, he was spellbound by the silhouette of Sam's shapely figure outlined by the flickering dim rays of candlelight piercing seductively through the thin layer of lace.

Eric issued one low pitch tone. "Whoa."

"Is this too strong an answer on how I feel?"

Eric reiterated his one syllable response.

"I guess this is all right for us, I mean our relationship..." but before Sam could finish, Eric was there, all around her. No mores words, no confusion, everything was clear between the two of them.

They moved into her bedroom and laid carefully onto the bed.

She unbuttoned his shirt and caressed his chest, as her heart pulsed, pushing blood through her muscles. Then his clothes disappeared. They touched each other softly, and joined flesh to flesh. Her breath deepened and her spirit rushed up from its hiding place, into her flesh, and then into his. Their lungs moved in harmony, each touch sent needles across his skin, up his arms and down his spine.

From the emptiness that had occupied her heart, the memory raced up and wedged between the two lovers. It reached out from that dark abyss where she concealed her painful secret. Like an icy rain, the vision from the past sent her spirit running back to where it had hidden for so long.

Eric sensed it, two souls surging across the sky, together, and then one fled, separating quickly. He must have felt her fall away; vanish into the dark, the raging fire quenched.

He slowly moved in next to Sam. He could feel her body shiver, not with the excitement that was there moments ago, but with fear.

"I'm sorry Eric, so sorry. I wanted to be with you, so much, but it haunts me, always. I was, I mean, it just...I guess I'm not ready yet. I thought I was, but it's still there. I'm so very sorry."

Eric gently stroked her shoulder. Then he reached around her chest and pulled her to him carefully. "It's okay. We can work this out, the two of us, together. When you're ready, you can share it all, whenever you choose, but maybe for tonight, we could just stay here, close like this. If that's all right with you?"

"You're okay with that, I mean just touching up next to each other?"

"I won't insult you and say it will be easy. Parts of me are about to blow a gasket, but I want you Sam, when it's right, and I will do nothing to risk that. Whatever it takes, I want you and Ronnie, as my family."

As Sam's breathing relaxed, and her body stopped quivering, she reached behind her and touched him softly on his bare thigh, "I love you Eric, for so long I've loved you."

"I do too, and I'll always be here for you and Ronnie, forever. Everything will work out. We've all the time we need. We'll chase out your ghost and destroy the fiend that haunts you. We'll do it together, you and me, so it's only the two us."

~ * ~

As she slept, Eric inhaled her scent, what was below the perfume, the body wash, and the shampoo. He smelled the pure essence of the beautiful woman beside him, her soft and mild fragrance, like a sweet honey melon. He traced the valley down her back, touched the dimples above her cheeks, the flowing curves of her hips. He felt her cool skin as her rump absorbed the heat from the blood rushing below his stomach. He placed his arms tenderly around her waist and held tight, pushing the demons from her soul. He caressed her face listened to her gentle breath, as her heart spoke to his, again and again.

In her slumber, there were no nightmares, no pain, no visions of being smothered, or scent of foul drunken breath. Tonight she dreamed of clipper ships that sailed across the sea on a deep blue carpet. The sandpipers scurried along the beach as white puffs tumbled through the sky, pushed slowly by the tropical wind. She felt the warm breeze on her face and the hot sand on her bare lower back. She lay contented, on the tiny isolated island, detached from the world, and her memories, with the waves beating to the rhythm of her heart. The strong trees reached down and gently stroked her breasts. The palms that held her tightly sheltered and protected her, from the sorrows of the past.

Eric softly pressed his hand against her back. *I love you Sam. I know your tender soul has been bruised, that he used your innocence against you, and he will pay. When it's right, he will pay. Then you can be free again. I'll wait, no matter how long it takes; I'll wait for you.*

Eric sensed the flow of blood in his body shift again and he pressed the sheet between them. His mind drifted off as the angel reached down, lifted him above the earth, and carried him to a small island with white sand. He glided above the trees and saw her nude body lying peaceful on the beach. The sweet scent of orchids filled his head, and the warm breeze enveloped his body. He belonged right there, beside her. The angel placed him next to the woman he loved. As the two lovers became one, the angel whispered, "Together, always." He knew, as he looked into her face, and her wings embraced their naked form, he would never be alone again, without someone that loved him, the way he loved her.

Eric startled awake. The dog across the courtyard was barking at the paper boy. Sam stirred. He bent down and kissed the curve of her neck. "Good morning, beautiful."

Sam pushed her hand down between their bodies. "My Lord, has he been awake all night long?"

"On and off through the night. I slept great, but he didn't catch a wink of peace."

At that moment, they heard the handle on the door turn.

"Crap." Eric quickly pulled the cover over his head.

"Good morning, Mom."

"Good morning, Ronnie."

The young man eyed the bulge tucked up next to Sam. "Did you have a sleep over, Mom?"

"What do you mean?"

"Like when Tommy used to come over and bunk with me."

"No."

"Then why is Eric bunking with you?"

Eric pulled the covers down from his head. "Morning, Ronnie."

"Morning Eric, is this a courtship thing again?"

"Sort of, Sport."

"Good, when you're done, you can come in and eat cereal with me. I'll fix you a bowl too Mom."

"Thanks, Ronnie."

Eric stared at the closed bedroom door. "Man that's a great kid, pure joy and kindness. You've done a wonderful job on your own."

Sam turned over and kissed him. Then she lifted the blanket. "Sorry, I didn't mean to wake him up again."

Eric sighed. "I don't think he got a wink of sleep all night. I'll close my eyes while you get dressed or I'll never be able to join you two for breakfast."

"By the way, I appreciated last night. I don't remember when I've slept so peacefully. I had wonderful dreams all night long."

"I'm glad. Now get dressed. I have to pee, and I can't go like this. Please put some clothes on."

Sam smiled and jumped up, taking the sheet with her, just to satisfy her curiosity. "Uh, I did miss something last night, didn't I?"

"Please, grant a man some dignity, will you?" Then he covered his condition with the pillow.

"Okay, I'll stop kidding around. I wouldn't want to hurt him or anything."

Eric waited for Sam to dress in the bathroom. He listened as she hummed some mellow tune to herself. From the kitchen, he heard a young voice announce, "Your breakfast is ready. Come and get it."

Sam walked out of the bathroom and looked out between the blinds. "It's a beautiful morning, isn't it?"

"Yes it is, as soon as I get to go to the bathroom. Please Sam, I'm dying here."

Sam headed into the kitchen and closed the door.

Eric jumped up from the bed and ran into the bathroom. "Not going to make it." After a few minutes, he washed his hands and sighed. While he headed for the kitchen, he murmured, "That was way too close."

Thirty

The senior Viper contractor leaned forward in his chair. He twisted his cufflinks then propped his large frame on his elbows against the conference table. "I believe all the changes we've discussed in the Viper test plan should satisfy your concerns. Major, here's the list of people you requested that participated in the last OPEVAL. Is there anything else?"

Eric looked around the room at each individual, with the exception of the colonel seated at the head of the table. "I'm still curious about one thing. On line twenty-three of your revised test plan, you call for modification to the standard targets they use on the firing range. Why?"

"As of March, the test facility began using the smaller drones for their training and test projects. The contract specification calls for a kill probability on targets of a specific Radar Cross Section or larger. The new targets they are using fall thirty percent below the minimum RCS for Viper. Our modifications to the target drones bring the RCS up to our required specs. Anything else?"

"Not now. If we think of anything, we'll call you."

After all the government representatives had left the room, the man with the cufflinks turned to the company employees left in the room. "I want to meet next week to discuss how we plan to correct these performance problems, and remember, do not discuss anything with the government representatives. Each of you is directed to forward all questions through one of us. It's unfortunate we have to do this, but the government reps have a tendency to misinterpret things. Such an incident would cost us a lot of schedule time and affect all our bonuses for this year. I am confident we'll figure out these problems in the target recognition software before we hit the field. There's no sense in getting everyone upset. Now I'd like to discuss some administrative issues. Would everybody except the management team leave? Thanks for the great job, good team effort."

Once the room cleared, Cufflinks turned toward his deputy. "Cheryl, I want you to call the senator. He needs to get these damn guys off our backs so we have time to work out these problems. He's getting paid for a reason. If this test falls through, then we lose our bonuses, and if we don't work out these problems, there goes our jobs. I'll be up in the Engineering Department.

When you get the senator's secretary on line, just patch the call through up there. One more thing, make sure the team keeps their mouths shut, especially the target reconfiguration guys. Cheryl, this interim solution to fudge the test was your idea. I strongly encourage you to help the senator understand how serious this is, and that his ass is in this just as deep as ours. Losing a job is one thing, but going to jail is something else."

~ * ~

Eric and Sam walked out of the multi-story building at Crystal City Two. "You should feel good about that meeting, Eric. They agreed with all the changes we requested. Why the sour puss on that handsome face?"

As they both got into his car, he asked, "I know your secondary career code is a 49, but isn't your primary code 14?"

"That's right. I took my air defense training at Fort Bliss. Why?"

"What systems did you specialize in?"

"The Hawk and Patriot PAC2 deployed at Corp and Echelons Above Corp."

"No Vulcan, Chaparral, or Roland systems?"

"Those are short range or SHORAD systems. That series is closed to women, but I do have some experience in supporting combat analysis of those systems. Why the twenty questions?"

"In all your dealings with Army air defense systems, have you ever seen one where the single shot kill probability approached anything close to 100%?"

"No, none."

"We watched three live fires at the Viper OPEVAL, and they were all direct hits. The telemetry showed a Target Location Error of zero on all four shots. With all the variables involved in getting two high-speed objects to converge their trajectory vectors, don't you think that a TLE of zero is unbelievable for all three shots? Then, when you look at the results of the developmental test data the contractor just presented to us, out of six life fires, all of them were kills. I know they are pitching Viper as the wonder of all air defense systems, but come on, nothing can be that perfect. Doesn't all that strike you as an extreme anomaly or something?"

"You're right, it is unbelievable. Even after all the modifications the Army has done through out the life cycles of our current air defense systems, none approach perfection, and they never will. There are too many uncontrolled variables in combat. That's why in critical area defense grids, like when the SCUDS were fired against Israel and Kuwait during Desert Storm, the Operational Concept is to coordinate multiple launches."

"My point exactly. I don't think any system is that good. None. There's a rotten egg in here somewhere, and we have to smell it out."

After they got out of the car and began the long walk from the Pentagon parking lot. Sam chewed on her lip while she thought. "Hey, what happened to lunch? I'll even treat."

"I can't. There are a few things I have to coordinate before the Viper tests next week. Here are my keys if you want to go out."

"It's no fun eating by myself. Guess I'll get something in the cafeteria."

"I promise, when we get these first two items off the general's list, I'll make it up to you. After I make some calls, I'll meet you in the cafeteria, say in an hour."

"I guess that's better than nothing."

"Let me see that list Duke gave us," Eric said. "I want to compare it to this one we just got from the Viper contractor."

Sam removed a piece of paper from her folder and handed it to him.

He pointed to the center of the page. "Look here. These two

guys are not on the list the contractor provided to us. I need to call Duke and see who they are, and what their function was during the test."

"Why?"

"Maybe it's just a coincidence, or maybe there's an intentional reason these two guys don't appear on the official contractor's list."

As they entered the Pentagon, Eric said, "Sam, when we go out for the follow-up tests next week, I think we should split up. You stay in the Control Center, watch what they do. I'll go down range. Make up an excuse if they ask where I am."

"Whatever you say Mr. Boss man. Did you call your friends at Derrick and CAA to discuss the Osiris Study?"

"I'll do that today after I talk to Duke. Now, go earn your pay. I'm going down to contracts. I want to check something out on the Viper contract. I'll meet up with you in an hour. Later, Woman."

Sam waved as she headed back to their office. "I have some of my own stuff to check out. Later, Man."

~ * ~

Judi stared at the blank computer screen. For the last two days, she had pondered and struggled with the guidance provided by her mentor. Eric was right. There was no easy way out. She could never look in the mirror again if she ignored this. She have to do it.

Judi sighed. Then she sat up in her chair, flicked on her computer, and began typing at the keyboard.

TO: Eric Emerson
From: Judi Cohen
Subj: Our discussion in the garden
I thought about what you said to me. I see no way out but to take the right path. I would really appreciate your help and guidance. I want to discuss with you what is going on with the Viper OPEVAL and what they had to do to make it work. I also discovered the true nature of the Osiris Study. I'm afraid no one understands what they plan to do. I need your help. Someone has to be told what they are really doing. Please let me know when we can meet and I will share with you what I know.
Judi

Judi reviewed her message and stared at the screen for

several minutes before reaching for the mouse. She touched the SEND button. *There, it's done. Whatever happens, I'm sure I did the right thing.*

Thirty One

Sam waved at Eric and walked over to his table. "I knew I'd find you in here stuffing your face."

"I'm only eating a hot dog. A man's got to eat. I can't be a little bird like you and eat that rabbit food you munch on."

She slid into the chair across from Eric. "A girl's got to watch her figure if she's going to maintain a man's attention. Did you find out anything interesting down in Contracts?"

"Yes. The Viper program is a CPAF acquisition."

"And why is that relevant to us?"

"On Cost Plus Award Fee contracts, the company makes its money on the award fee. In this case it's a fourteen percent incentive fee with nine percent of that award tied to the delivery schedule. The rest is linked to the probability of kill and other design requirements. That's a heavy weight assigned to the schedule. The Army did it that way because of other air defense systems that are scheduled for replacement by Viper. They did not want to extend those other contracts. If Viper is ready for production in four month, the company gets the full fee. If not, the profit decreases gradually each day they are late. If delivery is delayed beyond six months, they lose all nine percent. That's a hell of a lot of money."

"How much?"

"Viper is a multi-billion dollar program. You're not talking a few million, but hundreds of millions of lost profit. Executives and company managers lose jobs over that much money. That's some serious motivation to meet the schedule, and if things don't work when they hit the field, the company would get paid additional funds for modification."

"If it doesn't work, why would they get paid more to fix what they didn't do right in the first place?"

"Once the Army certifies system performance via the OPEVAL, the contractor would start production. After that, the Army may not figure out there's a problem until after the missiles were fielded during actual combat conditions, and the enemy was able to penetrate the Integrate Air Defense shield. By then, who the hell can prove that the OPEVAL was screwed up? That's why they were so pissed off when we showed up, and why everyone tried to hunt me down when our report came out."

"What are we going to do? It sounds like you're saying there's a cover-up going on here. Do we have any proof we can give to General Williams?"

"Not yet, but we will. We're not going to let this happen to the troops."

"But how?"

"Sam, I just found this out. You have to give me at least a few days to think things through. I also called Duke. He said he would check on those two guys that were missing from the list. The follow up tests are next week. He said he would call me back before that. What have you been doing while I was saving the world here?"

"I got tired of waiting on you to call your friend regarding the Osiris Study, so I did my own snooping."

"You're really into this aren't you, Ms. Nosy?"

"Yes I am. I sweet-talked Paul into letting me see a demo of the PRES model. I told him I didn't need to look at the classified data, just the capabilities of the system, like the inputs and outputs of the software."

"What did you see?"

"I thought you weren't that curious. You have to ask nice."

"Why do I always have to beg with you, woman?"

"Helps a girl retain control."

"Just tell me what you saw, damn it."

"The model uses estimates of how the human population is distributed across the world. Parameters are entered that depict how the population functions based on the technology and life style of each nation. The more advanced the country, the higher the consumption rates of natural resources, the longer the life span of its people, and the more proficient the government is at recovering from catastrophic events."

"Anything else?"

"As I said before, I told Paul that I didn't need to see the actual data or real model runs, but even though he cleared the data fields, the titles that define each of the headers were still there. The professor at Virginia Tech said he designed the model to evaluate all kinds of disasters, but this version was set up specifically to analyze two key drivers, one with the header BIOAGT and the other was PTRLM."

Eric thought for a moment. "I think it's obvious the first header refers to biological agents, but I have no idea about the second one, do you?"

"No I don't, but I agree on the bio agents. That's probably why Fort Derrick is involved in the study. Eric, maybe they're worried about terrorist elements using biological agents, and they're developing an operational plan to respond to such global catastrophic events. There's been chatter in the intel circuits for a long time that the bad guys have been studying distribution methods for bio vectors."

"It's possible, except...Why the compartmentalization of the study to only twenty four people? To counter such attacks would require hundreds of experts. I just can't figure this out."

"Maybe it's not just chatter, maybe they have verified threat data and they're concerned about mass panic."

"That's possible, but my gut tells me there's something more to all this."

Sam concluded, "At least you have to admit that we understand a little more than before."

"I would never give you that edge, it would swell you're head too much, and its big enough already."

Sam looked at Eric. "Boy, sometimes you just push the envelope a bit too far."

"I'm only kidding with you, Miss Sensitive. By the way, I called a friend of mine down in St Mary's County. He has a small powerboat and he said we could use it for the weekend. How would you and Ronnie like to go fishing this Saturday?"

"Let's see, you're offering me to spend a day smelling slimy fish and touching ugly worms. That is an attractive proposal."

"Come on. Ronnie is dying to go fishing, and we can make a day of it. Fish in the morning, and I'll take you to lunch at a great seafood restaurant on Solomon's Island. Is that better?"

"Guess I could sun on the boat in my bikini while you two boys do your guy thing."

"Bikini, huh? I like the sound of that. I'll have to bring my camera. You know, just in case we catch any fish. You want to tell Ronnie, or should I?"

"You go ahead. I'd wait until Friday night though, otherwise he'll bug you all week about the trip."

"I don't mind. I like being with him, almost as much as I like being with you. What do you say we quit early today? We've been putting in ten-hour days the last couple weeks. The two of us can stop on the way home and get your favorite treat."

"You mean share a banana split? You think that will make me forget that big head comment?"

"I was thinking more of getting one for each us. Last time we shared, I got the short end of the stick."

"You got a deal. Ice cream in the middle of the day, boy, what more could a girl want? Let me secure my safe and I'll be ready to go."

~ * ~

Sam blended three flavors of ice cream onto her spoon. Then she slipped in a question to the man across the table mesmerized on the woman licking the concoction off the spoon. "Did Judi get back to you on her problem?"

"No. I checked my emails before I left, but she hadn't sent me anything yet."

"Why didn't you just go down and talk to her?"

"I tried, but she wasn't there. She put a note on her screen that said she and Paul were downtown for a meeting with some of the Osiris people to discuss their data. She was leaving right after their meeting for the long weekend. She said earlier this week that she was going to drop Paul by his parents before she visits her sister in Sykesville for the three-day weekend. I just put a note on her desk that said we were going fishing at Solomon's Island on Saturday and I would see her Tuesday morning. I gave her my cell number in case she needs to talk to me this weekend. Does that make you feel better?"

Sam smiled. "I just didn't want her to be left hanging out there, that's all."

"Would you do me a favor? I'm not much on legislative affairs or governmental law, but could you check a few things out for me when we get back to work on Tuesday?"

"Like what?"

"Like whether Senator Clark or Robertson have any stock in escrow for the Viper contractor, or if the company made any campaign contributions."

"For you handsome, anything."

"Boy, you're in a good mood today. What gives?"

"Ice cream and gobs of chocolate do it every time."

Eric pulled out his small notebook and jotted something down.

"What are you doing?"

"I need to keep that fact under the heading 'Ice cream and chocolate can soothe a woman's fury' for when I get into trouble in the future."

"Are you planning on getting into trouble a lot?"

"A man never plans to get into hot water, it just happens. Women are sensitive like that."

Sam grinned and tossed a cherry at Eric's head. "I can see we're going to be spending a lot of time at the treat shops around here."

Sam finished her last bite. "I appreciate you taking us on the boat this weekend. I'm really looking forward to a day out with my two favorite guys. I actually bought a brand new black bikini just for this trip. Are you looking forward to tomorrow?"

"I am looking forward to going fishing. I haven't done it for quite a while."

Sam pinched Eric hard on his arm. "Maybe I won't bring the bikini after all."

Eric teased Sam as they left the restaurant. "Probably a good idea anyway. I'd have to keep my eyes covered the whole time to prevent an accident out there. Hell, you'd have all the other boats running into us. They've probably never seen a catch like that before."

"Men just don't know when to keep their mouths shut, do they?"

Thirty Two

The senator pulled the hair in his sideburns while he read the note Carlson handed him, "This is not good. How the hell did she find out?"

Carlson twirled his gold ring. "We have no idea, Senator. Maybe someone at the company shot off their mouth. It could be that your son was careless with the Osiris report and left them out somewhere."

"Bullshit," Perry shot back. "I lock those papers up every damn night. They've never been left out. Maybe you shot off your big mouth to impress some chick."

The senator slammed his hand on the desk. "Stop it you morons. Do you realize what will happen when he reads this? He's not going to ignore it. Some might, but he won't. It's your ass too, the both of you."

"Senator, there's no chance that he'll read that message. I have a filter set up on their mail server. I pulled this off before it reached him."

"That's great for now, but when he doesn't get back to her, she'll go see him."

"I've got that covered. I'll take care of the problem this weekend. I'm going to..."

"Stop right there, Carlson. I don't want to hear anymore, just fix it."

The phone rang on the senator's desk. "What? Tell her I'll call back. Fine, ring me when she's on."

"You two stay here while I take this call." Then the phone rang again.

"Hello Cheryl. No that's all right; I always enjoy talking to a lovely woman. I only have a minute though so what do you need? Yes. I understand, but I can't stop them from doing what the general tells them to do. Yes, I could call him, but what good would that do? Look, if they're not satisfied with the test, there will be no certification to begin production. I can't do that.

Young lady, I'm a U.S. Senator, I suggest you watch your tone. I will do something about it, but I can't stop them from doing their job, damn it. Even if I could, do you realize how that would look? I'm not talking votes here; I'm talking about someone calling for an investigation. Tell your boss the next time he wants to chew someone's ass out to send a man. That kind of language sounds coarse from a woman. Goodbye."

The senator slammed down the receiver. "Carlson, the Viper contractor is spitting nails. Do whatever is necessary to get these guys off their backs. Just do it discreetly."

Then he turned to his son. "Perry, I don't know how she learned about the true objective of the Osiris Study, but you better not let it happen again. The Viper thing could put us in jail, but if the purpose of the Osiris Study were to get out, it would get us hung. Do your job, or we're all in serious trouble. Now get out of here."

The senator pushed back in his burgundy leather chair, turned toward the window and placed his feet on the windowsill. He peered at the dark clouds that signaled the approach of a thunderstorm. He pulled at his eyebrows, and after several minutes, shook his head. "Damn. If anyone finds out...I don't like this at all, not at all."

~ * ~

Judi and Paul pulled up to the small sixty-year-old house in the community of Arbutus, just south of the Baltimore beltway. She turned on the overhead light and apologized, "Tell your parents I'm sorry they had to stay up so late."

"It wasn't your fault. That was a terrible accident on Interstate 95. I bet they don't get that jackknifed five-wheeler cleaned up till tomorrow. We were lucky to get through that mess and get here by ten. It's really late for you to be driving around by yourself. Why don't you stay in the guest bedroom tonight? You can head for your sister's in the morning."

"I appreciate that, but my sister has to leave early in the morning for a craft show she's doing this weekend. I have to be there to baby-sit for my two nieces."

"At least call me when you get there. I'll stay up until you call."

"I'm a big girl. I'll be fine. You go on to bed and I'll call you in the morning."

Judi leaned over and kissed Paul on the cheek. "Goodbye, Paul. I'll pick you up Monday around two o'clock. Have a nice weekend."

Judi waved as he walked into his parent's home. Then she departed the small community, turned back onto the Baltimore Beltway and headed toward her sister's in Sykesville. It never ceased to amaze her how many cars are zooming down the beltway this time of night. They must have worked late too, and were rushing off for the weekend.

Once she turned west onto Interstate 70, virtually all westbound traffic disappeared. Except for the occasional vehicle across the median strip that charged toward Baltimore, Judi was the only other vehicle headed west. With no radio, no passenger, just the darkness, she rode in silence. The same eternal quiet she had experienced all her life, but on the lonely road, this time of night, even Judi sensed her isolation.

In her solitude, she began to ponder her situation with Paul. The same doubt that always loomed over her shoulder and shaped her view of their relationship. Was it her inability to communicate like other women that kept him from committing? She cared so much for him, but he just won't take the next step. Maybe Eric was right. Perhaps he's too shy and she should push things forward herself.

Then she considered her job. She loved the work, but the way she was treated by her current team leader made for an unpleasant environment. His hostile attitude and nasty disposition, there had to be a reason. Perhaps it was her--something she did or didn't do. Was it because she was deaf? Is that why he didn't respect her contributions, because she couldn't communicate as effectively as other people?

She loved her job, the field she had chosen for her career, but would the label of whistleblower mar her future? All these uncertainties swirled in her young mind without the context of age to provide perspective. She remembered what Eric once said, "Girl, stop lamenting these little gnats circling your pretty head. As you get some more moss on your keel, you'll find life has a way of sorting out the stuff that's actually important, like those you love and your health. Ignore the stones, and only sweat the boulders. You'll learn that everything else is but a small bug buzzing in the distance-- nothing of real consequence. Chill out and enjoy each day, and save your worries for the real big things, like your family."

Maybe Eric was right. She needed to relax and let things work themselves out. All these things are just little stones. She could step right over them.

After she traveled several minutes along the isolated root section of the I-70 corridor, two headlights appeared in her rearview mirror, like the eyes of a wolf as it peered into the field at its prey. In no time at all the lights had closed to within one hundred yards.

As the vehicle that trailed her small Saturn passed on the left, Judi saw the reflective paint reaching back from the bridge that spanned the Patapsco River. The speeding vehicle cleared four car lengths ahead, and began to slow down.

The car looked familiar. Did she see it when she dropped Paul off? Before she could react, the large vehicle veered directly into her lane, and slammed on its brakes. Judi tried to maneuver around on the right side, but her right bumper caught the concrete guard at the leading edge of the bridge. Her small car spun like a top, and skidded rearward along the rail of the bridge.

When she came to a stop, roughly two-thirds down the length of the bridge, her rear fender was positioned sixty degrees to the guardrail, while her front bumper remained in contact with the steel rail.

Judi sat motionless, dazed by the collision. It took a moment for her senses to recover. She unhooked her seat belt, reached into the glove compartment for her flashlight, and got out of the vehicle to inspect the damage. While she scanned the side of her car, she noticed the red reflection of taillights on the inside of her glasses. She turned and saw the vehicle that had caused the near miss backing up along the side of the bridge. Thank goodness. They stopped and were coming back to help her.

Judi moved her flashlight up and down to let them know she was all right, but as they advanced closer, it was clear that they would not be able to stop in time. *They're too fast, going to hit me.*

She was trapped between her car and the bridge. Her throat tightened, the view of the red taillights charging rearward caused her chest to pound, and the veins in her neck to throb, as she frantically searched for an escape. *The rail, hang onto the rail.*

Judi climbed on top of the guardrail. When she grabbed the rusted steel of the rail, the flashlight slipped out of her fingers and tumbled end over end downward into the dark. The flashlight disappeared as it crashed onto the stone rocks along the sides of the ravine, bounced twice, and then splashed into the edge of the river.

Judi struggled to maintain her hold on the top steel beam of the guardrail, but she began to slip. At first the rail lodged into her armpits. When she struggled to climb back up, she slid down further, until she dangled from both arms wrapped around the rail.

In the glow of her taillights, a figure got out of the other car and approached. "Please hurry, I can't hold on much longer. Please, I'm slipping."

But as the figure stood over her, he did nothing.

"Please help me, please."

Still nothing.

Judi's left arm broke loose from the rail. Then, as her right hand provided the only remaining lifeline circled around the rail, the hand of the dark figure moved toward her.

Judi cried out, "Please hurry."

The large fist came down hard against her hand and, in the red glow; she saw the glistening star of a sapphire ring. When her fingers released from the rail, she panicked at the image of what waited below, the vision of her young body spattered against the rocks as her life seeped out. She tried to scream, but it was too late. She followed the flashlight into the void.

Thirty Three

Eric turned onto Route 5 headed for Solomon's Island. At four thirty in the morning, there were no other vehicles on the road. By the time he passed through Mechanicsville both his passengers had fallen asleep. At five-thirty, he stopped at a small diner outside of Hollywood, Maryland.

"Wake up sleepyheads."

Sam stirred slightly, but Ronnie remained motionless in the back seat. Eric reached over and softly stroked her face until she began to wake. "Eric, please let me sleep."

"Come on, we're fifteen minutes away. I thought you guys might want some breakfast."

Eric turned around and gently pressed on Ronnie's leg. "Come on Sport, what do you say we get some food?"

Ronnie sat up and opened his eyes wide. "Are we there yet?"

"Almost, we're stopping for a quick breakfast."

Sam and her son dragged themselves into the diner. "I had no idea we were going to fish in the middle of the night. Won't the fish still be asleep?"

"The fish don't sleep, silly. We have to get there in time for the change of tides. Day or night, that's when they feed, and that's when you have to catch them."

"Let's go sleep in the car till the tide changes around noon."

Eric smiled. "Doesn't work like that, Sam."

By now, Ronnie was fully energized with the excitement of the trip. "Yeah Mom, we've got to get them when they feed, right

Eric?"

"Right Sport. Now finish your cereal, and Sam eat your donut. We want to get there by the crack of dawn."

"I'm not going anywhere until I have a second cup of coffee," Sam said.

"Okay, but I suggest you make a pit stop. There are no toilets on the water."

"Things just get better and better. What the heck am I supposed to do if nature calls?"

"I got a blanket and a bucket, one's for a cover, and the other's for...well, you can figure it out."

Sam looked at the grin on Eric's face. "Forget the second cup of coffee, but it's going to take a few minutes in the ladies room." As she headed for the restroom she murmured, "I hope you two guys appreciate this."

Ronnie turned to Eric. "Sometimes she's a bit grumpy in the morning."

Eric smiled. "We are asking a lot of her, to get up at four in the morning to watch us guys fish, but I'm sure she'll perk up when we get out there and start catching all those big ones."

"You're right, that should make her smile."

As Sam returned, she said with a smile that looked forced, "Alright boys, let's do this thing before I chicken out and sleep in the car while you two go fishing on your own."

~ * ~

"Ronnie, here's a life preserver I got just for you. It's designed for guys your size. You have to wear it while you're on the boat."

"What about me?" Sam jested.

"I didn't want to cover up your bikini, but here's a PSD for you too. I assumed you would want to lounge up front, so just keep it by your feet."

They pulled out of the dock. "Boy it's chilly out here. I'm freezing."

Eric tossed a blanket to Sam. "It's just the morning dew. It will warm up in a couple hours. Here Ronnie, I brought an extra jacket for you."

"Eric, how long till we get there? I'm ready to fish. What are we using for bait? Where's my rod? Where do I sit?"

Sam looked through the blanket wrapped around her head and warned Eric, "You understand that he's going to be like that all day."

"That's why we're here. The morning is for him and the afternoon is for you."

"What about you?"

Eric cocked his head and wiggled his eyebrows. "I thought you brought the bikini for me."

Sam responded with a grin.

"Ronnie, you sit here beside me. This is your rod, and we're only going a half a mile to the mouth of Harper's Creek."

"I thought we were fishing in the Patux River."

"It's called the Patuxent River. Harper's Creek is a small feeder inlet to the river."

"Is it good fishing there?"

"It used to be when I was a kid. My dad took me fishing right off that point over there on the Naval Air Station when he was a civilian working for the Navy. The big fish, like Stripers and Blues, prowl outside the mouth of the creek and wait for the little fish and small crabs that flow in and out on the tides, so they can eat them."

"Neat. Where's our bait?"

"Right there in the cooler."

Ronnie reached in and pulled out a small crab and pointed it at Sam. "Look Mom, a crab."

"Put that down before it bites you."

"It's a soft shell crab, Sam. They're dormant after they shed their shell. It can't bite."

"You're going to put that whole thing on a hook?"

"No, you cut it into pieces."

Sam scrunched her nose. "That's gross."

"Maybe, but it catches fish."

Eric turned off the motor, walked to the front of the boat and picked up the small anchor. "I'll put the anchor back with us, Sam. That way you won't have to mess with it."

Eric baited two rods, tossed both lines in the water, and handed the smaller rod to Ronnie. "Here you go, Sport."

"Now what do we do?"

"We wait."

"How long?"

"It's up to the fish, sometimes it's five minutes, and sometimes it's an hour."

"How will I know?"

"You'll feel a tap-tap on your rod."

"Then what?"

"You set the hook like this." Eric snapped his rod tip quickly.

"Oh, I understand."

After twenty minutes, Eric saw Ronnie's rod tip jiggle. "You've got a bite, Sport."

The young boy reeled in his line to find an empty hook. "What happened?"

"He got your bait because you didn't set the hook. Let me put some new bait on it and you can try again."

Another five minutes passed, and Eric had a bite. "Here we go," he said, and then he reeled in his line and lifted the fish into the boat.

"Neat, can I touch it?"

"Sure, but keep your fingers away from his mouth. It's a bluefish and they can put a hurt on your finger if they bite it."

Ronnie stroked the fish. "He's cold. Here Mom, come touch the fish."

"No thanks, I'll leave all that fun to you."

When Ronnie looked up, Eric grinned. "Women."

Ronnie responded, "Yeah, women. Do we keep him?"

"No, he's too small. We toss this little one back and let him grow."

Eric placed his line back into the water. In ten minutes there was a tug on his line. He set the hook and turned to Ronnie. "Here Sport, this is my lucky rod. Let's switch."

The young boy took the rod and soon the line began to peel off the reel. "Pull back Ronnie, you hooked a big one."

The line began to run left, then to the right. Several times when Ronnie stood up, the rod almost pulled him in the water.

"Eric, he's going to fall in, cut the line."

"No way Mom, I've got this fish."

Eric gripped Ronnie's belt. "Just fight the fish and I'll keep you in the boat."

The battle raged for several minutes before both the fish and the boy tired. Eric helped Ronnie gain ground by pulling back on the rod and the fish finally came up next to the boat.

Eric reached for the net. "Good Lord, he's caught a whale. Looks like a twelve-pound sea trout."

"Mom look, I caught a monster!"

Eric tossed the camera to Sam. "Take his picture while we bring this beast aboard."

When the fish was removed from the net, Eric held the fish alongside the small boy. "Take his picture, Sam."

"Eric, we can keep this one right? He's big enough, isn't he?"

"You bet Sport, sea trout are great to eat. We'll put him in the cooler and cook him for dinner tomorrow."

Sam looked at the fish. "You're not going to kill that fish, are you? He's too pretty. Throw him back in the water."

"No way Mom, we're going to eat him."

"Sam, you fish to eat. That's why we came."

"That's right." Ronnie looked up at Eric. "Women."

Eric replied, "Exactly."

The temperature had warmed enough that Sam could sun on the front of the boat. She removed her robe, which distracted Eric as he baited Ronnie's hook. With his attention focused on Sam's bikini, he stuck the tip of the hook in his thumb. "Ouch, damn it."

Eric glanced at Ronnie. "You should always pay attention when you bait a hook, Sport."

The young boy replied, "I thought I was paying attention."

Eric looked back up to the front of the boat again and flipped the bail on his reel, but instead of his line falling into the water, it plopped back into the boat. Eric was so intent on the view offered by Sam that he was oblivious to the location of his line.

After a few seconds, Eric felt a slight tug on his sleeve. "Hey, Eric."

But Eric didn't flinch he just kept his vision focused on Sam. Then again, a bit louder. "Hey, Eric."

"Yes, what is it?"

The young boy pointed to the weight, hook, and bait stuck to the floor of the boat. "Shouldn't that be in the water?"

Eric came back from his daydream. "I was just giving you a head start on the next fish."

"What does that mean?"

"It was a joke, watch your line."

Eric saw Sam grin before she turned over away from the two males.

After two hours the tide changed and the fish stopped feeding. Sam noticed a forty-foot cruiser as it moved to their right. "Eric, what is that boat doing out there? It's passed by us several times."

Eric glanced at the vessel. "He's probably locked on that skimpy Band-Aid you're wearing up there. I can't say I blame the poor man."

"Don't be a smarty butt. Why does he keep running back and forth so close to us?"

"He's trolling. See the two lines behind his boat? It's just another way to fish. We're anchored and using live bait; he's dragging lures."

The cruiser continued prowling back and forth just outside the mouth of Harpers Creek. Sam continued to observe the man with the binoculars, and murmured to herself, "There's something familiar about that guy."

Eric reached over and rubbed the young boy's head. "Well, we've got three keepers. That's a good day's work. What do you say we reel in and treat your mom to lunch? She deserves it, don't you think?"

"I agree. Thanks for coming, Mom, and thanks Eric for teaching me how to fish. This has been the best day in my life."

"It was my pleasure."

Eric tucked the two rods under the seat and began to pull up the anchor when Sam pointed at the cruiser. "Should he be that close?"

He turned to see the cruiser maybe sixty yards away, only this time it was headed directly at their boat. Eric stood up and waved both hands. "Hey, wake up!" but the large boat kept coming.

Sam screamed. "He's going to hit us!"

"Sam, Ronnie!" Eric yelled. "Get down in the boat!"

Eric quickly untied the anchor line and tossed it into the water. He started the boat and began to move forward, but before he could get out of the way, the large boat crashed into the rear corner of the smaller boat and glanced off the back, stalling the motor.

"Stay down!" Eric yelled. Then he tried to restart the motor as the large boat circled around.

"He's coming back. Hurry!"

The large boat had drawn within fifteen yards when the motor started and Eric throttled forward, just as the cabin cruiser missed the rear corner by two feet.

"What's wrong with that man?"

"He must be drunk. They keep letting these idiots back on the water."

Sam pointed at the other boat. "Look he's pulling off."

"Did you see the number on the side of that boat?"

"No."

"Neither did I. Let's go back to the dock."

"I'm for that."

"Me too," Ronnie agreed.

As they pulled into the dock Sam asked, "Eric, what do you think happened back there?"

"If he would have come at us once, I would have assumed he was a moron. You see it all the time on the water. Some drunk gets out here and runs down another boat. Two months ago they had a drunk on one of those high-speed cigar crafts ram a pontoon boat and kill the entire family. He had been arrested twice before for DUI, but they still let him keep his license. In our case, the jerk came back a second time. That's something else."

"Like what?"

"Like...I don't know Sam, it was weird. If I could have made out his number from the side of the boat, I'd report his ass, but without it, that boat is just like a hundred other white cruisers that occupy these waters. Hell, even if they found him, I doubt they would do anything except give him a ticket. Let's not let that idiot spoil a great day. I'm ready for lunch, anybody up for seafood?"

"Best part of the trip," Sam answered.

Thirty Four

Sam removed her overnight bag from the trunk of the car. "You two guys decide what you want while I go to the ladies' room and change into something acceptable."

Eric smirked. "I think what you have on is totally acceptable."

Sam shook her head. "Men."

The two males studied the menu for several minutes, before Ronnie looked up. "Eric, can I ask you a question?"

"Always, Sport. What's on your mind this time?"

"When Mom removed her robe today, the way you looked at her, it was different. Why?"

Eric stalled, "I'm not sure what you mean."

"The expression on your face, it went blank, like you were hypnotized, or at least I think that's how you say it."

Sam overheard the last few words of the conversation as she returned to the table. "Who's been hypnotized? What have you two been discussing this time?"

"Eric was hypnotized today, Mom. I saw him, when he looked at you on the boat. It wasn't like the way he normally looks at you, why?"

Sam grinned. "Yes, I'd like to hear an explanation of that myself."

Eric looked at Sam, and then at Ronnie. "Oh crap."

"Go ahead," Sam repeated. "We're waiting for an answer, Mr. Emerson."

"Haven't you explained the facts of life to your son yet?"

"I didn't think it was necessary until today. You caused it, so why don't you explain to Ronnie why you eyeballed his mother today."

"You're really enjoying this, aren't you?"

"Yes I am, every wonderful second."

"Sport, when a woman is beautiful like your mom, it's a pleasure to look at her."

Sam smiled. "That was good."

"But it was different today, Mom. I've seen the way he looks at you before. This wasn't like that. Why?"

"You'll understand in seven years when your hormones pick up."

Ronnie wrinkled his nose. "What does that mean?"

Sam took pity on Eric. "I can see I've been delinquent in your education, Ronnie. I promise I will explain why Eric ogled your mother when we get home, alright?"

"I guess, but I don't understand why you just can't tell me now."

Eric picked up a menu and handed it to the young inquisitive boy. "Here, focus your attention on this for awhile, now that you've turned me into a pervert."

The young boy started to ask another question, but Eric pointed to the menu. "I'm hungry, let's figure out what we want to eat."

The young boy shook his head as both adults smiled at each other, and then studied their menus.

~ * ~

Eric decided to take a different route for the return leg of the trip along the back roads of Calvert County. "Except for playing bumper boats with that cabin cruiser, it was still a good day, wasn't it guys?"

"I really enjoyed catching that big fish," Ronnie admitted. "That was cool."

"How about you Sam, did you enjoy the trip?"

"I think I would enjoy any time I spent with you two handsome fellows."

"But?"

"I think I'll leave the fishing to you two men next time."

Eric glanced in the mirror toward Ronnie as he scanned the scenic countryside. When they passed the White Plains Park, Eric asked, "Have you guys ever walked along the beach of the Calvert Cliffs? You can find small fossils of prehistoric creatures embedded in the limestone. Maybe we could come back and visit here next time. We could even stop by the nuclear power plant and take a tour. What do you say about that, Ronnie?"

"Okay, but if it's okay with you, I'd rather not go where there are big boats again. That was kind of scary today."

"Roger that. Let's take some more peaceful trips," Sam said.

Eric smiled. "I think I understand. No gooey worms, no slimy fish, and no boat chases, right?"

"Right," Sam replied.

After the long day, it only took twenty minutes before the backseat became quiet. Eric glanced at the young boy asleep. "Looks like we wore him out."

"He had a ball. You're very patient with him. The two of you relate together very well. Ronnie's never had someone to bond with like you. It was good to watch. He needs a positive role model. He cares for you deeply."

"I told you, I love kids. I don't want to rush things, Sam. I understand that we need to take it slow, but someday I'd like to have two, Ronnie and a maybe a little girl that looks like you. Are you interested in another child?"

"Yes, I would love to have your child, but let's not wait too long. I am getting older, and my mom and dad hound me constantly for a granddaughter."

"You're the boss in this department. You just have to clue me in when we've vanquished these phantoms from your heart. I'll be there ready to jump right in."

Sam moved closer to him and softly placed her hand on his leg.

"Not there," he said, "it was hard enough watching you in that bikini all day."

Sam smiled and grasped his hand as they headed home.

~ * ~

When Eric turned south on Route 301, his cell phone rang.

"Hello. Hi Paul, what's up?"

Sam looked over at Eric. His expression was different, solemn.

"How did it happen?"

"What's wrong?" Sam asked, worried.

Eric held up his hand for her to wait a second. "When?"

"Where is she?"

"How bad is it?"

"I'm in Upper Marlboro right now. I have to drop Sam and Ronnie at their apartment. I'll be there in ninety minutes. All right, Paul. Goodbye."

"What is it?"

"Judi was in an accident. It's really bad."

"How bad?"

"They don't know if she'll survive. She has numerous internal injuries, broken bones and ribs. She suffered major damage to her right eye. As if it weren't hard enough to go through life deaf, she may be blind in one eye. It's uncertain right now."

"My God, how did it happen?"

"No one knows. Some hikers found her on the bank of the Patapsco River just west of Baltimore. Her car was smashed on the bridge above. They haven't figured out yet how she fell. It was a fifty-foot fall. She's been unconscious since they brought her into the hospital. I have to go see her, before it's too late."

"I'll go with you."

"She's really in bad shape. I'm not sure if Ronnie should see this."

The phone call woke up the young boy. From the back seat, a young voice answered, "I can handle it, Eric. We need to do this together. You need us to be with you."

Eric looked at Sam, then at Ronnie. He cleared his throat. "You're right. I do need you. This may be hard for you to see. This young woman is hurt bad. She may not make it, Ronnie."

"If you're going, we're going, right Mom?"

"Right, Son."

"All right guys, let's go see Judi, together."

Thirty Five

Eric hesitated outside the ICU. It was clear to Sam that there was more than just a friend behind the glass door. The girl that had reached into his heart and touched the place where he kept his sister was now in harm's way. She watched him struggle with his emotions, as if he were forcing something back.

Sam reached around his large shoulders, rose up on her toes and caressed his cheek softly. "You go in by yourself. I'll stay here with Ronnie. When you come out, if she's conscious, I'll go in. We'll be right here. You're not alone. We're always with you. Go ahead, talk to Judi. She's still there. Just talk to her."

Eric placed his hand around Sam's head, and pulled her to his chest. "I'll be back."

When he entered the room, he saw a young man kneeling by the bed with his face pressed down on a body, wrapped in bandages. There were bare spots on her arm where stitches crumpled the skin. Blonde hair extended from her head, but except for one exposed eye, her face was mostly covered in gauze.

When the young man looked up, Eric saw the tracks of moisture on his face. Eric fought the tightness in his throat. "Hello Paul. Has she come around yet?"

Paul used his sleeve to wipe his face. "Not yet, Mr. Emerson."

"Any change since you called me?"

"No. They tried to fix her inside, but she's still losing blood. They plan to go back in again when they get her stabilized."

"Do you mind if I sit with her?"

The young man pulled out his handkerchief and cleared his nose. "You go ahead. Judi's sister is trying to track down her parents. They're on vacation somewhere in Europe. I'll go see if she found them yet. Take as long as you need."

As Paul walked out of the room, Eric sat down next to his friend. He picked up her small hand and stroked her fingers gently. When he buried his face into the pillow next to her head, a shiver traced down his neck and along his back as the image jumped in front of him. Judi abandoned on an isolated riverbank, in pain, suffering in total silence, in the dark, with no one to help her. Then it came back from his past: the agonizing memory that haunted his nightmares.

The young girl imprisoned in a culvert on a desolate back road as she screamed, without words, for her big brother. In total darkness, crying in silence, for days, but no one came. Eric never came. The horrible visions that had plagued him for so many years; they were back.

The fury burned in his mind, it gnawed in his gut as he watched the fawn destroyed by the wolf, while he did nothing to stop it. Again, he had failed to protect those around him from the evil that prowled among us. The ones that consume the innocence and purity from those who trust, those who are blind to the demon until he swoops down and devours them.

Please, not again. Don't let it happen again. Not to this girl. Not like before. Tell me what to do this time. Anything, but please help her, I beg you. Eric brushed his hand across Judi's fine blonde hair. When he leaned over and caressed her forehead, she stirred as a droplet fell from Eric's face onto her cheek. Then she moaned and twisted her body in response to the pain.

"Judi, sweetheart, I'm here." Even though she had never heard his voice, he held her hand and talked to her. Eric turned her hand over, and signed: *"Judi, its Eric. We're here with you. Everyone who loves you is here. Your sister is trying to contact your parents"*

"Paul?"

"He'll be right back. He went to get your sister."

She moaned again, tried to talk, but could not. *"Why can't I talk? Why is everything foggy?"*

"I'm sorry sweetheart. The fall from the bridge; you were injured. You've damaged one eye, and your throat was punctured, but you're alive. I know you're going to make it. You're too strong and stubborn."

Eric looked into her face. He rubbed his eyes as he saw tears stream down her bruised cheek. "*Judi, can you tell me what happened?*"

"*The man, with the star ring, from work, he wouldn't help. He ran me off, and then came back, but he wouldn't help. He hit my hand. Why?*"

"I don't know, but I promise I will find out. Don't tell anyone about this man, just me. Trust me. Don't tell anyone. I will take care of it. He will never hurt you again."

"*Eric, the email I sent you. I saw the man with the ring and the colonel. I read their lips. The drone beam, the study, what they did, it's all wrong. What they are doing, the study, mass murder. We need to tell someone. Please Eric, tell someone.*"

"What do you mean it's all wrong? Sweetheart, I don't understand."

Judi moaned again.

A nurse came into Judi's room. "I saw a change at the monitoring station. She's awake?"

"Yes, and she must be in terrible pain."

"I'll be right back."

Judi twisted again, as if she wanted to get up and leave.

"Sweetheart, please relax. Let them help you and you will be all right. Don't fight. They'll give you something for the pain. Please sleep."

"*Paul?*"

"I'll get him. I'm going to take Sam and Ronnie home. I'll be back. I'll stay with you tonight."

With tears flowing down her face, she signed, "*Thank you.*"

Eric cleared his throat. He lost the battle and held his hands around his eyes, and he choked. Paul reentered the room with Judi's sister and the nurse close behind.

"Paul, Judi is asking for you."

As the nurse administered the sedative, Eric asked Judi's sister, "Please tell her Paul is here. Paul, please come outside with me for a moment."

The two men walked into the hall. "Paul, she needs to understand how you feel. You can't leave her now. You have to see the girl inside. You've got to tell her what's happened to her body, it doesn't matter."

"I would never leave her, Mr. Emerson. I love her. I want to marry her."

The emotions that Eric had suppressed broke through the surface. "Then why haven't you told her, damn it?"

Eric looked through the glass in the door at Judi and took a deep breath, before he returned his attention to the man next to him. "When she comes to and can understand, you must tell her. While you can, she needs to hear it from you."

Paul looked into Eric's eyes. "I will, I promise." Then he covered his face. "This is my fault. I should have dropped her off first, but she said no. She wouldn't be here if not for me."

"No. It wasn't you. Don't start down that path or you'll be haunted forever by false specters that'll ruin your life. Trust me. Be there for her, not in the past, but now. You must convince her that this affects nothing between the two of you. She must believe you, understand?"

"Yes sir, I understand and I will be there for her."

"One more thing, stay here while I'm gone. Don't let anyone near her unless you see a badge like the nurse is wearing."

"Why?"

"If you want to protect her, do what I ask. Even if it means being an asshole, don't let anyone near her that cannot verify who they are. I'll be back in a few hours after I take Sam and Ronnie home. When I return, I'll relieve you and stay through the night, okay?"

"Yes sir."

Sam leaped to her feet as he returned to the waiting room. "How is she?"

Eric paused, and then shook his head. Sam looked into his red eyes, and without asking again, she knew. She reached over and took his right hand.

Ronnie looked up at his friend and understood. He reached his hand up and grasped three fingers from Eric's left hand. Eric looked down at the young boy that felt so much for one so small. Ronnie saw the water in his friend's eyes, and he squeezed tighter.

With a slight tremor in his tone, Eric said, "Let's go home," and the three of them walked our together.

Thirty Six

"Sam, after I drop you and Ronnie at your apartment, I have to go back to the hospital. I'm going to relieve Paul and spend the night there."

"Do you think that's really necessary? You said she's sedated, I doubt she will even know you're there."

"I'll know I'm there, and until her parents get back from Europe, I don't want her to wake up and feel she's been abandoned, like before. Never again do I want anyone to feel they've been abandoned. Besides, I'm not comfortable with her being there by herself. Paul can't stay there the entire time, and I don't know when they'll be able to track down her parents. If I have to take leave to watch over her, I will. "

"I understand how you feel. I'm aware that Judi is very special to you. I just hate to see you drive all the way back up there this late at night, especially after the long day you've had."

"I'll be fine. There's something else. I don't believe what happened to Judi was an accident."

"What makes you say that?"

"When Judi became conscious, she told me that after a man ran her off the road, he backed up and tried to hit her when she got out of the car. She jumped over the rail to keep from getting run over. I don't think she realized it was a fifty-foot drop. The bastard actually let her fall. She cried for help and he slammed her hand against the rail. This was intentional. Whoever did this had a reason, a very cruel and calculated reason."

"Like what?"

"I don't know, but I can't leave her alone tonight, not until I figure out what's going on here."

"Did Judi recognize the man who did this?"

Eric hesitated for a moment. "No." They drove in silence for a few minutes before he asked, "Sam, have you ever heard of a project called Drone Beam?"

"No, why?"

"Judi visually overheard a conversation that was not intended for anyone else. Whoever it was that she saw talking said something that really bothered her."

"Did she say who it was?"

"Not yet. She was in terrible pain and the nurse came in and sedated her before she could tell me. That must have been what she was concerned over when she asked for my advice. She said they were doing something wrong with the Drone Beam project, or at least that's what I think she said. Some of it was incoherent. She was phasing in and out. I've never heard of that project or program before. She was also disturbed about the Osiris study. She associated it somehow with mass murder."

"My lord, what does she mean by mass murder?"

"I have no idea. The conversation was really difficult for her. I don't want to probe any further until she's recovered and out of harm's way."

When they pulled up to the apartment, Sam pointed to her son, asleep in the back. "Would you help me get him inside? All this activity wore him out."

"Sure." Eric gently lifted Ronnie from the seat, carried him into the apartment, and placed him on his bed.

"Please let me fix a thermos of coffee to take with you. It's been a long day. I don't want you to doze off on your way back to the hospital. You can spare thirty minutes, can't you?"

"I appreciate that."

Eric sat at the kitchen table while Sam made the coffee. "I think people that care so much for each other, should know everything, don't you?"

"I guess so."

"I understand you are close to Judi and she means a lot to

you, but I sense there's something else."

"I told you we're friends, that's all. It's just that she reminds me so much of my sister."

"I understand. I'm aware that she reminds you of your sister. I see it in your face and I feel it in your heart, but there's an agony in your eyes that I need to understand. I love you, Eric and I have to know the things that hurt you, that disturb the man I love. We need to share these things with each other. What really happened with you sister?"

Eric glanced at Sam. He knew she was right. She did need to understand everything, the events that plagued his thoughts and caused his nightmares. "All right, sit down."

Sam pulled out the chair next to Eric and as she sat, she reached for his hand.

Eric stared out the front window of the apartment for a moment. Then he began to share thoughts and emotions he had never confided to anyone. "When Robin was sixteen, she was killed by a child molester who had been released from prison a year after he was convicted of abusing several other young girls. He imprisoned my sister in a discarded culvert half buried off an isolated back road. He tortured and raped her for days. As she huddled in that vile place, bruised and starving, he assaulted her again and again, but that wasn't enough. In the end, when he had his fill, he devoured her life as he strangled Robin with the lanyard he wore around his neck. He had one of those big turquoise stone clasps. It left its imprint in her neck where he choked my little sister."

Sam reached over and stroked his hand. "I had no idea what…I'm so very sorry."

"For a long time, night after night, I was haunted by the image of my baby sister gasping for air, as she looked up into the empty eyes of this fiend while he robbed Robin of her life. He took everything from my sister, her dreams, her innocence, everything. She was nothing to him but a few stolen minutes of course physical release, then he cast her aside like a used rag. Almost every night, I dreamed of those last moments in Robin's short life, until you and Ronnie saved me from this agony. I don't want to go back to that place Sam, those dreams. Not again."

"I'm so sorry. I know it must be terrible to live with

something like that. If anyone hurt Ronnie I don't know what I'd do. I think I'd...I just don't know."

Eric sensed the rush of blood in his neck. The same anger he felt when he was faced with the terrible moral paradox of what he should do. "That's the problem. The very system that was established to protect our families puts these demons back on the streets to hunt down our children and use them as fodder.

I recently heard of a child molester that had abused dozens of children and kept being released by the judges that cater to the pacifists in our confused society. The courts are so concerned with the rights of these assholes that they forget about the rest of us. The only solution is to ignore the incompetence of our legal system and make sure our kids are never threatened again."

Sam cocked her head to the left. "What are you saying, that we should enforce the death penalty?"

"That would be great, but it will never happen. Today's legal system has too many faults. It's essentially defunct. No, I'm talking about ensuring that justice is served and our children are protected."

"So, are you saying we should take things into our own hands? What about the law?"

Eric turned away, shook his head, and then looked back at Sam. "I'm not referring to going out and randomly shooting a bunch of bad guys you have no connection to. You touched on it yourself when you said if anyone harmed Ronnie, you don't know how you would respond.

If someone hurts your family, your wife, your child, you are morally obligated to make sure that no one else has to suffer such pain. You know yourself every day we hear on the news where the law has let some killer, rapist or molester back out to harass us. Hell, the scum who tried to kill that little girl and me down in Virginia had been released on numerous occasions because no one was willing to stop him.

The problem is that most people have become so civilized they are no longer capable or have the will to do the right thing. In the majority of cases, the families of victims relinquish their responsibility. They leave the removal of these monsters to a legal system that has become so liberalized and flawed that it is essentially non-existent, except to act as a playground for the lawyers and judges that live off the pain of others."

"Then what are we supposed to do? If we go after the criminal, don't we become the criminal ourselves?"

Eric turned to Sam and reached for both her hands. He stared directly into her eyes. "It boils down to a choice between two paths in dealing with the ineptness in today's legal system. Move to the left and you ignore the current state of law enforcement, and its inability to protect us from those that wish us harm. It's the easy path, because each of us has been taught to place our defense in their hands, but it does carry a risk.

When you trust the government to protect your loved ones from the bad guys, yet that very system continues to focus its attention on the rights of the criminal, you're going to be exposed again and again to the scum they set free. When that happens, you end up with the loss that so many have experienced as the repeat offenders rape, molest and kill those we love. On the other hand, if we choose to take the right path, we can stop the insanity. When the courts funnel the demons back to walk among us, we can remove them from the flock and save someone else that might suffer from the pain they inflict."

"I agreed that our justice system is faulted, but you're talking about taking things into your own hands. Society's not set up for that, neither are modern people. They've become too civilized."

"That's the problem. The second path establishes a terrible moral paradox to the way we think and act as civilized people. We have been indoctrinated socially and spiritually that righteous men do not take the law into their own hands. That philosophy has worked in the past when we had a functioning legal system aimed at shielding its citizens. It doesn't work today when the protection of the citizen is secondary to the rights of the criminal, and the misplaced priorities of our judges multiplies the suffering and turmoil experienced by the victim's family. They become torn between whether to do what is socially acceptable, or to do what will protect the innocent. The victim's family becomes hounded by nightmares because they were unable to purge their soul and resolve this own moral dilemma. Few in today's society have the ability to compartmentalize their emotions, and take a course of action that will protect others from those that have been released back onto the streets."

"Is that something you feel you could do, set things straight?" Sam asked.

"Fortunately, in rare cases, there are a few who understand what needs to be done. They have resolved the moral paradox set up by the current state of the courts, and have the courage to do what's right. Unfortunately, there is a cost. I'm not referring to the turmoil that can result because it conflicts with someone's core values. That can be controlled once you adapt and separate yourself emotionally from the act. I am referring to the recourse the legal system will impose upon those courageous enough to point out the flaws in the courts. Such heroes can pay a heavy price."

"Like what exactly?"

"The legal system will turn, not on the evil ones that committed the atrocities, but on those that attempt to protect the innocent. Do you remember a few years ago when a child molester abused a small boy in California and the judge set the demon free to prey again on the children in the community? When the mother of the boy found out, she resolved her own moral paradox, hunted down the son of a bitch, and shot him. For the act of insuring the beast would not threaten her son again, the court system used her as an example to anyone that would point out their inadequacy. They prosecuted the woman and found her guilty, not of protecting her son, but of violating their unjust laws and she served many years in jail for defending her family."

Sam shook her head. "The man who took your sister—did they lock him up and lose the key?"

"Someone in the series of lost children he destroyed had the will to break the chain and stop the pain. They killed the bastard. The authorities searched for years wasting valuable resources to find whoever set things straight, but they never found them. The judge that let him out also had a taste of justice. A random act of violence broke his spine and he could no longer serve on the bench."

Sam reached over and softly kissed him. "You see Robin when you look at Judi suffering in that hospital."

"Yes, I do."

Sam caressed his forehead. "Then, you have to do what you think is right, but remember, you have two people here who adore you and plan to spend a long life looking at your handsome face. Please be careful."

"I will. Thanks for the coffee, and for being here when I need you."

Eric left Sam's apartment and started the hour drive back to the hospital.

Thirty Seven

As Eric pulled into the hospital parking lot, his cell phone rang. He parked in front of the main entrance and answered the call, "Hello."

"Mr. Emerson, this is Paul at the hospital. A man was just in here. He tried to do something to Judi's feeder line. I went to the bathroom for two minutes and when I came back he was here."

"Did he have a hospital badge?"

"No, sir. He wore a white outfit like the other attendants, but I don't think he belongs in this hospital. When I asked what he was doing he said it was time to administer her medication. When I requested to see his badge; he stated that he left it in his coat. When I insisted, he said he would get it and return."

"Did he mess with Judi's medication? I mean did he inject anything in the line?"

"He had just pulled the hypo out of his pocket as I walked in. I stopped him before he could do it."

"What did he look like?"

"He was stocky with a flattop haircut, blond hair and roughly forty years old."

"Was there anything else distinctive about him Paul, in terms of his attire or jewelry?"

"He did have a big gold ring on his left hand."

"Was there some kind of stone in the ring?"

"Yes, it was a dark stone. I think it's called a star sapphire or something like that."

"How long ago did he leave?"

"He just walked out. I'd say he left here two minutes ago. He probably hasn't even had time to leave the hospital yet. Should I try and catch him?"

"No Paul, I need you to stay there until I come back. It could be a few hours before I get there. Something has come up, but I will come and relieve you. Will you stay there?"

"Yes sir. I'm not going anywhere. I'll pee in this bucket here before I go to the bathroom again. Mr. Emerson, what is this all about?"

"I don't know, but I will find out and take care of it. See you in a few hours."

~ * ~

The man with the flattop haircut stared at the bare buttocks and firm breasts of the dancer circling the brass pole. His glazed eyes reflected the image of the full figured woman as she gyrated suggestively across the stage. Carlson chugged down the last swallow of the cheap booze. Then he motioned to the woman on the stage, and she danced to his side of the platform. She extended her pelvic region and he inserted the twenty-dollar bill in her G-string. He waved at the bartender as he staggered out the door, and stumbled into the parking area at the back of the bar.

The drunk reached into each pocket as he searched for something. "Where the hell are you guys?" When he pulled out the noisy tangle of keys, the heavy mass slipped out of his clumsy hands, clanked on the concrete and hid under the car. "Damn it."

He bent down on one knee. "Come here you little shits." He searched under the vehicle to locate the allusive metal objects. "There you are, you little farts."

As he retrieved them, he heard steps approaching from behind. He started to rise up from his knees, but before he could completely stand and turn around, something crashed into his cheek so hard that it forced his skull bone into his nasal passage. The impact twisted the stocky man's upper torso and momentarily lifted him off his left foot, just before he fell back to the ground and his face smashed into the concrete. The man was too drunk to feel the pain, or the blood streaming down his face. He started to rise up on his hands, but there was a loud crack when he was struck at the base of his neck. He fell back to the concrete, and his body shuddered for a few seconds. Then he lay motionless as blood began to encircle what was left of his deformed face.

As the lifeless corpse remained fixed on the ground, it was hit again around the head. The figure towering above Carlson reached down and extracted his wallet, and something from his hand. Then the empty leather enclosure fell down on the body, and the figure disappeared into the dark.

The raccoon searched along the shoreline for its nightly meal. The ringed creature paused, distracted by a vehicle that stopped on the bridge above. The animal started to wade into the water when a black bat splashed into the river, causing the raccoon to scurry up the bank. When it appeared safe again, the nocturnal animal approached the river's edge, reached under a circular object and removed a four-inch crawfish hidden beneath the discarded purple flashlight. While the raccoon chewed the head off the morsel, it watched green slips of paper glide down from the bridge above, land in the water, and one by one become swept away by the current in the river.

~ * ~

Eric entered the hospital and strode up to Judi's room. "Any change in her since I left?"

Paul glanced up from his chair beside the bed. "The doctor said the internal bleeding seems to have stopped. He said that her condition has improved. I think she's going to make it, Mr. Emerson."

"That's great. Has she come to again?"

"No, she's in a lot of pain. They've kept her sedated so she can rest and heal."

"I'll take over. Go home and get some sleep. How about if you or her sister switches with me early tomorrow?"

"I'll be back in the morning to take over, and Mr. Emerson, I'm going to ask Judi to marry me. I want to give her my grandmother's ring. I've just been waiting for the courage to ask. Do you think it's the wrong time?"

"No, it's exactly the right time, but she needs to hear you love all of her, no manner what this accident has done. She has to understand you've always loved her, but you were afraid she'd say no. You want to be there for her, for whatever she needs, forever. You can't live without her. Let her know that, and she'll give you the answer you want. She's been waiting for you to step forward, got it?"

"Yes sir. I will be there for her, for the rest of my life. I'll see you in the morning Mr. Emerson, goodbye."

Eric sat down beside Judi, and stroked her tiny hand. "Sweetheart, no one will bother you again. We all love you, Judi. You're not alone. You'll never be alone again." He softly caressed her forehead, settled back in his chair, and continued to hold her hand throughout the night.

Thirty Eight

As Perry walked into the waiting area, the receptionist warned him, "The senator is waiting for you, Colonel Clark. He's in a foul mood. He's been calling you all morning. You'd better go on in."

Perry took a deep breath and stepped into the senator's office, but before he could close the door behind him, the senator began his typical callous routine. "Where the hell have you been? I've been waiting over two hours for you?"

"I came as soon as I got your message."

"How am I supposed to get hold of you when you turn off your damn cell phone?"

Perry looked out the window and sighed. "I was in the SCIF. You're not allowed to have the power on your phone while in a SCIF."

The senator curled the gray hairs of his sideburns. "Do you know where Carlson is? I've tried for two days, but I can't get in touch with him. No one at the Pentagon has seen him. Damn it, he had orders to call me every day for a progress report. When was the last time you saw him?"

"Two days ago, right here in this office."

"Did he take care of the problem we discussed?"

"Partially."

The senator brought his hand down hard on his desk. "Look at me when you talk. What the hell do you mean partially? Did he fix things or not?"

The colonel began to raise the volume of his voice. "The girl is in the hospital. She is in serious condition. They're not sure if she will make it or not."

"What about the other two?"

"I have no idea."

"What the hell do you mean? Did he take care of them or not? Are you stupid or something? What the hell is wrong with you boy?"

Perry jerked his head toward his father. His expression changed from apathy to anger. The pitch of his voice transformed from monotone to rushed fury. In bold pronounced singular words, he rammed his hands down on the desk. "I mean I don't know!"

"Don't get smart with me, boy."

"I'm not your boy, or your dog, and I wish I wasn't your damn son!"

"Watch it, you're about to go too far. I'll bring a ton of hurt down on your ass, so watch yourself or I'll—"

"You'll what? Not hound me anymore? Not talk to me? Not command me to do your illegal crap? You've screamed and snarled at me every damn time I've seen your grumpy face since I was a kid. Do you have any idea what it's like to be the son of a control freak; a tyrant who runs over everyone he comes in contact with?"

The senator pointed his bent finger at his son. "You're just like your mother and sister. Neither of them was worth a shit either. You've turned out as useless as them."

"I wish I was like my mother. She was a compassionate woman before you drove her into the ground. Did you ever wonder why she drank herself to death? It was to get away from your controlling, hateful ass. Her only sanctuary was to commit suicide at the bottom of a bottle.

And as for my sister, you worked your magic on her poor soul too. You had to figure out why she did drugs, why she turned tricks to fund her habit. It was to get away from you. She searched for a father's love in any man who walked into that rundown apartment. She became a whore because of you; because of the times you made her feel small and insignificant. My sin is that I watched you do it. I stood there and let you destroy them. I have to live with that for the rest of my useless life."

"Everything I've done has been for you, you ungrateful runt."

"Bullshit. It's always been about you. Everything we've done since you became a senator has been to expand your power and fame, and no one else."

The colonel moved around the side of the desk and moved closer to his father. "In my entire life, I never heard you say you cared, not even one kind word, let alone any sign of encouragement. You've bitched at me constantly, every miserable minute we've been together."

The senator pulled back for an instant, unaccustomed to his son's display of grit. "I made you what you are. Without me, you would be nothing."

"You're right about that. You did make me, but if I were you, I sure as hell wouldn't be proud of what you produced, Father. Have you examined your creation lately? I'm scum, just like you. I've been molded in your image. You corrupted me, taught me how to screw everyone, and trust no one."

"You could have done a lot worse. Look at what I made of you."

"Are you blind? I have no one in my life. No wife, no friends. How the hell could it have been worse? I've contemplated what I might have been if I hadn't spawned from your loins. Maybe Senator Robertson, anyone but you. I've always wondered what I might have been if I had a father who wanted me, who loved me. Not a shallow self-serving jackass like you."

"You're culpable for your own actions, not me."

"I'm not shucking responsibility for what I've done. I let it happen, but you were the seed, the anvil that hammered me into submission, day after horrible day, and I've had it. No more of your bullshit, your rules, your orders. Get another fool to do your shit. We're through, and don't worry about the holidays, or fishing trips, or the football games you never spent with me. We never had a father/son relationship, just a pitiful master/slave domination. You're on your own, Father, like I have been all these lonely years."

Perry stood up and stared directly into the baggy eyes of the man he had hated all his life. Since his first memory of his father, he had felt nothing but coldness. Today, all that had changed. He no longer felt the vise on his chest

As the colonel turned to leave, the senator shot one last salvo. "Your ass is in this fiasco as deep as mine, Perry. If you don't take care of the problem, we'll both end up in jail. Is that what you want?"

"Frankly, I don't really care. There's nothing that could be worse than this, but I will finish what you failed to do. Not because I feel obligated to help you, but because those two have disrespected me for the last time."

"Then to hell with you and your screwed-up mother. She was a useless woman, and she produced a useless son. I wash my hands of you."

Perry reached the exit to the office. "She was a wonderful person who made a terrible choice in a mate. I was never your son, just your gopher."

Before the colonel could close the door, the senator issued one final order, "One more thing, get that reptile out of my vacation home. Your damn pet gives me the willies."

As he stood outside the door, Colonel Clark took a deep breath. He tucked in his shirt, straightened his tie, and closed that chapter of his life, forever.

The senator sat isolated in his large office. In silence, he stared at the door, alone, without anyone except his own wretched self. After several minutes, he looked down at his desk, placed his hands on his temples, and whispered, "My God, what have I done?"

~ * ~

Eric leaned back in his chair and examined the words *Drone Beam* that he had scribbled on the notepad on his desk. He scratched his forehead for a moment, before he picked up the paper and pulled forward in his chair. "That's it, that's what she meant."

Sam turned around. "What are you mumbling over there?"

"Let me see that slip of paper with the names of the people that conducted the first OPEVAL."

Sam searched through her files, located the sheet of paper and handed it to him. After staring at the page for a couple of minutes, Eric said in disbelief, "My God, could they have been that brazen? I just can't believe they would go that far."

"What?"

"I think Judi actually meant to say Drone Beacon, not Drone Beam."

"So?"

"Those crooks actually falsified the damn Viper test results."

"But how? We saw the missiles hit the targets."

"I need to check something out. If I'm right, I understand why Judi was hurt, and why someone tried to run us down when we were out on the boat."

"What, what? Tell me, darn it. What are you talking about?"

"Not until I'm sure, but if I'm right, there's a bunch of people headed for the slammer. Sam I need your help on this. I want you to witness the second OPEVAL on your own. I'll meet you right after the test."

"Where are you going to be?"

"If my hunch is correct, you'll know it because the test will fail. I plan to leave late tonight from the hospital and go directly to the airport. Judi's parents get in around nine to night and I want to meet them. I need you to go ahead and take the noon flight today. I'll meet you at the motel early in the morning, but once we pass through the security gates at White Sands, you're going to drop me off and go to the control center by yourself."

"If I'm going to help with this, you have to tell me what's going on."

"I'll share it with you on the way to the range, but I have to run. I need to call some old friends and set something up and I don't have much time."

Eric leaned over and kissed Sam. As he ran out of the door he looked back with a smile. "I think we've got them." Then he disappeared out the door.

Thirty Nine

"I'd like to draw everyone's attention to the platform," Colonel Clark informed the crowd. "You'll notice we have changed the format of this test in response to General Williams' concerns. The test rig is a fully configured HUMVEE with launch canisters, and only military personnel will perform all prescribed system operations. Also, once the first three standard shots are fired like in the first test, we launch a fourth Viper against a countermeasure-configured target."

Perry turned and looked directly at Sam. "Major, where is your friend? He's responsible for this repeat of the OPEVAL. He could at least grace us with his presence."

Sam turned her head away from the colonel. She began to speak, but as always, she stalled. She steeled herself, refusing to be intimidated again. Not this time, or ever again.

She looked up, and stood eye to eye with Clark. "Mr. Emerson wanted to witness the OPEVAL first hand. He's observing the tests down range so he can get a direct view when the missiles strike the drone...Colonel."

At first Perry was confused by her response, then he smiled at Sam, but she did not waiver in her resolve. She continued to stare straight into the dark eyes of her adversary.

As Clark turned back to the crowd, Sam sighed. *You don't scare me anymore.*

The colonel spoke to the observers in the control center. "If there are no questions, then Johnson, please instruct the drone center to launch the first target."

The man seated at the console spoke into the phone, "Launch the drone."

Sam watched the main viewer and after several minutes, a small speck traveled across the screen. Within seconds the system acquisition radar on the test vehicle sensed and located the target. The launch tubes swiveled clockwise on the support gimbal and a trail of vapor traced from the center tube toward the sky as the missile headed for the target.

"We should see an explosion on the screen momentarily," the colonel instructed those observing the test.

Everyone in the room waited. After twenty seconds the phone at the control console rang. The technician at the console picked up the phone. "What, it did? Are you sure? All right, get ready for the second shot."

The technician hung up the phone, and glanced at the colonel without saying a word.

"Johnson, what did they say?" the colonel demanded.

The technician responded, "It was a clear miss Colonel. Should I have them orbit the drone and fire the second shot?"

The colonel stared directly at the senior contract representative with an expression of uncertainty. "How the hell is that possible?"

"Even with a kill probability of ninety percent," the bald contractor replied, "you will get one miss out of ten shots."

Perry began to twirl his pen across his knuckles. He opened his mouth, but closed it without uttering a word. He turned back to the technician. "Start the second sequence."

The same process was repeated, with the same result. Once the missile launched at the target, there was no cloud of smoke to signal a hit, nothing but a vapor trail arching across the sky and vanishing with no terminal explosion.

Before she realized it, Sam blurted out, "My God, he was right, and he proved it."

The colonel snapped around. "What was that, Major?"

With a smirk, Sam replied without hesitation. "It appears that Mr. Emerson and I have been vindicated for requesting a second OPEVAL...Colonel."

Perry's face flushed. He began to respond, but closed his mouth. He paused for a moment as the major held her ground. The colonel turned to the bald man that stood stunned in the back of the room. "I'll assume two misses back to back would be unexpected. This is your system. Do you have an explanation for what we just witnessed?"

The bald man remained rigid and silent.

The colonel looked back at the observers. "I'm sorry everyone but it appears we have a wire crossed somewhere. We'll have to reconvene once we diagnose the problem."

~ * ~

Sam pulled up to the front of the drone control building. When Eric got into the passenger seat, Sam stated, "You caught them in the act, didn't you?"

"Yes indeed I did, and here's the proof."

Eric held up a small black box roughly the size of a pack of cigarettes. "They were using a homing beacon that could vector the missile directly to the target. That's why they had a kill probability of one hundred percent. I made them launch one of the larger drones that I had flown in last night from Fort Bliss. Since the older drone had a larger Radar Cross Section area, it should have been easier for the Viper radar to acquire the target."

"Didn't they put up a hassle when you walked into the drone center?"

"I called the center chief yesterday and told him my intentions, and why it was important. While I exchanged words with the contractor technicians, he launched the drone. When they attempted to contact the control center to warn them, that's when things got interesting."

With a sparkle in her eyes, Sam beamed. "What happened, did you have to clean their clocks?"

"Let's just say that I may be sued for assault, but once I caught them in the act, I think they have more serious concerns on the horizon. I will have to pay for the two cell phones I crushed, but it was worth it."

"Anything else?"

"Here's the rest of it." Eric held up a camera and two sheets of paper.

"I have pictures of how they hid the beacon in the drone, and I convinced the two guys that installed the device to provide a statement of what they did, of course all the time proclaiming their ignorance as to the purpose of the beacon. We've got them cold, Sam. We really did our job today. What was it like in the control center?"

"You should have seen their faces," Sam said. "The colonel and the lead contractor rep reacted like they had just witnessed the impossible. I actually had to squeeze my cheek to keep from laughing out loud. It was priceless. What's next?"

"We'll turn over all our evidence to the OIG when we get back. On the return flight, I'll write up what we've discovered and provide it to the investigators and General Williams. There will definitely be an investigation, and I'm pretty sure somebody will get jail time, I just don't know who yet."

"How deep do you think this goes?"

"It's hard to say. I'm sure some of the managers in the company who makes the Viper system are involved, maybe the colonel, and I'm convinced Senator Clark played a role in this corruption. I'm not sure about Senator Robertson yet, but it's possible he's also part of this."

"When will we know?"

"It will take time. As the investigation evolves, many of the conspirators will turn on each other, that's when we'll know for sure how wide the web extends."

"So what do we do now?"

"Not a thing. We've done our part. Once we turn this over to the Office of the Inspector General, they'll take over our investigation, and you can forget the Viper program. The entire production decision will be shelved. I'm not sure whether they'll cancel the entire contract, or call for deeper involvement by the government in the design and evaluation process. It will be up to the general Officers and suits."

"So now we can focus on the Osiris Study, right?" Sam asked.

"You bet, but for tonight we sleep well. What we did was very important for the troops and the taxpayer. It's unlikely that we'll ever get an *attaboy*, but you should take pride in what was done today."

"I am proud, especially of you, and how you gave me fortitude." Sam reached over and with both hands, pressed Eric's cheeks, and kissed him long and hard on the lips.

Eric looked inquisitively at the beaming face of his partner. "My lord woman, what happened over there that's got your blood pumping? How many cups of coffee did you have this morning?"

"I just feel refreshed and ready to take on the world. So good in fact, that I think its time for a treat before we head back?"

Eric raised his right eyebrow. "What did you have in mind, beautiful?"

Sam grinned. "The same thing you're thinking of, a big banana split at that restaurant next to the motel."

Eric smiled. "Not exacting what I was imaging, but if it's your treat, I'll tag along, as long as I get my own. We might as well go. Nothing they do from this point forward means anything anymore, they just don't realize it yet. Now switch seats with me. You're too hyped up to be behind the wheel."

"I don't think so, Mister. I've got the keys to the rental car. I'm driving, and you're just going to have to get used to it. In fact, I plan to drive a lot from now on."

Sam leaned toward the man she loved. "You got a problem with that, handsome?"

"I'm not sure I'm ready for this side of you. It's a little scary."

"Too bad, you're in for a lot of changes Mr. Emerson, so buckle up and close your eyes. I'll have us there in no time."

As Sam squealed the rear tires, Eric grabbed the console with both hands and closed his eyes. "Lord save me."

Forty

Upon returning from their trip to witness the Viper OPEVAL, Eric shifted his attention to unraveling the Osiris mystery. After calling the last member of the technical team working on the study, he hung up the receiver and stared at the STU phone. "Damn, tight as a drum."

Sam turned around from her desk. "Still nothing?"

"I've called everyone I know on your SAP list that's cleared for the Osiris program. No one knows crap. Either they are lying to me or this is the tightest compartmented program I've ever seen. Not one of them has any idea what the Oversight Board is doing with the data that each organization provides to the Osiris core team. It's like it gets sucked into a black hole. There's something really unusual about this study, Sam."

"Then why not go to the source?" Sam suggested.

"What do you mean?"

"If no one on the rim of the project is privy to anything, why not head for the center of the wheel."

"You really think if we go to the Board and say, 'We demand you tell us what the hell is going on right now,' that they'll greet us with open arms and tell us everything? I don't think so."

"Eric, you need to get away from your typical brute force approach. Use a little finesse on this one. They have no idea what we do and do not understand, do they?"

He hesitated, and then agreed. "You're right, they don't. We can tell Robertson that we're concerned over the direction that the study has taken, and unless he convinces us otherwise, we're going to report what we know up the line. Very good Sam, I like it."

"I thought you might."

"We can also let it slip that we've discovered how they falsified the Viper OPEVAL, and then watch his response. I'm pretty sure that either Robertson or Clark is in collusion with the contractor. Maybe this will flush them out."

Eric glanced at the window for a moment. "We now know that when Judi told me about the drone beacons, she was informing us about what they pulled on the Viper test. What if, when she signed 'mass murder', she was actually somehow referring to the Osiris Study?"

"That's a little extreme, don't you think?"

"Maybe not. Maybe they're trying to examine the global implications of a biological terrorist incidence, or maybe worse. It's possible they're evaluating an even more terrible scenario."

"Like what?"

"I'm not sure, but it must be something fairly severe. Judi was hurt and we were almost run down by that cruiser for some reason. It's either because we uncovered the Viper skullduggery, or because we've been snooping around on the Osiris effort. It's got to be one or the other, unless you've pissed someone else off and didn't tell me."

"I don't think so, Mr. Smarty."

"Then let's use it. Someone almost killed Judi for what she saw, let's assume that 'mass murder' applies to the study and use it against them. If we're wrong, they can prove otherwise. If not, God help us."

"So how do we set the trap?"

"Leave it to me. I'll call up Robertson's office and put out the bait, and we'll see if they take it, on one condition. I do it all on my own."

"No way Eric. Not this time."

"Then we don't do it. These guys play a serious game. I've just gotten you and Ronnie into my life; I'm not going to risk losing both of you."

"It works both ways. I don't want to lose you either."

"Damn it, Sam. Have you ever slit a man's throat, or broke

his neck, or killed anyone while you stared directly into his soul? Of course not. I have, and I can't take care of my ass if I'm worried about you."

Sam paused. "Maybe we should drop it, not do anything."

"You know we can't do that. We're still at risk until this is resolved one way or the other."

"I don't want to lose you. It's taken me too long to get you to wake up. Things are so good now, for all of us."

Eric pulled softly on Sam's chin. "Sweetheart, you have to trust me. I've dealt with far more capable enemies than these guys. It's what I was trained for, what I was meant to do. I promise, I'll be all right. First, I've got to get you to a place where I feel conformable about your welfare."

"What about my parent's house. Its time they met you face to face, don't you think?"

"That works for me. Let me call Senator Robertson and see when I can meet with him. Would you send an email to General Williams and his secretary Mary?"

"Sure, what should I say?"

"Attach a copy of the report I gave to the OIG, but don't say anything regarding the Osiris Study yet, or my visit to the senator. Tell Mary where we'll be, but ask her not to share it with anyone else. I'll drop you off by your apartment, before I go visit Judi. You pack up some stuff for a three-day trip for you and Ronnie. Call your parents and tell them that they've got visitors on the way."

Eric kissed Sam on the cheek. "I'll meet you at the main entrance in forty minutes."

~ * ~

Colonel Perry walked into the reception area for General Williams' office and sat down at the secretary's desk. When Mary came back from her visit to the rest room, she saw the colonel scanning her computer screen.

"Can I help you, Colonel?"

"I wanted to speak with the general."

"He's still at the Supreme Headquarters for Allied Powers in Europe. He'll return from the SHAPE conference next week. Would you like me to schedule a meeting with him?"

"No, I'll stop back by next week." Then Clark left the office.

Forty One

Eric got into the driver's seat to start the trip to Sam's parents. "You don't mind if I drive this time do you, Sam? After all, it is my car."

"I'll let it slide, but don't get used to it. How was Judi?"

"It's amazing, but with all the things that girl just experienced, she's still a ray of sunshine. They were able to repair her larynx, and she's going to recover some of the vision in her right eye. She has to undergo a long period of physical therapy, but she's got her life back. Oh, Paul finally proposed. And she accepted. They're not going through an extended engagement. As soon as she's out of the hospital, they're getting married. Kind of makes you think doesn't it?"

"Yes it does."

Eric looked into the mirror. "You're mighty quiet back there, Ronnie. What are you thinking?"

"I was listening to what you said, and I'm really happy about Judi. I like her a lot."

"Me too, Sport."

Sam asked Eric, "When are you going to drive back to DC and see Senator Robertson?"

"I'm scheduled to meet him day after tomorrow, but not in DC. He has a farm south of Winchester. That's where he is this week, so I'm going to meet him there, and get this. When I called to put our plan in play, the senator had already intended to meet with me. His aide said the senator has been planning to call me to set up a meeting."

"Did he say why?"

"No, but I'm sure I'll find out when we meet."

"I couldn't get you to change your mind and let me watch your flank, could I?"

"No. As long as I'm sure you two are safe, no one can harm me."

Sam folded her arms and stared out her window. "Always got to be Mr. Macho don't you? If you let anything happen to you, I'll..."

"Yes, what do you plan to do to me? I'm waiting."

"I'll bite you hard where it really hurts, and you will be in pain for a long time."

"Ouch, and where might that be?"

She glanced into the back seat, frowned at the driver, and stated, "You figure that one out."

When Eric looked in the mirror, he saw Ronnie shrug his shoulders to indicate that he had no idea what his mother was talking about.

After driving for a couple of hours, they turned down the dirt road to the small retirement community where her parents recently relocated. A large bulldozer and other excavating equipment were parked along the road.

"What are they doing here?" Eric asked.

Sam pointed to the hill on the left of the road. "Dad says they plan to take the hill down. This road we're on is temporary. It was put here so they could bring the equipment in and clear the home sites. Notice how sharp this turn is? You can't see around the curve. They plan to go straight through that field with the permanent road."

"How many people live back in here?"

"It's a small planned community for one hundred and forty homes. My parents bought the first house and moved in early because the buyer of their home in Newport News had to move in last month. Right now, they're the only people living in the community."

As they approached the midsize, one story log cabin, Eric scanned the mountains surrounding the development. "I can see why your parents moved here. I love the mountains. They have one terrific view. I especially like the small stream tracing along the road. It reminds me of my dad's farm back in North Carolina."

"Mom and Dad are crazy over this place. You know they've traveled all over the world. We were always on tour in some other country. Being in the military, we didn't see much of Dad. Since he retired three months ago, it's a whole new world for Mom and Dad, like starting their life over again together."

When they got out of the car, Ronnie ran ahead on the herringbone brick sidewalk. Before he reached the cabin, the front door swung open and a golden retriever leaped out, knocking the small boy to the ground.

"I missed you too, Tucker," Ronnie said, peering up at the big canine.

Eric bent down and petted the large dog. "What a beautiful animal."

Ronnie looked up from the ground while the dog repeatedly licked his face. "She's all mine."

"My dad got Tucker for Ronnie when he was four. They grew up together. When we moved to Fort Monroe, our apartment wouldn't permit dogs, so Tucker stays with Mom and Dad most of the time, but she still adores Ronnie."

Sam's father opened the door to the cabin. Eric reached out and the two men shook hands. "Hello General. Good to see you again."

"Good to see you, Eric. It's been quite a few years."

Sam looked between them. "What do you mean again? Have you two met before?"

"Yes."

"You didn't tell me that. Dad, why didn't you tell me you two already knew each other?"

Eric smiled at the general. "Men have learned that to survive in a relationship, they don't tell a woman everything."

She placed her hands on her hips, looked at Eric and frowned. "I can see we're going to have a long talk Mr. Emerson, and soon."

"You have to allow a man some secrets, Sam."

Sam shook her head. "No you don't. I'm supposed to be privy to everything. That's my right."

A grin spread across the general's face. "Just like her mother. She's been that way since she was five. Hit me with a thousand questions every day. That's why we call her Ms. Nosy."

Eric looked at Sam before returning his attention to her father. "Really? That's original. Now I know where your grandson gets it from. He's the same way."

The tall man shook his head. "Just like his mother. We call him little nosy around here."

Sam pushed through the two men and walked into the small cabin. "Mom, they're ganging up on me. I need your help out here."

Ronnie ran between the two men, "Jimmy! Grandpa, where's Jimmy?"

"He's probably in the bathroom in his little house."

Eric quirked his brow.

"That's his gerbil friend. Ronnie lets that little hairball run everywhere around here. Don't be surprised to see a tuft of fur darting around the house."

"The dog doesn't kill it?"

"No, that dog allows the fur ball to crawl all over her. Ronnie seems to think that Tucker and Jimmy are best friends. That's why he didn't take the rat with him when they moved. He was afraid they would miss each other. Tucker does seem to enjoy playing with Jimmy. I only let the rat run around the house when Ronnie's here."

As the two men walked into the cabin, Sam's father closed the door. "Here they come." A white ball of fur with one brown spot scurried between Eric's legs. The gerbil ran from the door, under the couch, and finally scampered up to the bathroom, with Ronnie close behind. Not to be left out, Tucker stepped through the pet entry at the bottom of the door, and took off after his friends.

"It can get a little noisy around here when Sam visits."

"I kind of like it General, just part of family life."

Later, as the family sat around the dinner table, Sam probed, "Dad, where do you and Eric know each other from?"

The elder man finished the last bite of his sandwich. "It's a secret."

Sam looked at Eric. "Okay, you tell me. I have more leverage on you."

"Your dad was our guardian angel on deep missions."

"What does that mean?"

"When a deep mission team goes out on assignment, someone has to be responsible for coordinating all inputs, demands, and intelligence to the team. Your dad was assigned to the theater Joint Special Operations Task Force and functioned as our SpecOps coordinator as a member of the Joint Intelligence Center staff. His role was to review all national and tactical intel reports funneled into the JIC to make sure the adversary remained blind to our presence. He saved our butts many times, right General?"

"At least a hundred times."

Sam rested her chin on her hands. "That's really interesting."

"Yeah Grandpa, that's really interesting," Ronnie, seated next to his grandfather, replied.

"Dad, why didn't you ever discuss this before?"

"Princess, I'm aware you think you're supposed to know everything that goes on in the world, but you're not."

Sam looked at her mother. "Dad's picking on me again. Make him stop."

"At least tell me if you ever met Eric in person before today."

"I did, once. It was when he was hospitalized after his last mission. I had to meet the man that literally fought the enemy to his last ounce of blood. I see the scars on your face have healed well. Have there been any residual problems?"

Eric smiled. "Actually the women love it. It gives me kind of a rugged look."

Sam stared at Eric. "You're really looking for trouble today, aren't you?"

"I wouldn't worry sweetheart," said Sam's mother from the other end of the table. "He's seated next to you, and from the look in his eye, I don't think he's going anywhere with anyone else."

"I told her that, Grandma," Ronnie chimed in, "but she never listens to me."

Sam bent sideways and looked directly into Eric's eyes. "Really, I must be missing something because I don't see anything in there."

"You're not looking hard enough, woman," Eric tossed back.

While Sam and her mother began clearing the table, Eric got up and started to help. The general informed his guest, "Don't worry about that. Let the women handle it."

Sam bounced back immediately. "Don't start that stuff, Dad. Just because Mom lets you get away with it doesn't mean I want Eric to get any ideas. Every time Ronnie visits you, it takes me a week to get that macho stuff out of him. 'If Grandpa doesn't have to help, why do I?' My men will share the load."

"She can get feisty," the general noted.

"Must be that red hair."

"It's all right sweetheart," Sam's mother said. "Just for today, let the men go bond in the living room."

"Okay, but only for today, and don't talk about me."

The general opened his desk drawer and pulled out a box of cigars. "Would you like one?"

"I appreciate the offer General, but I gave them up several years ago."

"What about me, Grandpa?"

"Your mother and grandma would both kill me. I can't survive the wrath of two women. Come on Eric, let's sit on the porch."

As the three males became comfortable in the wicker furniture, the older man asked, "Eric, I'm confident you're a good man, and I can tell you care for my daughter, but I need to be a bit traditional here. You have to be aware that my daughter adores you. I'd like to know, when are you going to do the right thing?"

Ronnie, seated across from the two men inquired, "Yeah Eric, when?"

Eric smiled. "There sure are a lot of matchmakers in this family."

"She's my only child, and I don't want to see her hurt. She has a very tender heart. I just want to hear your intentions."

"My intent is to love and protect your daughter and grandson for the rest of my life." Eric pulled a small box from his pocket and opened the top.

The young boy yelled, "Wow, look at that ring!"

Eric pressed his two fingers gently against Ronnie's lips. "Shhh. It's a secret."

"Oh, I understand. Man to man."

"You too have to remain quiet until the moment is right, okay Sport?"

"You got it."

The general smiled. "Then when?"

"I thought maybe this weekend, if the right moment pops up. Hopefully she'll say yes."

"Son, you don't have to worry. You've had her heart in your hands for years. She just hid it very well. Would you like us to take Ronnie and disappear tomorrow?"

"No General. This involves Ronnie too, right Sport?"

"Right, Eric."

"Can I give you a bit of advice? It should be only the two of you, and it doesn't matter where it is, as long as you two are alone. The moment is a big deal for women. You need to make it all about her. Don't you agree Ronnie, just your mom and Eric, together?"

"I guess so, as long as it happens soon."

"I don't want to push you, Eric…well maybe I do. I want to see Sam and Ronnie happy, and with a father and husband who will take care of them, and provide Ronnie with the role model he needs. You're that man. I want to be there to give my daughter away, and I'm not going to live forever. May I make a suggestion?"

"Sure, General."

"There's a real nice vista two miles back along this road."

"Yes sir, I saw it coming in."

"Just before you turned onto our dirt road is a small town. Sam loves dark chocolate ice cream. I'll ask you to go get some ice cream for dinner and give you a cooler with ice. Take two spoons with you, stop on the way back, and park at the pull off that overlooks the scenic vista. Tell her you want to spend a few minutes together. As you share a few bites of ice cream, ask the question.

"Do you think that's special enough?"

"Her favorite ice cream, a beautiful view, the two of you, sounds like the perfect recipe to me, right Ronnie?"

"I guess so, but don't let Mom eat all the ice cream. Make sure she saves some for us."

"You think that will work, General?"

"Guaranteed."

"Okay, let's do it."

The tall man stood up and yelled into the kitchen, "Ruth, I want ice cream for dinner. Sam, will you and Eric drive back to town and get a half a gallon?"

Ronnie corrected his grandfather, "No Mom, get a gallon so there'll be plenty for all of us to eat."

The two men looked at the young boy. "What? I didn't tell her. I know how Mom likes ice cream, right Eric?"

"Right, Sport."

Forty Two

Eric turned into the pull-off for the scenic overlook.

"What's up?" Sam asked.

He handed her a spoon and removed one of the four pints of ice cream from the cooler. "I thought it would be nice for us to have a moment together. With all that's been going on recently, we haven't really had any time alone, and you'll notice I gave you the bigger spoon. Let's sit on the hood so we can see the valley better."

As they sat on the hood, Sam moved closer to Eric and grinned. "Just so I get my share."

While she scooped her first spoonful from the ice cream container, Eric suggested, "It's really a nice view here, isn't it?"

"Yes it is. I love to watch the wonderful colors in the sunset."

"There's only one problem with that sunset. One very important color is missing."

"Like what?"

"Like that gorgeous green in your eyes."

Sam lowered her head and with a curious expression. "Nice. Corny but nice."

"This may not be the best time, but I don't want to wait any longer. I want to do it now and enjoy what we have together."

With a tone of jest, she asked, "Now what, don't tell me you're dying?"

"I understand you have issues inside that sweet and bruised soul of yours. So do I, but that doesn't mean we can't work them out,

I mean bonded together."

"What are you up to, Eric?"

"Sam, you have to sense how I feel about you, after all these years. How much you mean to me, how much I care for you and Ronnie."

Sam placed her spoon on the hood of the car. "I don't understand. What are you trying to say?"

"Hold on a second." Eric knelt down on the gravel. "Ouch, damn that hurts. This may be a bit old fashioned, but I love you, Sam. Whatever comes our way, whatever we have, I want the three of us to be a family." He handed her a small box he removed from his pocket.

"And?"

"Come on Sam, I'm dying here, the stones are digging into my knees. Tell me, is it yes or no?"

"What do you think, you silly thing? Of course I will. What the hell took you so long? Now give me a wet one, and let's go tell everyone there's a new man in our lives."

On the trip home, Eric noticed how silent Sam remained, fidgeting in her seat, like she was anxious to get somewhere, to tell someone, everyone what had just happened. Sam leaped out of the car, raced down the sidewalk, and reached the door twenty steps ahead of Eric. "Mom, come look at my ring! He finally did it."

Sam's father and Ronnie were seated on the couch when Eric came through the door.

With his thumb pointed up, Sam's father pronounced, "Way to go, Son."

Ronnie mirrored his grandfather's expression. "Yeah Eric, way to go."

As Eric sat down, the young boy remembered one vital question. "Hey Mom, you didn't eat all the ice cream did you."

Ronnie looked at Eric. "Eric, you didn't let her eat it all? You promised."

Eric held out the keys to his car. "Relax Ronnie. It's in the trunk. I bought an extra pint all for you, and no one else. I wrote your name on the top of the container, and no one gets to touch it except you. How's that?"

Ronnie grabbed the keys and headed for the door. "Wow, all

mine." He reached for the knob. "Thanks Eric. Thanks a lot."

After consuming their treat, Sam announced, "Okay guys, before the sandman comes to visit Ronnie, we need to work out the sleeping arrangements. Eric you take Ronnie's room. Ronnie can sleep on the couch."

"Sam, I'm not kicking Ronnie out of his bed. I used to hate it when my parents did that to me. Besides, I go to bed real late, and I'll be up early jogging. I'll sleep out here."

"All right, but Ronnie, keep Tucker in your room so she doesn't go in and out all night long."

Sam went to the linen closet, pulled out a pillow, sheet and blanket, and placed them on the couch. "Whenever you're ready you can fix up the couch. It's been a long day guys, and I'm really tired. I'll see you in the morning Mr. Independent. I'm going to bed."

As Sam headed for the bedroom, her mother inquired, "Sweetheart, aren't you going to make his bed up for him?"

Sam turned, glanced directly at her husband to be. "Eric told me explicitly he doesn't need my help. He's drawn and quartered all kinds of things. He can take care of himself, right Hon? Good night."

Eric looked at the expression on Sam's face. "Didn't see that coming."

The general whispered, "Issues?"

Eric shook his head. "Beats the hell out of me, but I guess I'd better fix my own bed. See you in the morning."

~ * ~

The A10 Warthog flew low over the desert and fired its 30-millimeter GAU-9 Vulcan gun, cutting the Iraqi T72 tank in half. Eric turned back toward the two-story cobble building and directed his target designator device at the upper floor. In twenty-two seconds the MK83 Laser Guided bomb slammed into the Iraqi headquarters. Debris spewed into the air and bounced across the desert. His eyes followed the sounds of the mechanized tracks turning in the sand and he searched for the silhouette of a Bradley Fighting Vehicle or Abrams Tank, but there was nothing.

Eric opened his eyes. He blinked several times to clear his head, sat up and walked to the front door. He listened in the distance, but there was nothing. He returned to the couch and in a few minutes he was asleep again.

The golden retriever stirred from its position next to Ronnie. She jumped to the floor, moved over to the window and scanned the distant dirt road for the source of the sound. After thirty seconds, she walked to the door and lay down.

The pet door opened slightly. Something dropped to the floor. It waited for a moment, sensed the air, moved left, and then stopped. Once it caught the scent, it headed toward the couch, paused by Eric's shoes, searched again for the smell, and continued up the steps.

Tucker jerked her head and stared through the bedroom door into the hallway. The retriever whined, and then quieted. She listened for a few seconds before lowering her head back onto the floor.

It reached the top of the steps, lost the scent, and then caught the faint odor again. It turned right, moved down the hallway, and stopped at the bathroom door.

Tucker jumped up and paced back and forth at the bedroom door. She sniffed under the crack, and scratched at the doorframe.

It pushed on the open bathroom door, and entered. It reached up to its prey, struck, and waited.

Tucker clawed the door, and then she growled.

Ronnie woke up. He rubbed his eyes, and shuffled across the room. "Move Tucker. I've got to go pee, and you're blocking the door."

Ronnie pushed the dog back in the room. "Stay girl, you'll wake up Eric and then I'll get in trouble." But when he closed the door, the latch did not engage.

The sleepy youngster moved toward the bathroom, turned the handle and began to swing the door open. From behind, the dog leaped past the boy, knocking him to the floor. In mid air, Tucker grabbed it behind the head as it struck at the small leg entering the room.

The dog lost her grip. It struck again. Tucker yelped. Then she bit down on the snake's head and shook violently, until it lay motionless on the floor.

Lights went on throughout the house. Everyone converged on the bathroom to the sight of Ronnie lying on the floor as his dog licked his face and stood over the corpse of a rattlesnake.

Eric reached down and lifted the limp body of the viper.

Sam looked at the dog standing guard over her son. "Ronnie, my God what happened?"

"Mom, why did Tucker knock me down?"

Eric held the snake across his hands. "She saved your life Ronnie. Your dog saved you from a lot of pain. Sam, check Ronnie to make sure there are no puncture wounds."

Eric pointed to the dead gerbil on the floor. "I'm sorry Ronnie, but Jimmy's gone. It must have smelled his scent and tracked him up to the bathroom. General, do you know whether rattlers are indigenous to this area?"

"I'm aware they have them around here, but I've never heard of any getting inside a house. It must have come in through the pet door. It's probably all the excavation around here. It must have disturbed its cover."

Eric examined the tail of the snake. "Maybe, but that doesn't explain who removed the rattle from its tail."

The general inspected the slit in the rattler. "How the hell did that happen?"

Eric looked at Sam. "Obviously, not by accident. Sam, this is why I told you to let me deal with these guys by myself. We were lucky this time."

Sam stared at Eric, and then at Ronnie, but didn't say a word.

Ronnie pulled on his mother's nightgown. "Mom, Tucker is bleeding."

Eric bent down and checked the retriever's leg. "Damn, the snake hit the dog. We have to rush her to the vet right now."

"Ruth, call the vet," the general ordered. "Tell him I'll be at the vet hospital in twenty minutes. Sam, come with me. You need to sit in the back of the car with the dog. You have to keep her still. Eric, please stay here with my wife and grandson. Let's move everyone."

Sam and her father put the dog in the backseat of the van, pulled out of the drive and headed toward town. When they neared the sharp turn three hundred yards from the cabin, he looked in the mirror. "How's she doing?"

Before Sam could respond she saw the monster in their path,

Michael W. Davis

"Dad!"

Forty Three

A car horn howled continually in the distant darkness. "Mrs. Cassidy, Ronnie, hurry!" Eric shouted. He peeled out of the driveway, and vectored toward the sound. Just past the sharp turn, the windshield of the van was impaled by the shovel of a bulldozer positioned strategically in the right lane of the road. Eric leaped out of his car and ripped open the side door of the van. The end of the dozer blade had crushed deep into the general's skull.

Sam's torso had been thrown into the front seat, while her left leg twisted rearward and dangled over the passenger seat. The fibula bone protruded through the muscle tissue in her leg. "God almighty."

Eric looked back to see Sam's mother with her hands pressed on her mouth as tears streamed down her face. He tossed his cell phone to the distressed woman. "I'm sorry Mrs. Cassidy, but you have to call 911. Tell them where we are, and tell them to hurry. Sam's bleeding badly. I've got to try and stop it."

Eric smelled smoke. He scanned the hood and saw dark blue smoke rising from the engine compartment. "We can't wait. You two move back from the car, now!"

Sam lay unconscious jammed against the console. Eric gently removed her from the front seat, but the pain from her wound brought her back to consciousness. She screamed in agony.

"I'm sorry Sam, but I have to move you."

He carried her thirty yards from the wreck, and placed her on the soft dirt. "Ronnie, here's my keys, hurry and get the blanket from my trunk, and the coat in my back seat."

"Mrs. Cassidy, push here on her femoral artery. We've got to stop the bleeding. I have to check your husband, now."

Eric went to the driver's side of the van and looked at the crushed skull of the driver. "Jesus." He reached in and pressed two fingers on the general's throat. No pulse. He ran back to the others waiting to hear what they already knew.

"I'm sorry Mrs. Cassidy, he's dead. He was such a great person, and now he's gone. I'm really sorry."

Eric looked at the face of the woman he loved as tears flowed down her cheeks. "Sweetheart, I know you're in pain, but I have to stop this bleeding or you won't make it. I need to put a tourniquet above your knee, but when I shut of the blood flow, you could lose your leg."

Sam looked into his eyes. "Do it."

Eric removed his belt and secured it around her leg. She winced in pain, "I'm sorry, but it has to be tight to stop the flow."

Eric felt a small hand on his shoulder. He turned to the face of a sniffling boy as he wiped the moisture from his eyes. "What about Tucker? Please Eric, don't let her die."

With his one free hand, Eric encircled his arm around the boy and pulled him to his chest. "Ronnie, I can't leave your mother, not till they get here."

Sam squeezed hard on Eric's arm to drive back the pain. "Eric, Tucker saved Ronnie's life. You have to get her to the vet."

"Not until they get here. I don't want to lose Tucker either, but I have to manage this tourniquet, I'm not going to lose you. Not now."

"Mrs. Cassidy, while we wait for the ambulance, you need to tell me how to get to the vet's office."

At that moment, a siren could be heard as it approached their location. "Ronnie, you have to be strong, Son. I need you to watch over your mom and grandmother. Can you do that?"

"But what about Tucker?"

"I will do everything I can to get your dog there in time, but I have to drive very fast, and I need you to take care of the family. Can you do that? Please, I need your help, Son."

"Yes, I will watch over them, but please take care of

Tucker."

"Mrs. Cassidy, go with Sam. I will come to the hospital once I take Ronnie's dog to the vet."

While the man from the ambulance moved around the dozer, Eric yelled, "She has a compound fracture, her artery has been nicked, and the tourniquet has been applied for six minutes."

As he hugged Ronnie, and kissed the woman he loved, moisture formed in Eric's eyes. "I love you guys." When he stood to leave, Eric told the EMT, "Please take care of my family."

He removed the dog from the van, placed her in his car, and looked one last time at the position of the dozer. "This was no damn accident."

Then he raced to the small town to try and save an important friend in the life of a young boy.

Eric rubbed the blond fur of the retriever. Her breathing had become shallow. "Seems like her breathing is distressed. Do you think she'll be okay, doctor?"

"I'm not sure, Mr. Emerson. Her size helps, and the fact that her leg was only hit by one fang cut down on the venom that was injected into her system, but it's been in her for quite a while."

"Will she lose her leg?"

"I'm not even sure whether she can recover, given the amount of time since the poison was injected. If she does live, there'll definitely be some residual muscle damage, likely a limp."

"This dog is very important to a young boy that just lost his grandfather. She has to survive. It doesn't matter what it costs. She took that bite trying to save the boy's life. A dog like that deserves to make it."

"I'll do what I can, but I would say she's got about a fifty-fifty chance."

"If this dog doesn't make it, you'll have to be the one that looks into Ronnie's small face and tells him his best friend is gone."

"We'll know more in twenty four hours."

"Ronnie wouldn't wait that long. I have to go to the hospital, but he'll want to see his pet in the morning."

"I'll stay here with her tonight. You can stop by in the morning, but she'll be sedated to keep her immobile."

"Thanks. How do I get to the hospital from here?"

"Go through the town. Half a mile past the police headquarters, you'll see it on the right."

When Eric entered the waiting room, he saw Ronnie tucked into the shoulder of his grandmother. The young boy looked up and immediately walked to Eric. He buried his red eyes into Eric's side, and then he glanced up. "Tucker?"

"She's resting at the vet's."

"Is she going to be okay?"

He looked down at the young boy struggling to understand the events of the night. Eric had always wanted to be a father, but this aspect of parenthood was unexpected. He had always believed in the truth, but what would that accomplish here.

Eric sat down in the closest chair so he could hold Ronnie's tiny shoulders. "I hope so. The doctor said we would know more in twenty four hours."

"I need to be with Tucker. She needs me. She doesn't have anybody there."

"She needs to rest. They gave her something to help her sleep so her body can heal itself. The doctor said we could visit her in the morning. Right now we need to be here for your mother, do you understand?"

The young boy hesitated, and then nodded.

Eric stood up and walked over to Sam's mother. "How is she?"

"She's in surgery. The doctor said he would come out and talk to us as soon as he could."

The woman rubbing her hands together was on the edge. Eric sat beside her and took her hand. "Mrs. Cassidy, I am so sorry for your loss. Your husband saved my life so many times. We lost a great man tonight, but you are not alone. The three of us will take care of you. I promise, we will be right there whenever you need us. I understand it's too soon, but when you've had time to adjust to this terrible loss, please come and be with us, as a family. At least think about it."

The elderly woman looked down and rubbed Eric's hands. They sat there mute for several minutes, before she looked up. "Why did this happen tonight?"

"Sam and I discovered certain things at work that people

didn't want anyone else to know. These people want to make sure what they did remain a secret, regardless of who gets hurt. The general and Tucker were merely collateral damage to them. All of our lives are irrelevant to these fiends. They think they're invulnerable, but they're wrong. I thought Sam and Ronnie would be safe here, but somehow they found out where we were. Mrs. Cassidy, do you and Ronnie have somewhere you can stay for a few days, I mean some place different from your house?"

"Max's brother has a place eight miles south of here. I'm positive we can stay there. Do you really think it's necessary?"

"Yes I do. Until I can level the battlefield, I have to be sure you and Ronnie are protected. Sam will be safe here. I'll take you back by your house in the morning after Ronnie visits Tucker so you can get some things. Then I'll follow you to your brother-in-law's. I should have this straightened out in a few days. Tomorrow evening I'm meeting with someone pivotal to what's going on."

The three people in the waiting area turned as a short husky doctor entered the room. "Mrs. Cassidy? I'm Doctor Feldman. Your daughter is resting peacefully. She lost a lot of blood, but fortunately at the crash site, someone made the right decision to risk her leg and save her life."

Eric rose and shook the man's hand. "I'm Sam's fiancé. Will she lose her leg?"

"We don't think so. The tourniquet was not on long enough to sustain major tissue loss, but there will be permanent damage. The impact splintered two inches of the bone in her lower leg. We had to remove a section and insert a small bar to fill the gap. We also had to repair the ligament in the knee. The tibia was pulled forward, rupturing the anterior cruciate ligament, often referred to as ACL."

"Will she be able to walk?"

"Yes, but there will be a pronounced limp, and she won't be doing any sprints. We won't know the full extent of the damage for six to nine months."

"Have you told her?"

"Not yet. She's still under anesthesia."

"Can we see her?"

"In a couple hours, but not for too long. She needs to rest. I have to go, but call me if you have any questions. With all she's been through, I think she's lucky to be here and still have both her legs."

As the doctor left, Eric turned to Sam's mother. "Instead of waiting around here, let's go back to your cabin and get what you need for a few days. We'll come back here afterwards and see Sam."

~ * ~

Eric was the first to enter Sam's room. As he approached her bed he scanned the metal frame that encased her leg. He bent down by her side, took her hand, and softly caressed her cheek.

Sam moaned, and slowly opened her eyes. A tiny smile creased her face. "Hello, handsome."

"Hey beautiful, how do you like the new leg? We're going to have to call you the bionic woman with all the metal they put in there."

"That should be fun at the airports. Still want to marry a one legged gimp?"

Eric smiled. "Let me get back to you on that."

"I'm glad you're okay, Mom." Ronnie moved around the left side of the bed and laid his head on Sam's shoulder.

Sam kissed her son on his head. "Is Tucker okay, did she make it?"

Eric looked down at Ronnie. "We'll know tomorrow. Personally, any dog that heroic is too tough not to make it."

"You have to take care of this. They can't harm our family ever again."

"I will Sam, I promise. Your mother and Ronnie will stay with your uncle till this is over. Mrs. Cassidy, I'll take Ronnie to see Tucker, then come back and follow you to your brother-in-law's. You can stay and talk to Sam. I'm sure you have a lot to discuss. Remember what I said, you'll never be alone. Sweetheart, I'll be back tomorrow. Try and stay out of trouble till I return. Come on Ronnie; let's go see that dog."

~ * ~

Ronnie stood next to the table and stroked the fur of his canine friend while she laid rigid on the gurney. "Tucker's going to be okay, right Eric? She's not going to die like Grandpa, is she?"

Eric felt an unfamiliar tautness in his chest when he saw the tears trickle down Ronnie's cheek. He removed his handkerchief, bent down on one knee, and gently cleaned Ronnie's face. He glanced at the veterinarian. "Doctor, you heard the boy. Will Tucker be okay?"

The doctor looked at the young boy, and then at Eric. "I hope so. She has a strong constitution and a lot of courage. Ronnie, we need to let her rest. She's sedated now, but her body is fighting hard to purge itself of the poison. I'm doing all I can, but it's really up to her. If she's still with us in twelve hours, I think she'll make it. That's the best we can do."

"Ronnie, we need to get back to the hospital. We appreciate your help, Doctor. Ronnie and his grandmother will be back tomorrow. I'll be out of town, but I'll check back when I return. Say good bye to Tucker."

The young boy hugged his dog, and as he moved toward the exit, he turned to the doctor. "Thank you for taking care of Tucker." As they walked to the car, Ronnie reached up and grasped Eric's hand.

"Son, I really believe Tucker will be all right."

"Me too Eric, I'm sure of it."

Forty Four

Eric stopped at Rudy's Diner thirty miles south of Senator Robertson's farm. He sat in one of the red leather booths that were positioned along the full wall of windows in the diner.

The young blonde waitress lifted the hinged counter top and raced to Eric's booth. "I've got him." The second waitress placed her hands on her hips, shook her head, and went back to washing the dishes in the sink.

"What can I get you today, Hon?" The blonde offered a suggestive smile.

"A cup of coffee, please."

"We also have homemade pie. We've won the contest for the best pies in the entire county for the last four years straight, see." The blonde pointed at the four framed gold ribbon awards entitled, *Best Pie in Page County*. "We make our own peach cobbler, apple, and blueberry pie. Are you sure you wouldn't like to try the blueberry, it's my favorite of all three."

"Thank you, but just the coffee for now."

Eric gazed out the window at the blue and gold metallic wind chimes that twisted and sang in the mild mountain breeze while he sipped his second cup of coffee. He was oblivious to the movement of the waitress as she floated around his booth. His attention was centered on the task that lay before him.

He had to make sure he played his cards right so as not to disclose what he did and did not know. He did not fully understand Senator Robertson's role in the Viper affair. He surmised that the senator had played some part in the corruption of the missile OPEVAL, but exactly what that role was remained uncertain. He was confident Colonel Clark was responsible for falsifying the test, along with his father.

But what if either Senator were involved, how could he make them accountable? That was the job of the IG office. If they were found culpable, and were not brought to justice, something else would need to be done. Eric did not want to consider the implications of that chain of events until it became absolutely necessary.

The question still remained: what would justify the actions over the past week that had been directed against Eric and his new family? The answer hovered just out of reach. He felt it deep inside, like a winter wind after being soaked to the skin, but the answer did not make sense. Could the contractor be so damn desperate that they would kill someone? Malfeasance is one thing, but murder? There must be something else. Perhaps the Osiris study was at the core of the attempt to silence Judi, Sam and himself, but why? What could they possibly be studying that would justify such criminally motivated activity? He just didn't get it.

Eric reviewed the events of last night, and what course he must take to resolve the menace threatening those he loved. The murderer had left his signature in his choice of methods, but only Eric recognized his mark. Who else would have removed the rattle from the viper to allow a silent entry into the Cassidy house?

He knew what he had to do, but as he pondered the nightmares and turmoil of his past, he shivered at the thought of opening the door again. He had cast out the demons haunting his soul each time he grappled with the moral paradox, but he saw no other option. There was no doubt, none, regarding who was responsible for the attempted threat against them last night. He was certain of the culprit that inflicted pain on his family, but no amount of proof could withstand the trickery of a defense attorney.

The courts would ignore the inevitability of what had occurred. They would allow the guilty one to go free and wreak havoc on his loved ones again, but that he would not allow, no manner what specters revisited his dreams.

A lanky man with a red cap and unshaved face momentarily distracted Eric. He had just entered the diner and stepped toward the cash register to pay for his fill up at the pumps outside. "Hey Bob, how in the hell can you double the price of gas in two weeks? I would expect such robbery in the big city, but not out here. Your friends won't forget this."

The overweight man behind the counter walked down to the cash register. "Tommy, I don't set the damn price, the oil company does. Haven't you heard the news? It's right there in the paper. One of the main pipelines sprung a leak and they had to shut it down. Until it's fixed, the price is expected to skyrocket."

The man with the cap wasn't open to any excuses. "That's bullshit and you know it. There's no way one pipeline could cause that kind of increase. It's the big oil companies screwing us again, and the government lets them get away with it. Those assholes in congress are in cahoots with them."

The heavy man at the cash register replied, "What the hell are you bitching at me for? I told you, I don't set the prices, they do."

The angry man ripped his cash up from the counter. "You're all a bunch of crooks, the hell with you." He stormed out the door.

Eric returned his attention to evaluating his current situation. The spoon scraped the side of the porcelain mug as he stirred the coffee again and again, his vision fixed on the sixty-year-old faded photograph behind the counter that depicted the original tin roof restaurant before it was refurbished into a modern diner.

The waitress mistook his stare. She removed a piece of blueberry pie from the canister and walked over to the handsome dark haired man seated alone at the booth.

The soft touch on his shoulder brought him out of his trance. He looked up at the shapely figure of the young blond female, and began to register the words directed toward him. "My uncle makes this pie fresh every night. You have to try it. Since you're new to our town, this piece is on us."

Eric began to decline, but decided that would be rude.
"I appreciate your kindness."

The waitress smiled as she traced a circle on the table with her slim fingers. "Is it okay if I sit down with you for a minute?"

"Uh, sure, go ahead."

The attractive female smiled. "What were you thinking about? You looked like you were slaying some evil dragon."

"Excuse me?"

"Just then when I came up, it seemed like you were somewhere else, with the weight of the world pressed down on those big shoulders."

Eric still had not picked up on the signals being transmitted by the young woman, in terms of her true intent for sitting at the stranger's table. "It's pretty rough. I'm not sure you really want to hear what I was thinking."

"Yes I do, please tell me."

Eric hesitated for a moment. He scanned the inquiring blue eyes seated across the table. He pondered how to convey something so complex and horrible with someone sheltered in this isolated community from the cruelty of real live. Perhaps there was a way to share his current struggle without being explicit. "All right then, here goes."

Eric placed his mug with the spoon at the center of the table. "I want you to focus on the spoon in my coffee. Think about someone close to you, someone you adore. Your whole life centers on that particular person. Do you have someone like that?"

"Sure, it would be my little sister."

"How old is she?"

"Sandy is sixteen."

"Imagine some terrible person reached out and threatened to harm Sandy, but he only told you, and no one else. What would you do?"

"I'd call the police and let them take care of it."

"In this case, that won't do you any good. The police can't do anything based on your accusation. It's your word against his. There's no recording, no confession, no proof of any kind, but you're convinced this person will do what he said. He doesn't care what's right or wrong. Your sister's life is irrelevant to him. He's not human, he's an animal and he intends to hurt your sister, unless you can stop him."

The waitress stopped looking at the spoon. With a distasteful expression, like biting into a lemon, she pushed the mug back toward Eric. "I don't like this game."

She started to get up, but he gently grasped her hand. "This is not a game. It takes place all the time. It happened to me. A molester from New Mexico who preyed on young girls destroyed my little sister because the courts let him back on the streets. After he had abused her, tortured her, raped her repeatedly, he strangled my little Robin with the turquoise lariat that he wore around his neck."

The waitress sat back down and stared at the dark haired stranger seated across from her. "I'm so sorry. What did they do to him?"

"Nothing. The judge declared that his rights had been violated. Without regard for what he had done in the past, the judge released the animal back into society to continue his reign of terror over our children."

Eric watched as the girl processed what he had said, before repeating the question, "I'll ask you again. Assume you are aware that some fiend is going to harm your sister and the legal system will do nothing to stop them."

Eric pulled the utensil out of the cup and positioned it half way on the edge of the tabletop. "Now look at the spoon."

The waitress did as requested.

"By tossing this spoon on the floor you will make that evil creature vanish, forever. He can never bother or harm your little sister again. Of course, the courts and bureaucrats will scream, 'Don't do it, it's not your job, he has rights,' but they won't do anything to protect your sister. They'll remain in their ivory towers pontificating the law. They'll hide in courts and ignore the threat they've allowed to roam freely among the innocent in our world."

Eric paused for a moment. "I'm sorry, what's your name?"

"April." She was locked in the parable, and intensely focused on the spoon teetering on the table's edge. The flirtatious smile had disappeared, replaced by taut cheeks as she folded her lower lip between her teeth.

"April, try to imagine that this is real, and not a game. Sandy's life depends on your decision here, today. If you toss that spoon, your sister is safe, and the predator who wished to devour her vanishes forever. There will be no legal foolery to allow him to harm her, and no one will ever know, except you."

"No one?"

"No one, only you."

"But what happens to him when he disappears?"

"Does it matter? He's an animal aimed at killing your sister."

"I need to understand what happens to him when I do it."

"Very well, he will be cast into hell and burn for eternity for the evil creature that he is and the terrible deeds he's done."

The waitress looked deep into Eric's blue eyes. She glanced back down at the spoon positioned at the very edge of the table. Her hand moved toward the spoon, and then she hesitated. Her hand drifted back and fought above the silver object that would determine the destiny of her sister. Finally, like a bolt of lightning darting through the night sky, the silver projectile arched slowly across the diner as a low guttural sound radiated from within the waitress' throat.

The spoon ricocheted off the counter and bounced into the glass cover of the cake canister. The sound cracked the silence in the diner. The few patrons in the small establishment turned in the direction of the commotion.

The waitress' face bore an expression of release and self-gratification at what she had just accomplished.

Eric smiled. He leaned back in the booth. "Exactly. That's what you should do. That's what I would do."

Eric removed a ten-dollar bill from his wallet and placed it on the table. "I'm grateful to you. You have helped me to resolve a personal dilemma I have been struggling with repeatedly in my life. I also appreciated the pie. It was indeed, the best blueberry pie I've ever tasted."

Eric pushed out of the booth and stood at the edge of the table. "I must leave for a meeting up the road, but I enjoyed our conversation. Good bye."

Michael W. Davis

Forty Five

Eric knocked on the door. After a few seconds, he heard a faint voice. "Come on in."

He opened the door and paused at the sight of the elderly man slumped in the wheelchair. He held out his hand and offered a reserved, but polite, greeting. "Good afternoon, Senator."

The senator shook Eric's hand weakly. "I'm glad we finally have this opportunity to meet. I have followed your accomplishments for some time. I appreciate you coming down to visit me in person. I felt we needed to talk face to face, and as you can see, it's become increasingly difficult for me to leave my sanctuary."

Eric knew the old man was waiting for a response. He wandered around the perimeter of the library. He reviewed the artwork, the elegant hand blown glass, and the variety of hand carved wooden figures of horses distributed around the room.

"Beautiful aren't they? My daughters have decorated my prison with TLC. I do love it in here, and I get such pleasure watching the wildlife come out and visit my pastures each morning and evening."

Again, without amity, Eric ignored the senator and continued to scan the room. After several seconds, he turned back to the man in the wheelchair. "Senator, when I called your aide to discuss certain concerns regarding various activities you are involved in, I was told you actually wanted to talk to me. Out of respect for the position, I'll let you go first. What is it that you want of me?"

"No pleasantries, right to the point. All right, but please call me John. Senator is too formal for two men that share so much in common."

"I don't know what you mean by that. Why did you call me here?"

"Answer something for me. I notice in your eyes that this meeting troubles you. Can you tell me why?"

"I don't like politicians. They're dishonest as shit and only care about maintaining their position of power, not for the people they were elected to represent."

"Boy, you are candid. I can see why you have raised so many eyebrows at the Pentagon lately. For myself, I actually find honesty refreshing. It's a rare commodity in today's world. I too have experienced your predisposition against many of my colleagues. I find their games and double talk tiring, but while in the playground you have to play by the same rules or no one includes you in their games. So let's agree not to bullshit one another, all right?"

Without cracking his austere expression, Eric said, "Fine, let's get to it."

"Please sit down over here. If not for yourself, take pity on an old man. This is killing my neck."

Eric complied and sat in the chair across from the senator.

"That's better. First, I see we need to establish some common grounds here. Otherwise, I doubt you will ever accept what I am about to share. I bet you weren't aware the two of us started our career both dependent upon the field of mathematics."

"Really? No, I was not aware of that."

"That's right. I wasn't always a politician. I started out as an economist. My specialty was macroeconomics and its role in world development. In the early days, I taught as a full professor in Charlottesville. Because of various papers I published in key journals, I began to be asked by various government organizations to consult on global trends. Over the years I worked for DOE, the Commerce Department, the CIA, and DOD. As I gained more notoriety, and more access to data dealing with the growth in global consumption of our natural resources, I noted a general pattern that disturbed me. As a species we are gluttonous. The human race has become oblivious to the true limits of resources available across the world. We operate as if there is no limit to the reservoir and the fact that it can run dry. Excuse me for a moment."

The senator picked up a glass of ice tea positioned in a holder built into his wheel chair. He drank the remaining fluid in the glass. "I get parched so quickly now. It's a side effect from the chemotherapy." The senator turned his chair toward the door and rattled the ice. "Rose, I need a refill."

The elderly man turned back to Eric with a grin. "My wife has her own blend of tea; it's the best I've ever tasted. She thinks that's why I married her. It was really her legs. They use to stop a young man's heart just to look at them. Would you like a glass of ice tea?"

"That would be nice Senator; lemon and sugar if you don't mind."

"Rose, bring a second glass, just like mine."

"Where were we?" the senator continued, "I remember. Do you recall a movie many years ago called *Soylent Green*? I think it was the last movie Edward G. Robinson made. Charlton Heston played the main character."

"Yes sir, I do. It was situated sometime in the future when the world had become so polluted that the food supply had dwindled to nothing."

"That's right. The movie had a profound impact on me. Probably because it resonated with my core belief that mankind has the potential to abuse the gifts bestowed on us by our maker. It was part of the reason I became so enamored with world growth patterns."

At that moment, a woman with white hair, and slightly bent posture came into the room. She handed the first glass of tea to Eric. "Here you go, tell me if you like it." She placed the second glass in the holder of the wheelchair. "You old crow, you must be downing a gallon an hour."

Both the senator and his wife looked at Eric and waited. Once he realized why they had focused their attention in his direction, he took a sip. "That really is good. I've never been into tea that much, but this could become addictive. Thank you ma'am."

"John, you're running off these skinny old legs of mine."

The senator smiled. "They still look mighty fine to me you cranky old woman."

"I know you're fibbing, but I still like to hear it anyway, you old charmer. Are you sure you'll be all right if I go play Mah Jong with the girls? I won't be back until after eleven."

"You've been landlocked in this house taking care of me every day for a month. It will do you good to go jaw with the old hens. I'll be fine."

"All right. I put your dinner in the refrigerator. All you have to do is place it in the microwave for four minutes. It was nice to meet you, son. Come back and have dinner with us next time. Bring your wife with you."

"I'm not married, but I'm working on it, thank you ma'am."

The two men watched as the woman left the room, and then they returned to their conversation. "Like I was saying, that movie left an impression on me. Out of curiosity, I had several graduate students create a first order back of the envelope model that correlated world resource consumption to trends in population, technology advances, and changes in our life style habits. We ran a ton of scenarios making various assumptions about world population, medical advances that extended life spans, petroleum dependencies, and a variety of related variables that influence the rate at which we use up our natural resources.

"And what did the models predict?"

"The results were alarming. In all but the most unrealistic assumptions about our habits, the world as a whole will consume itself to a slow death in the near horizon. What varied was the time required to screw ourselves into oblivion. Our very coarse model predicted that human civilization, as we currently know it, would cease to exist in seventy to ninety years."

The senator was beginning to earn Eric's attention. "Did you report your results to anyone?"

"You bet I did. I talked to economists at other institutions that had reached the same conclusions, but no one in the government gave credence to our findings. They claimed our data sources were faulty, or that our model did not account for non-linear effects, or our assumptions regarding technology advances were too restrictive. They came up with a dozen reasons to ignore us and wish away our results. They referred to our projections as the Chicken Little Scenario."

Eric was hooked. For many years, he'd sensed the world was blindly headed down a path that would eventually cause the demise of control and order. This was the first time anyone had actually tried to predict the point when all the lemmings would fall off the cliff.

"So what did you do?"

"The only thing I could. I got involved in politics. I figured if I got inside the decision making process myself, maybe I could actually affect a change. Frankly, I was very naive. No one wanted to deal with the issue. I guess they felt the slogan 'Change your habits or die' would never win any elections. They all suffered from the *next watch* syndrome, since it won't happen on their tour, the hell with it."

The senator paused for a drink of his tea, and then he continued, "I've never been one to give up easily, so I decided that I would use someone with more clout to conduct their own analysis. I needed an organization Congress could not ignore, and someone who had a record of leaking things to the media, like Langley. That way, Congress would have to respond when the report came out. The public would demand it."

Eric actually grinned. This smart old bastard had played two politically driven organizations against each other. He became aware that the tightness in his neck had disappeared. Ten minutes ago when he had entered the room, his muscles were coiled like a spring.

He actually started to admire the man seated across from him. As he looked into the tired eyes of this frail man in the wheelchair, Eric realized he had been wrong. The events of the past few weeks had caused him to create a false demon in the image of a seventy-four year old man that he now knew was not his adversary.

"So you set the two sides who had ignored the problem against each other. That's beautiful, absolutely brilliant."

"I would never admit to it, but that's a reasonable presumption." The senator returned the smile.

"Unfortunately, after Langley conducted their own analysis, no one could ignore the results any longer. They presented an absolutely catastrophic outcome. On our current course, the world will commit suicide in twenty years, plus or minus a decade. Most still feel that to be an extreme interpretation. They were fixed on projections made decades ago before two wild cards entered the equation.

First, no one envisioned China would begin to shift to a consumer driver society, and today they gobble up almost as much as we do. The second error in the old predictions was the assumption that people would change their habits, and that we would make leaps in internal combustion efficiencies, as well as major shifts to alternative energy sources. But we never did, at least not to the degree that it could make a significant difference in the time we have left."

"I'm actually familiar with the studies done over a decade ago. It was part of the research for my graduate thesis. Problem was, in the reports I read, no one offered any viable solutions."

"Before we can consider solutions to our dilemma, we need to discuss some real world facts. Currently we consume eighty million barrels a day to satisfy global appetites, and our production system is operating at between 96% to 99% of capacity. That's why little perturbations like a hurricane or one pipeline shutting down for maintenance has such an immediate and pronounced effect. We also understand that our ability to exploit new reserves and transform them into black gold is declining. Consider that fifty years ago we used four billion barrels per year and uncovered new supplies of thirty billion barrels. Today we demand thirty billion barrels per year and only come up with four billion each year in new sources."

The senator leaned forward in his chair. "I want you to consider the following scenario. Let's simplify the world and ignore the growth in pollutant levels, ignore the excessive demands being placed on our ground water, and forget about the depletion of critical metals. Those variables could be viewed as second order or delayed drivers. Just consider the marriage between our civilization and petroleum, and how critical it is to the success of our demanding society. To produce the massive amounts of food we need to feed our population, the farms are heavily dependent on oil for fertilizer, field operations, and agricultural distribution. Now imagine how the mega metropolitan areas across the world thrive.

Consider cities like New York, Baltimore, Los Angeles, DC, Paris, and London, as just a few examples of our high-density population centers. The fact is that in the US alone, over 80% of the population is clustered into large cities. These city dwellers survive by networks of five wheelers, titan ships, and hundred car trains flowing in and out to feed their massive appetites."

The abbreviation Sam had seen at the top of the PRES output, the variable they couldn't figure out. Now it made sense. The letters PTRLM represented the world supply and consumption of petroleum. "You've been analyzing global expenditures of oil, that's what the PRES model was used for, isn't it?"

The old man paused to take another drink of tea. "Like a queen ant being serviced by the rest of the colony, most of our industrial and agricultural machine is focused on supporting the voracious appetite and consumption of these population centroids. Imagine all the arteries that service these population centers shut down. There is no longer fuel to mass-produce food supplies or to distribute them into the population centers. Society, as we know it, will deteriorate into chaos. People who have lost all contact with self-sufficiency and dependency on nature will be on their own. Governments will disintegrate, riots will break out everywhere, there would be no time to redistribute to rural areas and learn to survive at a primitive level."

Eric leaned back in his chair. For many years, he had believed civilization was on a course toward self-annihilation, but not so soon. Not in his lifetime. "Are you saying…but I thought they were working on alternative energy sources."

"Our leadership still wants to paint this vision as some way out ravings by mad scientists, but it's a reality. Scientist have long projected the near term expenditure of our oil reserves, but our elected officials counter public fears by touting that, just over the horizon, there's some techno fix or bridge technology that can fill the gap and save us. The truth is that such innovations to solve our dilemma have not materialized. There are others that have pushed the *Caspian* myth that there is some mega oil reserve as yet untapped, but that too is just some self-fulfilling fantasy. Of course, there are the radical elements among us. They believe that the sheer greed of our capitalistic society will save us. They think that the ruling elite will not permit our lucrative economy, driven by its rampant attitudes for big cars and a greedy life style, to disintegrate."

"So when? How long do we have?"

"The real facts are that over half of our oil reserves have

already been extracted from our natural supply, and the remainder is becoming increasing difficult and costly to obtain. There are some who profess we could have better tackled the technology obstacles and resolved our dilemma if the petroleum industry had not thrown roadblocks up the entire way in order to maintain their stranglehold on the black cash cow. I happen to be one who accepts that theory, but knowing it still does not solve our approaching doom. As part of the Robertson report, I read a study that estimated we would move to the right of the supply bell curve next year.

Predictions are that the supply will taper off somewhere between 2012 and 2020. But the impact will not be felt in any gradual sense. Rather, it will be more like an immediate descent into a dark chasm. The shortage of the seventies and other perturbations, like hurricane Katrina, are nothing in comparison to what waits for us over the horizon. Back then, prices only doubled over a few months. We're talking about a total shutdown. There won't be any vehicles filled to capacity with goodies that march up to the food stores and large merchandizing outlets.

Law and order will quickly deteriorate, governments will falter, and currency will no longer be recognized as sound. People will roam the countryside looking for any means to survive. There will be looting, murder, and death on a massive scale as people begin to starve. Disease will spread across the large cities and no one will be able to stop it."

"I can't believe—There's got to be a way to stop it, before it's too late."

"Maybe in a hundred years, if we had developed cold fusion technology to support mass transportation and energy production, or some other revolutionary energy technology, we could survive at these consumption levels, but we will never make it. The reservoir will dry up way before we get there. That is of course, unless we do something drastic immediately. There's no time left to pass the problem to the next generation.

Given that we're stuck with the poor decisions and sins of our past, what the hell can we do? It's too late for a graceful solution. Any course of action that might have a chance at success will have to be draconian in its application. Are you with me so far?"

Now Eric understood. The Osiris report, what it was all

about, why the senator would commission such a study, the missing pieces to the puzzle that he and Sam had been searching for. He saw the answer, and the result caused goose bumps to run up his arms.

Forty Six

Eric now understood the purpose to the mysterious study only a handful of people were supposed to even know existed. The proposed solution to civilization's downfall still remained hidden. "I can see the implications of your argument, and I admit they are disturbing. That's where the Osiris Study came in. You're trying to derive an effective solution, a way to turn us around before it's too late."

"That's right. We used the name of an ancient Egyptian deity who represented life, death and rebirth. That's exactly what we're trying to accomplish, to bring back our civilization from the depth of the underworld before it's too late. But how do you solve such a broad behavioral problem? We can't create a miracle technology in twenty to thirty years. Nor can we change people's appetites for pleasure and the standards of life they've come to expect.

No one ever wants to make the sacrifice themselves, so what are our options? We are stuck with a moral dilemma. Do we step back and do nothing, and watch the world drift into oblivion, or do we make the most difficult and costly decision of our lives? Several on the board resigned, either out of fear if the truth came out, or because they lacked the backbone to make such a choice. They simply would not deal with the repercussions of such a decision."

Eric knew where the senator was headed. That undeniable conclusion of how, under these conditions, you can make an immediate impact to reduce resource consumption in developed countries. "My God. You're discussing a massive and rapid decrease in the world population. Not a sustained gradual reduction, but an immediate decrement over a few years."

"Exactly. The conclusion is inescapable, but it's the solution for achieving such an affect that's the real gut grabber. What means can be used to accomplish such a feat? We're talking massive quantities here. Not merely ten or twenty percent. That will not achieve the necessary impact. You have to think large numbers like fifty to sixty percent. Do you think people will voluntarily allow themselves to be designated as the unlucky ones? Hell no. The political and social implications of solving this dilemma are inconceivable, and that's why I asked for the study. We needed to evaluate our options for clandestinely realigning the world's population."

The senator paused and took a long breath. He watched Eric grapple with the significance and enormity of what he had just heard.

Eric started to perform a coarse analysis of his own. "To achieve those levels of population reduction, you would have to secretively cause a major catastrophe. It would have to be done covertly; otherwise there would be an uprising, people against people, against their government, and country against country. Lord, you're talking Armageddon. You couldn't do it by nuclear or chemical means. It would leave everything contaminated. That would counter your whole goal of saving the core of mankind."

Eric looked away for a moment and then back at the senator. "The only solution which would satisfy your restrictions and objectives would be biological."

The senator smiled. "The respect for your analytical reasoning abilities by your associates is not misplaced. You hit it exactly. We ran dozens of alternative solution strategies. We varied the technology we would employ to achieve the population realignment, as well as the severity of the course of action we would implement.

Like you, once we reviewed the results of the output from the PRES model, we rejected the nuclear and chemical options. It was clear the only viable solution was to depend on a biological vector. The question remained, just exactly how do we implement such a solution?"

"That's what Judi was working on. Clark must have tasked her to run the model without giving her an explanation of how the results would be used. When she found out the true intent of the study, she was devastated."

The senator removed his glasses. "I wasn't aware anyone on the team beside Clark knew the true nature of what they were being asked to do. The results were supposed to be generic. Only the Board was cleared for the truth. It's unfortunate the young lady had to deal with such a dark forecast of her future. So you already know the results?"

"No, just that she was using a system's dynamics model to evaluate alternative assumptions about population growth."

The old man rubbed his crooked fingers through his thin hair and replaced his glasses. "Using the model they developed, we evaluated four contingencies varying in terms of the severity of the tactics we would employ. Our options ranged from a zero action contingency, where we let nature take its course and blindly enjoy what years we have; and extended up to the extreme tactic whereby we would actively distribute biologic agents across the globe. I'm sure it would not surprise you that your friend Perry and his father opted for the Extreme Contingency."

"No, it doesn't surprise me at all."

"The board found the suggestion untenable and dangerous. We would end up with a repeat of the Nuremberg trials if in fact society did survive, because no one would ever admit we did the only thing that could be done. The Board elected to go with what we called the Medium Contingency to resolve our moral dilemma.

This course of action requires we wait for when a pandemic occurs, then allow it to take its natural path without the application of technology to thwart the extent of its damage. Such population adjustments have occurred in the past, in terms of actual global pandemic events. In the sixth, fourteenth and seventeenth centuries the black plague killed ninety percent of its victims. Consider the Spanish influenza of 1918 that affected thirty percent of the population and eventually killed over thirty million people."

"I'm familiar, Senator, with the pandemics of the past, but I wasn't aware there are potential diseases out there now that would achieve such major realignments. I mean, you hear the media trying to scare the hell out of everyone, but I always thought modern science would be able to minimize the impact so that you didn't get a repeat of the historical death tolls."

"Most in the political arena prefer to discount that there are actually natural agents out there today which can achieve the intent of the Medium Contingency. The reality is we have epidemics waiting to break out and repeat history, only with a greater death toll this time. In the field of epidemiology, we have known for several years that in the incubators of Africa and Asia, there are various diseases currently working their way up the chain who will eventually spread on a global basis during the next four to five years. These infective agents are so lethal that, without treatment, the mortality rate is extensive, possibly enough to help solve our problem.

Consider the hemorrhagic virus weaving its path through Africa. Hell, the strain that ran across Angola early in this decade had a mortality rate of roughly ninety five percent. Then there's the well-publicized avian flu where everyone is holding their breath. Many in the profession of fighting such afflictions think it is inevitable that it will become a global blanket of death. Right now the avian virus is only able to vector from fowl to humans. The fear is that the current strain will eventually mutate to a form that has human-to-human capability."

"I thought I read somewhere that they're working on an inoculation against the avian flu?"

"They are. The CDC was so concerned about such an event they actually engineered an avian strain for human-to-human transmission of the disease. They were able to take the H gene that allows the virus to penetrate the target cell, and engineer it with a key so it can unlock entry into a human cell. Then they altered the N gene so it could break free of the infected cell and spread the replicated viral elements throughout the lower more vulnerable regions of the lungs. By forcing nature's hand, we developed not only the vector that might initiate a pandemic, but also the counter agent that can be used to inoculate humans from the particular strain."

Eric saw the ugly reality, the only hope for mankind was to perpetuate a lie, and that was part of the plan. Even with a means to defeat the disease, it would never be used. "Sounds a bit ironic, doesn't it? Our government has the means to prevent the pandemic, but no intent to use it."

The senator confirmed Eric's supposition. "The problem is that if we interfere with the dark angel, we will prevent the very solution we seek. The Medium Contingency calls for our government to consciously amplify the effect of these agents, not by actively spreading the disease, but rather by not having sufficient counteragents except for a controlled set of the population. We can easily limit production and distribution through selective incompetence, but we haven't worked out yet how the selection will take place. That's a rather tricky problem."

Eric shook his head, started to speak, but failed to come up with the right words.

After a moment of silence, the senator continued, "I'm aware it sounds horrible to consciously allow millions to die. As a religious man, I pray the Lord will forgive us, but what choice do we have? If we permit things to continue as they are today, the loss will be even more extreme.

It will take several hundred years to recapture our technology-based edge, if we ever can. At least this way we will have time to readapt to new forms of technology. This is not for the old; we will be the ones that go first. It's to preserve the world for our children and grandchildren. It's a terrible thing, to stand by and watch millions die when you have the capacity to save them, but what choice do we have, other than to allow three thousand years of civilization to disappear."

Eric pondered the senator's plan, and then offered an observation. "But, even if the Osiris solution were successful, there would still be chaos and carnage across the globe. Pandemic events occur in waves. It would take years for the full impact to ripple around the world, and during that period the infrastructure of our society would falter. Law enforcement, military resources, distribution systems, medical services; with so many dying within each element, the fabric comprising our society would stall. Mayhem and disorder would still be rampant."

"Exactly Eric, but the duration and extent of the damage would have a less severe impact on the recovery of our civilization. To restore some semblance of a technology-based society after such a major pandemic event would probably take ten to fifteen years.

Without petroleum resources to fuel the recovery, it would require hundreds of years to regain a technology driven society, if ever."

Eric sat in silence. There was nothing to say. No resolution to offer. Eric didn't like it. He tried mentally to turn away from the course before them, but the inevitability of it kept coming back right in his path. The senator was right. There was no way out. Any other course of action Eric envisioned would eventually cause more pain and suffering than what the Board had selected.

When he came out of his momentary trance, he saw the senator's gaze locked on his face. He felt the old man was visually begging for a reprieve. It was as if he thought the young man could put forth some innovative new approach that was not as drastic or seemly inhuman. Eric noticed something else not there before. Or maybe it was and he had blocked himself from seeing it. The figure lounged in the wheel chair had become worn. The physical burden of fighting cancer and the mental torment of this decision had truly taken a toll on the 130-pound figure.

As he searched the wrinkled face of the fragile old man, he saw it. The inevitable similarity that they shared, the decisions that had haunted Eric for so many years, to choose between doing what is right, or doing what is socially acceptable. Deep within the spirit of the old man, he saw the same specters that plagued his own soul. That fed the terrible nightmares that hound you, rob you of any peace. Eric examined the stark comparison between his own history, and the monumental choice the Board had elected to implement. If you terminate someone who will cause pain and suffering, are you morally righteous or evil? If mankind were allowed to continue on their current path, there would be absolute pain and suffering.

Eric empathized with the extreme burden of the moral paradox the senator had confronted and conquered. He felt compassion for a man who could have ignored such responsibility and turned away, but instead accepted the imperative to make such a decision for mankind. No one would ever appreciate what the senator had done, nor would they listen to the reasoning and logic behind why he had made such an enormous and controversial choice. If made public, the entire Board would be lynched. The old man knew that, yet he wrestled his demons and cast personal risk aside.

Now Eric had to grapple with his current ethical dilemma.

He could blow the whistle, but what would that achieve? The problem would still be there, growing worse as each year passed until there was no solution left. Even the perception of these men as villains or heroes was uncertain. Were they to be viewed as evil for allowing so many to die by a conscious decision, or were their motives morally sound to try and extend the life span of civilization?

Eric looked at the planked wooden floor. Issues of right and wrong, pain and suffering; they buzzed in his skull like a swarm of bees. He leaned forward and placed his hands on his forehead as the memory leaped backed from his past. The choice to ignore social standards and protect those you love caused significant emotional turmoil; he had found that battle and won. But to allow millions to die so that civilization could survive...

Without a word, Eric shook his head. The question before him was beyond his spiritual and ethical plane to judge its compassion or sickness. Only divine judgment would know how to sort out the goodness or punishably of this decision. He raised his face, peered into the eyes of the old man, and sighed. He realized that his original feelings of hostility and dishonesty that he imposed against the senator had faded. Now he felt empathy for this man who'd tried so hard to do what he thought was right for a world he would soon leave.

Forty Seven

Eric released the air in his lungs and drew a fresh breath. "Senator, I understand everything you've shared. I'm not sure I have the guts to make such a decision, nor the willingness to meet God with this one on my slate. I will not expose your Osiris study, or your elected course of action. You have my word. I do respect you for your strength in trying to help mankind out of a pit you were not personally responsible for. I don't know if it is right or wrong. I can't give you the relief you are searching for, but I do admire your courage."

The old man's shoulders slumped and his eyes issued gratitude for the sympathetic words. He looked exhausted.

Eric regretted pushing into the last dark corner of the discussion, but he had to hear what he already surmised. "I'm sorry to ask this, but what happens if the anticipated effects of the Medium Contingency do not materialize? I mean, what if the natural biological agents do not cooperate and appear in the next few years?"

The senator took off his glasses and squeezed the bridge of his nose as if to press out the pain he was feeling. "You've already figured the answer to that, haven't you?"

Eric nodded. "If one were to accept the results of the Osiris analysis, you would have to escalate your actions to one of the more severe contingencies by actively disseminating a biologic agent."

The old man nodded to confirm Eric's conclusion. "The truth is, I don't think any leader in this country would ever pull the switch. They don't have the moral strength. We're not even sure on a collective basis that we could gain approval for the Medium Contingency, let alone something more severe. Most in the chain of command are old men that figure they can toss the dice for the next generation and ignore the problem since they will all be gone by the time the chaos occurs."

"John, I wish I could offer you some relief from your spiritual turmoil, and with the specters that will haunt your remaining days. This is the best I can do." Eric stuck out his hand and lightly grasped the wrinkled fingers of the senator, before adding, "You have my respect and admiration as a man of commitment and strength, though no one will ever understand or commend you for what you plan to do.

I also want to apologize for being curt and abrupt when I came in today. The last few weeks have been rough. I have witnessed a dedicated young woman severely injured, had someone try to kill me, and have seen the father of my fiancée murdered, all over what they feared I would do to expose either the Viper collusion, or the Osiris report. I mistakenly assigned responsibility for those acts to your hand, and I am truly sorry."

"Me? I've always been one of your strongest supporters. I was the one who had General Williams assign you to the Viper evaluation and suggested he find a position for you at the Pentagon. Why did you think I would do anything to harm you?"

"Lack of information," Eric admitted. "And a willingness to jump to conclusions."

"Do you have any idea who is responsible for trying to harm you?"

"I have a suspicion Perry Clark is involved, but I also believe his father played a role in the decision. What I'm not sure of is the culpability of the contractor in these retaliatory activities. Everything will come to a head shortly. I turned in a scathing report to the IG that exposes how the contractor falsified the Viper OPEVAL. There's no need to try and silence us anymore."

"Don't fret over Senator Clark. He has numerous skeletons in his past and I know where they are buried. I will make one call and no further actions will be taken."

"Thank you. I pray you will find peace shortly. Now I need to leave. You have graciously allocated enough time to me. Good luck to you, and good luck to all of us."

Eric leaned forward in his chair to stand, but the senator touched his arm. "Son, when I told you earlier that I had admired your career for many years, that was the truth, but it goes beyond respect for what you have done for this country. I know of your unique ability to accept impossible gut-wrenching missions and your moral strength to carry them to a successful conclusion, no matter how unpleasant the course may be."

The senator reached down under his wheelchair, removed a manila envelope, held it tightly in his hands, and stared at the object for several seconds. Then the true purpose to the senator's invitation to meet today leaped into Eric's soul. He felt a cold shudder ripple throughout his body as he peered into the horrible reality inside the envelope. Everything discussed over the past thirty minutes flashed through his mind, and lead Eric to the realization of why he was here, the role the senator had envisioned for him, all along.

Eric pushed back hard in his chair, until the joints in the wooden frame actually creaked. His typical taciturn expression had been replaced with disbelief at the responsibility that was about to be imposed on his soul. Although he already surmised the extreme consequence of continuing with the dialogue, he would listen. The ethical fabric of Eric's core values mandated that he consider the only salvation that society might have, through his hands.

Eric saw a pained and sorrowful expression edge across the senator's face. "Eric, as an Operations analyst, you understand that for a mission as important as referenced in the Osiris Study, there must be a contingency plan. You noted yourself it was unlikely our leadership will have the guts to do what they must do. Add to this the fact that I only have maybe six months to try and hammer the necessity of this action into their weak spirits, and you must see that it is imperative we have a *Hail Mary* backup plan."

With those words, the senator handed across the envelope. Eric gazed at the object, and then back into the expectant eyes of the old man in the wheelchair. Eric opened the envelope, unfolded the single sheet of paper, and read the hand written words scribbled onto the page. Once he finished, the senator took back the message, moved over to the fire, and tossed the only copy into the flames.

"No one else but you and I know what you just read. This

exchange is strictly between the two of us, and when I'm gone, there will be only you. Such absolute secrecy is essential if we are to guarantee that no retribution is ever waged against our country. The key in that envelope opens a refrigerated storage unit in my basement. Inside you will find what is needed should the medium contingency fail, along with instructions to help with its execution. I do not seek your answer to my request here. That is strictly between you and your maker. However, if I cannot achieve our goal, or I am taken from this world too soon, I place upon you the responsibility to struggle with the most difficult decision any one man has ever been asked to make.

It requires that you resolve a moral quandary beyond anything we on the Board have had to deal with. I'm sorry to place this weight on your shoulders, but I do not apologize for my selection of you as the reserve element to save our civilization. There is a terrible cost associated with this responsibility. You will have to make peace with your maker and yourself for eternity. But there is also a significant reward. Follow the instructions provided with the package and your family will survive the catastrophe."

Eric peered deep into the eyes of the old man. "Why me?"

"I needed an unknown independent maverick with an iron core. Someone immune to political forces or motivations, an element outside the bureaucracy who will surely delay the decision to the point where any corrective action is too late. The agent had to be familiar with life and death choices, like those made by our SpecOps resources during any deep penetration mission.

The person had to possess the analytical capability to understand that this course is the only hope for the survival of our civilization. Most importantly, it had to be someone who could compartmentalize the emotional and moral dimension of their spiritual existence. It had to be the rare individual who can see past the immediate suffering caused by their action, and see the true humanitarian nature of what they've done. Was I wrong? Do you disagree with my assessment?"

Eric gazed at the senator for a moment, and then at the envelope the old man held in his hands containing the key to Eric's unwanted destiny. Finally, Eric removed the extreme solution to the worlds pending disaster, and placed the key in his pocket. As he stood to depart, the elderly gentleman made one final request. "Would you help me onto the couch? I'm kind of tired and I'd like to take a nap before dinner."

"What do I need to do?"

The senator rolled the chair toward the couch. "Hold out your hands and let me pull against you."

Eric did as requested and as the senator was positioned comfortably, he asked, "By the way, what time is it? I don't keep any clocks in here." He looked at his watch and noted it was just past six. "It's seven thirty. If there's nothing else, I need to get back to my family. It's a long drive."

"Our talk today actually brought some relief for me. Thank you, and goodbye."

Eric took one last look at the senator and his sanctuary, before excusing himself and headed back to do what needed to be done.

Forty Eight

The young girl watched as her partner worked hard to earn their pay for the night. She pretended to participate, but her attention was diverted to the expensive furniture and accessories scattered around the room. *Come on, get it over with it. You're taking so long.*

Perry moaned. The older woman rose up from her knees. "Are you done?"

Without looking at her face, Perry reached for his wallet and tossed several large bills onto the bed. "I'm done, you can leave now."

He reached for the iceless drink on the end table and tossed it down. He poured an inch of scotch from the pint container, raised it to his lips, and the bronze liquid disappeared in one swallow. Then he wiped his forearm across his mouth.

The older woman tried to reach out and touch the heart of the cold man. She smiled. "Is there one left in there for me?"

Perry stared at the middle-aged woman and her female partner for several seconds. Without any facial gesture, he picked up the pint and lobbed it at the woman sitting naked on the bed. Then he walked to the closet, removed a robe, and disappeared into the bathroom without a word.

The two women could hear the shower running in the next room. "Okay Tammy, I think he's done with us for the night. Put your clothes on and let's get out of here. I want to get home so I can take a bath and wash another night away."

She picked up the clothes she had discarded around the room

when they had first arrived. The younger girl, being more energetic, and having only disrobed from her waist down, was ready first. She strolled around the large area as she inspected each artifact and knick-knack distributed across the room.

The petite young girl peered into the empty aquarium on the dresser. "I wonder what he keeps in here." Then she moved out on the balcony to wait for her partner.

The breeze came up from the cavernous valley below the terrace. It swirled around the naive face of the girl causing her long blonde hair to obstruct her vision. She removed a scrunchy from the pocket of her tight faded jeans, gathered together her swirling hair, and formed it into a ponytail.

The girl looked between the two mountains and gazed at the glow of lights below the horizon four miles away. The pattern of the streetlights declared the existence of a town in the shadow of the large mountains on each side.

The young female turned to greet the second woman as she stuck her head through the doorway. "Come on Tammy. We've been paid. We need to get out of here before he comes out."

Without acknowledging the request from her partner, the young girl continued to scan the vista. "Doesn't he have a beautiful view out here? Look at what a steep drop off there is below this balcony. It's almost straight down."

The other woman stepped onto the platform and moved over to the railing. She inhaled the crisp fresh air and agreed. "Yes, it is a beautiful view up on the edge of this rise."

The girl folded her arms around her exposed shoulders. "Boy, it would be so nice to live here, to be able to get up each morning and watch the sun peer over that ridge. I miss that a lot. I used to get up early every morning before I had to do my chores, so I could see the sun rise above our mountain back home. I would listen to the animals in the woods as the world came alive for the day."

"This guy doesn't own the house. His dad does. Senator Clark uses it as a vacation home. I bet he's only here two or three times a year. The senator gave his son a key, and the sun comes up and uses it whenever he wants."

"A senator, that's impressive. Has he ever been your client?"

The older woman scanned the bedroom to make sure it was

still empty. "Yes, I've worked for him before, but he's worse than the son."

"You mean because he's so old?"

"Hon, who cares about their age? You're confusing the job with emotions again. The son is cold, like an iceberg, but his father is cruel. Frankly, they both give me the willies, but at least they're safe, and they pay well for our discretion."

"That's too bad. This sure is a pretty place. I really like it out here. It reminds me so much of where I came from in Tennessee."

"The place is definitely isolated. There's no one around to bother you for miles. I've been here in the winter with the senator when snow blankets the mountainside. Now that is really something to see."

The young girl took a deep breath and leaned out over the rail. "We sure are lucky, aren't we?"

With a confused expression, the older woman looked over at her partner. "How do you figure we're lucky?"

"Back home, I would never get to be in a house like this. It's wonderful, and the money is unbelievable. I would have to clean tables for a month to make what we did in one night. Don't you think we're lucky to have all this?"

As Sharon scanned the smile on the inexperienced, but jubilant young face, she recalled when her view of the world, of life, of this profession, was different. Now she understood completely what she had thrown away, so long ago. All these years alone, she had been with so many men, but still she was all alone. She knew that regular people would classify her career as many things, but no one would consider her profession to be a fortunate choice.

"What kind of life do you think I have? I'm thirty-eight. In a few years, no john will want me. Then what will I do? How will I take care of myself? I have no one permanent in my life. No husband, no children. Even my parents won't acknowledge I still exist in their world."

Sharon pointed to the scar running down her neck. "See this." She pointed above her eye. "And this. It's part of the trade. They're souvenirs from the tricks who took out their hatred for women on me. And most girls like us have experienced far worse. It doesn't matter that what they did was wrong and hurtful. Only other angels of the night care about our welfare. No one else gives a damn about us, whether we live or die, except our clients, when they need a release. After that, we're just shadows no one wants to acknowledge exist in their world."

The young girl was taken aback by the bluntness of the woman that had been her role model for the past year.

"Tammy, you have to realize what you've done, how this last year has cast a cloud that will affect you for the rest of your life. Do you need proof? Go into a restaurant or grocery store and introduce yourself as a prostitute. How do you think the people will greet you, with a smile and a handshake? No, they'll back off like you have the plague, especially the women. I've never figured that out. Do you think any of them would be proud to call you their friend? Do you think they would label you a lucky whore? Hon, I'm not trying to be mean, but you need to wake up to the realities of the vocation you've chosen."

Sharon turned toward the distant lights. Her voice turned soft. "Do you think I will ever have a real man, one that will want me for who I am, not what I can do for him for the moment? I mean, someone who will greet the years with me reminiscing about our lives and memories together. Someone who will look at my aging face with tenderness not disgust. Do you think I'll ever have children to love me, respect me, and take care of me when I'm old? While other women celebrate Christmas with their family, I'm turning tricks for some dude who thinks I'm trash. Every john over the past twenty years has taken a small piece of my soul. I get depressed each time I have to put makeup on and look at this face no one really cares for anymore.

Tammy, for God's sake, is that what you envisioned for yourself when you ran away from home? Sweetheart, you're repeating the same mistakes I made twenty years ago. And in a few years, like me, you'll be locked in, with no way out."

The smile that had filled the young girl's face a few minutes earlier vanished. She looked at the poignant expression on her friend, and saw herself, not to far into the distant future, if she stayed on her current course.

"You're still young. You have a chance to get out before it's too late. You've only been turning tricks for a very short time. Take what you've saved and get as far away from here as possible. Never tell anyone what you've done. Find a young man who will hold you each night, the same man. Someone who will caress your soft skin, look into that pretty young face, and see the angel you are inside, not the whore you're trying to become. And have kids, Tammy, lots of kids before it's too late."

At that moment, Perry stepped into the patio doorframe. "I thought you two were gone."

"We just wanted to make sure you were done with us for the night."

"I said I was done. It's time for you to leave."

The two women stepped back into the bedroom, picked up their coats and walked toward the front of the house. As the older woman sauntered out the front door, she turned and offered, "Call anytime. We enjoyed the drive, and would be glad to see you again."

As Sharon slipped into the driver seat she motioned toward the garage, "You left your garage door open."

When she turned to back out of the driveway she shook her head. "He's a cold hard man, but at least he's safe." After a few minutes of silence on the secluded road, Sharon turned to her friend and asked, "You're awfully quiet over there. You were beaming ten minutes ago. What are you so deep in thought about?"

"I've really enjoyed our time together. You've taught me many things I could never have imagined back home. Please don't get upset or hurt, but I've decided this way of life is not for me anymore. Tonight was my last time. I'm going home. I miss my family."

"If that's what you think is best. I'll miss your perky face, but you have to do what's best for you, Hon."

Perry opened the door in the house that entered into the garage. He flipped the switch, and the garage door came down. He walked back into the bedroom, removed his robe and flopped into the bed. He listened to the mild wind sing as it pushed its way through the pine trees that lined the hillside. Just as he began to doze off, he was startled by a muffled noise in the garage. He opened his eyes and waited. When he heard it again, Perry murmured to the invader, "I knew you'd come. I've got you this time you son of a bitch."

He reached into the night table and withdrew a 44-magnum revolver. He moved quietly to the garage door and turned off the hallway light. He turned the doorknob very slowly until he could open the door into the garage. He stepped into the room with the intruder, and closed the door behind him. The silence in the large house was shattered by the massive repercussion of the large caliber pistol. Then a second shot reverberated into the house.

Perry turned on the garage light and looked down at his victim. Then he kicked the body lying on the concrete floor. "You won't ever do that again will you, you bastard."

He bent down, picked up his victim by its ringed tail, and surveyed the trash tossed around the refuge container. In the buff, Perry opened the garage door and walked around the side of the house to the edge of the cliff. He swung the carcass of the raccoon twice and tossed the dead creature down the ravine into the darkness. "Enjoy the fall you damn pest!"

He walked back into the garage, closed the door, and when he reentered the house, he declared with pride, "Now maybe I can get some sleep."

As he dropped on the bed on his stomach, he turned his head toward the balcony and watched the curtains at the open doorway wave in the breeze. While the clouds edged across the full moon, Perry slowly drifted into slumber.

In his sleep, he fell into a deep pool. It was dark and he couldn't see who had pushed him into the water. Each time he tried to come up for air, a hand forced him back down. He struggled to penetrate the surface, but the figure would not let him breathe. He could see the silhouette that belonged to the hand, but not the face. He began to drown, in the dark, with no one else around to save him, or to grieve his death.

Perry awoke from his nightmare to the taste of latex. Something pushed hard down on his back. He could not move. He struggled, but the harder he fought, the more violent his assault became. Perry could not break free from the weight pushing his head deep into the covers while it pressed the air from his lungs.

He heard breathing, hard deep breathing. As he was jerked up and down, there were no words, no voice, but he sensed the fury of the one who controlled his destiny.

He was terrified, a fear like he had never felt before. His heart pounded. He heard it throb in his chest, his neck. He felt panic as he gasped for air. He was lost. There was nothing he could do. He just lay there, frightened, quivering, as he waited for whatever came next.

He felt someone's breath in his ear; the harsh words whispered slowly, deliberately, in a deep voice, "I know who you killed, you selfish bastard. I know who you raped. In these last moments of your life, I want you to think about all the pain you've caused. I want it all to swirl around in that evil mind of yours as I send you through the gates of hell. I suggest you beg your maker to forgive you for the terrible things you've done. As for me, don't squander your last breath. You're a waste of skin, and I'll never quarter you one ounce of absolution. Prepare for your descent into the pit of eternal damnation, you prick."

At that moment Perry heard a slight cracking sound. He felt a sharp intense pain fire down his spine just before his vision faded. There was a slight rush of air as the last breath exited his body. Then he was gone, forever.

The figure towered over his victim, and for a moment, he surveyed what he had done. The heavy breathing diminished as the pent up rage subsided. The shadow lifted the limp body from the bed. Like a rag doll, he threw the corpse over his shoulder and carried it toward the balcony.

Two arms lifted the last remains of the colonel above the rail. Something howled, like a furious beast that broadcast its victory and retribution to the world. The corpse arced through the air as it hurdled into the void. The silhouette on the platform watched the body tumble down the sharp ravine, and disappear, consumed by the dark. After several moments, the landscape became peaceful again, and the shadow vanished back into the night.

Forty Nine

The doctor helped Sam up from the edge of the bed and into the chair. "Ms. Cassidy, you'll have to ride in the wheelchair till you're out of the hospital. Use the crutches to get in and out of your vehicle. Try to stay off your feet for at least four weeks. It will take that long for the bone to begin to bond around the metal pins we inserted."

"Will I be able to do all the things that I used to do?"

With a smirk, the doctor replied, "That depends on what you used to do."

"You know what I mean. Will there be a total recovery, or will I have some residual loss from the accident?"

"You'll always have a limp Ms. Cassidy, but we were able to restore the anatomical integrity of your knee. You need to gradually start the exercises that are illustrated in the pamphlet we gave you, and eventually expand to the advanced ones with your physical therapist. If you have any problems, ask your therapist to help with the exercises. In two to three months you should be able to walk around without the crutches. If you have any questions, please feel free to call me."

At that moment, Eric burst into the room, slightly out of breath. "I bet you thought I forgot you."

"Yes, I did. Where have you been? Where are Mom and Ronnie?"

"They're fixing a cake and decorations for your welcome home party, so you have to act surprised. They've put a lot of effort into everything, so don't give it away and get me in trouble."

"Fine, but why are you so late?"

"I'm sorry I was late. I'll make sure it never happens again. I had some minor car problems last night on the return trip from my meeting with Senator Robertson. I didn't have a flashlight in the vehicle so I had to walk four miles until I found someone to loan me one."

Eric pulled out a bundle of flowers from behind his back. "Am I forgiven?"

Sam smelled the roses, and then she looked up with a grin. "Yes, you are."

He bent down toward Sam and turned his head sideways. "No kiss?"

Sam reached up and turned Eric's face toward her. Then she moved toward him slowly and caressed his mouth with a juicy penetrating kiss.

"Damn. Guess I'll have to be late more often."

"I'm afraid not, Mr. Emerson. You're never supposed to keep a woman waiting. I'm the only one permitted to be tardy in this relationship, understand?"

Eric moved behind the wheelchair. "Yes ma'am."

While he pushed her toward the car he informed his fiancé, "Don't get used to being pampered like this. In a few months, your butt's going to help Ronnie and me get your mom's house ready to put on the market."

"The market, they've only had the house a few months. What's going on?"

We'll talk about that later. For the moment, enjoy being treated like a queen."

"I think I will."

When they pulled out of the hospital parking lot, the announcer on the radio was discussing the news. *"On the Washington front, Colonel Perry Clark, the son of Senator Clark, was found dead at his father's cabin near Winchester, Virginia. A preliminary investigation is underway, but initial results do not indicate foul play. Apparently, the colonel had been drinking heavily and fell to his death from the balcony. We'll keep you up to date on any further developments."*

"Before she realized it, Sam blurted out, "He's dead. He's finally dead." After a moment, she turned toward Eric. "How do you feel about that? I mean about the colonel being gone."

"The world has been purged of an evil person. No one will shed a tear for the loss of that asshole, especially not me."

Sam reached over and turned off the radio and sat silently for several minutes. Finally, Eric tapped her leg. "You still alive over there? That pin they put in your knee, they didn't staple your vocal chords by mistake, did they? I couldn't stand that. I depend on you to fill the air between us."

"I'm fine. I was just considering how I felt about the colonel dying. I think you're right, no one will lament the passing of this particular person, and that's sad."

"Are you saying you'll mourn the loss of this scum?"

"No, that's not what I said, but the fact that so many will not mourn his passing, that's sad. Personally, in this case, I agreed with your typically stark perspective. Clark was bad, by his own choice. Whatever turned him down a path to cause so much pain to others, to lose all compassion and remorse for the people he affected, was unfortunate, but it was his choice. Nothing justified the suffering he inflicted; all the terrible dreams and sleepless nights he caused. No, I'm glad he's gone. Perhaps there are people out there he's hurt that will sleep better, now that he's gone forever."

"And you always accuse me of exhibiting such a dark side to my personality."

"Maybe I do, but in this case, it's justified."

Sam remained quiet.

Eric pinched her ear. "Hello in there. Are you with me or what?"

Sam rubbed Eric's leg. "Sorry, I was thinking about something. Why don't you tell me about your meeting yesterday with Senator Robertson?"

"We had the old guy all wrong, Sam. He wasn't responsible for any of the things that we've been through recently."

"Did he discuss the Osiris study? Was it as bad as we thought?"

At first, Eric considered that maybe he should refrain from the total truth to protect her from the bitter reality of what was in store for all of them. When he scanned the trusting face on the woman he loved, it was clear she deserved to know everything; no matter how hard the truth might be to accept, but he had to release the reality of their situation gradually, so she could adjust.

"The senator explained what they intend to do, and why. We were correct regarding a lot of it. The objective of the study was to analyze the state of the world's consumption of natural resources, but it's worse than we originally imagined, far worse. We're running out much faster than any of us have been told.

Just over the horizon, when supplies are exhausted, our civilization will disintegrate. Everything we depend upon, our society, the way we live, it will all disappear. Our day-to-day existence will change drastically. Survival will become our primary concern. The prognosis is bad, really bad."

"Can't they do something? Aren't they going to try and fix it?"

"They plan to try, but even the solution is pretty rough. That's what the study is all about, but the breakdown of our culture, our humanity, I believe it's destined for our future. I don't think anyone in the government has the guts to do the right thing."

"So this is real. It's not some wild scientific theory. It's really going to happen to us, in our lifetime?"

"It's our fate, Sam. All these years the governments across the world have stuck their collective heads in the sand, and ignored the problem, and it will happen. In seven to fifteen years, it's just a question of when. I always knew we were headed down this path. I just didn't think that we would see it in our lifetime, maybe the next generation, but not us."

Sam chewed on her lip as his words hit home. She turned to Eric and asked the only possible question. "What do we do?"

"We survive. By adapting the way we live, our family will survive."

"But how?"

"We have to be prepared to live in a whole new world with a totally different set of rules. Sam, you're going to have to change, to be willing to protect your family on your own, with help from no one in the government. Most in our society will be incapable of doing what is necessary, and they will perish.

When it starts, in the beginning, almost everyone will become our enemy. Neighbors, friends, the man at the store, they all will be forced to struggle, to scratch, to defend, like we will. They must adjust to a new set of principles, and they won't be ready. They're not prepared to deal with the moral contradictions they'll face. They won't be able to make the right choices. They'll still be fixed on the old ways, doing what is socially acceptable, not what is right, for them and their family.

Those that cannot adapt to the new moral standard will not survive. But the evil elements in our society that have no morality, they will already be prepared to wreak havoc. They now wait in the shadows weaving hate and pain along the edges of the legal system. The scum allowed to roam freely today will no longer be restrained by boundaries that control their primal urges, and they will thrive among the carnage as our world falls apart."

"What are you trying to say, that we can't trust anybody? What about the government?"

"The government won't exist anymore. Once the fuel is gone, food can't be delivered, people will start to starve, there will be riots, and law enforcement will collapse. The cities will become war zones, and who around us can we depend on, our neighbors, our friends? They will be struggling to live; everyone will exist on the edge. For those who survive, their attitudes toward anyone with food or supplies will change. No, Sam. We cannot depend on anyone anymore, except each other."

The words echoed deep inside her mind, and Sam was afraid, like when you peek under the bed in the dark, only this time there was a monster in the form of her uncertain future. It clawed at her instincts that there would always be tomorrow. A chill crept up her back and Sam shivered. Her confidence in the security of her world began to crumble.

"I'm not ready for that. Things can't become that bad. They won't let it."

Eric knew it would take time for her to overcome the initial shock. Anyone would resist the finality and inevitability of such a radically different existence. She would come to accept their only recourse, at her own pace. He would help her all he could, but she had to meet their new life on her own terms.

Sam sat silently, her face in her hands, until she felt an arm slowly ease around her shoulders. She looked up to see a new expression on Eric's face; one she had never encountered before, empathy.

"There has to be something they can do, some solution that can turn things around, before it's too late."

Eric felt she was ready. "Listen to me for a minute. Sometimes people are faced with very difficult and confounding decisions. Dramatic events occur in their lives where they have to make a terrible choice between doing something that is logically just and right, or doing nothing and letting others suffer.

We've talked before about the moral dilemma of stopping a killer or sex offender so that they never hurt anyone again. The judgment, whether to terminate a person that is evil, or to turn away, that choice is on a personal level, but what about when you're left to make the ultimate decision for the innocent.

Consider someone that witnesses a sixty-year old man and a newborn infant caught in a burning house, but they only have time to save one. What about the reported incidences when ships go down and there is only enough space on the lifeboat for a small fraction to survive? Stretch this quandary to a level a billion times greater in terms of the loss of human life.

Do you really thing anyone in our government has the strength and courage to select the only solution possible to save a semblance of civilization as we know it? Even with the means at their disposal, do you thing they have the balls to resolve such a moral paradox? No Sam, we're stuck with the path predicated by the gluttony and blindness of our society. We don't like it, we didn't cause it personally, but we're been dealt a hand and we have to play it out, no matter how much it hurts.

Our only hope is that a small group of men will have the fortitude to make the right choice, not the easy one. If they do, we can slow the rush to self destruction, but I don't hold out much hope that they will be able to collectively push the Osiris solution to its necessary conclusion."

Eric watched Sam's face. He saw her struggle with the undeniable truth. No matter what they did, it would come, and they must confront it together. It was obvious she didn't like it, that it scared the hell out of her, but he knew she would have to accept it. She would have to be strong, and change her philosophies of right and wrong, for her family.

Sam looked over at Eric, "So where do we begin?"

Eric could see she was ready. "Over the next few years, we have to prepare for what's coming, and there's a lot of work for us to do together. Now that I've shared the downside, let me offer some hope. When my father passed away eight years ago, I inherited a 640-acre parcel of land near Brevard, North Carolina, outside of Ashville. Two years ago, I sold roughly four hundred acres to a lumber company. The bottom-line is that we will have plenty of money to get ready, to establish the capacity for self-sufficiency. I know what needs to be done to survive. Everything will be ready when it gets here. That's why we need to sell your parent's house and move to our farm as soon as possible. Your tour ends in five months. At that time I'll resign and all of us will prepare for our new life together. How does that sound?"

Sam smiled. "I want to see operational, tactical, and strategic plans on paper before I approve anything."

"Yes ma'am, now let's go tell everyone about their new adventure." Eric decided to withhold the ultimate truth regarding the destiny of the Osiris solution. He knew that, no matter how strong their bond, to share such information could condemn their love forever, and levy a burden of knowledge so great that it would crush Sam's tender spirit. As with every covert mission he had performed in the past for the survival of his country, only he would know the course of action that he decided to execute.

When Eric wheeled Sam up the walk, the door opened and the first one out was a hobbling dog. The golden retriever with the bandaged front leg limped into Sam's lap. She rubbed the dog's head and with a smile stated, "Tucker, you're all right."

Ronnie and Sam's mother joined the hug fest. Eric pushed the chair into the house as Sam and her mother chatted over a dozen topics.

He shook his head and grinned, *Two women in the house, one in a wheel chair, a gimpy dog, and a nine year old tornado; man, is my life about to become really complicated, but I wouldn't have it any other way.*

Fifty

Ruth grabbed her grandson by the hand, "Okay young man, go get your coat. Tonight is all for you. We'll start with miniature golf, then we'll get you a hamburger, and we'll wrap it up with some ice cream."

"Wow, all my favorites, why am I so lucky tonight, Grandma?"

Ruth smiled. "The newlyweds deserve some quiet time all to themselves. Would you like a little sister?"

"I'll have to think about that. Can Tucker come with us?"

"Sure she can, let's really make it a special night for your parents."

Sam grinned. "I appreciate it, Mom."

"I was young once, a long time ago. Besides, I'd like another grandchild while I'm still alive. Maybe a girl this time. Do you think that's possible?"

"I'll see what I can do."

"Why the frown, Sam? I'd expect you to be ecstatic after all this time."

Sam looked down at the metal brace that enveloped her leg. "I sort of envisioned our first night together to be a bit less encumbered."

"Sweetheart, do you really think Eric cares about that? At least you're out of the wheelchair, now that would be a challenge. I guarantee that once things get started; you won't even notice that little inconvenience. I remember when your dad fell off that ladder and broke his leg. The cast never stopped us. He was a fireball, and I wasn't bad either. It was right after you were born and..."

"Stop right there. That's way more information than I ever wanted to hear about you and Dad. Now you guys get out of here so I can prepare myself before Eric gets back from the real estate office."

Ronnie headed for the door. "Hey Mom, are you sure you don't want to come with us? Grandma says she's going to get some ice cream."

"Tonight you get to hoard all the ice cream for yourself, so enjoy it."

"Don't you think Eric might want to come with us?"

Sam smiled at her mother, before she replied to her son. "I think tonight he'll have something other than burgers and ice cream on his mind."

"I don't know what could be better than that, but suit yourself."

Sam's mother opened the front door and shook her keys. "Come on Ronnie, I'm headed out the door."

When Ronnie reached the door, he looked back at his dog slowly limping toward him. He yelled outside, "Grandma, Tucker can't move that fast, please wait for us." He hurried back to assist his friend and encouraged the struggling pet, "Come on, Tucker. You'll get a hamburger too but you have to hurry before she leaves us."

Sam watched as her son pushed his dog from behind. Then she closed the door and went back into the living room to prepare for her husband's return. As she passed the kitchen counter, she paused by the newspaper with the headline: "Senator Robertson dies of cancer."

Sam folded the newspaper and tucked it away in the magazine holder at the end of the couch. No sense complicating Eric's thoughts tonight. She wanted him focused on the events she had planned for the evening. She would tell him about the senator in the morning.

~ * ~

The front door opened as Eric stepped into the house. "Hey Sweetheart, I'm back with dinner. Where is everybody?"

Crutches and all, Sam moved toward the entry of the

bedroom. She leaned against the frame. "I've got a different treat planned for you over here."

She attempted to project an enticing image as she propped herself up by two crutches. She saw Eric turn toward her and focus, not her precarious balancing act, but on what was being offered beyond the vapor thin veil of nylon. He scanned the candles and wine next to the fireplace, and finally looked back to his wife as she hobbled her way toward the couch.

"I had imagined our first night together to be a bit more seductive and without all this hardware," Sam said, "but I promise it will be different than before."

At first, she was anxious that the crutches and metal frame bracing her leg would be too much of a distraction, and quench the appeal she might have in the eyes of her husband. But when she looked at Eric's midsection she smiled.

Eric glanced down. "Sorry. It's difficult to hide isn't it? It has been a long time."

He pointed at the fire and candles. "I guess you figure to get lucky tonight, don't you, Mrs. Emerson?"

"I was counting on it, but with these crutches, looks like you'll be doing most of the work.

"I'm up for it, so to speak."

Eric helped ease his wife down gently off the crutches onto the floor next to the couch. "I'm impressed. What else can you do with those beautiful legs; anything I'd be interested in?"

"It won't be the best you ever get, but I think you'll still enjoy it."

After a few minutes of light foreplay, Sam stopped. She leaned up on her elbows. "I have to tell you something. It's really important."

"Now? You have to tell me now? Can't it wait until later?"

"No, it can't wait. I need to share this with you first."

"Sam, you're driving me nuts here."

"I need to tell you about Ronnie. You have to know who his father is…was, and how it happened."

"You don't have to tell me anything."

"I have to get this out. There can be no secrets between us."

"I already know, so let's get back to where we were."

Eric attempted to pull her toward him, but she pushed away. "How could you possibly know? I never even told my parents."

Eric grinned, and continued to try and nibble on Sam's ear. "You forget; both of us are operations analysts. We see events and predict how they came about. I see all and know all."

"Stop it, I'm serious. I want to hear how you could possibly understand what happened to me ten years ago."

He took a deep breath, and sat up on the couch. "You think I'm a light switch don't you? Up, down, up, down. You're killing me here."

Based on the expression on Sam's face, and her folded arms, Eric could see that his current goal was dead until the issue of his insight was clarified. "All right Sam, but you owe me on this one. You'll remember that I was there the night we turned in the optimization model for our class project.

The four of us on the team went for a drink afterwards to unwind. I didn't stay with you because I had been away from the apartment so much studying that I wanted to get home to be with my wife. I figured you could take care of yourself. Guess I was wrong.

The next day in class, your whole demeanor morphed. You were no longer Miss Sunshine, and you wouldn't look anyone in the face, especially him. Four months later, before graduation, you began to show signs of a little tummy. I used to spend a lot of time secretly admiring those tight buns of yours, and I could see the change. Then almost to the day, nine and a half months later, I got word that you delivered Ronnie."

Sam now realized that the man she loved had known all along, but there was one part of the equation he could never have figured out. "I need to tell you how—"

"No you don't."

"If you're going to want to jump my bones, I have to explain this to you. It's important to me."

"Sam, you don't need to bare your soul to me, I have always known that you were raped."

Sam's emotion of attrition was shifting to frustration. "Stop doing that. How could you possibly have known that I was raped? You weren't there, and neither was I mentally."

"Sam, it was obvious. If it had been consensual, you would

never have reacted to his presence the way you did afterwards. Whenever he would come into the room, you would leave or turn away."

"Listen Mister, I want you to sit there and hear what I have to say. I've spent a lot of time figuring out how to tell you this, and you're going to hear me out, understand?"

"Yes ma'am."

Sam began to reveal the secret that she had held in her dark place all these years. Even if her husband felt that the exposure of that night was unnecessary, she had to hear herself say the words to the man she loved. "After you and Captain Ryan left, I went to the ladies room. When I came back, I finished my wine and started to call a cab. He offered to drive me to my apartment, and since I didn't really understand how he was at the time, I thought it would be alright. After all, he was a fellow officer.

By the time we got to my apartment, I began to feel dizzy and disoriented, so he helped me into my room. That's the last I remember. He must have slipped something into my drink. I wasn't aware I was pregnant until I started tossing my cookies two months later. Then I figured out what he did. He was a superior officer and I had no proof that he forced me. None. There was nothing I could do, and I wasn't going to make Ronnie suffer for my naiveté."

"Frankly, I always assumed you had better taste in men than that jackass. Did you ever tell him about Ronnie?"

"No, I lied to everyone, including my parents and Ronnie. I implied that it was a friend who was killed overseas. I didn't want Ronnie to hear the anguish his birth had caused, and the fact that he wasn't conceived in love."

"That was a good decision. Ronnie is a wonderful boy. I don't think you could have done any better raising that terrific kid on your own. It would have caused him nightmares and identity problems if he knew he was spawned from a pool of evil. We know he got all your good genes and attitudes on life. He would always wonder about his true nature. If it were me, I would never put that monkey on his shoulders."

"I don't plan to, and you're the only other person on this planet who knows."

Sam looked down at the floor after baring her soul, admitting to sins she never committed. She had tried to clear her conscience from the self-recrimination that had hounded her heart and caused barriers in her mind to the progression of their relationship. But something remained; all the demons had not been purged. There was still shame, still uncertainty in how her confession would be received. How it would affect the man she loved.

She raised her face and stared thought the pool of moisture in her eyes, and waited.

He took her hand and ran his fingers across her palm. "Sweetheart, everything is alright. There is no blame for you in what he did. I've always admired your strength in dealing with this on your own, in not taking the easy way out. You need to flush these fears out of your mind. There should never be any doubt in your heart for how I feel. I still love you, as much as before, and I always will."

"You don't care about what happened? It doesn't matter?"

"Hell yes, I care. I wish I could have ripped the bastard apart with my own hands for what he did to you, tossed him down into the pit of hell myself, the way he made you suffer all these years. It makes the blood ring in my ears when I think of it. But Sam, nothing will stop me from loving you, not even when you turn my arousal switch on and off and drive me up the wall.

No one can fill that lonely place in my heart except for you. You are not the bad one here; nor should you feel ashamed for trusting someone, and having them misuse your innocence. You did nothing wrong, nothing Sam. Your only mistake would be if you continued to allow this thing to haunt you. You have to purge these thoughts from your mind. There can be no guilt for something you did not cause."

"What about Ronnie?"

"What about him?"

"It doesn't matter who Ronnie's father was?"

Eric displayed a slight smile as he consoled his wife. "I couldn't care more for Ronnie than if I had been lucky enough to be his real father. I really mean this, I love that kid. You need to look into my eyes and see for yourself, so you can understand how much I care for our son."

Eric caressed her palm. "You two have pulled me out of the

depths of hell. All the hate and anger that had imprisoned my soul for so long, it's gone. I can actually sleep at night, undisturbed, because of both of you. What more could I want. Except maybe a little girl someday."

Sam scanned his face, peered into his eyes, and then she knew it was true. Everything he had said was from the heart. He had committed himself to the welfare and happiness of his new family, and Sam agreed. What more could she want?

She reached around Eric's neck and whispered, "Thank you for being my husband, my friend, and the father of my son. You have released my soul from all those years of darkness. My heart will always be yours."

Eric gazed at Sam's beautiful face. "Can I ask one favor? You think we could work on that little girl now, before Ronnie and your mom get home?"

Sam looked down at Eric's waist and grinned. "Men. God love them."

"It has been a long, long time. You keep lighting my furnace and not releasing the heat. I feel like I'm going to explode."

"Well we can't have that, can we Mr. Emerson? We'll take care of that right now."

With those words, a man and a woman who had suffered for so long were set free. Their spirits bonded in the way that can only be achieved by two people that are truly in love. And to Eric's delight, the physical confirmation was repeated several times, until they both fell asleep, spent.

Enveloped in each other's arms, they shared the dream again: the white sand cushioned their nude forms, while the waves gently caressed the beach. They shared each other's warmth, as the clouds encircled the small island and secured them from the rest of the world.

Fifty One

Eric tightened the noose that was attached to the eyelet at the top of the windmill. Then he looked over his shoulder at the young boy seated in the ATV. "Okay Ronnie, pull ahead very slowly, and listen for my voice."

The young boy started the engine. When he moved the vehicle forward, the turbine and prop portion of the windmill begin to cantilever upward.

"When you hear the shaft drop into the hole, you have to stop."

A few more seconds and the shaft of the windmill slid down into the hole Eric had dug in the ground, and oscillated back and forth, slowly dampening to a total vertical position.

"Great job, Sport. I knew you could do it. All we have to do is backfill this hole with quick-set cement, and then make the electrical connection. At that point, we'll actually have our own power supply."

"Is this all we need to power our house?"

"No. Over the next six months, you and I are going to install a small generator over there at the waterfall, and also a solar panel in that backfield. It won't give us unlimited power like we have today, but when the energy plants go offline; we will be able to meet most of our energy needs. For the rest, we'll have to change our life style."

After Eric secured the shaft in place, he turned to his son. "What do you say we go catch a couple catfish for dinner?"

"That works for me."

"Go into the shed and get two poles, I'll dig up a few worms and meet you on the dock, and remember…"

"I know Eric, always wear my vest."

~ * ~

Eric perched atop a white bucket on the dock, relaxed in the afternoon sun, and glanced down at Ronnie cooling his feet in the water. He caught the movement of their bobbers, swinging slowly left, then right. Like a lazy dog wagging its tail, the red and white bobbers waved to the motion of the ripples created by the mild breeze.

The falling leaves formed a blanket on the surface of the twenty-acre lake. "It looks like fall's coming. That means we'll be able to hunt soon. I'll start you off with a .22 rifle. You can bring home squirrel for dinner. In a few years, I'll teach you how to use the 30-30 Winchester to hunt deer."

"Is that the gun over the door?"

"It sure is Sport, and remember…"

"I know, never touch the gun without your permission. You don't have to tell me all the time. I remember the rules."

"I'm sorry, I keep telling you these things because I don't want you to get hurt. We need guns to survive here, but you have to respect them. Anytime that you want to see them, all you have to do is ask."

"I understand."

"You're a good boy."

Ronnie looked up at Eric, then back down at his bobber. "Eric?"

"Yes, Sport?"

"When we signed those adoption papers, it meant that we're really a family now, all of us, the baby too, right?"

"That's right."

"Then what should I call you?"

"What do you want to call me?"

"How about Dad, would that be okay?"

"I would like that, a lot. What should I call you?"

"Sport is okay, but I like *son* better."

"Me too."

Eric continued to stare at the sunbeams darting across the

water. He looked down and observed his son gazing along the surface of the lake. "Kind of nice to relax like this, isn't it?"

"It's very nice. I like it now that we live by the water. I can go fishing all the time."

"I always liked to fish here when I was a small boy. My grandfather created this lake from that stream over there. He passed this land to his son, then my father to me, and some day it will be yours. My dad and I actually built that log cabin we all live in. After my mom and sister died, he stayed here alone for many years. He never remarried."

After a few moments, Eric continued, "I guess Dad always kept his heart full of the memory of mom and my sister. I wish I had visited him more. He was all alone out here. I tried to come to stay with him at least one week each year, but I was deployed overseas all the time, and with my first marriage so messed up, it was just so hard."

"Dad? Can I ask you sort of a personal question?"

"Sure, you can always ask me anything."

"Did you tell your dad you loved him, like when you came to see him?"

Eric paused for a moment. "No I didn't, and I wish I had. I've thought about it a lot, especially since he's been gone. It's sad guys don't do that. We're taught to be tough, but that shouldn't stop us from telling people important to us how much we love them."

"I agree. Dad?"

"Yes?"

"I love you."

"I love you too, Son."

Eric sat quietly with his son for a few minutes. "Ronnie, over the next few years I'm going to spend a lot of time showing you how to do stuff you've never had to deal with before."

"Like what?"

"Things like how to hunt, fix mechanical equipment, grow crops, and a bunch of other talents that will be new to you."

"Why?"

"You're going to need those skills in the future. You'll also have to teach your sister, or brother, how to do this stuff. That's very important."

"Wow, I get to be a teacher. I can really live with that. When will I need it?"

"I don't know for sure, but soon. Maybe when I'm old you'll even have to take care of your mom and me."

"I can do that."

~ * ~

Sam stepped out on the porch and rested both her hands on the bulge in her abdomen. She smiled contently as she watched the two males enjoy their break from the work they completed over the last two months.

She waved. "Lunch in twenty minutes. Clean up boys."

Eric and Ronnie returned the wave, and she walked back into the log cabin.

"Dad. Do you want a boy or a girl?"

"I have a son so I think I would like a little girl. Maybe she would look like your mom. How about you, would you prefer a boy or a girl?"

"A brother could help with all these chores we have to do around here. That would be nice."

"What if it's a girl?"

"A sister would have a lot of girlfriends I could meet. That would be nice too. I don't know Dad; it's a hard choice. I'll have to think on that and get back to you. What if we had one of each?"

Eric smiled. "I would love that. It would drive your mom nuts, but you can ask her. You had better do it soon. The baby will be here in a few months."

Eric placed his hand gently on his son's head. "I think you've got one nibbling at your bait. Remember what I told you—"

"I know, wait till it goes under, count to three, and then set the hook."

When the bobber went under the water, the boy counted out loud, then he jerked his rod, and started to retrieve his catch.

"You did that real good. That's a three-pound catfish."

Eric glanced at the ripples emanating from his bobber. "Now it's my turn." After a few seconds, Eric raised his catch out of the water.

"They're both the same size. There must have been a pair of them prowling for minnows under the dock."

"I think mine's bigger than yours."

Eric grinned at his son. "Perhaps you're right, yours is a little bit bigger. This will be enough for dinner. Let's save the rest of the fish for another day. We'll put them in the bucket, and you can go show your grandmother what you caught. I'll be there in a minute to teach you how to fillet a catfish. I have to go give your mom a hug. You know women need that kind of stuff."

"I've noticed that, especially since she's been pregnant."

Eric chuckled, rubbed Ronnie's head, took the pole from his son, and the two men walked toward the cabin for lunch.

Fifty Two

After enjoying his meal, Eric decided to relax for a while in the double hammock on the front porch. Sam walked onto the porch carrying a small green shoebox in her arm. "I've been unpacking the cartons we brought with us, and I found this in the last one. I think it's yours. It's full of little odds and ends. What is this stuff?"

"Just things that keep the past fresh and alive in my mind, the decisions I've made, the paths I've taken, stuff like that."

Sam extended the box toward Eric. "Do you still want it?"

Eric thought about all he now had. "I don't think I need it anymore."

As Sam turned to re-enter the house, Eric pondered the choices and events he knew were approaching all of them. "On second thought, maybe I should hold on to these things for awhile longer. They may give me the strength I need to deal with what lies ahead for all of us."

He took the box from her hand, and placed it on the floor below him.

Sam sat on the hammock next to her husband and inhaled a deep breath of the musky mountain air. She smiled as she rubbed her abdomen. "The baby is really starting to kick. Here feel."

Eric gently pressed his hand on her stomach. "Wow, doesn't that hurt?"

"No, not a bit, but my back is really sore."

"Here sweetheart, let me rub it for you."

As Eric pressed his warm hands along Sam's back, she

moaned. "Ah, that feels good, don't stop."

After a few moments, Eric sensed the change in her breathing. The momentary release of pain and the motion of being rocked back and forth allowed her to sink into one of her peaceful dreams.

Eric continued swinging gently as he watched his new son do what boys do so well, enjoy the simple pleasures of an autumn day on an isolated lake far away from the rest of the world. Ronnie dangled his feet from the dock into the water, tracing crazy eights with his big toe as he watched the cool fall breeze chase the colors off the trees. With his finger, he followed each leaf as it performed its final ballet descending across the air currents to the waiting ripples in the lake. When he tired of the lack of interest from even the smallest fish, he commanded his bobber to dance by smashing his toes on the surface until ripples raced outward and dashed his beacon madly up and down.

Eric smiled as he watched his son drink in the wonder of youth. *I haven't quite taught him the art yet, but at least he enjoys the sport.*

He looked down at the woman cuddled beside him, and the baby she carried. He considered his life, the pain, and the pleasures. He had learned so much from his past, and would use it in his future to protect those he loved so dearly.

Eric now knew the moral paradox he had struggled with for so long did not offer the clear and pure solution he had once envisioned. To do what was right, and morally just, could cause unexpected repercussions, sometimes to the extreme.

When he chose to confront the gang leader and terminate his reign of terror, it cost Karen her life. When he elected to violate the rules of engagement, and save the young Iraqi girl, each member of his deep penetration team paid a horrible price. The choice to expose the corruption behind the Viper fiasco levied a heavy toll on his friend Judi, and on Sam's father. And the action to relinquish Sam's demons and free her spirit had vanquished the biological father of his new son, and set in motion the guilt and confusion of whether some day he should share the truth with Ronnie.

He understood the decision to resolve sorrow caused in the past could cascade into a chain of events that transferred the suffering into the future.

This new enlightenment did not change the direction he would take, but rather demanded an awareness of the total implications of his choices. The alternative of trying to ignore the moral dilemma and placate the evil among them carried its own recourse and was unacceptable.

Eric reached down and picked up the green shoebox that he had retained since the loss of his sister. He examined each turning point and struggle in his life: the turquoise lanyard, the star sapphire ring, each gold earring, the insignia of an Iraqi General, and a Colonel's silver eagle. Each object was a symbol of how he had made the hard choices and conquered his nightmares. To help the eternal shepherd rectify the sins of others, there were occasions that mandated he take justice back from a faulted system, one that had forgotten the people for which it was built to protect. And he understood that unless someone was willing to accept a terrible responsibility for the survival of mankind; civilization, as we know it was doomed.

Eric tucked in tightly against Sam on the hammock, and placed his arm gently on their unborn child. As he inhaled the sweet scent of the woman he loved, he gradually drifted off and began to dream.

From the top of the hill, he remained bound to the tree, only this time when he pulled at the chains, the shackles he had struggled with all his life dropped from his wrists. He picked up the sword at his feet and ran toward the center of the plateau. The pack of wolves gathering for the slaughter of the small flock encircled on the knoll.

Eric launched toward the pack, but they escaped over the ridge and ran down the hill. At the edge of the knoll, he saw sheep expanding to the horizon, but there was no grass, nothing to graze. The wolves merged into the endless flock causing chaos across the herd. The air was filled with the cries and sorrow from the flock as they panicked.

He watched as they began to starve and be devoured by the wolves. Eric raised his arms and heaved his sword down into the crowd. He closed his eyes and screamed. When he looked back at the mayhem there was only silence, everything was dead. The innocent and the beasts that attempted to feed on the carnage, all lay rotting in the barren fields. Eric walked back to the pond on the knoll where the small flock gathered to drink. When he gazed at his reflection in the pool, he no longer saw the image of a man, but instead the profile of the wolf.

Eric was startled by a hand on his shoulder. He looked up to see his mother-in-law extending a glass of lemonade. "Sorry, I didn't mean to scare you. I figured you two might want to share a cold drink."

As he accepted the beverage, his mother-in-law noted, "I thought you would want to know. I just heard on the radio that a new viral strain is moving across Asia. They're concerned it will reach pandemic levels shortly and jump to other countries. The government is meeting this week to discuss what can be done if it moves our way. Thank God you concluded your trip overseas last month when you quit your job and came home early. Otherwise, you might have been caught up in all this."

Sam awoke from her nap and looked at her husband. "Sounds like it's finally begun."

Eric glanced at Sam, and then at her mother. "Maybe, but we'll all be safe right here."

Sam looked at Ronnie, and then her stomach. "Eric, will those flu shots we got last month work against this mutated strain?"

"I hope so, but we are fairly isolated up here on this plateau. I have sensors set up on the gate this side of the ravine that leads onto our property. You ladies may want to think of any last minute items and tomorrow we'll head down into the town for one final trip. If this virus does jump to the states, we could be up here for a very long time."

Eric turned and scanned the horizon. Dark clouds approached from across the mountain. "Get up sweetheart. There's a big storm headed our way."

Sam sat up and gazed in the same direction. "Boy, it looks like a bad one."

"Don't worry, we'll be ready when it gets here. Go inside and help your mother close the windows. I'll get Ronnie and we'll make sure the livestock are put away."

From inside the cabin, Sam's mother approached the kitchen

window and stood beside her daughter. The two women watched Eric and Ronnie protect their essential food source. Sam glanced at her mother, smiled, and gazed back outside.

"What is it sweetheart?"

Sam replied, "I was just thinking about how fortunate we are, at this time in our life, with all that's about to happen, to have someone like Eric. Ronnie now has a father, someone that sees Ronnie as his son, to guide and mentor through the hard days ahead. And I have a wonderful caring man who loves me with all his heart. Someone that will care for all of us with his skills, his strength, and resourcefulness. Because of the things Eric was forced to do in his past, he'll make whatever difficult choices are necessary to ensure the safety and welfare of our family."

"Yes, we are lucky, but so is he. I see what's inside you for that man, how much you love him, and from what I can see, he's a very happy person with his new family."

"He does seem happy, doesn't he? I've never seen such contentment in his face. All these years I've known him; I've never seen Eric smile so much. And I do love him, Mom. I have since the first day I saw Eric in class, only then, I could never say anything. I had to watch him suffer from a distance. Not anymore. Now he's all mine, the man I always wanted. I just wish Dad could be here, to see how happy I am, we all are."

The old woman nodded and glanced back outside as the storm began to churn the leaves on the trees.

Eric closed the gate, grabbed Ronnie's hand, and headed toward the house. He looked up at the two women staying at kitchen window. He smiled, waved, and then walked inside to weather the storm with his family.

About Michael

Michael was born in North Carolina. At seventeen, he fell in love with his wife and they married two years later. In the next decade, he obtained a degree in Aerospace Engineering and a Masters in Operations Research. They raised two sons. Before retiring in 2007, he supported his family by working for the military and the intelligence sector. They now live in the Piedmont, VA where he began his new life as a writer. Visit Michael's website: Davisstories.com

Visit our website for our growing catalogue of quality books.
www.champagnebooks.com